ZOMBIESLAYER

'It was Krell,' rasped Gotrek.

Von Geldrecht blinked. 'Who? Who is Krell?'

'Krell the Holdbreaker,' said Gotrek. 'The Lord of the Undead.'

'The Butcher of Karak Ungor,' said Rodi. 'The Doom of Karak Varn.'

'Whose name is written a hundred times in the Book of Grudges,' said Gotrek.

'Who so hated dwarf-kind that he returned from the dead to seek vengeance upon us,' said Rodi.

'My doom,' said Gotrek.

'*My* doom, said Rodi.

Gotrek glanced at the young slayer and gave him a vicious smile. 'He may well be, beardling,' he said, then wiped blood from his wounded leg and looked at his hand. 'But he has already killed me.'

A WARHAMMER NOVEL

Gotrek & Felix

ZOMBIESLAYER

Nathan Long

BLACK LIBRARY

To Keith, for instruction on zombie law.

A BLACK LIBRARY PUBLICATION

First published in Great Britain in 2010 by
The Black Library,
Games Workshop Ltd.,
Willow Road, Nottingham,
NG7 2WS, UK.

10 9 8 7 6 5 4 3 2 1

Cover illustration by Geoff Taylor.
Map by Nuala Kinrade.

A CIP record for this book is available from the British Library.

US ISBN: 978 1 84416 881 1

Distributed in the US by Simon & Schuster
1230 Avenue of the Americas, New York, NY 10020, US.

See the Black Library on the internet at
www.blacklibrary.com

Find out more about Games Workshop
and the world of Warhammer 40,000 at
www.games-workshop.com

Printed and bound in the US.

THIS IS A dark age, a bloody age, an age of daemons
and of sorcery. It is an age of battle and death, and of the
world's ending. Amidst all of the fire, flame and fury
it is a time, too, of mighty heroes, of bold deeds
and great courage.

AT THE HEART of the Old World sprawls the Empire, the
largest and most powerful of the human realms. Known
for its engineers, sorcerers, traders and soldiers, it is
a land of great mountains, mighty rivers, dark forests
and vast cities. And from his throne in Altdorf reigns
the Emperor Karl Franz, sacred descendant of the
founder of these lands, Sigmar, and wielder
of his magical warhammer.

BUT THESE ARE far from civilised times. Across the
length and breadth of the Old World, from the knightly
palaces of Bretonnia to ice-bound Kislev in the far north,
come rumblings of war. In the towering Worlds Edge
Mountains, the orc tribes are gathering for another assault.
Bandits and renegades harry the wild southern lands of
the Border Princes. There are rumours of rat-things, the
skaven, emerging from the sewers and swamps across the
land. And from the northern wildernesses there is the
ever-present threat of Chaos, of daemons and beastmen
corrupted by the foul powers of the Dark Gods.
As the time of battle draws ever nearer,
the Empire needs heroes
like never before.

'There was no end to the horror. No sooner had we felled the beast-shaman and sundered the stone that might have destroyed the Empire, than a new threat arose, deadlier and more gruesome than the last, an army of the living dead, ten thousand strong.

In the dire days that followed, when madness and despair were our constant companions, it seemed certain that his doom had found Gotrek at last, though in a form no slayer would ever wish for. But despite the danger and hardship and the threat of an unworthy death, Gotrek's most painful challenge came not from our enemies, but from his oldest friend. To save the soul of Snorri Nosebiter, Gotrek's sacred oath to Grimnir would be tested as never before, and I could not be sure which would break first, the friendship or the vow.'

– From *My Travels with Gotrek*, Vol VIII, by Herr Felix Jaeger (Altdorf Press, 2529)

ONE

Felix Jaeger stared in horror as eerie laughter echoed in unison from the dead throats of the encroaching zombie horde. Dead man and dead beastman alike, they all laughed with the same voice.

'Hans,' he said, edging back. 'Hans the Hermit is behind this.'

Gotrek Gurnisson hefted his rune axe. 'Should have gutted him the first time I saw him,' he growled.

Kat wiped her blood-grimed brow with the back of a bruised hand. Her skin, in the sick green light of Morrslieb, looked as dead as that of the walking corpses. 'We just killed them,' she groaned. 'Now we have to do it all over again?'

'Good,' said Rodi Balkisson, smoothing his braided slayer's crest. 'Maybe this time we'll find our doom.'

'You may, Balkisson,' said Gotrek. 'But Snorri Nosebiter will not.'

The Slayer turned and helped Snorri up from the makeshift stretcher he and Rodi had carried him on after Snorri had lost his right leg. He slung Snorri's arm over his shoulder as Rodi did the same with Snorri's other arm, and with Felix and Kat following, the three dwarfs stumped towards Baron Emil von Kotzebue's troops, who were closing ranks and lowering spears against the undead army in the centre of the narrow valley.

'Snorri wouldn't mind slaying a few more beastmen, actually,' said Snorri, looking over his shoulder at the shaggy undead monsters that groped and stumbled after them.

'Sorry, Father Rustskull,' said Rodi. 'No slaying for you until you make your pilgrimage, remember?'

'Oh, yes,' said Snorri mournfully. 'Snorri forgot.'

As rally horns blasted bright tantaras and cannons roared from the hills, weary handfuls of spearmen and knights fought through the dead towards the relief column from every corner of the battlefield – cutting down corpses that wore the same uniforms as themselves.

That was the worst of it, thought Felix. Though half the zombies that threatened the living were risen beastmen, the other half were men he and the rest of the Imperial force had been fighting alongside not a quarter of an hour before. All around, valiant soldiers who had ranked up with their brothers in desperate besieged squares against the raging sea of beastmen, now instead lurched along with those same horrors and attacked their old comrades with blank-eyed ferocity – in death becoming traitors to their own kind.

Felix parried a blow from the corpse of Sir Teobalt von Dreschler, who, until he had died in Felix's arms, had been a noble templar of the Order of the Fiery Heart. Now he was a horrible, animate cadaver, with a dangling jaw and a glistening red wound in the middle of his caved-in chest. Kat hesitated when she could have hamstrung the old knight, and nearly lost a hand when he lashed out at her.

'How can I strike him?' she moaned. 'He was our friend.'

'Who he was is gone,' said Gotrek, cutting down a beast-corpse. 'Kill it.'

With a sob, Kat buried her hatchet in Sir Teobalt's knee as Felix hacked off his head with Karaghul, a relic of the old templar's order which Teobalt had bequeathed to Felix only days before.

'With his own sword,' said Felix bitterly as the old man fell.

Felix was so battered and tired as they pushed on that he could barely lift the blade against the dead that stumbled towards them. An hour ago, he and Kat and the three slayers had charged into the circle of standing stones atop the hill known as Tarnhalt's Crown and attacked Urslak Cripplehorn, a powerful beast-shaman, attempting to stop him from completing a ceremony that would have turned every human within the Drakwald into a beastman. Half an hour ago, with Urslak dead, they had raced down into the valley below the Crown to join the armies of Viscount Oktaf Plaschke-Miesner and Lord Giselbert von Volgen in their ill-advised attack on the shaman's ten thousand-strong herd. Ten minutes ago, the forces of Baron Emil von Kotzebue had thundered into the valley and slammed into the flanks of the beastmen, and the young lords' doomed armies had been saved – though it was too late for the young lords themselves. One minute ago, Morrslieb, the Chaos moon, had eclipsed its fairer sibling, Mannslieb, at precisely midnight on Hexensnacht, the last second of the old year and the first second of the new, and all the dead on the battlefield, both man and beastman, had risen together in undeath and turned their dull, staring eyes upon the living. Felix had not stopped fighting in all that time.

The hulking corpse of Gargorath the God-Touched, the war-leader of Urslak's massive herd, staggered in front of the slayers, moaning and swinging the cloven-hoofed leg of another beastman as if it were a club. The hole that Gotrek's rune axe had made in the beastman's chest when the Slayer had earlier killed it did not appear to be troubling it in the least.

'You want to die twice?' rasped Gotrek as he, Snorri and Rodi ducked the meat-club.

The stumbling beast-zombie turned after them, but Gotrek left Snorri to Rodi and swung his rune axe in a high arc behind him. The blade *chunked* into the side of Gargorath's black-furred neck and severed its spine.

'So be it.'

The dead beast toppled forwards as Gotrek wrenched his axe free and stepped back under Snorri's arm. They hurried on, falling in with other survivors and hacking in every direction. Fortunately, the zombies were still only rising in ones and twos, and it did not seem that Hans the Hermit yet had full control of their limbs. They jerked and twitched, and fell as often as they walked, or wandered off in the wrong direction, but with each passing second, their movements grew more certain and their attention more focussed – all turning towards von Kotzebue's besieged column like blind mosquitoes attracted by the scent of blood.

The closer Felix, Kat and the slayers fought to the column, the thicker the mass of zombies became, until it was a solid wall through which Felix could see almost nothing.

'Dress ranks! Square up! Square up!' shouted a

sergeant from somewhere beyond the corpses.

'Wounded on the carts! Them as can walk, carry them that can't! Move!'

'We will retreat in good order, curse you! If you want to fear something, fear my boot, or you'll get it up your backside!'

'Heads, necks or legs, gentlemen! Heads, necks or legs! All other strikes are worthless!'

This last came from a splendid-looking old knight in the colours of Middenland, who Felix saw over the heads of the zombies, lashing about vigorously with a long sword from the back of a heavily barded charger. His close-shaved head was bare, and he shouted his orders through the largest, whitest and most magnificent moustaches Felix had ever seen. This must be von Kotzebue, Felix thought – their saviour. Fighting beside him was a thick-necked, broad-chested nobleman, with a pugnacious bulldog face that Felix almost recognised. He wore a surcoat of mustard and burgundy over his plate, and the crowned eagle of Talabecland on his shield.

'My son!' the Talabeclander was shouting. 'Find my son!'

Hearing that, Felix recognised the face at last. It was a middle-aged mirror to that of Giselbert von Volgen, one of the young lords who had led his tiny army against the overwhelming might of the beastmen. This must be Giselbert's father, and he was shouting in vain. Giselbert was dead now, alas, killed by Gargorath, and raised again like all the other corpses on the field. He would not hear his father's cries.

Ten yards from the column, Felix, Kat and the slayers found their way blocked by a supply cart, stranded amidst the swarming undead. Its driver and cargo men fought for their lives atop its load – the neatly stowed canvas and sticks of a score of officers' tents – as their horses kicked and screamed.

'Help us!' shouted the driver towards the troops.

But with a ragged blast of bugles and a roar of 'Company, march!' the knights and foot soldiers began to push their way south, fighting for every step.

Gotrek nodded Rodi towards the cart as the driver wailed with dismay.

'Here,' said the Slayer, hooking a zombie aside with his axe and shouldering his way to the tailgate. 'Up, Nosebiter.'

He and Rodi shoved Snorri up onto the pile of canvas, then fanned back the zombies and climbed up after him. Felix kicked back a corpse that had him by the leg, then pulled himself up as Kat clambered up beside him, panting.

'Drive!' Gotrek called to the driver as he and Rodi swiped back at the undead beasts and men that closed in after them. 'We'll hold them.'

'Oh thank you, sir dwarf,' said the man. 'Thank you!'

He took up the reins as Gotrek, Rodi, Felix and Kat joined his cargo men along the sides of the wagon and began hacking and kicking at the encroaching horde.

'Manling, little one,' barked Gotrek. 'Keep them off the horses.'

Felix groaned with fatigue, but crawled past the driver with Kat, then hopped awkwardly onto the backs of his carthorses. The terrified animals bucked and shrieked as Felix and Kat clung to their backs and slashed at the clawing zombies, but when a path had been cleared, they took it, and strained slowly towards the retreating column through a fetlock-deep swamp of twice-dead corpses.

Then a voice rose above the din of battle. 'My son! Stop! We must go back!'

Felix looked up. Lord von Volgen was pointing directly at the wagon, his eyes wide.

'Von Kotzebue!' he cried. 'Stop the column! My son!'

His son? Felix looked back, frowning. A figure in beautifully crafted armour was pulling itself up onto the tailgate of the cart at the head of a throng of undead. It wore the same mustard and burgundy as Lord von Volgen, but its face under its dented helmet was as withered and lifeless as when Felix had last seen it – when it and the corpse of its cousin, Oktaf Plaschke-Miesner, had moments ago shambled towards him in a horrible mockery of life.

Gotrek and Rodi brained and decapitated the young lord's corpse, then kicked it back into the rest.

A wail of anguish rose from the column. 'Giselbert! No! My son!'

A claw raked Felix's arm, and he had to return his attention to the zombies around his horse, slashing and hacking and kicking them away as Kat did the same on the second horse. The strikes of the dead were clumsy and easy to block, but they were so many, and so relentless, that it was all she and Felix could do to keep them at bay and stay on their mounts.

After what seemed an hour, the cart reached the column, and the line of spearmen who were desperately staving off the shambling horde parted and let them through. Once behind their ranks, Felix and Kat flopped across the necks of their horses and just lay there, panting. Felix was as exhausted as he had ever been, and now that his limbs were at rest, the pain began to seep into the dozens of wounds he had taken during that long, long night. He was cut, bruised, scraped and battered from head to foot. There was nowhere on his body that didn't hurt.

'Well, that's that, then,' said Rodi, behind him. 'We

can go back and find our dooms now.'

'You can,' said Gotrek. 'I stay with Snorri Nosebiter until the column wins clear.'

'But…'

Felix looked back as Rodi turned from the sea of zombies to glare at Snorri, who lay in the middle of the cart, tightening the tourniquet that was wrapped around his severed leg.

'All right,' Rodi grunted at last. 'I owe him that, but afterwards, no more waiting. There is a great doom here.'

'Aye,' said Gotrek. 'No more waiting.' He jumped down from the cart and started towards the left flank of the column. 'Come on, beardling. We'll warm up with these.'

Rodi hopped down after him, grinning. 'Good. The sooner these manlings get away, the sooner we have the rest to ourselves.'

The two slayers shouldered forwards to join the side-stepping line of spearmen who stabbed mechanically into the surging mass of undead as the column marched out of the valley.

'Heads, necks and legs!' roared Rodi, bashing around at the zombies with his hammer.

The spearmen cheered and echoed his call. 'Heads, necks and legs!'

Gotrek didn't join in. He was too busy slaying.

'We should help them,' said Kat, rising wearily from her horse's neck.

'Aye,' said Felix, 'we should.'

But when he tried to push himself upright, his arms shook so much he knew he would be useless on the front line. He would only add himself to the dead, and he didn't fancy Gotrek slaying him for becoming a zombie. Still, there was other work that needed to be done.

Felix saw that the surgeons' assistants were overwhelmed by the number of wounded and dead falling back from the flanks and the rearguard. They were carrying them to the baggage carts as fast as they could, but men were still being left behind for want of bearers to carry them.

He dismounted and beckoned to Kat. 'Come on,' he said. 'This we can do.'

A GREAT CHEERING arose and Felix and Kat looked up from laying another wounded spearman on the cart that had brought them there. It was following von Kotzebue's ragged column of knights, spearmen and halberdiers up through a low pass between two hills at the southern end of the valley of Tarnhalt's Crown, and all the men were shaking their weapons and roaring and thrusting up two-finger salutes back towards the battlefield.

Felix blinked. He and Kat had been so focussed on carrying the wounded that they hadn't noticed the column's progress. There were no zombies around them. The shambling dead were all further down the slope, funnelled together by the constricting hills and held back by a rearguard of spearmen that blocked the narrow pass – a noble sacrifice that would allow the rest of the army to escape.

'We – we won free,' said Kat, staring.

'And now we're going back,' said Gotrek, as he and Rodi joined them at the tailgate.

Felix's heart thudded in his chest. This meant that he and the Slayer were parting ways at last. He didn't know what to say.

But as he opened his mouth in the vain hope that something appropriate would fall out, a cold wind, reeking of death and earth, blew up from the valley and made the brave cheering falter and die. Lightning flashed above them, and thunder followed it, a deafening crack that went echoing across the endless Barren Hills.

Felix and the others looked up with the rest of the column. The two moons were now hidden behind a pale scrim of clouds, and had pulled apart from their earlier eclipse. Now they looked like the glowing eyes of a warp-dust addict gleaming through a mask of dirty gauze. And before them, stepping out of a fading cloud of shadow at the crest of the hill above the pass, was the twisted figure of Hans the Hermit, laughing maniacally.

'Yes,' he hissed, as the soldiers shivered and stared. 'Flee to your masters. Tell them I am coming. Tell them that every castle and town between here and Altdorf will fall before me. Tell them their dead will become my army. Tell them I will take Altdorf with a hundred thousand corpses, and that the Empire of Sigmar will become the Empire of the Dead.'

Pistols and long guns cracked at the hermit, and Kat unslung her bow and sent an arrow speeding his way, but he paid them no heed, and none of the missiles seemed to find its mark.

'You may outrun the tide now,' the hermit said. 'But soon the sea of death will overlap your walls and drown you. Then you will rise and walk with us. All will die. All will be one. All will be mine.'

The spearmen and knights roared defiance at this pronouncement, breaking ranks to start up the steep slope of the hill, and Gotrek and Rodi followed, bellowing dwarf curses, but before any of them could take more than three steps, mist and shadows coalesced around the hermit and he was gone as suddenly as he had appeared, and the ridge was empty.

Felix shivered and pulled his red Sudenland wool

cloak tighter around his shoulders as the men whispered prayers of warding at this sorcerous disappearance. He hoped Hans's words were only boasting, but after seeing how the supposed hermit had tricked him and Gotrek and the others into destroying Urslak's herdstone so that he could work his dark magic, he wasn't willing to bet on it. Whoever he was, Hans was a powerful and cunning necromancer, and Felix feared they had only seen a fraction of his power.

'Come on, Gurnisson,' said Rodi. 'The manlings have picked a good place. We'll be able to hold the corpses there for a good long time.'

Gotrek nodded. 'Aye.'

'Snorri could help if he had a crutch,' said Snorri, sitting up in the cart.

Gotrek turned and scowled at him. 'You are going to Karak Kadrin, Nosebiter. This is not your doom.'

Snorri hung his head. 'Snorri forgot again.'

Felix and Kat stepped to the slayers.

Felix swallowed. 'So… so it's goodbye at last,' he said, inanely.

'Aye, manling,' said Gotrek, and though he tried to be solemn, Felix could see he was finding it hard to keep the eagerness from his voice. 'Remember your pledge. Bring Snorri Nosebiter to the Shrine of Grimnir and you are free.'

'I'll get him there,' said Felix.

'Goodbye, Gotrek,' said Kat. 'Goodbye, Rodi. May Grimnir welcome you to his halls.'

Felix held out his hand, but as Gotrek made to clasp it, a thunder of hooves shook the ground. A score of knights were galloping down the column, Baron von Kotzebue and Lord von Volgen at their head, and pulled up at the back of the wagon, making a ring of horseflesh and pistols and naked swords around Gotrek, Felix, Kat and Rodi.

'There!' said von Volgen, pointing at the slayers with his broadsword. 'There are the inhuman berserkers that murdered my son!'

TWO

FELIX STARED AT von Volgen as Gotrek and Rodi went on guard. What was the lunatic talking about? Hadn't he seen his son's withered face? Hadn't he seen him attacking the slayers with the other zombies?

'You will die here, dwarfs,' choked von Volgen.

'Aye, we will,' said Gotrek, looking past him into the valley, where the zombies were starting to push back the rearguard. 'If you get out of our way.'

'You stand between us and our doom,' growled Rodi.

The two slayers started straight for the two lords. 'Kill them!' shouted von Volgen, waving at his men. 'Execute them for the murder of my son!'

'Come and try,' said Gotrek, still striding ahead.

'Wait, my lord,' called Felix, running forwards as von Volgen's knights dismounted. 'The slayers did not kill your son! He was already dead!'

Von Volgen turned, glaring. 'What foolish lie is this? I

23

saw it with my own eyes! My son was trying to escape the undead, and these wretched dwarfs cut him down without a second glance.'

The knights were stepping forwards to encircle the slayers. There would be bloodshed any second.

'He wasn't escaping the undead,' said Felix desperately. 'He *was* undead! He died fighting the beastmen before you arrived and was raised with the others!'

'It's true,' said Kat, stepping up beside Felix. 'Please. I saw him die. It was a hero's death, but–'

'You question my eyes, peasant?' Von Volgen's face was purple with rage. He turned to his men. 'Stand back from the dwarfs, or die with them!'

'Somebody help Snorri stand,' said Snorri, from the cart. 'He wants to die with his friends.'

'Hold!' called von Kotzebue, and such was the command in his voice that the knights paused.

Von Volgen was furious. 'You order my men? You are in Talabecland now, sir. You have no authority here.'

'Perfectly correct,' said von Kotzebue, bowing from the saddle. 'But it occurred to me that, as both you and the dwarfs want the same thing – namely their deaths – you should let them do it slaying our common enemy, rather than getting into a fight that will wound, and likely kill your own men.'

Von Volgen scowled. 'How is it punishment to give them what they desire? If they wish to die, then it will be by execution!'

'Very well, my lord,' said von Kotzebue. 'But by my recollection, execution only comes after a trial, and it seems–'

'There is no time for a trial!' cried von Volgen, flinging out an arm to indicate the encroaching undead. 'We are about to be overwhelmed!'

'Precisely,' said von Kotzebue. 'Which is why I

recommend you let the slayers go to their doom and let us be on our way.'

Von Volgen chewed his lip, his angry eyes shifting from von Kotzebue to Gotrek and Rodi to the zombies and back. Felix didn't know who was more insane, the lunatic who wanted to kill them, or the madman who seemed perfectly happy to debate points of law while an army of zombies bore down upon them.

'No,' said von Volgen at last. 'We will take them with us and have your damned trial once this is over.' He motioned to his knights. 'Arrest them!'

Gotrek and Rodi raised their weapons as the knights began to move in again.

'Try it and you'll have your murder,' said Gotrek.

'Gotrek, please,' whispered Felix. 'These are men of the Empire. They are our allies.'

'Not if they try to arrest us, they aren't,' said Rodi.

'Aye,' said Snorri, dragging himself onto the tailgate. 'No one stands between a slayer and his doom.'

'Noble dwarfs!' called von Kotzebue. 'If you are reluctant to spill the blood of men, hear me out. We travel to Castle Reikguard, six days to the south-west, to bolster its defences and send warning to Altdorf. If you accompany us there without violence, I will guarantee two things. One, a fair trial within its walls, and two, this shambling horde will be only days behind us. If you prevail in your trial, there will be ample opportunity to find your doom when they arrive. What do you say?'

'Since that one has already decided our guilt,' said Rodi, nodding at von Volgen, 'we say nay.'

Felix groaned, but drew his sword and stood beside the dwarfs. He didn't want to fight Empire men, but nor would he watch while Gotrek was attacked. Kat pulled her hatchet from her belt and crouched beside him.

'If you fight, Gotrek,' she said, 'I fight.'

'And so does Snorri' said Snorri, balancing on one leg.

Gotrek grunted, then, with a Khazalid curse, he lifted his head and levelled his one eye at von Volgen. 'Stop,' he said. 'We will go.'

Rodi turned, stunned. 'We will?'

'We will,' said Gotrek, not looking away from von Volgen. 'We will wear your chains and submit to your trial.'

Felix and von Kotzebue let out relieved breaths. Von Volgen's eyes gleamed.

'Arrest them,' he said. 'Take their weapons and shackle them to the cart.'

Rodi bristled at that and went back on guard, but Gotrek let his axe thud to the ground, his face cold and impassive. Rodi stared at him, as did Felix.

'Drop it,' said Gotrek, turning on the younger slayer. 'Or I drop you. You too, manling. And you, little one.'

Felix shrugged and unbuckled Karaghul, then laid it next to the Slayer's axe. Kat threw down her hatchet as well, but Rodi stood defiant for a long moment, trying to withstand the baleful glare of Gotrek's glittering eye, then he cursed and tossed his hammer beside the rest.

Von Volgen's men stepped forwards with chains and led Felix, Kat and the slayers to the wagon, then urged them onto it. When they were seated, the men chained them to the gunwales, even Snorri. They gave the key to the driver and told him and his cargo men that they had the care and feeding of them, then returned to their masters.

'Gotrek Gurnisson,' said Rodi as von Volgen and von Kotzebue galloped away. 'I want an explanation. You have robbed me of my doom.'

'And myself as well,' the Slayer said, then turned his eye on Snorri, who was looking back towards the valley, oblivious. 'Never involve yourself in another slayer's doom,' he muttered, and that was all.

As they got under way again, the last of the rearguard fell, and the zombies welled up after them through the pass like pus bubbling from an open wound.

IT WAS A grim march. Though most of the men were wounded and painfully weary from fighting two terrible battles back to back, there could be no stopping to rest and bind their cuts with the undead horde so close at their heels. They had to limp on, shambling like zombies themselves, through the long dark hours of the night, and then far into the day, without proper rest and eating from their packs at dawn before trudging on again over the endless wasteland of the Barren Hills.

As he slumped in the back of the open cart, the hood of his cloak pulled low against the ever-present wind, Felix had to smile at the favour von Volgen had done them. If the lord had let the slayers go to their doom and allowed Felix, Kat and Snorri to march with the army, they would be slogging along beside the cart with the others, mile after mile. Instead, as prisoners, they rode where the others walked, and slept when they could.

Felix's mood was soured, however, as he saw men wounded far worse than he die on their feet around him. Over the course of the day dozens toppled to the ground in mid-step as their exhaustion caught up to them, or bled white while carrying the stretchers of comrades worse off than themselves. Still more died on the carts before the surgeons could get to them – and when they died, there was no time to bury them properly, nor could they be granted the dignity usually accorded the dead.

At first, to be sure they did not rise again, the heads of the fallen were cut off and wrapped in their shirts so they could be buried together later. Unfortunately, that procedure had to be abandoned after all the severed heads started talking in unison, whispering from their bags that the men should give up, that they should just lie down and let the sweet release of death come to them. After that, the heads were all smashed with hammers and left behind as the armies plodded on.

VON VOLGEN AND von Kotzebue finally called a halt in the early afternoon and let their troops rest until nightfall. Word came down the line that, for the rest of the march, the force would be allowed to nap during the day, when the zombies were at their weakest and it was easiest to see them coming. The march would resume at nightfall to keep ahead of them.

During that first daylight halt, weary pickets patrolled the perimeter and wearier field surgeons worked straight through, trying to save the lives of knights and spearmen and handgunners whose wounds had been left too long. Because they were prisoners, the surgeons passed Felix, Kat and the slayers by, but the driver, Geert, and his two cargo men, still grateful to them for saving their life and cargo, browbeat a surgeon until he consented to see them, and their wounds were cleaned and bound. The surgeon even found some hot tar to cauterise and seal Snorri's severed leg.

Kat shook her head as she looked at the slayer's black stump. 'We fought so hard for nothing.'

'Not nothing,' said Felix, scratching under the bandage the surgeon had wrapped around his upper arm. 'Didn't we stop a great evil that might have caused the downfall of the Empire?'

'Yes,' she said, bitterly. 'And another sprang up in its place before it breathed its last breath. Will there never be peace?'

'Never,' said Gotrek, who was also looking at Snorri's

leg. 'We will never win.'

'Then why bother to fight?' asked Kat.

'So we don't lose.'

Kat frowned. 'I don't understand.'

'It is a lesson the dwarfs learned of old,' said Rodi, lifting his head. 'We fight to hold ground. In some battles we win back a hold or a hall. In others we are driven back. But if we stopped fighting...' He shrugged.

Kat slumped against the side boards, not liking it. Felix reached out to put a hand on her shoulder and found his chains wouldn't let him.

'Snorri thinks this is good,' said Snorri from where he lay. 'It means Snorri will never run out of things to fight.'

Gotrek turned away at that, and glared out at the endless hills, and Rodi glared at Gotrek, while Snorri closed his eyes and went back to sleep, blissfully ignorant of the turmoil he was causing amongst his fellow slayers.

Gotrek and Rodi had been at silent war since they were chained up, and the tension between them felt like a sixth person on the back of the cart – a sleeping ogre so large that it crowded the rest of them into the corners and made them unable to look at each other. Despite the discomfort, Felix did not try to talk the two slayers out of their anger. He knew better. Dwarfs were stubborn, and slayers the most stubborn of dwarfs. And what could he say anyway? The problem of Snorri seemed insoluble.

A dwarf became a slayer to make penance for some great shame, swearing to Grimnir that he would die in battle against the most dangerous of enemies as recompense. If he died in some other fashion, or if his courage failed him, or if he gave up his quest, he would not be welcomed into Grimnir's halls, and would spend eternity as a miserable outcast spirit, wandering through the dwarfen afterlife. Snorri had done none of these forbidden things. He had never turned from his quest and he remained brave to the point of foolhardiness, but despite this, because he had lost his memory, he was in grave danger of dying without Grimnir's grace, and facing eternal damnation.

The trouble was that a slayer was also required to die with his shame firmly in mind, and Snorri could not remember his. Too many blows to the head, too many nails pounded into his skull to make his rusty slayer's crest – whatever it was, Snorri had trouble remembering even Gotrek, who had been his friend for over fifty years. He would regale Gotrek with tales of his old friend Gotrek, and not remember him as the same dwarf who sat next to him now. But the worst of this forgetting was his shame, which he last remembered remembering before the siege of Middenheim, but now could not recall at all.

The news had struck Gotrek hard. Snorri was one of his greatest friends, and Felix could see that the thought that the old slayer would be denied entrance to the dwarfen afterlife pained Gotrek more than any wound he had ever taken. Indeed, it had caused him to free Felix from his vow to record his doom in an epic poem so that Felix could instead escort Snorri on his pilgrimage to the slayer Keep of Karak Kadrin to pray at the Shrine of Grimnir, the slayer god, for the return of his memory. Once Felix completed this task, he would be free from his vow, and able to live his life as he chose for the first time in more than twenty years.

Unfortunately, Gotrek was finding that keeping Snorri alive was interfering with his own doom, and worse, had caused him now to interfere with Rodi's as well. Felix knew Gotrek had not liked telling Rodi he couldn't fight von Volgen's men, but if the fight had happened, Snorri might have been killed, and that was unthinkable. And so, until the problem of Snorri was somehow resolved, Rodi glared at Gotrek, and Gotrek glared at Snorri, while Felix and Kat tried to rest and ignore the slumbering ogre of their anger as best they could.

THERE WERE NO attacks during that brief afternoon stop, at least not from outside the camp, but men who had laid down to sleep barely alive later woke up dead and attacked their tent mates. Felix was twice jerked awake by sudden screaming before the orders came down that any man in danger of dying before he woke was to be tied into his bedroll and gagged so he couldn't bite.

But even when the screaming stopped, Felix found it hard to sleep, for he kept hearing the distant howling of wolves, and when he did at last doze, the howling invaded his dreams and he thought he heard something snuffling under the cart. Needless to say, it was not an easy rest, and he breathed a sigh of relief when, just as the sun was setting, the ragged army got under way again, leaving behind them a roaring pyre of burning, headless corpses – and limping south all night over the grey, changeless landscape.

Though the wolves howled all night long, and the half-heard flapping of wings had the men looking into the sky at every step, the column saw nothing of the undead that night, and fought only the icy wind that blew stiff and cold and ceaseless from the east. Felix's shackles froze his wrists and ankles. His fingers went numb. Kat curled up inside her heavy wool clothes and hid her face in her scarf. The slayers didn't even shiver.

The morning brought relief from the wind, but none from fear or cold, for a thick fog smothered the hills, filling in the valleys and bringing with it a wet, seeping chill that made bones ache and teeth chatter. It was so dense that Felix could barely make out Rodi where he sat in the far corner of the cart, and flapping wings could be heard in its depths, while the howling of the wolves seemed even closer than it had been at night.

Von Kotzebue and von Volgen kept the men marching long past dawn in hopes that the fog would lift and they would be able to see when they made camp, but when it had failed to dissipate by noon, there was nothing they could do but call a halt. The men were too tired to go on.

The commanders ordered double pickets, set a ring of fires around the perimeter, and had their knights make constant long-range circuits of the camp.

None of these measures reassured Felix in the least. The fog was somehow more terrifying than the night. It couldn't be pushed back with torches, and it played tricks with the ear, making some sounds seem closer, while hiding others entirely. He stared out into it, unable to sleep, his eyes shifting from place to place, searching for unseen movements and shadows that weren't there.

A hoarse cry echoed from the camp.

'Another dead man waking?' asked Kat, looking up.

'I don't know,' said Felix.

He craned his neck but could see no further into the fog. Another cry came from the left, and then another from behind them.

'Wolf! Kill it! Kill it!'

Horns blared from every direction and sergeants bellowed.

'Companies, assemble!'

'Out of those tents! Up! Up!'

Running footsteps thudded past very close by.

Felix and Kat swivelled their heads towards each new

sound, straining on their chains, but Gotrek, Rodi and Snorri only stared into the fog, unmoving.

'How can you just sit there?' Felix asked. 'We're being attacked.'

'*We're* not being attacked,' sneered Rodi. 'They are.'

'And if they turn on us?' insisted Felix. 'I thought you submitted to these chains to keep Snorri safe.'

'Snorri doesn't want to be safe,' said Snorri.

'Snorri Nosebiter will not meet his doom here,' growled Gotrek, wrapping the slack of his chains around his fists. 'No matter what happens to the humans.'

Felix heard movement and voices from Geert's tent, only a few paces away, and turned towards it.

'Geert! Release us! Give us weapons!'

But the driver and his cargo men ran out and into the fog, swords and cudgels drawn, calling to their comrades.

'Bastards,' grunted Kat.

An angry snarl brought their heads around. A young spearman ran out of the fog, panting and wide-eyed, and turned to sprint past the cart, but a huge black shape hurtled through the air and brought him down.

Felix and Kat drew back, sickened, as blood and limbs flew. The beast was twice as big as it should be, with rotting muscle showing through mangy crawling fur and a skinless skull for a head.

Another spearman appeared and charged, his spear raised.

'Hoff! Hang on!'

He struck the wolf's shoulder and it whipped around, snarling, to take a second thrust in the chest. The spear snapped, and the wolf slammed the spearman to the ground right next to the cart, tearing his throat out with its skeletal jaws.

Felix and Kat held their breath as it finished him off, wincing at the sound of crunching bones. Go away, thought Felix. Go back to your masters. There's no one else here. There's nothing left to hunt. The monster raised its head, sniffing the wind, then turned its red eyes straight towards him.

'Bugger,' said Felix.

He heard the sharp snap of breaking chains and turned. Gotrek and Rodi were standing and flexing their wrists.

Snorri had broken his chains too, and was struggling to sit up. 'Snorri will–'

'Snorri will stay where he is,' said Gotrek.

The wolf was padding towards them now, circling to come around the back of the cart.

Rodi took up the slack of his broken chain and held it tight between his fists. 'I'll hold it,' he said. 'You kill it.'

Gotrek nodded.

The wolf sprang.

Rodi ran to meet it, and beast and dwarf slammed together in mid-air, then dropped out of sight behind the tailgate as Gotrek leapt the side boards and snatched a spear from one of the dead spearmen. Violent thuds shook the cart and the monster heaved up again with Rodi on its back, choking it with his chain.

The wolf rolled, trying to crush him, but Gotrek leapt at it, spear high, and stabbed its exposed throat with such power that the point punched out the back of its neck and nearly put Rodi's eye out.

The wolf went limp and Rodi pushed it off. 'Are you trying to make me like you, Gurnisson?'

Gotrek let the spear drop and climbed back into the cart. 'You'll never be like me.'

'Grimnir, I hope not,' said Rodi, following him. 'Still chasing my doom twenty years from now? No thanks.'

A twinge of anger flashed across Gotrek's face as they sat down again, but he said nothing, only picked up the sprung link of his broken chain, slipped both ends into it, then twisted it closed. Snorri chuckled and did the same, and Rodi followed suit.

Kat stared in wonder at this casual display of strength and was about to say something when Geert and one of his cargo men limped out of the fog, their faces bruised and their clothes torn. The other cargo man wasn't with them.

'Sigmar's blood!' cried Geert when he saw the dead spearmen. 'Here's two more!'

He and the cargo man ran to the dead boys, then saw the wolf and cursed again. Geert looked from the dead beast to his prisoners and back, glaring suspiciously.

'Show me yer chains!'

Felix, Kat and the slayers obligingly lifted their chains. Geert grunted to see them whole.

'Then who killed this here wolf?' he asked.

Rodi nodded to the dead spearmen. 'They did.'

'And who killed them?'

'The wolf did,' said Gotrek.

Geert and the cargo man looked dubiously from the wolf to the spearmen and back.

'And how did they kill each other when they was so far apart?'

'It was something,' said Felix, getting into the spirit. 'You should have seen it.'

Kat stifled a laugh and Geert glared at her, but after a moment he just shook his head and stomped off to his tent with the cargo man following.

'Snorri wishes there had been another wolf,' said Snorri. 'So he could have fought one too.'

Gotrek grunted at this, but said nothing, only glared into the distance and twisted his chains. Rodi in turn glared at Gotrek and stroked his braided beard, while Snorri lay back, oblivious, humming an off-key tune. The same tortuous round again, Felix thought as he looked at the slayers. The same irresolvable tangle. He sighed and sat back and returned to watching the fog for loping black shapes.

FOR TWO MORE days, the pattern remained the same – a pyre of the day's dead as they broke camp at nightfall, a dull march across the featureless landscape during the hours of darkness, and shadowy hit-and-run attacks all through the fog-bound day. It was impossible to tell what progress the army was making when every mist-shrouded hill and valley looked the same as the one before, but to Felix it seemed the column was marching slower and slower, the sleepless, terror-filled days and nights taking a toll of weariness and despair.

And perhaps the column truly *had* slowed, for, two hours before sunset on the evening of the fourth day, a squad of von Volgen's knights came thundering into the camp, shouting that the zombies were not more than an hour away.

As their troops scrambled to dress and pack and get into march order, von Kotzebue and von Volgen and their captains convened at the north edge of the camp, looking into the grey fog as if they might see the encroaching horde from there. They talked near where Geert had left his cart, and Felix could hear them plainly.

'They have marched night and day,' said von Volgen, 'while we have only marched nights.'

'Yes,' said von Kotzebue. 'It is as I feared. Slow as they are, they never stop. We will not outrun them before we reach Castle Reikguard. At least…'

'At least the foot soldiers won't,' said von Volgen when

the baron trailed off. 'Yes?'

Von Kotzebue nodded. 'I have less than three thousand foot troops left, and most of them wounded, starving and exhausted. The horde must number more than ten thousand. If my men stand and fight, they will die, and do nothing but add to the necromancer's ranks. If they run, it is the same. Your two hundred knights, however–'

'We will not abandon you, my lord,' said von Volgen, drawing himself up.

Von Kotzebue tilted his head, and Felix thought he saw him smile through his enormous moustache. 'I was thinking more that we would abandon you.'

Von Volgen frowned. 'I don't understand.'

'It is this way,' said the baron. 'The necromancer says he is driving for Altdorf, and plans to take the towns and castles in his way to bolster his troops. Castle Reikguard must be his first target, for it has the largest garrison, and he cannot afford to have it at his back. But to take it, he must act swiftly, before a concerted defence can be brought against him. Therefore, I believe if our infantry were to turn away from his line of march, he could not afford to follow. He could not spare the time.'

He looked west. 'We are almost due east of Weidmaren here. If I were to march west and bolster their garrison, while you and your knights raced south-west to do the same at Castle Reikguard, we would starve him of fresh troops, and make two of the strongholds he absolutely must take that much harder to win.' He turned back to von Volgen. 'What say you?'

Von Volgen stroked his heavy chin. 'I see the sense of it, but I wonder if Graf Reiklander will welcome an armed force of Talabecland men within his walls.'

'In the face of an enemy such as this necromancer, my lord,' said von Kotzebue, 'surely Empire must come before province.'

'Aye, baron,' said von Volgen. 'I only hope my lord Reiklander sees it that way.' He shrugged. 'Well, if you will take my foot troops and my wounded as well, I and my knights will speed south-west as you suggested.'

Von Kotzebue bowed. 'Of course. I will give my sergeants their orders.'

The two lords and their captains turned from the fog-shrouded vista, but before they had taken more than a few steps into the bustling camp, Rodi raised himself up in his chains and called after them.

'Hoy, lordling!' he barked. 'Aye, you. The one who can't tell the dead from the living. If you're running away, why not free us instead? We wouldn't want to slow you down.'

Von Volgen's brutish brow lowered into a scowl, and he turned his eyes to Geert. 'Make your cart ready to go,' he said. 'And find some extra chains.'

Geert saluted and the lords walked away.

'At this rate, beardling,' said Gotrek without looking around, 'you'll live long enough to learn when to shut your mouth.'

FOR THE NEXT two days, von Volgen and his two hundred knights rode hard to the south-west, with Geert's cart rattling along behind the other supply wagons. At noon on the first day, they plunged into the dark forest that bordered the Barren Hills. The narrow track they followed was old and often overgrown, and for all von Volgen's urgings that they make haste, sometimes the servants and cargo men were forced to stop and shoulder the carts over thick roots that humped up out of the path, or to guide them across rushing streams.

Each time this occurred, the dwarfs would watch from the cart, smug, as the men did the heavy work because von Volgen refused to unchain them. Felix was too uneasy to enjoy the irony. Whenever they slowed, he would stare into the depths of forest, fearing that at any moment undead horrors would lurch out of the shadows and attack. Adding to his nerves was the fact that von Volgen had sent his field surgeons along with his wounded to join von Kotzebue's train, so if an attack did happen, there would be no one to patch them up.

But no attack came. Not that day, nor that night when they made camp in a cramped glade not far from the track. Felix dreamed again of wolf howls and black wings, but when he woke, sweat freezing on his brow, he heard nothing, and there were no alarms from von Volgen's sentries.

The next day was the same as the first, except with freezing rain. The forest was so thick over their heads that even though the winter trees were bare of leaves the raindrops did not reach them, only great fat drips from the black branches that nonetheless soaked them to the bone. Felix tried to drape his cloak over himself and Kat, but they were chained just too far apart, and neither of them were fully covered. The dwarfs still showed no discomfort, except for wringing out their beards and flipping their drooping crests out their eyes. Snorri's crest of nails made little red rivulets of rust that dripped off the end of his bulbous nose like blood.

The next morning, the rain stopped, though the clouds remained. Unfortunately, the downpour had made a mud bath of their track, and there were many stops to pull the wagons out of wheel-sucking ruts, but at last, in the middle of the afternoon, the column came out of the forest and into a wet patchwork of dreary farmland, the fields black and brown and bare under stone-grey clouds.

Felix sighed with relief to be out of the woods, and it

seemed the knights shared his mood. They had been almost entirely silent for the last two days, talking only when necessary, and laughing not at all, but now they began to chat and joke amongst themselves.

Geert stood up on the buckboard of the cart and pointed ahead. 'That'll be Castle Reikguard, or I'm a goblin,' he said to his surviving cargo man, Dirk.

'Soon be warm and dry now,' said Dirk, nodding.

'And on trial,' said Rodi, without looking up.

Gotrek didn't raise his head either, but Felix and Kat stood as high as they could in their chains and craned their necks. A dull gleam, far in the misty distance, was the Reik, snaking north and west towards Altdorf – and rising from it, like some massive, high-prowed stone ship, was a towering castle, heavy walls of dark granite circling a craggy hill to surround a stern old keep. A great tower jutted from its black slate roof, rising so high its pennons were lost in the lowering clouds.

Felix had seen the castle often as a boy travelling with his father on business. It had been a familiar landmark to be watched for on the way to Nuln, and he was surprised what a sense of nostalgia and comfort he felt seeing it again. The castle was the hereditary seat of the Reikland princes, and also Karl Franz's summer home, as well as the home of the garrison that had guarded the Reikland's north-eastern border since before Magnus the Pious. He felt, suddenly, that after his long trek through the wild and dangerous Drakwald, he was back in the civilised heart of the Empire. This was where his people were their strongest. This was home.

A thudding of hooves behind them made him turn his head. One of von Volgen's rearguard knights was galloping towards them down the forest road, his horse's flanks flecked with foam and his eyes wide and staring.

'My lord!' he cried as he reached the tail of the column. 'My lord! They're coming!'

The knight thundered on towards the vanguard before Felix could hear who was coming, and he and Kat and the slayers looked back towards the forest, as did Geert and Dirk.

'What did he mean?' babbled Geert. 'Not them corpses? They couldn't have caught up with us so fast, could they?'

The knights were turning too, wheeling their horses around to face the woods, now a half-mile behind them, and a moment later von Volgen and his captains cantered back to stand with them and stare at the distant wall of trees.

'You are certain?' asked von Volgen, when nothing happened.

'Yes, my lord,' said the knight, panting along with his horse. 'And the wolves with them. They–'

Then they appeared.

From the dark of the forest came a swift, roiling blackness, shot through with flashes of white and steel and bronze, like shooting stars in a turbulent sky. Then the flashes resolved themselves. The white was bone – skull-faced riders leaning low over the necks of bone-shanked horses. The steel was swords and axes and lance-tips, held in gauntleted hands. The bronze was helms and breastplates and greaves of ancient design. And as the skeletons rode, the clouds in the sky above them lowered and blackened, so that the green fire that flickered in their empty eye sockets glowed brighter.

Felix swallowed, fear clutching at his insides. This was no shambling mob of clumsy corpses, mindless and unarmed. These riders were charging towards them in a disciplined line, as fast as smoke before a strong wind. A spike-helmed warrior in full plate led them, a black sword held high in one gauntleted fist, while the low black forms of dire wolves loped between their steeds like silent shadows.

'About eighty, my lord,' said one of von Volgen's captains, fighting to keep the fear out of his voice. 'Perhaps a hundred.'

Von Volgen's heavy jaw tightened and he wheeled his horse around. 'Make for the castle,' he said. 'Now!'

He galloped for the front of the column with his captains bawling orders to the wagons and the knights as they raced behind him.

Geert called up a prayer to Taal and slapped the reins over the backs of his horses as the column started forwards. 'Come on, Bette! Come on, Countess!'

The cargo man, Dirk, drew a hatchet out from under the driver's bench and made the sign of Sigmar.

Felix watched, mesmerised, as the undead riders surged closer behind them and von Volgen's knights and the other wagons pulled away ahead of them. Weaponless aboard the slowest of the wagons, he and Kat and the slayers were worse off than they had been against the wolves in the fog. The skeletal knights would ride them down before they were halfway to Castle Reikguard.

THREE

'WILL YOU ALLOW this doom, Gurnisson?' asked Rodi, sneering. 'Does it meet with your approval?'

Gotrek glared back at the encroaching riders. 'It does not,' he said, then snapped his chains and stood.

Rodi and Snorri took that as a sign and broke theirs too, while Gotrek freed Felix and Kat.

'Thank you, Gotrek,' said Kat, rubbing her wrists.

'Then what are you doing?' asked Rodi. 'Are you going to fight?'

'I am going to see that Snorri Nosebiter reaches the manling castle,' Gotrek said, and pulled up one of the tightly rolled lengths of canvas tenting that lay on the bed of the cart.

Rodi snorted. 'We could do that by jumping off and facing them.'

'Do what you will,' said Gotrek, and heaved the first roll off the cart.

'Snorri doesn't want to go to a castle,' said Snorri, trying to stand on his one leg. 'Snorri wants to fight.'

Rodi shot an angry glance at the old slayer, then cursed and started throwing off the canvas as well. Felix and Kat joined him.

Geert looked back, alarmed, as he heard the canvas rolls splat behind them on the muddy road. 'Hoy! What are y'doing free? And those are my tents!'

'You want to go back and get them?' asked Felix as he and Kat pitched another roll off the back.

Geert groaned unhappily, but only turned back and cracked the reins again.

The cart flew faster with every canvas they unloaded, and was soon bouncing and lurching in a terrifying fashion, but it was still not fast enough. They had caught up with the other carts, but von Volgen's knights were pulling further ahead, and the undead riders kept gaining.

Kat bent to shove off some of the tent poles that lay stacked in the centre of the cart, but Gotrek stayed her arm.

'Wait until they'll make a difference,' he said.

Felix looked back at the riders. Now that they were closer, he saw that not all were ancient skeletons. Some still had flesh on their bones, and wore the colours of Plaschke-Miesner or von Kotzebue or von Volgen. He stared, shocked. They must have been knights who had fallen at Tarnhalt's Crown, but like their bronze-clad comrades, their movements were swift and sure, not the vague stumblings of zombies. Was the necromancer controlling them like puppets, or had he somehow found a way to let them retain the skill they had possessed in life?

'How does a mad beggar like Hans have such power?' Felix mumbled.

The cart boomed over an ancient stone bridge that crossed a wide, winding stream. Felix looked around. The castle was closer now, and he could pick out details such as spear-tips glinting on the battlements and the yawning arch of its main gate, but it was still too far.

Behind him, the dead riders bounded over the broad stream as if they had wings, then touched down in a spray of mud and surged closer, pushing before them an icy, foetid wind that made Felix shiver with more than just cold.

Gotrek picked up one of the tent poles, nearly as long as a pike and heavier, then stepped to the back of the cart and heaved it like a javelin, straight at the spike-helmed warrior at the front. The rider danced its bone horse to the left and avoided the pole, but it bounced and knocked another dead knight from the saddle. The rest swerved around him and came on.

Snorri laughed. 'That looks like fun. Snorri wants to try.'

'Not with one leg, you won't,' said Rodi as he and Gotrek picked up more poles. 'You'll fall off the cart.'

Snorri sulked. 'Snorri never gets to do anything.'

Gotrek hurled his next pole low and to the left, and Rodi did the same to the right. They bounced in front of the lead riders, hitting their horses at knee height and sending them crashing neck-first to the turf in an explosion of armour and bones. More crashed down behind them as riders dodged and slammed into each other, but the fallen swiftly vanished behind the blurring hooves of the others, and the dread warriors closed ranks and came on.

Gotrek and Rodi bent to take up new poles, and Felix did the same, grunting at the weight. The long length of oak was an awkward, unwieldy weapon, and he marvelled again at the strength of the dwarfs to have pitched theirs with such ease and accuracy.

As he raised his to vertical the cart bounced and he overbalanced, falling against the side boards. Kat yelped as the pole banged down on the driver's bench between Geert and Dirk, and Felix lost his grip.

'Hoy!' said Geert. 'Watch it!'

'Leave it, manling,' said Gotrek, hurling his pole and bending for another.

Snorri snorted. 'Snorri could do as well as *that.*'

Felix recovered, flushing, and drew the pole back, letting the weight rest on the bench.

'Ah!' he said. 'That's a better idea.'

'What?' asked Kat. 'Not falling off?'

Felix ignored the dig and slid the pole out to the side of the cart, resting the weight of it on the side boards like it was an oar.

'Ah!' said Kat. 'I see now.'

The skeletal riders leapt a low stone wall and came parallel with the cart. Gotrek and Rodi swung their poles left and right at them, denting bronze helmets and knocking them out of their saddles.

Felix lowered the end of his close to the ground and swept it at the knees of a skeletal horse as Gotrek bashed at the rider. The pole ripped from his hands as it got tangled in milling forelegs, but the horse went down and the rider fell under the wheels, armour crumpling and bones snapping.

'Good work,' said Gotrek as Felix bent for another pole.

'Now *this* Snorri can do,' said Snorri.

The old slayer grabbed a pole and came up on his knees, then hung it out over the right side of the cart while Felix did the same on the left, but by the time they were in position, most of the dead riders had already passed by, converging on the head of the column. Only a few of the loping wolves remained behind, dodging the slayers' swipes and trying to leap up onto the cart.

Snorri punched one in the eye with the butt of his pole and sent it stumbling into a tree trunk. Gotrek knocked another off the tailgate and lanced a third, but the knights were faring less well. The undead riders cut them down at the gallop, but when the knights slashed back, their swords rang harmlessly off the skeletons' armour. Only a knight with a warhammer did better, shattering skulls and femurs, but he went down too, brought low by a dire wolf that tore his horse's left hind leg off with its exposed jaws.

Another knight went down right in front of a supply wagon, sending it vaulting into the air as its right wheel bounced over the falling corpse. The wagon crashed down on its side, pulling its draught horses with it and throwing its driver and cargo men into a field. The wagons behind it barely swerved aside in time, and Geert nearly ran into the ditch.

'Pull up! Pull up!' roared von Volgen as his bugler blared distress calls. 'Form a square!'

The lord might be a blind man who couldn't tell his son from a corpse, but Felix had to admire his courage and tactical sense, and the training of his men. When it was clear they wouldn't outrun the undead cavalry, he did not panic and keep fleeing. He ordered a defence, and his men obeyed neatly and without question, despite their mortal terror of the enemy they faced.

The echo of von Volgen's order had not died away before the column of knights had split – two files to the left, two to the right – and pulled up smartly, allowing the surviving wagons to slot between them so they were soon in the middle of a hollow square of knights, all facing out and fighting for their lives.

Geert and Dirk let out relieved breaths as they pulled

the cart to a stop, but then Geert turned on Gotrek, Felix and the others. 'You shouldn't have broke them chains! I told you I'd…' He sighed. 'Well, I'm glad you did, though. Saved our bacon and no mistake. But I'm begging ye,' he added as he and Dirk took up their weapons, 'stay on the cart. If von Volgen sees you free, it's my hide.'

Gotrek shrugged. 'It's your hide if we do nothing.' He turned to Rodi. 'You seek a doom, Rodi Balkisson? Now is the time.'

'I don't need your permission, Gotrek Gurnisson,' snapped the young slayer.

The two slayers jumped from the cart and started towards the head of the column.

'Aw, now, gentles,' whined Geert after them. 'Don't do this to me. Haven't I done my best for ye?'

'And we go to do our best for you,' said Felix, heading after the slayers with Kat.

'Snorri wants to come,' said Snorri.

'You can't walk, Snorri,' said Kat. 'Defend the cart.'

Felix and Kat hurried on, edging between the wagons and the shifting, surging battle line of knights and warhorses as Geert and Dirk called after them and the blasts from von Volgen's bugler were finally answered by an echoing horn from the castle.

Felix looked up at the noise. Help was coming, but would it be soon enough? On every side of the hollow square, knights were falling to the ancient swords of the undead riders. Von Volgen's men might outnumber them three to one, but the skeletons fought with a relentless mechanical savagery that knew no pain or panic, while the cold wind of fear that breathed from them paralysed the knights and made them falter. It would be mere minutes before the formation collapsed completely.

The slayers found von Volgen at the far end of the square, cursing and standing over a dead horse as his chosen knights held back the undead riders and his squires scrambled to bring him a remount.

'Lordling!' barked Gotrek. 'Return our weapons if you want to live!'

Von Volgen glanced over his shoulder as his squires led a horse forwards. 'Go back to your chains, murderer,' he said, swinging into the saddle.

Gotrek's brow lowered and Rodi balled his fists. Felix could see they were an inch from returning to the cart and sitting on their hands while the knights died all around them. Felix couldn't stand by and let that happen. He stepped forwards.

'My lord,' he called. 'Will you let good men die while we sit safe behind them?'

Von Volgen drew his sword and turned his horse back towards the melee, and Felix wondered if he had heard or cared, but then, as he made to spur forwards, he looked along his line and saw how close it was to collapse. His lantern jaw clenched and he called towards the wagon that carried his baggage. 'Merkle. Give them their weapons.'

And with that, he sank his spurs into his horse's flanks and punched back into the line, severing the head of a recently-dead knight in black and gold as he shouted a challenge to the spike-helmed warrior who led the riders.

Gotrek and Rodi grunted with satisfaction, then turned with Kat and Felix as the driver climbed into the back of the wagon and unlocked a chest. He threw back the lid and tried to lift something out, then tried again.

'Leave it,' said Gotrek.

He climbed onto the wagon, then reached into the trunk and pulled out his rune axe with as little effort as it took Felix to lift a pen. He slung it over his shoulder, then handed down Rodi's hammer, Felix's sword and Kat's hatchet, bow and quiver. Felix felt emboldened as he strapped Karaghul on again. Now he was ready to fight.

Without another word, the slayers shouldered through the stamping, side-stepping warhorses of von Volgen's line, and plunged swinging into the mass of skeletal riders. Kat watched as they were buffeted this way and that by the maelstrom of surging bone and horseflesh, and shook her head.

'I wouldn't last a minute in all that,' she said.

'Nor would I,' said Felix, looking around. A few yards away was a steed that had lost its rider. 'Here!'

He ran to it and pulled himself into the saddle, then hauled Kat up behind him and drew Karaghul as she drew her hatchet. The warhorse seemed to know where its duty lay and plunged into a gap between two knights with only the lightest touch of the heel, and Felix and Kat found themselves suddenly in the middle of the swirling, clattering melee.

A dire wolf snapped at the horse's neck. Felix chopped through the beast's spine, then decapitated a bronze-helmed rider that trampled over it to lunge at him. Kat shattered the skull of another rider with her hatchet, but it got caught in its helmet, and as she tried to yank it free, a second wolf clamped its jaws around her wrist and almost pulled her from the horse.

'Kat!' shouted Felix, slashing awkwardly at the thing.

Kat pulled against its teeth, trying to free herself, and stabbed left-handed at its skull with her skinning knife, popping one of its eyes. Felix finally twisted around enough to get a strike at its neck, and half-severed it. It fell away, twitching, and Kat righted herself behind the saddle.

'Are you all right?' asked Felix, looking back.

She nodded, hiding a wince as she slashed at another rider. 'It got mostly coat, I think.'

Felix nodded, hoping she wasn't being brave, and they fought on.

To their left, Gotrek and Rodi were hewing like woodsmen through a forest of bone and flesh horse legs. Despite their recent arguing, the slayers were an effective team. Rodi would smash through the forelegs of a horse with his hammer, bringing it crashing to the ground, and Gotrek would chop off the rider's head, then on to the next. They were getting kicked and kneed and crushed by both sides, but they just took the pummelling and kept on killing.

Then, with a tantara of horns, two score knights appeared, galloping over the fields, the white and red banner of Castle Reikguard cracking above them in the wind. Von Volgen's knights gave a great cheer at the sight, and renewed their attacks on the dread riders. Von Volgen himself, however, didn't look like he would live long enough to be saved. He was in desperate trouble. The heavy black sword of the spike-helmeted skeleton had cut his plate to ribbons, and he was reeling in the saddle.

But then, just as the dread knight knocked von Volgen's sword from his hand and raised its black blade for the killing stroke, its skull-headed horse shuddered beneath it and staggered sideways. The sword missed von Volgen by a hair's breadth and the dead rider turned to aim a cut at something below it.

The strike never landed. Instead, the bone horse toppled forwards and the ancient warrior fell with it, vanishing under the seething combat. Felix saw an orange crest of hair bob up and an axe-head flash down, and a shout of triumph burst from von Volgen's men.

It was immediately echoed by the war cries of the Reikland knights as they slammed into the flanks of the dead riders, lances lowered. A score of ancient warriors went down under the charge, smashed from their horses and ridden over in a splash of shattered bones. Felix and Kat surged forwards with von Volgen's knights, yelling and slashing at the dead riders from the front as the Reiklanders bashed at them from behind.

In the face of this double assault, the ancients turned and raced back the way they had come, but not like any living troops Felix had ever seen. They didn't break in ones and twos, nor throw their weapons away in panic. Instead, it was as if an unheard voice had whispered a single order for, as one, they and the wolves wheeled and fought free of the melee to race away without a backwards glance or any attempt to rescue their fellows who had been laid low behind.

Felix exhaled grimly and slid from the borrowed horse, then helped Kat down as all around them von Volgen's captains called for perimeters to be set and for the wounded and dead to be counted and collected.

'How is it?' asked Felix, as he saw Kat pressing her arm.

Before she could reply, Rodi's booming voice rose from nearby. 'By Grimnir!' he shouted. 'Do humans have no honour at all?'

Felix and Kat exchanged a glance, then hurried around a knot of knights to find von Volgen, his powerful frame hunched with pain, supporting himself with the aid of his sword and standing before Gotrek and Rodi while his men moved in to surround them. Rodi was sputtering with fury, while Gotrek was staring at the wounded lord with cold, silent menace, his rune axe at the ready.

'Curse them,' said Felix, then hurried forwards with

Kat running beside him.

'You are still my prisoners,' von Volgen was saying as they reached the confrontation. 'You will not be allowed your weapons.'

'You don't trust our word,' growled Gotrek, 'after we saved your life?'

'I don't trust your restraint,' said the lord. 'You might kill anyone in your frenzy.'

Gotrek's eye got colder still, and Felix's heart lurched. He had to say something before there was bloodshed, though he had no idea what.

'My lord!' he called, pushing through von Volgen's men. 'My lord, I–'

He stumbled over the body of a knight in red, black and gold and glanced down to step around it. The knight's severed head lay staring up at the sky from under his left arm. Felix stopped. He knew the knight's face, and all at once knew what he would say to von Volgen as well.

'My lord,' he called. 'If you intend to try my companions for the murder of your son, then perhaps you should submit yourself to trial as well – for the murder of your nephew, Viscount Oktaf Plaschke-Miesner.'

All heads turned his way.

'What is this nonsense, vagabond?' the lord snarled, wincing as he turned to face Felix. 'I haven't killed my nephew. I was told he died at Tarnhalt's Crown.'

'And yet he is here, my lord,' said Felix, indicating the body over which he stood. 'And cut down by your hand, if I recall, only moments ago. Perhaps he didn't die at Tarnhalt after all. Perhaps he was trying to escape these skeletons when you struck him.'

Von Volgen paled and stumped forwards to stare down at the boy in black armour. He wrinkled his nose. Oktaf smelled like a week old corpse, which of course he was. His blond hair was matted with filth and his beautiful face marred by a terrible wound, black and rotting at the edges, that showed his back teeth. Flies crawled around his lips.

'You did not recognise him when you cut off his head, my lord?' Felix asked. 'You didn't wait to be sure he wasn't still alive? From where I fought, it looked like he was coming to help you, not kill you. Were you so certain he was a zombie? Will you be able to look his mother in the face and tell her–'

Von Volgen's fists clenched. 'Enough, curse you! You've made your point!' He glared at Felix, his bulldog face flushed. 'I concede that my son may have... that he might possibly have been...'

'He *was*, my lord,' said Kat, stepping up beside Felix. 'He was dead before you arrived at Tarnhalt. We saw him die, killed by the beastmen's war-leader.'

Von Volgen turned his terrible eyes on her, and Felix gripped his sword, ready should the lord try and strike her, but instead he turned away, shoving his men aside to limp on his own back towards his horse.

Gotrek and Rodi and the knights remained on guard as he lurched unsteadily across the muddy, trampled harrows, then, halfway to the horse, he staggered to a stop and closed his eyes.

'Release them,' he rasped.

The knights relaxed, lowering their swords and hammers, and Gotrek and Rodi nodded, smug.

'But, hear me!' cried von Volgen, turning and standing straight. 'I will have my vengeance! Before Sigmar and Taal, I swear the foul necromancer who defiled my son's corpse and disturbed his eternal rest will die for his depredations, and all his works shall be cast down!'

His men cheered, raising their swords high. 'Death to the necromancer! Long live Lord von Volgen!'

'Well spoken, my lord,' came a new voice. 'But please tell me what trouble you have brought into the domain of Graf Falken Reiklander.'

Von Volgen and the others looked around to see two armour-clad noblemen in red and white approaching on a pair of sturdy warhorses. The one who had spoken was a tall, trim knight of middle years, with a jutting black beard and fierce brows, who rode ramrod-straight in his saddle. At his side was a florid, heavyset older man, whose breastplate bulged over his saddlebow to accommodate his belly, and whose face and neatly-trimmed beard were running with sweat. The rest of the Reikland knights gathered behind them.

'You are Reiklander, then?' asked von Volgen.

'I am General Taalman Nordling,' said the black-browed knight, bowing from the waist in his saddle. 'Acting commander of the castle until Graf Reiklander can resume his position.'

The red-faced lord mopped his jowls. 'The graf is recovering from wounds he received during Archaon's invasion,' he said, then bowed as well. 'Bardolf von Geldrecht, his steward, at your service. And to whom do I have the honour of speaking?'

'I am Rutger von Volgen, vassal of Count Feuerbach of Talabecland,' said von Volgen, returning the bow. 'And I thank you, my lords, for your timely intervention.' He looked around at the wounded and the dead and the skeletons that littered the field, then sighed. 'I did not wish to bring you trouble, but to warn you of its coming. These are but the vanguard of an army of the undead some ten thousand strong, which is led by a necromancer of great power who marches on Altdorf, and means to swell his ranks with the corpses of every garrison in his way.'

Nordling blinked. The knights around him

murmured amongst themselves. Von Geldrecht's red face paled a little.

'Ten thousand?' he asked. 'You are certain?'

'Perhaps more,' said von Volgen. 'Many of my men now walk with them, turned against me in death. They are less than two days behind us, perhaps only one. We–'

He cut off as a spasm of pain made him wince and he nearly fell. His men rushed to him and steadied him.

Felix saw von Geldrecht whisper to Nordling as von Volgen recovered himself, and wondered if the men were going to turn them away, but finally General Nordling turned back to von Volgen and bowed.

'Forgive me, my lord, for ignoring your wounds,' he said. 'You and your men are welcome to Castle Reikguard. Enter and bring your wounded. The graf will be informed of your grave news.'

Von Volgen waved weakly, and his retinue picked him up and carried him to his baggage wagon while his knights and servants gathered their wounded and dead. Felix and Kat helped, guiding or carrying maimed men to their horses or the wagons, and the slayers did the same, picking up fully armoured men with ease. Gotrek and Rodi also cut off the heads of those knights who had been killed in the battle. Von Volgen's men, long since aware of the necessity, did not object, but Steward von Geldrecht was outraged.

'What are you doing, you horrible savages?' he said, trotting up on his horse. 'You defile the bodies of my men!'

Gotrek glared up at him as he moved to the next body. 'Better now than later.'

'I don't know what you mean,' insisted von Geldrecht, and turned his horse to block Gotrek's way. 'By Sigmar, I should have you slain on the spot.'

Gotrek growled and readied his axe.

'He means,' said Felix, hurrying to them, 'that when the necromancer comes, he will raise the dead, foe and friend alike. If we don't do this now, my lord, we will be facing these same men in battle later.'

Von Geldrecht sputtered, his red face growing redder, but with the evidence of Plaschke-Miesner's corpse and the rest of the recently risen knights, there was no argument he could make.

'If it must be done, it must be done,' he said at last. 'But we will tend to our own. Leave them alone.'

Gotrek shrugged and returned to helping the wounded, and Felix and Kat did too. But Kat nearly lost her grip on the first knight they helped, and hissed as she clenched the arm the dire wolf had bitten. The cuff of her wool coat was black with blood.

Felix cursed. 'I thought you said it got mostly coat.'

'Aye,' said Kat. 'Mostly, but not all.'

Felix wanted to tell her there was no need to play the hero, but he resisted. She had long ago made him promise not to coddle her. Instead he followed as she went in search of more wounded, and helped her carry a handful of knights to the column – but he made sure he did the bulk of the lifting.

Finally, they could find no more, and returned to Geert's cart, where things had not gone well. Snorri was fine, and had crushed a dread rider with another tent pole, but Geert was binding a deep cut on his leg, and Dirk was dead, lying across the driving bench with an axe wound in his chest.

'I'm sorry,' said Felix, as he and Kat climbed aboard.

Geert shrugged. 'If you'd stayed in yer chains it would have been all of us.'

They laid Dirk beside Snorri, and Felix closed his eyes while Kat whispered prayers to Taal and Morr over him, then pried the hatchet from his rigid hand and slipped it into her belt. Felix smiled as he sat down next to her. Respect and pragmatism – the marks of a veteran.

At the head of the column, von Volgen signalled the company forwards, and the last of the wounded were hurried to the wagons as the captains and sergeants relayed the order down the line.

As they moved out Gotrek returned and pulled himself up onto the tailgate. Rodi appeared a moment later and did the same.

'You're not leaving, Balkisson?' asked Gotrek as Rodi sat. 'You're free now. And doom awaits in the wood.'

Rodi shot Snorri a glance, then shook his head. 'Doom will come to the castle too, Gurnisson. I can wait.'

FOUR

MEN CHEERED FROM the walls of Castle Reikguard as von
Volgen's and Nordling's knights rode over the drawbridge and under the arch of its massive gatehouse.
Felix looked around at the defences as the wagons followed them in. The moat over which the drawbridge lay
churned with swift-flowing river water, diverted from
the Reik, which looked as if it could sweep away any
attacker smaller than a giant. The high stone walls that
surrounded the courtyard were thick, strong, and in
good repair, and the inner keep, looming above the
courtyard on top of a steep rocky hill and reachable
only by a narrow and easily defended stair, looked even
stronger – a square, brutish fortress of massive granite
blocks.

The courtyard contained all the things a castle was
expected to have – a smithy, a stables, a temple of Sigmar and half-timbered residences butted up against the

inside of the exterior walls – but it also had a more unusual feature: a small harbour. The castle was built right on the bank of the Reik, and a water gate, almost directly opposite the main gate, opened to the river to let boats in and out. There were several boats moored at the wooden docks – two big sloops, kitted out with cannons and swivel guns, as well as a few smaller oar boats. There was also a warehouse and a two-storey barracks at the quayside.

What the place did not seem to have, at least not in any great abundance, was men. Felix had expected to see companies of spearmen ready to march out in aid of the knights. He expected scores of grooms standing by to receive their horses. He expected dozens of field surgeons and scores of servants rushing out to help the wounded. Instead, there was one surgeon, a hunched little crow of a man with a meagre handful of assistants, and a plump old Sister of Shallya with a few very young-looking initiates to help her. There were no more than a dozen grooms, and though the spearmen who manned the main gate looked hale enough, too many of the fighting men who hurried from the out-buildings and down from the walls to greet the returning knights were wounded and maimed.

There were spearmen on crutches, handgunners with slings on their arms, greatswords with bandaged heads, artillerymen with missing hands and legs. They limped and hobbled forwards along with their more whole comrades to help the battered knights off their horses with admirable selflessness, but they were hardly better off themselves. A chill came over Felix as he watched the scene. The garrison of Castle Reikguard didn't look ready to stand up to an army of ten thousand undead.

Von Volgen, being helped from his baggage cart by his men, must have noticed this as well, for he rounded on

Nordling, who was handing off his lance to a squire and swinging down from his horse.

'General, what is this?' he asked. 'Where are the rest of your troops? Is your graf undefended?'

Nordling lifted his black-bearded chin, glaring. 'The majority of Graf Reiklander's troops are likely where many of yours are as well, in northern graves. Talabecland was not the only province to march against the invaders.'

'I did not say–' said von Volgen, but Steward von Geldrecht interrupted him.

'The Reikland too gave of its best and bravest, Lord von Volgen,' he puffed, stepping up beside the general. 'My lord Reiklander marched north in support of his cousin, the Emperor Karl Franz, at the head of three-quarters of Castle Reikguard's strength. Only a month ago he returned with less than one-quarter still with him, and many of those gravely wounded. Because of this, we are at less than half strength.'

Von Volgen's jaw clenched. 'That is... unfortunate. I – I had hoped Castle Reikguard would be a bulwark against this necromancer's hordes.'

'It will be, my lord,' said Nordling, hard. 'We may not be at full strength, but we will not falter for that.' He turned to von Geldrecht. 'Lord steward, consult with the graf. I will gather the officers and we will meet in the temple to hear his will.'

'At once, general,' said von Geldrecht, bowing, and hurried towards the stairs to the keep.

Nordling looked back at von Volgen. 'My lord, if you are well enough, perhaps you will join us and tell us what you know of this threat.'

'Of course,' said von Volgen. 'Once my wounds are bound, I am at your service.'

Felix watched, frowning, as Nordling bowed and

strode towards the barracks, while von Volgen's men helped him onto a stretcher and started to remove his armour. If Nordling was in command of the castle until Graf Reiklander recovered his wounds, why was it Steward von Geldrecht's job to consult with the graf?

'There will be a good doom here when the necromancer comes,' said Rodi approvingly as they all started to get down from Geert's cart.

Snorri nodded. 'Snorri thinks so too.'

'Aye,' said Gotrek heavily.

Gotrek put his shoulder under Snorri's arm and helped him as they crossed to where the wounded knights were waiting for the castle's surgeon and Sister of Shallya to see them. They sat, and Kat shrugged out of her big wool jacket, then unlaced the sleeve of her hardened leather jerkin. Felix winced as she peeled it back. There was a dark, U-shaped bruise from the dead wolf's jaws on her forearm, half a dozen bloody puncture wounds perforating it like rubies on a purple ribbon.

'Wait here,' he said. 'I'll get some water.'

'I'll go too,' said Gotrek.

Snorri laughed at him. 'Water? What does a dwarf need with water? Snorri thinks you should get beer instead.'

Felix too thought it was strange that Gotrek wanted water. The Slayer almost never drank the stuff, and hardly ever washed, but as Felix filled his canteen at the castle's well, the reason was revealed.

'You and the little one will take Nosebiter away tomorrow morning before the necromancer comes,' said Gotrek, looking back at Snorri.

'Aye, Gotrek,' said Felix. 'As I promised. To Karak Kadrin. Though… though it feels strange that I won't be here to record your doom.'

Gotrek shrugged. 'My epic is long enough.' He spat on the ground and started back to the others. 'Too long.'

Felix finished filling his canteen and followed the Slayer.

'IT WILL WAIT,' said the pinch-faced little surgeon, glancing briefly at Kat's bite before stepping to the knight who lay beside her.

The plump priestess of Shallya and an assistant followed behind him, making notes in a ledger.

Felix stared after them, then stood, angry. 'Surgeon, the wounds are likely poisoned or diseased. Haven't you some ointment, or–'

'What I have,' snapped the surgeon, rounding on him with a beaky black glare, 'is a courtyard full of wounded *fighting men*, who will have to fight again, soon. Peasants, women and vagabonds will have to wait until those who contribute to our defence are seen to.'

'How do you think she got that?' asked Felix, pointing to the wound.

'Aye,' said Rodi. 'The girl's a match for any two of your *fighting men*.'

'It's all right,' said Kat. 'He'll see me when he can.'

'No it isn't,' said Felix levelly.

The priestess of Shallya looked over her shoulder, guilty, but the surgeon continued on, ignoring them, until Gotrek stepped in his way and folded his arms over his bearded chest.

The surgeon glared and opened his mouth, but Gotrek just kept staring at him, and whatever he had intended to say withered in his throat. Finally he snorted and turned back. 'Very well. Very well.'

He crossed to Kat and pulled her arm straight with more force than was necessary. She stifled a hiss, then sat stoic and grim as he prodded and squeezed the bite.

'A job for you, Sister Willentrude,' the surgeon said at last. 'Whatever poisons the beast carried are already in the bloodstream.' He looked back at his assistant. 'Fetterhoff, let the sister make her prayers, then salve it and bind it.' He stood and started back to the wounded knight. 'And be quick.'

'Yes, Surgeon Tauber,' said the assistant.

Felix and the slayers watched him go with sullen eyes as the priestess and the assistant got to work. The sister took Kat's arm in gentler hands than Tauber's, and murmured over it while touching each of the punctures with her plump fingers. The assistant opened a leather case and took out a pot of salve and a length of gauze.

'Where is the mess in this place?' Rodi asked the assistant. 'All that fighting made me hungry.'

'And thirsty,' said Snorri.

Before the assistant could answer, Sister Willentrude finished her prayers and smiled. 'The mess hall is in the underkeep,' she said, pointing to a pair of tall iron-bound doors set into the rocky hill upon which sat the keep. They were swung wide, revealing a shadowy interior. 'Evening mess is at sunset, but there's always food for valiant fighters at Castle Reikguard.' She smiled over her shoulder as she started after the surgeon and the assistant started salving Kat's arm. 'And beer as well.'

The slayers brightened considerably at this, and Gotrek and Rodi helped Snorri up, then put his arms over their shoulders. But before they could take a step towards the underkeep, a young knight in the mustard and burgundy of von Volgen's troops hurried towards them and made a tight bow, blocking their way.

'Your pardon, meinen herren,' he said. 'Lord von Volgen requests your presence in the temple of Sigmar. His son's scouts say you have some knowledge of the necromancer behind all this.'

The slayers glared at him and kept walking.

'We don't know any more than he does,' said Gotrek.

'Nevertheless,' said the young knight, backing up before them. 'I'm afraid I must insist.'

'Will there be beer?' asked Snorri.

'Will there be food?' asked Rodi.

The young knight scowled. 'This is a council of war, meinen herren.'

'Who has a war council on an empty stomach?' asked Rodi. 'Come see us after we've eaten.'

The young knight was turning red in the face. 'But – but, meinen herren...'

Felix grunted. 'I'll go,' he said, then stood and looked down at Kat, who was waiting as the assistant tied off her bandage. 'I'll find you in the mess.'

She smiled up at him. 'I'll make sure they save you some beer.'

THE TEMPLE OF Sigmar was just to the right of the main gate – a squat, sturdy stone building with a simple wooden hammer hung above heavy wooden doors. Felix followed the young knight into the stark, unadorned interior and made to stand behind the other men who were gathered there, but von Volgen, leaning wearily against the heavy stone altar next to Nordling and von Geldrecht, beckoned him forwards with a splinted hand. Despite his wounds, or perhaps because of them, he looked even more of a brute out of his armour than in, his battered head growing out of his shoulders without a hint of neck, and his broad chest swathed in bandages under his open doublet. Wounded, thought Felix, but in no way weak.

'Mein herr, welcome,' he barked. 'Now, tell us what you know of this cursed necromancer.'

Felix stepped to the altar, then turned, feeling

awkward with all eyes upon him. The men were a hard-looking bunch, as befitted the officers of one of the great castles of the Empire, but also hard-used, with many a fresh scar and bandage among them. He saw no one he thought might be Graf Falken Reiklander.

'Well,' he said. 'We first saw him as we were leaving Brasthof, on the trail of the beast herd. He said his name was Hans the Hermit, and he offered himself as a guide who knew the Barren Hills. He seemed… a bit mad, but he knew his business. He led us to the beasts, and then showed us tunnels – old barrows – that led under their camp to Tarnhalt's Crown. He said he was a grave-robber.' Felix smirked ruefully. 'And he is at that, I suppose.'

Nobody laughed, so he continued. 'We – we should have known he was more than he seemed. He smelled of death, and slipped out of shackles that he shouldn't have been able to escape.'

'Did he speak?' asked General Nordling. 'Did he betray any weaknesses, any schemes?' Without his helmet, the black-browed knight revealed a ring of short black hair around a bald head.

'Not before he raised the dead,' said Felix. 'But after… after, he spoke through the corpses as they closed on us, all of them talking in unison. He said the beast-shaman's magic had interfered with his own, and he had led us to them because he knew Gotrek's axe could destroy their herdstone, which was the source of their power.' He turned to von Volgen. 'I'm afraid that's all I know of him. You were there for the rest, my lord. He set the dead against us and threatened to sack Altdorf.'

Von Volgen nodded, then looked around at the others. 'Have any of you heard rumour of such a villain? Have any fought him before?'

The officers all mumbled and shook their heads, but

then a gravel voice spoke from the back.

'What did he look like, this necromancer?'

Felix looked up and saw a long-jawed old priest of Sigmar sitting on a stool behind the others. He might once have been a powerful man, but he was frail now, and blind. There was a rag wrapped around his eyes and he held a cane instead of the traditional hammer. A skinny Sigmarite acolyte stood at his left shoulder, and the plump old sister of Shallya stood at his right. Another woman stood beside her – a noblewoman of about forty years, with braided blonde hair coiled tightly to her head. She was beautiful and richly dressed, but carried a sadness in her eyes that was painful to look upon.

'He looked like a beggar,' said Felix to the priest. 'A wild-eyed old madman with a long dirty beard and filthy robes. No one wanted to touch him, let alone stand downwind of him.'

'Do you know him, Father Ulfram?' asked von Geldrecht.

The priest frowned, wrinkling the bandage over his eyes. 'No, no. That is not the description I feared to hear. This man is unknown to me.' He sighed. 'There are so many wicked men now. So many turn away from Sigmar and… and…' He trailed off, staring blindly at a point over the altar, his mouth still open. Felix stared. How did such a feeble old man come to be priest for a garrisoned castle? Why wasn't there a warrior priest here?

After an uncomfortable second, his acolyte patted Father Ulfram on the shoulder and the old priest subsided, muttering, 'Thank you, Danniken. Thank you. Was I saying something?'

'Yes, Father Ulfram,' murmured the acolyte. 'And well said it was. Very well said.'

A sturdy handgunner captain with a short brown beard and a plain, open face stood and coughed. 'Lord general,' he said. 'I don't know about the others, but if this fellow can raise ten thousand corpses, it doesn't matter if he's mad. We haven't enough men now to stop him.'

'I'm with Hultz,' drawled a scrawny, sandy-haired spear captain who slouched against a pillar. Despite a recent scar that puckered the whole left side of his face, his eyes glinted with the sly humour of a barracks tale-teller. 'I went north with four hundred. I came back with seventy. We've done our bit. Let somebody else take the first charge for a change.'

The handgunner captain and a short red-cheeked, red-headed man in the canvas breeks and jacket of a boatman murmured their approval, but a tall young greatsword captain with a bushy blond beard stood and rounded on the spearman.

'Our "bit" never ends, Zeismann!' he barked. 'We are soldiers of the Empire. We never shirk our duty.'

'Easy, Bosendorfer,' said Zeismann. 'I didn't say my lads wouldn't fight. I just think we should do it from a better position.'

'That is not an option,' said General Nordling, then nodded to von Geldrecht. 'The steward has informed me of Graf Reiklander's decision. We are to defend Castle Reikguard to the end.'

Von Volgen grunted, clearly unhappy. 'Forgive me for speaking plainly, my lords, but I fear you are just not equipped to hold here. If – if you were to allow me to speak to Graf Reiklander, perhaps–'

'You may not,' said Nordling, cutting him off.

Von Geldrecht was more polite. 'I'm afraid the graf is extremely ill from his wounds,' he said, 'and must not be unduly disturbed. Is that not the case, Grafin Avelein?'

The blonde woman at the back nodded dully. 'Yes, steward. It is so.'

Von Geldrecht leaned towards von Volgen, embarrassed. 'She lets no one but myself see him,' he whispered. 'I suppose because I am a cousin.' He shrugged. 'It is an awkward situation. Please forgive it.'

'I– I see,' said von Volgen, glancing from Avelein to von Geldrecht to Nordling. 'I did not know his wounds were so grievous. Forgive me.'

'The fault is ours for not telling you earlier.' Von Geldrecht turned to the officers and raised his voice again. 'But the graf was adamant. He said that it matters not that we are at less than full strength. This is the ancestral seat of the Reikland princes. It is Karl Franz's family home. It is the Reikland's eastern bastion. For both strategic and symbolic reasons, it must not fall.'

'The question, then,' said General Nordling, 'is not whether we should defend the castle, but how? I have sent ten messenger pigeons to be certain that one reaches Altdorf. Once the message is received, it will take at least six days for a relief force to arrive, if one can be assembled quickly. We must therefore be prepared to hold out for a week or more.' He nodded to von Geldrecht. 'The lord steward tells me we have enough food and fresh water for three months of siege. Now I wish to hear from each of you the status of your forces – men, supplies, weapons, ammunition.' He turned to von Volgen. 'My lord, if you would begin.'

Von Volgen winced and pressed a hand to the bandages around his ribs, then nodded. 'I had roughly two hundred knights when I left the Barren Hills,' he said. 'I lost more than a dozen to harrying attacks along the way, and many more during the fight today. I cannot say how many, but I would guess twenty or more dead, and as many wounded. So, perhaps one hundred and fifty ready to fight, though I'm afraid their kit is not of the best at the moment.'

'Thank you, my lord,' said Nordling. 'My knights will be happy to supply you with anything you need. Zeismann?'

The spear captain touched his forelock with a hand that was missing its two middle fingers. 'As I said, general, seventy men fighting fit. Maybe twenty more could fill in if things got desperate. The rest...' He showed his mutilated hand. 'They got worse than I did, and can't hold a spear with both hands no more. Our kit's in good shape, though. We've more spears than men, sad to say.'

Nordling nodded. 'Hultz?'

The handgunner captain saluted. 'Not many of my boys left, as you know, general,' he said. 'Too many buried at Grimminhagen.' He shrugged. 'Fifty-two, counting me, but six of them in the sick tent. Our guns are in good order, and we have plenty of powder, but...' He shot a glance at the man beside him, a gaunt artillery captain with one white eye and one blue, and waxy burn scars all over his bald head. 'But Captain Volk tells me...'

Volk straightened. The burn scars made him look like a half-melted daemon, but he talked like an Ostermark farmer. 'We're low on shot, m'lord,' he said, 'fer cannon and hand weapons both. Firing stock fell low up north and the new order from Nuln tain't arrived yet.'

'How soon is it meant to?' asked Nordling.

'Any day now,' said Volk. 'But I hear they been slow filling orders lately. Lot of folk looking to restock just now.'

'Exactly how much shot have we left?'

Volk pursed his lips. 'Enough for a few small engagements, m'lord, but if we was to be asked to keep up a steady rate of fire…' He scratched his scarred chin. 'Three hours or so with all seven cannons going. Less for the handguns, if all fifty o' Hultz's boys was firing away at speed. Maybe two hours.'

'That is grave news,' said the general. 'And your crews? Have you men for all seven cannon?'

'Oh aye,' said Volk, then made a face. 'Well, enough for five, at least. But these corpses won't be sailing up on boats, will they? So we can likely leave the riverside guns cold.'

'We can but hope,' said Nordling. He turned to the greatsword captain. 'Bosendorfer?'

The young man snapped a sharp salute. Too eager by half, thought Felix. 'Yes, general,' he said. 'Thirty men fighting fit and eager to serve. Our kit is polished and in good repair, and our greatswords sharp.'

'Any wounded?'

'Eight, my lord,' said Bosendorfer, 'but recovering quickly. I did not include them in my count.'

'Thank you, Bosendorfer. At ease.' Nordling turned to the red-headed boatman. 'River Warden Yaekel?'

The man saluted, but chewed his lip before answering. 'You know we didn't go north, general. Our duties on the river kept us here same as Steward von Geldrecht here. So we have a full complement – two fully armed and stocked river sloops, twenty-man crews for each, and a few skiffs and longboats, but – but, my lord, I have to agree with Zeismann and Hultz. There ain't no point in staying here. We'll never hold for so long. We have to retreat.' He took an involuntary step forwards. 'Please, let me and my men sail to Nadjagard and arrange things for your coming. We will–'

'No, Yaekel,' sighed Nordling. 'You won't be going anywhere. No one will. The graf has spoken.' He turned to the last man in the group, a hangdog-looking fellow with greasy brown hair spilling from his cap. He wore a doublet that proclaimed he was a Nordland forester, but breeches that suggested he was an officer of the Nuln city guard. 'And you, Captain…? Captain…?'

'Captain Draeger, m'lord,' said the man in a voice that announced him as a native of Altdorf's slums, and therefore not likely to have won any part of his uniform legitimately. 'Beggin' yer pardon but this ain't our posting. My lads are on their way home to the old city and just stopped for the night – thank you kindly fer the hospitality. But if it's all the same to you, we'll be on our way again.'

Nordling glared at him. 'It is *not* all the same to me,' he said. 'You're Reikland militia, are you not?'

'Aye,' said Draeger. 'Altdorf muster. Gallows Lane's finest.'

'No doubt,' murmured the general. 'Well, Captain Draeger, the Reikland still needs you. You will stay. How many men in your company?'

'Er, about thirty,' said Draeger, his eyes widening. 'But – but, m'lord, we was demobbed in Wolfenburg. They gave us our pay and sent us home. We–'

'Don't try it, my son,' said Zeismann. '"We done our bit" won't fly for you any more than it did for us.'

'It most certainly will not!' said Nordling. 'You have officially re-enlisted, captain. And fear not,' he said, as Draeger began complaining again, 'you will be paid.'

'Rather be gone than paid,' muttered Draeger, and folded his arms.

Nordling ignored him and stroked his black beard, thinking. 'Well then,' he said. 'Combined with the graf's knights – at least those who are fighting fit – we have roughly five hundred men, and when all the tenant farmers are brought in from the graf's lands, we will have another five hundred or so bowmen to add to our complement, making it an even thousand.'

'Against ten times as many,' said Yaekel bitterly.

Nordling turned hard eyes on him. 'Enough, river warden. The walls of Castle Reikguard have never fallen. I have every confidence we will survive.'

He turned and surveyed the others. 'Now, are there any further questions? Any further objections?'

No one said anything.

'Very well,' he said. 'Steward von Geldrecht will take the information you have given and consult with the graf as to strategy. In the meantime, you will inform your men of our situation and prepare for imminent attack, understood?'

The men all grunted their assent.

'Very good,' said Nordling, then saluted the others. 'You are dismissed. Long live the Emperor and may Sigmar protect us all.'

'Long live, Sigmar protect,' came the answering murmur, and the men began to talk amongst themselves as they started for the door.

Felix watched them as he followed them out. Except for the river warden, Yaekel, and Draeger, the militia captain, he thought the defence of the castle seemed in good hands. Bosendorfer was young and excitable, but full of fire, and von Geldrecht was a pompous ass, but he only looked after the stores. All the rest seemed hard, seasoned men.

'Herr Jaeger,' said a rough voice behind him.

Felix turned. Von Volgen was limping up behind him.

'My lord?' said Felix warily.

Von Volgen read his expression and scowled, embarrassed. 'I– I wanted to apologise, mein herr,' he said. 'I treated you and your friends abominably on our journey here. I hold the rule of law sacred above all things, and do my best to live by it, but the death of my son...

deranged me for a time, and I let anger rule instead of logic. Please forgive me for the lapse.'

Felix blinked, surprised. The lord's gruff manner had not prepared him for such a speech. He inclined his head. 'I understand, my lord. It must have been a great shock. But it wasn't me you swore to kill. You should speak to the slayers as well.'

'I will,' he said. 'And I thank you for your understanding.' And with that he bowed, and strode out through the temple door and into the courtyard.

Felix watched him go, bemused. He had expected the bulldog to act like a bulldog. Strange to find him a nobleman after all.

As he started to follow von Volgen out, he heard voices behind him and looked back. Avelein Reiklander was kneeling before the altar, head bowed to the hammer, while Sister Willentrude hovered behind her.

'Grafin,' the sister whispered, 'are you sure you wouldn't like me to look at your husband? Shallya has been known to work miracles.'

The grafin finished her prayer then stood, shaking her head. 'Thank you, Sister Willentrude, but my husband needs nothing but rest and peace. He will recover.'

The sister looked doubtful, but only bowed her head as the grafin turned for the door. Felix turned too, and hurried out, not wanting them to have caught him eavesdropping, and also wondering just what sort of wounds the graf had taken in the north.

'YOU ARE WELCOME to stay in any empty room you find,' said Captain Zeismann as he handed Felix and Kat bowls of stew from the mess line. 'And there's plenty empty. Most of the former occupants are sleeping in the ground north of Grimminhagen now.' He waved a magnanimous hand. 'Take some of the knights' rooms.

Y'don't want to bunk with the likes of us. Filthy peasants, all of us.'

This got a laugh from his men, who stood in line as well. They were in the cavernous underground mess, just one of the many chambers of the labyrinthine underkeep, which also contained barracks, store rooms, kitchens and workshops, as well as Tauber's surgery and a Shallyan shrine. The mess hall was loud with a hundred conversations, and warm from the heat of a huge fireplace at one end of the hall and the kitchens at the other.

'Very generous of you,' said Felix. 'But shouldn't we ask the knights first?'

Zeismann scowled towards the household knights, who sat all together at a dozen tables on the right edge of the room. 'Nah,' he said. 'They'll only say no if y'ask. But no one'll say anything if y'just take 'em.'

Felix smirked. 'Well, if they do, I'll tell 'em it was you who told us we could.'

Zeismann laughed. 'You do that.'

'Snorri thinks your bowls are too small,' said Snorri, looking dubiously at what the serving girl had handed him.

'Are you sure your stomach isn't too big, Father Rustskull?' asked Rodi.

'Come back for seconds if you like,' said Zeismann. 'We're always well stocked at Castle Reikguard.'

'Aye,' said Artillery Captain Volk. 'Till the war, the biggest danger the castle garrison ever faced was gettin' fat.' He grinned down at his skinny frame. 'Be a while 'fore we get some meat back on our bones after our long winter's jaunt, though.'

'Worry not, Captain Volk,' said Zeismann. 'At least ye'll be safe from the zombies. They'll think yer one of them!'

Everybody laughed, then started for the tables.

Felix scanned the room as he, Kat and the slayers followed. The various companies seemed to stick to their own kind, the handgunners at one table, the spearmen at another, the river wardens closest to the kitchens, while the household knights sat at the tables closest to the right wall. Bosendorfer, the towering, blond-bearded young captain, was laughing with his greatswords at a table near the fire. They were all big, broad-shouldered fellows like himself, and all wearing slashed doublets and hose and the most elaborate facial hair they could manage. It seemed they were having a contest to see who could spit into the flames from where they sat.

Von Volgen, as a noble guest, was dining with Nordling and von Geldrecht in their private quarters in the keep, which left his eight-score Talabeclander knights to eat here, sitting in a huddled crowd to one side, not quite comfortable in a room full of Reiklanders. The castle's other guests, the slovenly free-company captain, Draeger, and his motley militiamen, sat whispering over a table as far from the others as they could find, and looking often over their shoulders.

Felix, Kat and the slayers crowded in with Zeismann's spearmen at their table as they shoved aside to make room. They seemed a cheerful bunch, but Felix noticed a gauntness of cheek and hardness of eye among them that he had seen in other soldiers returning from the fighting in the north. Some, at the edges of the group, didn't join in the jokes and jibes at all, only stared dull-eyed at horrors hundreds of miles away and months in the past. Felix had seen that look before too.

'All dwarf work,' said Gotrek, looking up at the arched stone ceiling as he shovelled stew. 'All this underwork.

And better built than that human pile that sits atop it.'

'Reikguard is the finest human-made castle in the Empire,' said the artillery captain, Volk.

'*Human*-made, aye,' said Rodi dryly.

There were some glares at that, but Zeismann spoke up before things could get uncomfortable. 'The slayer is right, though,' he said. 'All this down here was built some eight hundred years ago, back when Gorbad Iron-claw was on his rampage. Emperor Sigismund ordered it to be converted into an Imperial fortress. It had to be turned from the Reikland princes' family seat into a citadel capable of holding a thousand soldiers and staff, and there was no one he trusted more than the dwarfs to do the job. They carved this little hill into a honeycomb, and built the harbour and outer walls too.'

'Trust dwarfs to put all our living quarters underground,' grumbled Volk. 'The knights' quarters have windows, air, the sun.'

'Wooden shacks,' said Rodi, between swallows. 'They'll fall down if you fart in them. You're safer here.'

'You haven't smelled Captain Volk's farts,' said one of the artillerymen.

Everybody laughed along with him, even Volk, and the tension eased. But as Felix took a swig from his mug, Kat trod on his toe under the table. He looked around and she nodded for him to bend down to her.

Felix frowned and looked around the hall as he leaned in. Had she spotted something strange? Was something wrong?

'What is it?' he whispered.

'We are leaving tomorrow with Snorri, yes?' she asked.

'Aye.'

'And Zeismann says we can have a private room tonight?'

'Aye,' Felix said again. 'If we want one, we are welcome–'

His eyes widened as he followed her train of thought to its conclusion. Though they had admitted their attraction to each other weeks ago, on the night she had saved him from freezing to death in the Drakwald, they had not, in all the time since, had any time to be alone together. Privacy had been fleeting on the trail, and being chased by beastmen was not particularly conducive to a romantic mood. The abject terror tended to get in the way.

But now, though a horde of undead was marching ever south towards them, they were for once in no immediate danger, and they would not be sleeping with only a thin sheet of canvas between them and their travelling companions.

'Ah,' he said. 'I see.'

Suddenly he couldn't finish his stew fast enough.

But though they practically raced across the courtyard – now filling up with the tenants coming in from Graf Reiklander's outlying farms – when they had finally found a room and closed the door behind them, they were strangely shy to begin.

For almost a full minute, Felix stood by the simple, neatly made soldier's bed, stroking Kat's hair and shoulders.

'Are – are you having second thoughts?' Kat asked at last.

'About you?' Felix laughed. 'Gods, no. It's only, having waited so long, I'm afraid we might have built up so great a mountain of expectation that... that we might not be able to get over it.'

Kat smiled shyly. 'You mean, "Now that we can, can we?"'

'Aye,' said Felix. 'Exactly.'

Kat shrugged. 'Well, there's only one way to find out.'

And with that, she tugged down on his collar until he bent to her, then went up on her tip-toes to kiss him. They came together hesitantly at first, but then Kat's lips parted and their tongues met. Filled with the strength of it, Felix crushed her to him, lifting her off her feet, and they toppled slowly to the bed.

FIVE

FELIX AND KAT walked together on a forest path. They were only a mile or so from Bauholz, where they were going to visit old Doktor Vinck. Felix was happy. It was an early spring day, still cold in the shade of the trees, but with a warm sun finding his face every now and then as they passed through a clearing, and he hadn't a care in the world. Gotrek wasn't there. Snorri and Rodi weren't there. Only he and Kat walked the path, and they were in no hurry, nor under any obligation.

Felix squeezed her hand. She squeezed back, and they stopped under the budding branches of an ancient oak, but as they leaned in to kiss, a distant cry reached Felix's ears – a bird of prey perhaps. He ignored it and bent closer, but Kat pulled back and looked around.

'Screaming,' she said.

'It's only a hawk,' said Felix.

'No.' Kat stepped away from him, back onto the trail.

'Can't you hear it? People are being killed.'

She started towards Bauholz again, jogging now.

'Kat, come back. It's nothing.'

She ignored him and ran on. He grunted in annoyance and started after her. The day was too perfect for trouble. He wanted her to come back and kiss him.

They ran out of the trees. The log walls of Bauholz rose beyond the fields before them, black smoke drifting in a cloud above them. The screams were clearer now. They were coming from the village.

Then they were at the gates, though Felix didn't remember running to them, shouting and pounding on the rough logs. Cries of terror and rage and the sharp reek of burning came from within.

Kat kicked the door. 'Get up!' she bellowed. 'Arm yourselves! We are under attack.'

Felix thought it was a very strange thing for her to say.

FELIX BLINKED AROUND, disorientated. He was not at the gates of Bauholz. He was in a dark room, lying in a cramped cot, his right side warmed by Kat and his left freezing where it pressed against the wall. But though the dream was fading, the shouting and pounding were getting louder and closer.

'Up, Reiklanders!' came the harsh low voice, and Felix wondered how he could have thought it was Kat's. 'To the walls!'

He raised his head and groaned, a terrible crick in his neck. Kat was sitting up beside him, naked and pushing her hair out of her face. The white streak in the middle of her dark brown tresses gleamed green in the light filtering through the room's diamond-paned windows. It looked like the castle had sunk beneath a sea of poison.

'What's going on?' Kat mumbled.

'I don't know.' He tried to sit up, then winced. His left

leg was completely asleep.

The door slammed open and one of Nordling's knights leaned in. 'Up and out! The dead–' He stopped when he saw Felix and Kat. 'What in Sigmar's name are you doing here? These are our quarters!'

He waved an impatient hand and ran on, banging on the next door down the hall.

'The dead?' echoed Felix.

He and Kat looked at each other, then scrambled to their feet and started grabbing for their armour and weapons.

SPEARMEN, GREATSWORDS AND knights hurried past them as Felix and Kat climbed the stone steps to the top of the castle wall. Torches glinted off their swords and spear-tips as they ran to their positions, and gleamed on the gun barrels of the handgunners who crouched between the crenellations, but the flames couldn't blot out Morrslieb's sickly green glow, which made the lowering clouds look like fat phosphorescent maggots, and turned everyone's skin a pasty grey.

To the right as they reached the parapet, Felix saw von Volgen talking earnestly with his knights, while to the left, Gotrek, Snorri and Rodi peered down over the battlements. Snorri had acquired a peg leg from somewhere, freshly sawn off at the bottom to fit his short frame, and had his hammer back, while Rodi had a new axe of dwarfen make to replace the one he had broken at Tarnhalt's Crown. Felix wondered where it had come from. A gift of the garrison?

'Snorri wants to go down and fight them,' Snorri was saying as Felix and Kat crossed to stand beside the slayers.

'Don't worry, Father Rustskull,' said Rodi. 'They'll come to us soon enough.'

'Too soon,' said Gotrek, shooting a grim glare at Snorri.

Kat and Felix leaned out over the walls to see what the slayers were looking at. The wan moonlight confused Felix's eyes, and at first he saw only twisted shadows lurching through the winter grass, but after a moment the shadows resolved themselves into walking corpses, both beast and man, hundreds of them converging slowly but inexorably on the castle. Already a thick crowd of them milled restlessly at the edge of the swift-flowing moat, while more and more stumbled forwards to join them, a moving carpet of the undead that stretched into the night for as far as he could see.

Gotrek was right. The dead had come too soon. Felix and Kat had planned to leave with Snorri the next morning, and be well on their way to Karak Kadrin before the horde arrived. Now they were trapped in the castle with everyone else. Gotrek must be furious. He had denied himself and Rodi a certain doom at Tarnhalt's Crown in order to get Snorri away from the undead, and now it was all for naught. Snorri was in worse danger than before, and Gotrek had done nothing but make an enemy of Rodi.

On the other hand, this wasn't necessarily the end of everything. Felix had fought the undead before and survived. He knew he was more than a match for any ten of them, and Gotrek was more than a match for a hundred. Still his stomach sank and his mouth went dry just looking at their lifeless, upturned eyes. And it wasn't just the dread of something dead returning to a travesty of life that chilled his blood, though that was horrible enough. It was the sheer, mindless inevitability of them. They were like ants, or water. A raindrop or a single ant was no threat. He could flick them away without effort. But a million ants, or a flood of water, those would find cracks in any wall, would spill over any barrier, would pull a man down and drown him in sheer numbers.

That was the true horror of the walking dead. They couldn't be reasoned with, couldn't be panicked into running away, couldn't be bought off or convinced to change allegiances. They were an unnatural force, as relentless as time or tides, and like time and tides, they would eventually wear you down, as mountains were worn down into hills and dead cattle were slowly stripped to the bone by thousands of tiny jaws. Zombies were as inevitable as death, for they were death.

'Look at 'em all,' said a spearman, his eyes dull. 'Endless. Endless.'

'And there's beasts among them,' said a handgunner, making the sign of the hammer. 'Sigmar, if that necromancer can make zombies of them monsters, what chance have we?'

'We must all pray to Morr,' said an artilleryman, touching a pin in the shape of Morr's raven on his cap. 'He will settle them and set us free.'

'Less of this talk!' cried General Nordling. 'We are Reiklanders! We fear nothing!' He was striding along the wall at the head of six household knights, with Steward von Geldrecht, and blind Father Ulfram and his acolyte, Danniken, following behind.

The men turned as the general stepped up into a crenellation and faced them, his back to the zombies. Felix could see that he was pale behind his jutting black beard, but he kept the fear out of his voice.

'Yes, our enemy is terrifying,' he said, as more men gathered around him. 'Yes, it is legion. But you are the strongest of the strong, the bravest of the brave, forged in battle against the Empire's greatest foes. Did we not hold the line together at Wolfenburg? Did we not drive back the fiends at Grimminhagen?'

'Aye!' cried the men. 'For the Empire! For the graf!'

Von Volgen and some of his men filed in at the back of the crowd, listening as Nordling continued.

'Neither do you stand naked and alone in the field against these horrors!' shouted the general, slapping the stones of the wall. 'You are protected by the defences of the finest castle of the Empire. Ogres could not ford our moat without being swept away. Dragons could not tear down our walls, so what chance have these poor corpses? Our battlements are dwarf-built and woven with powerful wards against the undead. They have endured for eight hundred years. Never has Castle Reikguard fallen, and never will it fall!'

The men cheered again, until Nordling raised his hands again. 'Quiet now for Father Ulfram, who will lead us in a prayer to Sigmar to give us strength for the coming–'

Something black and swift swooped out of the sky and slammed into him before he could finish, smashing him into Father Ulfram and knocking him off his feet.

'General! Father!' cried von Geldrecht, ducking and running to them as the black thing swept into the air again on leather wings.

'Kill it!' shouted a handgunner, pointing.

'Shoot it!' shouted a spearman.

Then the rest came.

Felix could not count the number of black shadows that streaked down out of the dim green sky and slammed into the defenders. It seemed as if the night had shattered and fallen in upon them. All along the walls, people were knocked to the courtyard, armour crushed and flesh torn, while others twisted and flailed as the things rode their backs, looking for all the world like lunatics dancing in flapping black cloaks. More were attacking the refugee farmers who had set up their meagre tents around the harbour. The peasants ran screaming as the ragged shades shredded their shelters and snatched up men, women and children to drop them to the flagstones or into the dark water of the harbour.

Felix ducked a swooping silhouette and drew his sword as Kat fired an arrow after it.

'Sigmar! What are they?'

Gotrek sheared the wing off one and it crashed at their feet in a spray of maggots and clotted bile. Felix recoiled at its rotting, snoutless face.

'Bats,' said the Slayer.

'Giant bats!' said Snorri, delighted.

'Giant *dead* bats,' said Rodi, wrinkling his bulbous nose. 'Grungni, what a reek.'

'So much for wards against the undead,' grunted Gotrek.

He and Rodi clambered onto the battlements and slashed around like whirlwinds as more black bodies dived at them. Snorri tried to follow, but couldn't manage with his new peg, and so stood guard with Felix over Kat as she continued loosing arrows.

A bat flew straight at Felix's face. He slashed with Karaghul and opened its chest to the bone, but momentum drove it into him, and it scrabbled at his chainmail shirt with diseased claws as teeth like black coffin nails snapped an inch from his cheek.

He retched, nauseated, and shoved it away, then cleaved its decaying head with his sword. It spun down over the wall, and Kat sent another after it, the fletching of her arrow sprouting from its eye. Felix made to turn back, but Kat laughed and pointed down towards the moat.

'Look at them!' she cried. 'Come on, you bone bags! More! More!'

Felix followed her gaze and saw that the undead, apparently stirred by the fighting over their heads, were pushing towards the walls – and toppling straight into the moat, where they were swept away by the roiling current. Dozens were floating downstream, and dozens more were falling.

Kat smiled grimly. 'At this rate the whole horde will be washed away!'

Gotrek chopped a bat out of the air directly above her head. 'Forget them, little one,' he rasped. 'Fight what you can hit.'

Kat scowled and she and Felix turned back to the bats on the walls, dropping them with sword and bow as they wheeled and swooped.

All along the parapet, the handgunners, knights and spearmen had rallied around their officers and were now fighting off the black shadows in good order, but they had already suffered terrible losses, and more fell every moment – punched from the parapet by the heavy bodies of the bats and torn apart by their claws. On Felix's right, the greatswords were sweeping their huge blades in wide circles over their heads, protecting Captain Bosendorfer as he pulled one of their number back onto the battlements. On his left, General Nordling had recovered, and was forming a square with his retinue around Father Ulfram and his acolyte while Steward von Geldrecht, bleeding badly from a wound on his leg, limped after them. Further on, Lord von Volgen and his men were fighting their way down the far stairs while the bats slammed down into them like black meteors.

In the courtyard Captain Zeismann and his spearmen were trying to herd the peasants towards the wide double doors of the underkeep as their tents burned down around them, but the farmers were being picked off as they ran, and many spearmen fell as well.

Then, with a sound like windmill blades turning in a gale, something huge swept over the wall, blotting out the sky. Felix ducked, and the thing skidded to a landing on the parapet beyond him, ploughing through Nordling's knights and knocking them flat with its enormous wings, as the armoured warrior on its back swept around it with an ugly black axe.

The beast was a wyvern – or perhaps a crude patchwork of several wyverns. It had a wyvern's vast leathery wings and whipping tail, and a cruel, horned head that snapped at the end of a long neck, but its scaly skin was ten different colours, the wings black, the head green, the body grey and red and brown, and in ten different stages of decay, with thick scars and stitches holding it all together; but as gruesome as it was, the rider mounted athwart its hulking shoulders was more terrifying still.

He looked more than a yard taller than Felix, and was encased in scarred black armour of ancient design. A heavy-browed skull, etched with age, glowered out from under a horned helm, green flames kindling in his empty eye sockets. He swung from the wyvern's saddle and waded into Nordling's retinue, his black axe trailing a glittering cloud of dark specks like the tail of a comet. Three knights died instantly as the fell weapon shredded their armour like parchment, and the rider trod their corpses underfoot to stride towards Nordling and Father Ulfram as von Geldrecht crabbed out of the way, gibbering with fear.

Gotrek, Rodi and Snorri stared. The ancient rune of power on the head of Gotrek's axe was glowing red.

'Mine,' he said.

'No, mine,' said Rodi.

'Snorri's!' shouted Snorri.

The three slayers charged as Nordling raised his sword and stepped in front of the skeletal warrior to protect Father Ulfram. The rider's flaking axe snapped the general's sword in half and smashed him off the parapet to bounce down the roof of the temple of Sigmar and into the courtyard.

'Face me, wight!' roared Gotrek, chopping into the wing of the undead wyvern as he dodged past it. The wyvern shrieked at the wound and leapt into the air as Rodi and Snorri ran under it.

'Face *me*!' called Rodi.

'Face Snorri!' bellowed Snorri.

'Come on,' said Felix, hacking at the swooping bats and starting forwards. 'We're safer near them than away.'

Kat dropped another bat point-blank, then followed, shouldering her bow and drawing her hatchets.

Gotrek reached the armoured wight first, and slashed for his knees just as he was turning from von Geldrecht to see what the commotion was. The dread warrior roared and blocked, and a choking cloud of obsidian dust shivered from his black axe as it clanged haft to haft with Gotrek's, covering the Slayer in black grit. Rodi struck next, but his blow glanced off the ancient black armour without leaving a mark. Snorri's hammer did no better. The wight seemed hardly to feel their attacks, and hacked back at them.

'Stand aside, Gurnisson!' shouted Rodi. 'You owe me this doom for that which you denied me at Tarnhalt's Crown!'

'I owe you nothing!' barked Gotrek. 'Take it if you can.'

Kat and Felix fell in behind the slayers, then turned as the wyvern *whumped* down again behind them, snapping and shrieking. Felix cursed and dodged right as Kat dived left, almost falling off the narrow parapet.

Trapped with the slayers between the beast and its master. Oh yes, much safer. What had he been thinking?

Kat buried her hand-axe in the beast's scaly neck, and it whipped around, crushing her against the wall.

Felix slashed, and Karaghul sheared off one of the wyvern's heavy horns. It roared and snapped, and he fell back into Snorri as the slayer was dodging back from the wight. They went down in a heap and the wyvern raised up, its fanged jaws distending as it snapped down at them.

Snorri swung his hammer up and knocked the scaly head aside. Its snout slammed into the parapet inches from Felix's shoulder, shattering the stone, and he and the old slayer scrambled up – only to have the wyvern's wing sweep them off the wall.

Felix froze, certain he was about to be smashed to a bloody pulp on the cobbles of the courtyard, but the impact came sooner than he expected, and he found himself rolling down the slanted roof of the temple of Sigmar in a scree of broken slates. He slid to a stop inches from the edge, then grunted as Snorri crashed on top of him.

Kat leapt down to the roof as the wyvern's jaws clacked shut inches behind her. She skidded to a stop beside him.

'Are you all right?'

'Aye,' wheezed Felix as he and Snorri untangled themselves. 'You?'

'Snorri is fine,' said Snorri. 'He landed on something soft.'

They scrambled up the slant again, dodging and swiping at bats as Snorri's peg leg slipped on the broken slates. Above them, the tide of the battle had turned. Rodi was driving back the undead wyvern, his axe making gruesome cuts in its head, neck and breast, while

Gotrek was backing up the armoured wight and matching him strike for strike as his axe traced rune-red swipes in the air.

But as Gotrek blocked a blow to his head, the champion turned his swing and cut at the Slayer's legs instead. Gotrek dodged back instinctively, but not quite quick enough, and the blade of the black axe grazed his thigh, cutting through his striped trews and slicing into his flesh.

The wound only seemed to anger the Slayer, and his next strike was so strong that it nearly knocked the undead champion over the parapet, and left him fighting for balance. Gotrek chopped at his flailing left arm and sheared through it at the elbow. The wight's armoured forearm bounced away along the parapet and became nothing but a lifeless bone rattling inside a battered vambrace.

He staggered back, as Gotrek pressed his advantage, denting his armoured legs and torso. The undead warrior had had enough. He jumped back from Gotrek, then barged past Rodi and leapt into the saddle of the reeling wyvern, spurring it savagely. The two slayers raced after him, but were too late. The wyvern flared its massive wings and knocked them back, then dived over the battlements and away.

'Come back, you coward!' bellowed Gotrek.

'How can the dead be scared to die?' shouted Rodi.

'Snorri missed the fight,' said Snorri.

'There are still plenty to fight, Snorri,' said Felix, helping Kat back onto the parapet.

But all at once, there weren't.

As if an order had been given, the bats flapped clear of their combats and flew after the dead wyvern and its malefic rider. Within a matter of heartbeats, the battle was over but for the groaning of the wounded and the weeping of the peasants in the courtyard.

While officers called orders and soldiers called for the surgeon, Gotrek and Rodi turned from the battlements, their faces hard and angry. The wound in Gotrek's thigh had drenched his trews red to the knee, but he paid it no mind. Instead he crossed to the severed forearm of the undead champion and picked it up. It began to disintegrate as soon as he touched it, the armour rusting away in brown flakes and the radius, ulna and finger bones within it crumbling to dust.

Gotrek crushed it in his meaty hand and looked out over the walls. 'A worthy doom,' he said.

'Aye,' said Rodi, glaring at him. 'For me, Gurnisson.'

Gotrek turned on the young slayer. 'I did not rob you of your doom at Tarnhalt, Balkisson. You put down your hammer for the same reason I put down my axe.'

Rodi snarled and stepped closer to him. 'You forced me to it.'

'You were free to defy me,' said Gotrek. 'As you were free to walk into the wood today.'

Rodi's hands balled into fists, and his face, already red, turned a deep vermillion. Gotrek put his axe on his back and waited, hands at his sides, meeting Rodi's furious glare with his single contemptuous eye.

'Snorri thinks he would have found his doom tonight,' said Snorri, trying to climb back onto the parapet as Kat helped Felix up, 'if some coward hadn't pushed him.'

Gotrek and Rodi held their staredown for another second, then broke off to take the old slayer's hands.

'Lucky for you, you didn't,' said Rodi.

He and Gotrek pulled Snorri onto the wall and Felix breathed a sigh of relief. Snorri couldn't have done it on purpose, but he had intervened at just the right time. The last thing Castle Reikguard needed just now was a pair of slayers brawling across the ramparts.

'Dwarfs!' gasped von Geldrecht, limping forwards on the arm of a knight, and followed by Father Ulfram and Danniken. 'Dwarfs, I owe you my life, and I thank you. You, more than anyone, drove that hellish wight away and saved me from its axe. But – but did you not tell us the leader of the undead horde was a mad old man?'

'That wasn't Hans the Hermit, my lord,' said Felix, shivering. 'I don't know who it was, or what. I have never seen it before.'

'It was Krell,' rasped Gotrek.

Von Geldrecht blinked. 'Who? Who is Krell?'

'Krell the Holdbreaker,' said Gotrek. 'The Lord of the Undead.'

'The Butcher of Karak Ungor,' said Rodi. 'The Doom of Karak Varn.'

'Whose name is written a hundred times in the Book of Grudges,' said Gotrek.

'Who so hated dwarf-kind that he returned from the dead to seek vengeance upon us,' said Rodi.

'My doom,' said Gotrek.

'*My* doom,' said Rodi.

Gotrek glanced at the young slayer and gave him a vicious smile. 'He may well be, beardling,' he said, then wiped blood from his wounded leg and looked at his hand. 'But he has already killed me.'

SIX

Felix frowned, certain he couldn't have heard the Slayer correctly. 'Killed you?' he said. 'Gotrek, it's just a scratch. You've taken worse. Far worse.'

'No, manling,' said the Slayer. 'I have not.' He held out his hand. The blood that dripped from his thick fingers was peppered with tiny black flecks. 'The Axe of Krell leaves behind splinters of obsidian. They burrow to the heart and bring slow death.' He smiled again, a grim flat line. 'I have found my doom at last.'

Felix's heart lurched. His head swam as he tried to take it in. Could he have already witnessed Gotrek's doom without knowing it? It seemed impossible. The Slayer couldn't die in such a sad, inglorious way.

'Gotrek,' he said, stepping forwards. 'You have to clean the wound. You can't let this happen.'

'Of course he can't!' said von Geldrecht, limping forwards. 'Sigmar's beard, herr Slayer, you must see our surgeon immediately. These splinters must come out!'

Gotrek turned a cold eye on the steward. 'Is it my doom that worries you, lordling? Or your own?'

Rodi laughed at this, while Von Geldrecht's red face got even redder.

'Certainly, Slayer, you are a great boon to our defences,' he said. 'But you mistake me. I am merely concerned for your wellbeing–'

'A slayer's "wellbeing" is his own business,' growled Gotrek, and started for the stairs to the courtyard with Rodi and Snorri following. 'And it doesn't matter. The slivers are already at their work. There's no getting them out now.'

Felix swallowed and stepped after him. 'Surely it's worth trying, Gotrek. Poison is no death for a slayer.'

Gotrek waved him off and continued. 'Leave me be, manling. I need a drink.'

Kat put a hand on the Slayer's arm as he passed her. 'Gotrek. Please. It might let you live long enough to face this Krell again.'

The Slayer stopped and looked at her for a long moment. 'Aye. It might,' he said at last. He nodded. 'Very well.'

As they started for the stairs again, Felix shot Kat a relieved glance, and von Geldrecht let out a breath.

'Thank you, fraulein,' he said, limping after them. 'You have done us a great service with this–'

She stopped and snarled back at him. 'I didn't do it for you!'

Felix turned away so von Geldrecht wouldn't see him smirk at his stunned expression.

'I'm sorry, Felix.' said Kat. 'He doesn't give a damn about Gotrek's "wellbeing".'

'Don't apologise,' said Felix. 'I'd have done the same if I had any guts.'

* * *

RODI GROWLED AS they started across the ruined courtyard towards the underkeep. 'Two thousand years of grudges crossed off in the book when Krell died,' he said.

Kat looked at him, amazed. 'You have fought him for two thousand years?'

'Aye,' said Rodi. 'Ever since he gave himself to the Blood God and came for our holds.'

'Karak Ungor and Karak Varn both suffered beneath his axe before that pup Sigmar killed him,' said Gotrek.

'And now he lives again,' spat Rodi. 'And all those grudges must be written back into the book as unavenged.'

Gotrek nodded, his one eye distant. 'Aye, but the slayer who gives him a true and final death would be remembered in the histories forever.'

'Aye,' said Rodi, thumping his chest with his fist. 'Rodi Balkisson, Slayer of Krell.'

Gotrek shot him a hard look. 'We will see about that.'

'Snorri thinks Snorri Nosebiter, Slayer of Krell, sounds better,' said Snorri.

Rodi grunted at that, and Gotrek ground his teeth, and they stumped on in silence. Felix shook his head at the dwarfishness of it all. Cut by an axe that seemed certain to kill him, and Gotrek was still more concerned with wrongs done to his ancestors thousands of years before – and of course by how he would be remembered by the dwarfs who would come after him. It seemed sometimes that dwarfs lived more in the past than they did in the present.

As they continued across the courtyard, however, Felix's grim amusement faded, to be replaced by a growing sense that something was terribly wrong in the castle. The dead and dying were of course everywhere, and the air was filled with the stench of burnt tents and roasted flesh, but there was something else, something worse behind it all, though he couldn't put a finger on what.

Dead knights, farmers, spearmen, greatswords, hand-gunners and river men lay where they had died, their faces and necks shredded to red ruin, and their bones smashed by falling from the walls. There were corpses burning amidst the smouldering tents, and bumping against the hulls of the boats in the harbour, and the wounded looked hardly better, howling and sobbing with deep claw marks in their backs and their limbs crushed and bent.

Zeismann's spearmen and von Volgen's knights helped the farmers pick through the carnage, dragging the living to one side, and piling the dead on the other. The tenants wept pitifully when they found loved ones, and some could not continue. A mother hugged her child to her breast, the blood from his torn throat drenching her tunic. A young girl shrieked ceaselessly for her parents.

The men of the castle gathered their wounded as well, carrying them into the underkeep on stretchers as they moaned and wailed.

The wailing.

Perhaps that was it.

Felix couldn't tell if it was his imagination, but the screaming of the wounded seemed even more agonised than was usual after a battle. Even the cleansings and salvings of the Shallyan initiates and Surgeon Tauber's assistants appeared to hurt them beyond bearing, as if they were being bathed with fire instead of water, and it got worse as Felix and Kat followed the slayers into the underkeep.

Wounded men were laid out in the mess hall and along the corridor leading to the surgery, all in

incredible pain. There was a smell about them too – a
sick, sour reek of neglect that Felix associated with
overcrowded poverty wards. He would have expected
such a smell if the soldiers had lain here for weeks, but
not so soon. Their wounds were fresh – minutes old.
The place should smell of blood and burnt flesh, but
not the charnel house. Not yet.

Captain Zeismann stood from lowering a spearman
into a cot, and gave Felix, Kat and the slayers a weary
salute.

'Well done, friends,' he said. 'Y'did heroes' work up on
them walls tonight. Saved old Goldie's bacon for him
and no mistake.'

'Goldie?' asked Felix.

'Von Geldrecht,' said Zeismann. 'He ain't much, but–'

A roar of anger from the surgery cut him off, followed
swiftly by the crash of overturning furniture and bellowed accusations.

'Murderer!'

'Poisoner!'

'You're in league with the necromancer!'

'Yer tryin' to turn us all into zombies!'

'Please!' cried a higher voice. 'It's got nothing to do
with me!'

Felix recognised the voice as Tauber's, strained to
breaking with fear.

'Aw, what's all this now?' groaned Zeismann, and hurried for the surgery door, which was clogged with
knights and foot troops, all shouting and trying to get in
at once.

Felix, Kat and the slayers followed as Zeismann
shoved and elbowed at the back of the mob, raising his
voice to a parade-ground bark to be heard.

'Step back! Step back! What's the trouble?'

The three slayers bulled through the crowd as if it

weren't there, and Zeismann followed gratefully in their wake, with Felix and Kat taking up the rear.

Inside, Greatsword Captain Bosendorfer and a semi-circle of men had backed Tauber and his assistants into a corner. Tauber shrank from them, a scalpel in his shaking hand. His assistants wielded stools and buckets and mops. It smelled worse in there than in the corridor.

'You may have killed us, you traitor,' said Bosendorfer, 'but we'll take you with us.'

'And take your head off too,' said a spearman. 'You'll not be joining your zombie brothers.'

'Hoy, now!' said Zeismann. 'What's this about?'

'I haven't poisoned anyone,' cried Tauber. 'It must be something else! The claws of the bats!'

'A liar as well as a traitor,' sneered Bosendorfer. He pointed to one of his men, sweating on a cot like he was in an oven and clutching an arm wound that glistened with oozing green pus. 'Pulcher was cut by falling slates. Those horrors never touched him!'

'Then I don't know what it is!' said Tauber. 'But I've got nothing to do with it.'

'That's just what you would say,' said Bosendorfer, starting forwards. 'Grab him! Bring him out to the yard where I can make a proper swing. And fetch out his minions too.'

'Wait, now, Bosendorfer! Wait!' shouted Zeismann, getting in the greatsword's way. 'I know you don't like old Tauber, but these are serious charges. Let's take it to General Nordling.'

Bosendorfer shoved the spearman into Felix. 'Stay out of it, Zeismann! You don't outrank me!'

The greatsword charged at Tauber with the mob barging in behind him, fists flying.

'This is bad,' said Kat. 'Gotrek needs him.'

'We all need him,' said Felix, setting Zeismann on his feet. Tauber might be a pinched little man with the bedside manner of a mollusc, but he had patched up nearly a hundred wounded the day before and none had sickened – not even Kat, not even after Felix had threatened him. Whatever his crimes, Felix doubted this present evil was one of them.

He caught Bosendorfer's arm as he started to drag Tauber out of the room. 'Wait, captain! Are you really going to kill the only man who can patch you up?'

'Aye,' added Zeismann, stepping beside him. 'Are y'daft?'

Bosendorfer glared down at them from his impressive height, and looked like he was going to shove them aside, but the slayers moved in behind them and he only snarled.

'He's not patching us up,' he said. 'He's murdering us, like he did up north!'

'He didn't murder anyone up north, Bosendorfer,' said Zeismann, exasperated. 'That's all been sorted out. He just couldn't save everyone. You know that.'

'I know nothing of the sort!' snapped the greatsword. 'I said then he was with the Kurgan, and now I say he's with this necromancer, trying again!'

Felix blinked, confused. The warrior sounded mad. 'If he's with the necromancer,' he said, as calmly as he could, 'then why didn't he poison everybody yesterday after the fight?'

Bosendorfer's cheek twitched as he locked eyes with Felix. 'Who are you, that we should listen to you? Are you with the necromancer too? Are you, Zeismann? Get out of our way! We've a traitor to kill!'

The men roared in agreement, and this time Bosendorfer did shove Felix and Zeismann, but as he started to drag Tauber between them, Gotrek, Snorri and Rodi stepped in his way.

'If you insult the manling,' said Gotrek, 'you insult us.'

Bosendorfer paused at this, looking uneasily from slayer to slayer. 'I– I didn't insult him. I only told him to get out of the way.'

'You said he was with the necromancer,' said Rodi.

'Snorri doesn't know any necromancers,' said Snorri. 'And neither does young Felix.'

Felix could see that Bosendorfer would have liked to back down in the face of three so fearsome opponents, but the men behind him were shouting insults at the dwarfs and egging him on. He was trapped, and it made him angry. 'I don't care who you know or who you are!' he shouted. 'You have no authority here! I am Graf Reiklander's captain of greatswords. I order you to get out of my way!'

The slayers said nothing, only raised their fists. Felix and Kat did the same as the mob roared and Zeismann called for calm. But then, over all the noise, came a bellowing from the hall.

'Surgeon Tauber! Clear your table!'

Felix recognised von Geldrecht's voice, and so did the rest, for they all stopped shoving as the steward limped through with two household knights behind him. He was using a cane to walk.

'Tauber!' he gasped. 'You must see to General Nordling at once. He has a pestilence in his–' He stopped as he saw the scene before him. 'Bosendorfer, what is this? Unhand our surgeon!'

'My lord,' said Bosendorfer, saluting. 'It is Tauber who has caused the pestilence. Look!' He flashed a hand around at the wounded, all moaning and putrefying in their cots. 'Look at their wounds. He has poisoned them!'

'You don't know that, Bosendorfer!' said Zeismann.

Von Geldrecht cringed as he looked from horror to horror, then turned back to Tauber, a frightened look in his eyes. 'Is– is this true, surgeon?'

'No, lord steward,' said Tauber. 'I don't know what has caused it. I swear to you.'

'He's lying!' shouted Bosendorfer. 'He's killed us all!'

'My lord,' said Felix, 'I don't think he has. If he was responsible, wouldn't he have tried to slip away? He has been at his post, tending the wounded.'

'He has been sickening them!' cried Bosendorfer.

'How d'ye know it was him that did it?' said Zeismann. 'It could be anyone!'

Everyone began shouting at once, with von Geldrecht bellowing over them all for silence, but then, into the room pushed four household knights with General Nordling on a stretcher between them, and the cacophony died away to a whisper of murmured prayers and indrawn breaths.

The general, so straight and proud when Felix had first seen him, now lay on the stretcher like a victim of famine. His limbs, under the bloody shirt that was his only cover, were bone-thin and swollen at the joints, and his face was gaunt and grey. His breath came shallow and fast, like a panting dog. Felix saw only one wound on him, but it was terrible. A spike of broken bone jutted out of his left leg above the knee, and the gash through which it stuck was black and bubbling with green pus, and stank of death.

Zeismann choked as the knights put Nordling on a table. 'Sigmar, what happened to him?'

A frightened field surgeon who had trailed in behind the knights shook his head. 'He was well enough after he fell from the chapel roof. Just the broken leg, and he made jokes about it as we carried him to the barracks, but only moments after we cleaned the wound he was like this. I don't understand it.'

Von Geldrecht turned to Bosendorfer and motioned to Tauber, who was still pinned in the greatsword's iron grip. 'Release him. Let him work.'

Bosendorfer reluctantly let go, and Tauber stood erect, his limbs shaking.

'Thank you, lord steward,' he said, bowing to Von Geldrecht.

'If you are responsible,' said von Geldrecht, putting his hand on his sword, 'you will reverse the poison. If you are not, you will cure him, or it will be the worse for you.'

Tauber swallowed, and a look passed between the two men that Felix could not read. 'I– I will try.'

The surgeon motioned to his assistants and approached the table as they began to prepare his implements.

'Tell me everything you did,' he said to the field surgeon as he checked Nordling's pulse and pulled back his eyelids. 'Omit no detail.'

'We did only what we always do,' said the man. 'We removed his armour and clothes, examined him thoroughly, then washed his wounds clean of dirt and gave him strong wine to drink so that he would feel it less when we put the bone back. But... but we never got so far as that. He sickened too fast. He wasted away before our eyes!'

Tauber frowned, seemingly baffled, then looked back uneasily at von Geldrecht, who gripped the hilt of his sword with white knuckles. 'I am not sure what to do, my lord,' he quavered. 'He appears to be dying of dysentery, but to reach such an advanced stage of the disease should take days, not minutes.'

'I care not what it is,' said von Geldrecht. 'Only heal him.'

'But, my lord, to heal a man in this condition takes

days – weeks. He will not get better in a matter of moments, no matter what I do.'

Von Geldrecht said nothing, only drew his sword, his face white. Tauber sighed and turned his assistants. 'Wash his wounds clean of pus and spoon-feed him water,' he said. 'After I salve the wound we will set the bone.'

The assistants nodded. One dipped a cloth in a basin beside the table, then began dabbing at the black meat of the wound as the other tugged Nordling's mouth open and began tipping water into it from a spoon, one drop at a time. Tauber crossed to a shelf and began pulling down pots and vials. But as he laid them out on a tray, there was a commotion in the hall and a woman's voice, high and strained.

'Let me through! By all mercies, let me through!'

The soldiers at the door parted and Sister Willentrude pushed in between them, her round face red and shiny, and her heavy chest heaving like a sail. Her eyes widened when she saw Nordling on the table, and she shot out a hand.

'Stop!' she cried. 'Do not touch him with that cloth! Take away that spoon!'

The assistants cringed back and Tauber turned, staring at her.

'What is this, Sister Willentrude?' he asked. 'Is there something–'

'The water,' she gasped as she tried to catch her breath. 'The lower well has been poisoned. And every jug, canteen and horse trough I have checked.' She turned to von Geldrecht. 'My lord, you must tell everyone. Do not drink or wash with water until we can test it all.'

'You see!' cried Bosendorfer, turning back to Tauber as von Geldrecht stared. 'The traitor has poisoned us all.'

SEVEN

Von Geldrecht turned on Tauber, eyes filled with fear and questions. 'Surgeon–'

Tauber stumbled back. 'My lord steward, I assure you! I have not done this thing. I haven't any such power. I am just an ordinary man. You know that.'

'Don't listen to him!' shouted Bosendorfer. 'He's poisoned me before!'

'Please, lord steward,' said Sister Willentrude. 'I can't believe it could be Tauber. He is a fine surgeon, a dedicated man of medicine! It couldn't be him!'

'Can you prove it wasn't?' asked Bosendorfer. 'Can you prove he is innocent?'

Von Geldrecht said nothing, only stared at Tauber as Bosendorfer and the sister continued to argue.

Felix couldn't take it any longer. He stepped forwards and shouted at von Geldrecht. 'Steward! Are you going to stand here while the men of the castle are still drinking and bathing in tainted water? Give the order!'

Von Geldrecht's eyes snapped around to Felix, hot with anger, but then he stopped, paling with realisation. He turned to the men. 'On my order,' he said. 'Speed to every corner of the castle. No one is to drink or touch water until I say. Go! Spread the word.'

The men, cowed by the horror of Nordling's condition, hurried out of the surgery without argument, yelling to everyone in the hall and leaving von Geldrecht and his knights, Bosendorfer, Zeismann, Felix, Kat and the slayers standing around Tauber and his assistants, who looked shaken and sick.

'Water,' Tauber mumbled. 'How was I to know? How was I–'

A breathy rattle interrupted him and everyone looked at General Nordling. His shallow panting had stopped, and he lay absolutely still. Tauber went white and stepped to him, taking his pulse again and listening to his chest. He closed his eyes and murmured a prayer, then stood.

'He– he is dead, my lord steward.'

The household knights groaned and lowered their heads, but Bosendorfer spun to von Geldrecht.

'Kill him, my lord,' he said. 'Kill him as you said you would!'

'No!' cried Kat. 'He must see to Gotrek! Tauber has to clean the Slayer's wound!'

'My lord, you mustn't kill him,' said Sister Willentrude. 'Without water, we will have to find other ways to clean and dress wounds. We will need his expertise.'

'His expertise is in death,' snarled Bosendorfer. 'Hang him! Or the men will do it for you!'

Von Geldrecht had said nothing through this storm of argument, only held eyes with Tauber, but at this last he shot a sharp look at Bosendorfer.

'With General Nordling's death,' he said, cold and quiet, 'I am now acting commander until Graf Reiklander recovers. And as commander, I will not allow a man to hang without trial, nor will I allow him to be subject to barracks justice.' He turned to the household knights. 'Classen,' he said to a young knight sergeant with tears in his eyes. 'Lock up the surgeon. He will stay in the dungeon until we get to the bottom of this.'

'But, my lord,' said Sister Willentrude. 'That is no better. How will he do his work from a cell?'

'How will he clean Gotrek's wound?' asked Kat.

'Until I know where his loyalties lie,' said von Geldrecht, 'he remains under lock and key. Take him away, Classen. And his minions too.'

The young knight nodded, then motioned to the others to arrest Tauber and his men.

'Now,' said von Geldrecht, sighing. 'We will check the stores. I want to see if anything else was tainted.'

Kat looked like she was going to protest Tauber's arrest again, but the Slayer shook his head.

'Forget it, little one,' he said. 'It's all part of the doom.'

FELIX GAGGED AS Gotrek knocked in the top of a barrel of salted meats with his axe. Fat maggots crawled all over bubbling beef and the stench of rotting flesh burned his eyes. Kat cut open a sack of beans, then choked as clouds of mildew spores billowed up from it. In other parts of the vaulted cellar von Geldrecht and the rest were finding similar horrors. Sister Willentrude was opening a sack of onions that had become black balls of slime. Bosendorfer was picking distastefully through apples and turnips gone brown and runny while Zeismann was cringing away from the hard sausages that hung from the beams, their casings split and giving birth to a swarm of flies.

From the far side of the room came a dismayed dwarfen shout. 'Not the beer, too!'

Felix and Kat looked around. Rodi was standing on tip-toe staring into a keg almost as tall as he was, his hands white-knuckled on the lip. Snorri was staggering back, awkward on his peg leg, waving a big hand in front of his bulbous nose.

'Snorri thinks that's the worst beer he's ever smelled.'

Von Geldrecht blinked at the two slayers, then turned and hurried to a long rack of dusty wine bottles. He grabbed one and broke the top off by knocking it against the wall, then inhaled over the open neck. He coughed and winced, holding the bottle away from him and covering his face in the crook of his arm.

'This flour might be saved,' said Zeismann.

The rest came over to look at the sack he had split open. The flour that spilled from it was crawling with tiny beetles, but did not appear rotten.

Von Geldrecht looked revolted, but nodded. 'It will have to be sifted, but it seems we have flour at least.'

'Yes,' said Bosendorfer. 'Though no water to mix it with, thanks to Tauber.'

'Mmmm,' said Zeismann, rubbing his skinny belly. 'Dry flour, with bugs.'

Sister Willentrude shook her head. 'The necromancer has nearly defeated us in a single night,' she said. 'The bats killed scores of men. The poisoned water has killed scores more, and hunger and thirst will finish the rest. It is impossible that the castle can still stand.'

Von Geldrecht glared at her. 'It *must* stand! We must hold until our relief gets here.'

'But how?' asked the sister. 'A man might live a week on biscuit, though he will be as weak as a child, but a week without water? Impossible. Four days at the most, and much less if he is forced to fight.'

'And we *will* be forced to fight,' said Felix.

'Can't you pray to Shallya?' asked Bosendorfer, holding up a disintegrating apple. 'Can't you make it all wholesome again?'

'The food is fouled beyond redemption,' said Sister Willentrude. 'But prayers to Shallya might purify some water, though how much I couldn't say.'

'What about taking water from the river?' asked Felix. 'Surely the necromancer can't have poisoned the whole Reik?'

'He don't have to,' sighed Zeismann. 'We're downstream from the Reiker Marshes. The water for miles below that stinking swamp ain't fit to drink unless it is boiled.'

'So start boiling,' said Gotrek.

Von Geldrecht swallowed, looking as pale and sick as one of the poisoned defenders. His first moments as acting commander of the castle had not been auspicious ones. 'Yes,' he said. 'Start boiling. And pass word to the men that the food has been poisoned as well. I… I will consult with the graf.' And with that, he turned and limped out of the room.

As THEY LEFT the store room and Bosendorfer and Zeismann went to tell the castle about the spoiled food, Kat stepped after Sister Willentrude.

'Sister,' she said, 'can you look at Slayer Gotrek's wound? It must be cleaned or he may die.'

The sister turned, smiling patiently. 'Child, I must begin my prayers. The danger we face is bigger than the wounds of one dwarf.'

'But he isn't only a dwarf,' pleaded Kat. 'He is a slayer. Who else is strong enough to fight the wight king if he comes back?'

Rodi snorted. 'You'd think he fought the bastard

alone,' he said under his breath.

Gotrek ground his teeth. 'I told you to forget it, little one.'

But Sister Willentrude was frowning, considering. She looked at Gotrek. 'I saw you fight on the walls, herr dwarf. You are indeed worth a score of men. But where is this grievous wound? I see only the scratch on your leg.'

'That is it,' said Felix quickly. 'It was made by Krell's axe, which leaves poison splinters that seek the heart and kill in time.'

'And it is too late to remove them,' growled Gotrek, impatient. He turned and started for the courtyard. 'There are worse wounded, priestess. See to them.'

'No, herr Slayer,' Sister Willentrude called after him. 'You are key to our defence. For the sake of the castle, if not your own, I will ask you to come with me.'

Gotrek kept walking, but Kat caught up to him and put a hand on his massive arm.

'Please, Gotrek,' she said. 'Let her try.'

Gotrek walked for a few more steps, but at last he stopped. 'For you, little one,' he said, 'I will go.'

The sister smiled as he turned back to her. 'Thank you, Herr Slayer. Follow me.'

She led them back towards the surgery, talking over her shoulder as she went. 'It isn't just for your fighting skill that I wish to keep you among the living. You lot have cool heads, and with General Nordling dead now, we will be needing all of those we can lay our hands on, I'm thinking.'

They entered the surgery, where Sister Willentrude's initiates were tending to the moaning rows of wounded, and followed her to a pantry-sized shrine of Shallya at the back.

She pointed Gotrek to a bench as she gathered

forceps, lens, jug and cloth, and pulled a stool up in front of him. 'General Nordling ran the castle well,' she sighed. 'But with him dead and the graf unwell, that leaves von Geldrecht, and I fear old Goldie ain't up to the task.'

The sister took up the jug of water and began praying over it as Felix and Kat watched and the slayers waited at the door, Rodi still muttering about Gotrek not being the only one to have fought Krell. The Slayer's gash was not deep, but it was grimed with little black flecks.

Finishing her prayer, Sister Willentrude tasted the water, then, satisfied, poured it liberally over the wound and sponged it with the cloth. The flecks lessened, but did not vanish. Next she took up the lens and the forceps.

'Yes,' she said, prodding the wound. 'There are slivers well buried in the muscle. Many of them.'

Gotrek sat stoic, his jaw set, as she gripped and pulled with the forceps, removing splinter after splinter from his flesh and wiping them onto the cloth.

'So, Graf Reiklander is confined to his bed?' asked Felix as she worked. 'He is that ill?'

Sister Willentrude sniffed. 'I know not. I saw him once, the day he returned with his troops, and he was gravely wounded, but since then the Grafin Avelein has not seen fit to let me see him, only Tauber. Only he and von Geldrecht are allowed into his rooms, and they tell me nothing other than, "his lordship is recovering".'

'Is that why von Geldrecht would not allow Bosendorfer to string Tauber up?' asked Felix.

'Very likely,' she said. 'Thick as thieves the steward and the surgeon have been since Graf Reiklander returned.' She shook her head bitterly as she removed another sliver. 'I wish the graf were well again – or that his son would return from university in Altdorf. The graf was an able commander, wise and strong, and Dominic a sharp-minded lad. Neither would have locked Tauber up for fear of Bosendorfer. They would have locked Bosendorfer up for insubordination. Now I must do double duty as physician and sister, and spend time and strength I don't have praying for pure water. Hopefully von Geldrecht will come to his senses. Besieged like this we cannot survive long without a real surgeon.'

'Is Tauber a good surgeon?' asked Kat.

The sister chuckled without looking up from her work. 'Felt the lash of his tongue, have you? Well, he's never been a friendly sort, and going north only made that worse. So many men dead. So many men he couldn't save. It left him bitter, but you'll find no more talented bone-cutter in the Empire. He treats Karl Franz himself when he summers here.'

With a sigh she sat back and mopped her brow. 'Well, I've removed all I can see,' she said. 'But there are more. I'm certain of it.' She pushed to her feet and stepped to her cupboard again, where she began pulling down pots and jars. 'I will prepare a poultice that will, Shallya willing, draw out more, but I don't know if even that will get them all.'

Gotrek shrugged as she began to mix ingredients in a bowl. 'As long as I live long enough to face Krell again, I don't care.'

'Don't think I'll back off because of this, Gurnisson,' said Rodi. 'You'll still have to beat me to him if you want him.'

'Don't worry, Balkisson,' said Gotrek. 'I will.'

THICK SMOKE WAS rising into the pink sky of pre-dawn as Felix and Kat stepped wearily out of the underkeep with the slayers. A great pyre of headless bodies burned in the middle of the courtyard, and the air was filled with the queasy smell of sweet pork. Father Ulfram and his acolyte stood in front of the pyre, chanting, the blind priest holding his warhammer unwaveringly above his head and clutching the holy book to his chest unopened. In a circle around the pyre, their heads bowed in silent prayer, the survivors of the battle stood – the household troops, the knights, von Volgen's men, the servants and refugee farmers who had thought the castle would protect them.

In the front row, their faces carved into stark, flickering relief by the glow of the fire, were the various commanders and captains – von Volgen, with new bandages to add to the one around his chest, von Geldrecht leaning on his cane, Bosendorfer glaring at the fire as if it were the enemy, Zeismann chewing his lip and shuffling his feet, Yaekel, the river warden, asleep on his feet, and Draeger with his thumbs hooked in his belt, looking like he'd rather be anywhere else.

Many of the farmers and servants wept. Many more just stared dully, shocked by the suddenness and savagery of the attack. The knights and household troops, veterans of the war in the north, only looked tired and resigned. Felix knew the look. He had seen it many times before, in the faces of those he had fought beside over all his long years with Gotrek. The loss of comrades in battle was never easy, but for the professional soldier, it was a familiar pain, and caused neither shock nor anger, just a weary sadness they locked away where it would not interfere with their work. The pain would be let out later, when all was safe, and would escape as drinking and fighting and whoring and the singing of raucous songs. But it was hidden now, and would not show itself while the threat of further battle remained.

Felix and Kat started across the courtyard towards the pyre, but the slayers were talking amongst themselves and didn't follow. Felix paused, wondering if they were still arguing about Krell, but it was something else entirely.

'Pay your respects, manling,' said Gotrek. 'We want to have a look at these so-called ward-woven walls.'

'"Enduring",' sneered Rodi. 'Aye. As enduring as an elf's honour.'

Felix nodded and he and Kat joined the mourners as the dwarfs stumped off in the opposite direction. After seeing the squabbling between Bosendorfer, Tauber and von Geldrecht, Felix was a bit envious of the slayers' ability to put aside their animosities and work for the common good. He knew that Gotrek and Rodi were still angry with each other, but they wouldn't let it get in the way of what was important. If only humans could learn that skill.

When Father Ulfram's chanting ended and everyone had murmured a last 'Sigmar preserve us', the crowd broke up – the surviving refugees returning to clear away their blackened tents, the household troops to begin repairing the defences, but the officers gathered around von Geldrecht and Father Ulfram, who were talking together in low tones. Von Volgen joined them too.

Felix edged closer with Kat, wanting to hear whether Graf Reiklander had told von Geldrecht to hold or retreat, but it was Father Ulfram who was speaking.

'No, I can't be certain,' he quavered. 'But I fear it must be. In the histories, they are always mentioned in the same breath. If the dwarf spoke true, and it was Krell he fought on the walls, then the necromancer is who I feared he was from the first – Heinrich Kemmler, who raised Krell from a thousand-year slumber to serve as his champion.'

The name seemed to mean little to most of the

officers, and it stirred only vague memories from university lectures in Felix, but von Volgen knew it.

'It can't be Kemmler,' he said. 'He was slain over twenty years ago, in Bretonnia.'

'It might be,' said the priest, nodding. 'It might be, but the deaths of necromancers are often greatly exaggerated. And if it is he, we face a terrible threat. Terrible. Kemmler was said to be one of the greatest necromancers since Nagash, defeating the most powerful magisters and priests of his age. If he is returned, then dark days have befallen the Empire. Dark days.'

Zeismann snorted. 'And that's a change, is it?'

Von Geldrecht smiled and clapped Zeismann on the shoulder. 'Thank you, captain,' he said, with forced cheer. 'That is the true Empire spirit. Knowing the name of our enemy changes nothing. We have faced worse before, and spat in their eye. We will do the same now.' He turned to the others. 'Now, gentlemen, your reports. Bosendorfer?'

The men all looked at each other, clearly not fully confident in their new commander, despite how hard he was trying – or perhaps because of it.

'Ten men dead, sir,' said the greatsword at last. 'Four from Tauber's poisons.'

The steward coughed. 'Enough about Tauber. How many can fight?'

'Thirteen,' said Bosendorfer, sullen. 'Only thirteen.'

'Zeismann?' asked von Geldrecht.

'Thirty-three dead or wounded,' said the spear captain. 'Thirty-nine fighting fit.'

'Thirty-seven knights dead,' said von Volgen. 'Fifty-five well enough to fight. Forty more are wounded or sick from the tainted water. I do not include the knights who died or were injured in yesterday's engagement.'

'Eight dead,' said Artillery Captain Volk. 'We'll have to

drop to two-man crews if y'want all the cannon firing, my lord.'

'Eleven men dead, sir,' said Yaekel, 'And my barracks and the canvas on my sloops burned. My lord, I–'

Von Geldrecht held up a hand. 'Yes, Yaekel. You wish to retreat. So noted.' He turned to the handgunner captain. 'Hultz?'

'Twenty-eight dead, my lord,' said the man. 'Only – only eighteen left alive. Them bats, sir. They done for us something terrible.'

'I know, Hultz,' said von Geldrecht sadly. 'I know.' He nodded towards the slovenly free-company captain. 'And you, Captain… what is your name again?'

'Draeger, yer worship,' said the captain. 'Er, three dead and twenty-seven alive.'

Everyone's head turned.

Von Geldrecht glared. 'You didn't fight.'

Draeger squared his jaw. 'We guarded the stables, yer worship. Barred the door and watched them horses like they were our own.'

'The stables were never under attack!' roared Bosendorfer.

'Aye,' said Draeger, smug. 'Thanks to us.'

The other officers all started barking at once, but von Geldrecht held up his hands. 'Enough! Never mind! We will deal with this later.' He turned to the young knight sergeant who had wept at Nordling's death. 'Classen?'

Classen pulled his eyes away from Draeger and saluted. 'Thirty-two dead, sir,' he said, then swallowed. 'In-including General Nordling. Fifty still living and able.'

'And at least a hundred of the servants and farm folk dead,' said Father Ulfram. 'With more wounded and sick.'

Von Geldrecht sighed and stared into the fire. 'So,' he said. 'More than a third dead or incapacitated after one attack, and any reinforcements at least six days away – once they actually start their march. It… will be difficult.'

'It will be impossible!' cried Yaekel. 'Forgive me, my lord, but we have no chance here! We must take to the river and escape! There is no other way!'

'Be silent, Yaekel!' barked von Geldrecht. 'I have told you–'

Zeismann cut in before he could continue. 'Much as I hate to admit it,' he said, 'I'm afraid I've to side with Yaekel. We're too reduced now t'do any good. Let's fall back to Nadjagard where we can make a proper defence.'

'I agree,' said von Volgen. He bowed as von Geldrecht rounded on him. 'Forgive me, lord steward. I am your guest, and will follow your orders, but this attack was only a quick jab to test our mettle, and it killed a third of the garrison. When the necromancer brings his full strength to bear, what will be the cost then?' He shook his head. 'I fear the castle is a lost cause. We can do more good in Nadjagard.'

'Thank you for your opinion, my lord,' said von Geldrecht, very stiff. 'But though I see the wisdom of it, Graf Reiklander is adamant that Castle Reikguard be held to the last man, and I will not disobey him.' He turned to his captains. 'You will second men from each of your watches to help with the construction of hoardings and other defences, and–'

'But, my lord!' wailed Yaekel, interrupting. 'What will we eat? What will we drink? Even if the zombies don't get us, we'll die of thirst!'

'Sister Willentrude is purifying water to be used for the washing of wounds,' said von Geldrecht. 'And the kitchen staff are preparing fires to boil water for drinking and cooking. We will have water and a hearty meal of... of flat cakes very soon.'

'If I might make a suggestion, yer worship?' said Draeger.

'If it involves you running away, you can forget it,' growled Bosendorfer.

'Not at all,' said Draeger. 'Only, we're not completely cut off here, are we? Why don't we send out Warden Yaekel's boats on a foraging mission? Go downriver to some village where the zombies ain't, and bring back some food.'

Everyone looked around, taken off guard by the sensibleness of the idea. Von Geldrecht nodded.

'That is an excellent suggestion, Draeger,' he said. 'We will do just that.'

'Thank you, yer worship,' said Draeger. 'And if I might–'

'You will have no part in it,' said von Geldrecht, cutting him off, 'as I fear that you might somehow get lost while ashore.'

'Oh no, my lord,' said Draeger, his eyes wide. 'I assure you–'

'Enough!' said von Geldrecht. 'Zeismann, you will take fifteen of your men and escort Captain Yaekel and his crew downriver to requisition food and supplies from the villages there.' He paused as Yaekel's eyes lit up, then continued. 'And you will make sure that Captain Yaekel and his crew do not get lost either.'

Yaekel's face fell as Zeismann grinned.

'Yes, sir,' said the spear captain. 'There'll be no men overboard on this trip.'

Kat clutched Felix's arm as the conversation continued. 'Felix!' she whispered. 'This is our chance to get Snorri away!'

'Aye,' said Felix. 'Let's find Gotrek.'

* * *

THEY FOUND THE three slayers at last in the narrow tunnel that ran under the castle's outer walls and connected its towers. They stood together, holding a lantern close to a square stone set in the wall, and staring at the angular dwarf rune that had been chiselled into it.

'Gotrek,' called Felix, as they approached. 'Von Geldrecht is sending out a foraging party by boat. We'll be able to get Snorri…'

He trailed off as he saw that the slayers weren't listening. They just continued to stare at the rune.

'Is something wrong?' asked Felix.

Gotrek pulled his attention from the rune and looked at Felix. His one eye blazed with fury. 'It is broken.'

Felix and Kat stepped in and peered closer. A hairline crack split the stone from side to side, and cut through every arm of the rune.

'This is why the dead could cross the walls,' Gotrek rumbled. 'With this crack, the power forged into the rune has escaped.'

'And every rune we've found is the same,' said Rodi.

'But how did it happen?' asked Kat. 'An earthquake? Settling?'

Rodi shook his head. 'Since the Time of Woes, the dwarfs have made such runes impervious to natural wear. And this happened only days ago. A week at the most.'

'Snorri thinks it stinks of magic,' said Snorri.

'Aye,' said Gotrek. 'A hammer couldn't touch such a rune. A chisel couldn't make a mark. This was the work of sorcery.'

'So it was Kemmler's doing?' asked Kat.

'Kemmler?' asked Rodi. 'Who's Kemmler?'

'Father Ulfram says that if the wight is Krell,' said Felix, 'then the necromancer must be Heinrich Kemmler, who raised him from his tomb.'

'Never heard of him,' said Gotrek.

'Whoever he is,' said Rodi, 'if he broke the runes, he must have slipped into the castle himself.' He pointed to the floor of the tunnel, then to the stone again. 'You see where someone tried to brush away their footprints? You see the imprint of a hand there?'

Felix and Kat looked at the stone again. At the very centre, overlapping the broken rune, were a few smooth patches where it looked like the rough stone had been glazed. It reminded Felix of the shiny scars left on flesh by a branding iron, but the patches formed the shape of the palm and fingers of a hand.

Kat shivered. 'A touch that can crack stone?'

Rodi nodded. 'And the same marks are on every one we've found.'

Felix swallowed as a thought came to him. 'Kemmler wouldn't bother to wipe away his footprints. He wouldn't care. But someone who was afraid of being caught...'

Gotrek nodded. 'Aye, manling. The saboteur is in the castle.'

EIGHT

Felix groaned. On top of everything else, there might be a saboteur among them, and a powerful one – powerful enough to destroy centuries-old dwarf runes.

'We must tell von Geldrecht,' he said. 'We must find who did this.'

'Aye,' said Gotrek. 'And kill them.'

The Slayer walked towards the exit, then looked back as Felix, Kat and the other slayers followed.

'You said something about a boat, manling?'

'Uh, yes,' said Felix. The revelation of the broken runes had momentarily knocked everything else out of his head. 'Von Geldrecht is sending a boat downriver to forage for food. It seems a perfect opportunity to get Snorri out and on his way to Karak Kadrin.'

'Why would Snorri want to go to Karak Kadrin when there are zombies to fight?' asked Snorri.

'You've forgotten again, Father Rustskull,' said Rodi.

'You're going to the Shrine of Grimnir to get your memory back.'

'Oh, right,' said Snorri. 'Snorri forgot he forgot.'

Gotrek shook his head. 'It won't work.'

Felix blinked. 'What do you mean? There are no zombies blocking the river gate. What would stop us?'

'I don't know,' said Gotrek. 'But the broken runes are proof the necromancer has planned this well. He would not forget the boats.'

THE COURTYARD WAS a hive of activity as Felix, Kat and the slayers stepped into it. Behind the pyre of the dead, still burning near the stables, carpenters and defenders were laying out lengths of wood and putting together the wooden roofs of hoardings, while more were winching pallets of blackpowder barrels and cannon shot up to the walls. Even the knights were bending their backs, von Volgen's Talabeclanders working side by side with the household knights. At quayside, Zeismann and his picked men were lining up as the river wardens made the largest of their sloops ready to sail. Von Geldrecht was giving Zeismann and Yaekel, the boat's captain, last-minute instructions as Bosendorfer and von Volgen waited to speak to him.

'As important as food is shot,' von Geldrecht was saying as Felix, Kat and the slayers neared them. 'We must keep the guns firing. Take all you can.'

'My lord von Geldrecht,' called Felix. 'We have grave news.'

The steward broke off and turned, mouth pursed in annoyance. 'Everyone has grave news, mein herr,' he said. 'It will have to wait.'

'It can't wait, my lord,' said Felix. 'It affects this foraging trip.'

Von Volgen and the three captains turned to listen.

Von Geldrecht's bearded jowls worked angrily. 'Very well,' he snapped. 'What is this desperately important news?'

'You have a traitor in the castle,' said Gotrek. 'Someone has destroyed your warding runes.'

'With magic,' said Snorri.

'Your walls wouldn't keep out an undead flea,' said Rodi.

Von Geldrecht, von Volgen and the officers stared, then looked around at their men nervously. But it seemed only they had heard.

The steward limped closer and lowered his voice. 'You are certain of this, dwarfs?'

'Certain as steel,' said Gotrek.

'But can they be repaired?' asked von Volgen. 'Can you fix them?'

Gotrek and Rodi snorted.

Snorri laughed. 'Snorri thinks you don't know much about runes.'

'A rune cannot be repaired,' said Gotrek. 'It must be replaced.'

'It takes a master runesmith years to make a single rune,' said Rodi. 'And we are not master runesmiths.'

'Someone in the castle?' von Geldrecht asked as he looked around at the soldiers and officers who were hard at work cleaning up the wreckage of the previous night's battle. 'Are you certain?'

'The footprints of he who did it were deliberately wiped away,' said Felix. 'Whoever did it had reason to hide.'

'Tauber!' cried Bosendorfer, triumphant. 'It was Tauber. He poisoned the water and destroyed the runes!'

Von Geldrecht blanched, but Zeismann just rolled his eyes.

'You've got Tauber on the brain, greatsword.'

'You think it's somebody else?' sneered Bosendorfer. 'Who, then?'

Von Geldrecht shushed them frantically as the men in the courtyard started to turn towards their raised voices. 'None of that! None of that! Let us have no unfounded speculation. We mustn't alarm the men.' He turned to Felix. 'I thank you, sir, and you, friend dwarfs, for your information. But please be quiet about this. I will take the necessary steps.' He turned away. 'Now, forgive me, I must see off Captain Zeismann and–'

'The boat won't come back,' said Gotrek.

Von Geldrecht's head jerked back around. 'I beg your pardon?'

Von Volgen and the three officers stared too.

'If this necromancer is cunning enough to plant a saboteur into your castle,' said Rodi. 'he isn't likely to have forgotten you could sail away, is he?'

'Yer saying he'll stop the boat?' asked Zeismann. 'How?'

Gotrek shrugged. 'It will be stopped.'

Von Geldrecht's head swivelled from slayer to slayer, eyes blazing, then he threw up his hands. 'This is mere supposition! How could he stop the boat? The sun is in the sky. Krell has gone. I see no bats. No, I am sorry, friends. We must eat or we will be too weak to fight. I must risk it.'

'My lord, please,' said Felix, stepping forwards. 'Gotrek is rarely wrong in these things. He–'

'Well, he is wrong now!' Von Geldrecht turned away and motioned to Zeismann and Yaekel, who, along with Bosendorfer and von Volgen, had been listening with uneasy expressions to the whole exchange. 'Go on,' he said. 'On board. Cast off. Just come back before sunset.'

'Lord steward,' coughed von Volgen, murmuring in von Geldrecht's ear. 'The necromancer has so far left nothing to chance. I fear–'

'There is no time for fear!' snapped von Geldrecht. 'Graf Reiklander orders me to act!'

'But, my lord–' said Zeismann, hesitant.

'Do you want to live on biscuit and water for seven days because you were too afraid to cross a river in broad daylight?' shouted von Geldrecht, his jowls quivering. 'Do you want our guns to stand cold when those horrors come for the walls? Get on the boat! I'm ordering you! Graf Reiklander is ordering you!'

Zeismann looked like he was going to make another objection, but then only saluted. 'Aye, my lord,' he said stiffly. 'Very good, my lord.'

The spear captain gave Felix, Kat and the slayers a curt nod of farewell, then turned and marched onto the sloop with his men following behind. Yaekel hesitated at the foot of the gangplank, looking suddenly less than eager to depart.

Von Geldrecht fixed him with a glittering stare. 'Have you some complaint, captain?' he growled.

Yaekel swallowed and shook his head. 'No, my lord.'

'Then cast off! Open the river gate!'

'Aye, my lord!'

Yaekel ran onto the sloop and shouted at his boatmen as they pulled in the gangplank and took up their oars. The pilot at the stern turned the wheel, then raised a horn and blew a loud blast. In answer, there was a clattering and creaking from the towers on either side of the harbour gate, and the heavy iron lattices that served it as doors began to swing open. In the waist of the sloop, Zeismann made the sign of the hammer, then turned to his men.

'To the sides, lads,' he called. 'Spears at the ready, and

keep your eyes on the water.'

As the sloop oared away from the quayside, Felix looked at the faces of the men who watched it go. Bosendorfer was pale, and von Volgen grim, but the most stricken of all was von Geldrecht, mopping his ashen brow with a trembling kerchief. For the briefest second he raised the cloth and Felix thought he was going to call back the sloop, but then he lowered it again and only wiped his mouth.

Gotrek shot a one-eyed glare him, then started towards the men who were assembling the hoardings. 'Come, manling,' he said over his shoulder as Rodi and Snorri followed him. 'There's work to be done.'

Felix looked from the slayers to the sloop. 'What work?'

'If the wards are broken,' said Gotrek, 'then hoardings are the best defence. Smartest thing the manlings have done yet.'

Felix glanced again at the sloop, which was pulling in its oars and unfurling its sails as it neared the water gate, then looked questioningly at Kat.

'I have to see,' she said. 'I have to.'

Felix turned back to the slayers. 'We'll find you.'

The dwarfs only grunted and kept on.

Felix and Kat hurried for the closest stair. Von Geldrecht and von Volgen were ahead of them, climbing in uneasy silence. The steward was met at the top by Captain Hultz of the handgunners.

'All quiet, my lord,' he said, saluting.

'I hope so,' said von Geldrecht and stepped past him with von Volgen to look over the battlements.

Felix and Kat found a spot a few paces to their left just as the sloop was passing through the water gate. Unnerved by Gotrek's warnings, Felix half-expected huge jaws or monstrous tentacles would rise out of the waves and drag it under, but nothing of the sort happened. The waters were undisturbed but for the sloop's bow wave, and though its passage was provoking movement amongst the zombies on the shore, they didn't appear to be any threat. The corpses shuffled clumsily in its direction like iron shavings being pulled upon by the influence of a lodestone, crowding the riverbank and pawing limply at the air as it passed, but that was all.

Von Geldrecht laughed and slapped the wall. 'You see? They can do nothing!'

Forbidding laughter wafted to them on the wind, an eerie echo of von Geldrecht's laugh.

Felix's heart clenched, for he knew that laugh. It was Hans the Hermit – or Heinrich Kemmler, if Father Ulfram was correct. Felix looked around, sweeping the horde of zombies with his eyes, but it was Kat who spotted him first.

'There!' she said, thrusting out a finger as she lifted her bow off her back.

Felix followed her gaze. A hundred yards downstream, a spindly figure in dirty robes, so like the army of corpses he had raised that he was nearly impossible to pick out, was moving from the bank onto a half-submerged outcropping of rocks and waving after the retreating sloop as it angled towards the opposite shore.

Quicker than Felix could follow, Kat had an arrow on the string and loosed it in Kemmler's direction. It went wide, but only just. She nocked another and fired again. The arrow seemed to curve away from the necromancer as it reached him.

'Fire at will, lads!' called Hultz, as his gunners raised their weapons.

'Yes!' shouted von Geldrecht. 'Kill him! A hundred crowns to the man who brings him down!'

But as the gunners sighted down at Kemmler, it became clear that the necromancer's arm-waving was not mere madness. Shadows blossomed around him, billowing from his dirty cloak to surround him in unnatural darkness until he vanished in a floating smudge of smoke.

The guns thundered, splintering the rocks around where Kemmler stood and sending up splashes in the shallows. Had they missed? Kat certainly did not. Her third arrow lanced straight through the heart of the smoke, precisely where Kemmler had been standing, but to Felix's dismay, it met no resistance, and stuck quivering in the ground beyond.

The darkness dissipated again, revealing nothing but empty rocks. Felix heard men running up the stairs behind him, drawn to the walls by the firing. He didn't turn. He was too busy searching the horde for Kemmler.

'Where's he gone?' cried von Geldrecht. 'Find him!'

'The boat,' croaked von Volgen, pointing.

Felix and Kat looked towards Yaekel's sloop as spearmen and greatswords crowded the battlements on either side of them. A swirl of shadow, almost impossible to see in the darker shadow of the sails, was coalescing behind the sloop's pilot. No one had seen it yet. Zeismann's spearmen were still following his orders and watching the waves. The crew were at their duties.

'The necromancer!' shouted one of Hultz's handgunners. ''Ware behind you, boys!'

The crowd that now thronged the walls joined him, all waving and shouting at once, but the distance was too great. The men on the sloop stared back at them, uncomprehending, as the darkness clotted behind them and became opaque.

Finally, one of the spearmen – was it Zeismann? It was hard to tell so far away – turned to call to someone, and froze as he saw the patch of misty blackness that was spreading across the aft deck.

Though Felix heard nothing, Zeismann must have shouted, for all at once the other spearmen whipped around, and the crew turned and lifted their heads.

What followed seemed somehow more horrible to Felix because it played out in the silence of distance – a sad, sickening pantomime that he and Kat and the others on the wall were powerless to stop.

As the pilot fled before the spreading cloud, Zeismann and his spearmen crept towards it cautiously from all sides, spears extended. The river wardens closed from all corners of the ship, brandishing cutlasses and boarding pikes. A flash of red hair showed Felix that Yaekel was at their head, a pair of pistols at the ready.

Then, as Zeismann prodded nervously into the churning dark with his spear-tip, black tendrils of writhing smoke shot out from its centre in all directions at once, impaling the spearmen through their breastplates and bringing them up on their toes in a paralysing rictus.

The crowd on the wall gasped.

Kat cried out. 'Zeismann! No!'

Yaekel and his crew drew back in terror as the shadowy strands reeled the spearmen closer and closer to the spreading cloud while they squirmed like worms on hooks. Zeismann, with seemingly superhuman willpower, stabbed convulsively into the dark as it drew him into its embrace, but his attacks did nothing, and he vanished with the rest.

Felix tore his gaze from the horror and stepped to von Geldrecht and von Volgen.

'Lord steward!' he said. 'Send the other boat. Let us on it! We must save them!'

'Aye, my lord,' said Hultz. 'Something must be done!'

The others on the wall echoed him, begging to be sent

to the rescue, but von Geldrecht shook his head, his eyes never leaving the sloop.

'It's too late. Too late.'

'Not for vengeance!' said Kat. 'Let us go. We will kill the necromancer for the deaths of your men.'

'Aye!' said a spearman who had stayed behind. 'Zeismann must be avenged.'

The steward didn't answer, but von Volgen coughed.

'I'm afraid the lord steward is right,' he said. 'We must not be drawn. The rescuers will only die and the castle will lose its second boat.'

Felix groaned, and the others cursed as they turned back to watch again. The lord was undoubtedly right, but it was hard to swallow.

With no one at the wheel, the sloop's rudder flopped free, and it turned with the current, its sails loose and snapping. Beneath them, Yaekel, with more bravery than Felix expected of him, was waving his crew back and advancing on the black cloud alone. The darkness now covered all of the aft deck and was curling down into the waist like a heavy ground fog. He aimed his pistols at it and shouted something, but clearly didn't get the response he'd hoped for, for he shouted again.

A figure emerged from the pall and Yaekel jumped back, frightened, but then, as it came into the light, it was revealed as a spearman, staggering like a drunk, his spear clutched in his hands. Yaekel spoke again, but this time seemingly in relief, and stepped forwards, lowering his pistols. The spearman stabbed him in the chest, burying his spearpoint between his ribs.

The river wardens cried out as Yaekel fell, and the distant pops of pistols carried across the water as they fired at his killer. The spearman twitched in the volley of lead, but did not fall, only jerked his spear free of Yaekel and stumbled down to the waist. More spearmen followed him out of the black mist, all with the same lurching gait, and fell upon the river wardens with ungainly savagery.

'Not our lads,' murmured the spearman who had spoken before. 'Not the captain.'

The crew fought valiantly, but the outcome was inevitable. Only seconds after his death, Yaekel rose again and turned to join the spearmen as they tore at his erstwhile men. And more and more of the river wardens followed him – falling as their guts were pierced by spears, only to rise again almost instantly, lifeless slaves to Kemmler's will, and leaving the living swiftly outnumbered.

Then, as the slaughter came to its grisly conclusion, the black cloud vanished from the deck and reappeared on the shore at the edge of the zombie horde, dissipating to reveal Kemmler, who once again laughed and waved to the sloop. In response, the newly risen zombies turned and staggered to the gunwales, then toppled into the water one after the other until there were none left on board, and the sloop drifted away down the river, unmanned.

'And that's that, then,' said a handgunner, staring hollow-eyed. 'Good men dead and drowned by the hand of that filthy grave-robber. May Morr watch over them.'

But that wasn't it, for as Felix, Kat and the others watched, there was a churning in the shallows near where Kemmler stood on the shore, and a cluster of helmed heads and armoured shoulders broke the waves, streaming water and blood. In ones and twos, the spearmen and river wardens from the sloop rose up and walked out of the river, then shambled past Kemmler to merge with the endless anonymity of the ten-thousand-strong horde as the necromancer's laughter again drifted to the castle on the wind.

Kat turned her head. 'Poor bastards. Poor Zeismann.'

'Aye,' said Felix, glaring at von Geldrecht. 'Damned short-sighted fool.'

The steward stood beside von Volgen, staring blankly after the receding sloop. The men around them wore the same expression, as if all hope had been pulled out of them in a single instant.

Suddenly, Draeger, the free-company captain, turned on von Geldrecht, his eyes blazing with fury. 'Y'fat bastard, y'trapped us! We could've got out yesterday but you wouldn't! If we all die here, I'm hanging it 'round your neck! It's you who've killed us, and nobody–'

Von Geldrecht slapped him across the face. 'Pull yourself together, captain!' he snapped. 'Or I'll have you in the gaol! There is no room for such an outburst here.'

Draeger balled his fists as the men on the wall held their breath, but at last Draeger just turned on his heel and stalked off.

Von Geldrecht glared after him, then seemed to remember he was supposed to be the commander, and drew himself up. 'Back to your duties!' he said. 'Back to your posts! If you want vengeance for this terrible loss, then shore up our defences. Sharpen your weapons, build the hoardings, carry shot and powder to the walls so that they are there when our gunners need them. There is no need to go to the enemy. The enemy will come to us, and when they do, we will make them pay tenfold for what they have done today!'

The men cheered this speech and broke up in better spirits, but as they filed past Felix and Kat towards the stairs, Felix heard some grumbling as well.

'If I wanted vengeance,' muttered a spearman, 'I'd baste ye in butter and send *you* out to forage, y'fat ham hock.'

'Two captains dead,' said another, 'and nothing to

show for it. Nothing. Go back to the counting house, Goldie.'

'My lord steward,' said von Volgen, as the last of them left the walls. 'If I might make a suggestion?'

Von Geldrecht stiffened. 'What is it?'

Von Volgen nodded towards the river gate. 'We have seen now that zombies don't drown. I am therefore concerned that there might be a gap between the bottom of the lattice doors and the river bed. If the corpses were to find it…'

Von Geldrecht paled. He looked overwhelmed. 'Good thinking,' he murmured. 'Thank you. I will ask if a solution can be– Ack!'

Von Geldrecht ducked and flinched as something swooped out of the sky and squeaked and flapped around his head. Von Volgen drew his sword and Kat had an arrow on the string in an instant, but what fluttered around the steward's head was not a bat, but the strangest bird Felix had ever seen. It looked something like a pigeon, with a round body and smooth head, but its feathers glinted like metal and it whirred and clicked like an angry insect.

'Hold!' cried von Geldrecht, waving Kat down. 'It is a messenger pigeon.'

Kat held fire, but kept her bow at half-draw, staring as von Geldrecht raised his arm and the thing settled on his wrist.

'It… it is a machine,' she said, wonderingly.

Felix stared too. Now that it was standing still, he could see that it was indeed mechanical. The wings were made of steel and brass, the legs and claws hinged with screws, and the eyes made from glass lenses. He shook his head. He didn't remember the Empire having anything like this before he had left it for parts east. Engineering had come a long way in twenty years.

Von Geldrecht twisted the cap off the end of a brass tube affixed to the bird's chest and withdrew from it a twist of paper. He uncurled it with nervous fingers and peered at it.

'From Altdorf, my lord?' asked von Volgen.

Von Geldrecht nodded and let out a sigh, though Felix couldn't tell if it was one of relief or worry. 'Yes,' he said. 'The Reiksguard are coming, and as many state troops as they can recruit along the way. Graf Reiklander's son, Master Dominic, is returning with them. They left late yesterday.'

'Praise Sigmar,' said von Volgen.

'Aye,' said von Geldrecht, his eyes distant. He crumpled the paper. 'And pray his deliverance isn't too late.'

NINE

THE REST OF the day was hard labour, with no one exempt. Even the knights worked, falling in beside the handgunners, spearmen and artillerymen to proof the castle as best they could against the undead. Directed by Reikguard's master carpenter, Anders Bierlitz, half the garrison cut, nailed together and fit wooden hoardings to the tops of the walls, while nearly as many worked just as furiously dismantling the stables, the privies and whatever other wooden structures could be spared, in order to provide usable wood for the builders to build with.

Gotrek, Rodi and Snorri, meanwhile, set to dismantling the officers' residence for its stone. There had been much argument earlier about the best way to prevent the zombies from crawling under the water gate, with some wanting to sink the remaining riverboat in front of it, and others wanting to drive the gates down into the mud of the river bottom, but at last it was decided that the surest plan was to pile up heavy stones below the gates to plug the gap. Unfortunately, the castle wasn't a quarry, and taking them from the exterior walls was obviously not an option.

And so all day the slayers used hammers, chisels and their bare hands to dismantle the corner tower of the officers' residence from top to bottom and tumble the stones down to river wardens, who then winched them onto oarboats and rowed them the short distance to the gate to dump them over the side as close to the iron doors as they could manage.

Felix and Kat, being neither capable carpenters nor stonemasons, went to work with the demolition gangs, and pried apart the weathered planks of the hayloft then pulled out every nail that could be salvaged. Even on a freezing late winter day, it was hot, dusty work, and they were soon working in their shirts, steam rising from their shoulders into the chilly air.

Ordinarily, this kind of labour would not have worn Felix out. Years of wandering and fighting had left him in good shape, and he was used to hardship, but even the toughest man could not go long without water, and there wasn't nearly enough to go around. Every vat and pan and pot in the kitchen was busy boiling water for drinking, but the process wasn't quick, and the rationing was severe. Every man got a ladleful to go with their single biscuit in the morning, and another in the afternoon, and some got less than that. Both times the crews were called to the mess, the water ran out before everyone got their share.

Gotrek, Rodi and Snorri never drank, though whether that was because they didn't need to, or out of sheer stubbornness, or just because it wasn't beer, Felix wasn't certain. Regardless, they each did the work of ten men, and never complained or showed any sign of weakness.

The same could not be said for the men. There were fights at the water barrel when some tried to drink more than their share. Others passed out or vomited from dryness. Felix was nearly one of them. By the late afternoon, he was staggering, and almost fell through a hole in the floor he was prying up. Only a swift grab by Kat stopped him from breaking his neck. Hunger and thirst weren't entirely to blame, however. Part of his clumsiness stemmed from his inability to keep his mind on the work. He couldn't stop wondering who the saboteur was.

All day long he watched his fellow defenders, wondering which one hid the power to shatter a dwarf rune – which was in league with Kemmler. Was it Tauber, like Bosendorfer believed? That would be tidy, for Tauber was already locked up, but somehow Felix doubted the castle was that lucky. But then who? It couldn't be anybody who had travelled with von Volgen, since the runes had been broken before his force arrived. Was it von Geldrecht? Had he ordered the garrison to hold the castle just so Kemmler could kill them all and swell his ranks with their corpses? Was it Bosendorfer, sowing discord by accusing others of crimes he himself was committing? Was it Father Ulfram? Was his blindness and seeming senility a cover for corrupt power? Was it Sister Willentrude, hiding an evil nature behind a kindly smile? Was it perhaps Graf Reiklander himself, or the Grafin Avelein, hiding in the keep and manipulating the rest of the castle for Kemmler's gain?

But why did it have to be one of the leaders? It could be anyone – a knight, a spearman, a groom, a scullery maid. There were too many choices, and too little to go on. It was maddening.

At least von Geldrecht was following through on his promise to take the necessary steps. As the day wore on, Felix saw him quietly pull aside each of his remaining officers and whisper in their ears, after which those officers began to look suspiciously around at their comrades. Felix supposed that removed von Geldrecht from the list of suspects, but perhaps not. What if he was telling his men to look for the traitor in order to throw them off the scent, or to create suspicion that would weaken the morale of the castle?

Felix cursed as his mind curled in on itself again, and forced himself to get back to the task at hand. Ceaseless suspicion would not find the saboteur. What they needed was proof, but Felix had no idea what to look for.

LESS THAN A third of the hoardings were in place by the time the sun vanished completely. The towers of the gatehouse and the sections of wall to the right and left of it had been covered, but that was all. Felix, with little knowledge of these things, thought it was a poor showing, and the slayers grumbled about 'manling laziness', but Bierlitz, the castle's carpenter, seemed well pleased, saying that given the lack of food and water the men had accomplished more than he expected.

Nor did the construction stop with the coming of darkness. After Bierlitz dismissed Felix and Kat and the rest of the men who had worked all day, he commandeered men from the night watches to keep at it, and the slayers of course continued without a break.

Felix left them to it, and stumbled with Kat into the underkeep as the mess bell clanged.

It was time for another biscuit.

* * *

'To Captain Zeismann and all our fallen brothers,' said a young sergeant of spearmen, standing and holding up his mug. 'He'd not relish being toasted with water, but until we have beer again, let us honour him as we can.'

The rest of the spearmen stood from their tables in the mess and raised their mugs as well, and Kat, Felix and the other men in the room joined them.

'To Captain Zeismann and the spearmen,' said the crowd, and everyone knocked back their meagre ration of water in a single slug.

As they all sat again, a burly river warden stood from among his comrades and raised an empty hand. 'And as that was all to drink till morning,' he said, 'I ask that you salute Captain Yaekel and his crew with a pledge.' He closed his hand into a fist. 'Vengeance!'

The whole room raised their fists, and the walls echoed with their pledge.

'Vengeance!'

The warden inclined his head and sat again, but before everyone could lower their fists, Bosendorfer sprang up onto the table where he had sat with his greatswords.

'I ask a pledge as well,' he cried. 'In the name of greatswords Janus Meier and Abel Roos, and the score of other men who died last night and today from the poisoned wounds that murdered them in their beds.'

He raised his fist in the air and the room followed suit, with many a 'hear hear' and 'well said'.

'Death to the poisoner,' said Bosendorfer. 'Death to Surgeon Tauber.'

Felix and Kat paused at that, and they weren't the only ones. Though many of the men joined in wholeheartedly, just as many were murmuring and lowering their fists instead of making the pledge. Even some of Bosendorfer's own men looked uncomfortable.

Bosendorfer glared around, his eyes blazing. 'What is this? Will you not honour my fallen men as you honour Zeismann and Yaekel?'

Captain Hultz stood from his handgunners. 'With a will, captain, if you choose a different pledge,' he said.

Bosendorfer sneered. 'You do not wish the death of our enemies, Hultz?'

'We don't all think it was Tauber who done it,' said Hultz. 'Choose another enemy and we will pledge.'

'Sigmar's hammer, I will not!' shouted Bosendorfer. 'I will honour my dead as I see fit, and if you will not join me, then be damned with you!'

Men stood all over the hall now, choosing sides and shouting at each other, as Bosendorfer continued to rave.

Felix shook his head and leaned to Volk, whose table he and Kat were sharing. 'Why does he hate Tauber so? I remember he spoke of Tauber murdering people during the fighting up north. Was the surgeon accused of worshipping Chaos?'

Volk shook his head sadly. 'Only by Bosendorfer,' he said, then sighed. 'When we marched north, the boy was only a sergeant. His brother Karl was the captain of m'lord's greatswords. But at the end, during the battle of Sokh, one of them Norse shamen blasted our whole left flank with purple fire, and afterwards, some of the men... well, they started to change. Bosendorfer's brother was one of 'em. His hands – they grew teeth, and other things.'

The artillery captain swallowed, then went on. 'It was standard procedure when that happened, to kill the man on the spot – for his own good, you understand – and Captain Karl was in the sick tent with a broken arm when he started to show, so–'

'So Tauber did it?' asked Felix.

Volk nodded. 'As gentle as possible. Laudanum, then poison. He just... fell asleep. But young Bosendorfer wouldn't believe it. He claimed it was Tauber who had made his brother's changes come, and that he'd killed Karl when he wouldn't pledge to the Ruinous Powers.' He looked over at the greatswords' table. 'Graf Reiklander himself talked to Bosendorfer, and got him to agree it wasn't true. Gave him Karl's commission too, which might not have been wise, as Bosendorfer ain't the man his brother was, not by a long shot, but it was a nice gesture, and the greatswords appreciated it, so...'

'But Bosendorfer doesn't seem to have really believed Tauber was innocent,' said Felix.

Volk shook his head. 'He's kept quiet about it till now, but no.'

Felix watched as Bosendorfer continued to rant. He could see the grief behind the young man's wild anger now, and felt sorry for him, but one could feel sorry for a savage dog that had been abused, and still not want to be trapped in the same room with it for days – or weeks.

He finished his last few crumbs of biscuit and turned to Kat. 'Shall we?'

She nodded, glaring at the greatsword captain. 'Aye, Felix,' she said. 'I'm starting to get an earache.'

They walked out of the underkeep and into the courtyard where, under the yellow light of flickering lanterns, Gotrek, Rodi and Snorri continued to knock apart the officers' residence, while the boatmen dumped another load of building stone at the river gate, and the carpenters and the men from the night watches kept on framing the hoardings and carrying them up to the walls.

Kat looked at all their industry, then shook her head. 'None of this is going to matter, is it? We won't stop them.'

'Not for long,' said Felix. 'But maybe long enough.'

A cold wind whistled down over the parapet, bringing with it the stench of corpses and the howling of wolves. Felix shivered and put his arm around Kat, and they hurried into the knights' residence and up to their borrowed room. By the time they had pulled their boots off and lay down on the narrow bed, they were too tired and hungry to do more than curl together and close their eyes.

SECONDS LATER – OR SO it seemed – Felix was jerked awake by shouting and cursing and heavy boot steps shaking the residence building.

Kat came awake too, and blearily reached for her weapons. 'That's on the floor below,' she mumbled. 'What's going on?'

Felix crawled to the window and looked out. It was still night, and he could see little but the shadows of men running to the door of their residence and going in. Three slower, heavier shadows followed them, walking along with their weapons out.

Felix grunted. 'We'd better go down.'

He threw on his padded jack and squirmed into his chainmail as Kat pulled on her leathers and the shouting continued. When they were ready, they hurried down to the ground floor, but the shouting was now coming from the cellar, so they continued down and, after following the cacophony through a series of cramped stone passages, came at last to a small round room that was filled with a jumble of machinery, and far too many shouting men.

The room appeared to be the base of one of the circular towers that rose at the corners of the castle walls, and a great brass and iron contraption of gears and levers and pistons that had a very dwarfish look to it rose in the centre of it. It also looked very broken, with one of the main gears cracked in half, and a piston ruptured and bent.

Cowering in the lee of the machine were Captain Draeger and his militiamen, while surrounding them were von Geldrecht, his bulk wrapped in a nightshirt and brocade robe, von Volgen, and a crowd of knights and foot soldiers, all holding lanterns and torches and shouting questions while the slayers watched from one side, their brawny arms folded across their beards.

'I swear to you, m'lord,' Draeger was saying. 'It wasn't us! We heard something suspicious and came looking, and found someone tampering with it. Sigmar be my witness it's the truth.'

Von Geldrecht laughed, and then waved a hand for quiet. 'So, you heard something suspicious, did you?'

'That's right, m'lord,' said Draeger. 'Woke us up. And–'

'You were sleeping in the underkeep and heard something suspicious in the cellar of the knights' residences *on the far side* of the courtyard,' continued von Geldrecht.

'Well, m'lord...'

The steward barged on. 'And so, you decided you would investigate this noise, with *all your men*?'

The knights and foot soldiers all laughed at this. Even von Volgen allowed himself a flat smile.

'Er, well,' stammered Draeger, sweating now. 'I know it seems strange on the face of it, m'lord, but–'

'It seems traitorous on the face of it!' bellowed von Geldrecht. 'By Sigmar, captain, if you've done what I think you've done here, you will die where you stand.'

Draeger cringed back. 'No, m'lord. Honest. We never touched it. It was the man we found tinkering with it. He wrecked it!'

Von Geldrecht rolled his eyes. 'One man wrecked

this? Don't lie to me, captain. You have committed this sabotage, and you will pay for it with your life.'

'But we haven't!' cried Draeger. 'I swear to you!'

'Then why *did* you come here?' asked von Geldrecht, then sneered. 'And don't tell me you heard a noise.'

Draeger lowered his head and slanted a look to his men, then sighed. 'We… we was looking for a way out. A secret passage, like.'

Von Geldrecht stared. Someone in the back laughed.

'You were trying to escape,' said von Geldrecht.

'Aye, m'lord,' said Draeger, his chin going up with sudden defiance. 'We told you from the first we was already demobbed. This ain't our fight. We're free men.'

That brought another round of laughter, and a combined snort from the slayers.

'Kill the lot,' said Gotrek, disgusted. 'We don't need cowards.'

Von Geldrecht inclined his head to him. 'Would that we had the luxury to choose who fought beside us, herr dwarf. But alas, it cannot be.' He turned back to Draeger. 'No, your punishment, captain, is to fight for your life with the rest of us.' He snapped his fingers at the young sergeant of spearmen who had toasted Zeismann earlier in the mess. 'Sergeant Abelung, lock these men up. They are only to be let out to fight, yes?'

'Aye, my lord,' said the sergeant.

But as he began to herd them towards the exit, von Volgen looked Draeger in the eye.

'One question, captain,' he said. 'The man who was tinkering with the machine. Was he another lie?'

Draeger shook his head, glum. 'No, m'lord. We saw him, right enough.'

'And what did he look like?' asked von Volgen.

Draeger frowned. 'I didn't get a good look, m'lord. He wore a robe. Covered him head to toe. Couldn't see his face, or anything about him. Not a big man, though, and went like a rabbit.'

Von Volgen nodded and stepped back, and Sergeant Abelung led the militiamen to the door, but as they filed out, there were running footsteps in the passage beyond, and a handgunner squeezed past them into the room.

'My lord,' he said, panting as he crossed to von Geldrecht. 'It is as you feared. The dike locks have been closed and the moat is dry. The zombies have already crossed it, and are at the walls.'

Von Geldrecht cursed as the crowd of soldiers and knights murmured in dismay and began to hurry out. 'And until the lock mechanism is repaired,' he said, looking at the wrecked machine with a sigh, 'we cannot flood it again. Our saboteur is very thorough.'

Von Volgen turned to the slayers. 'Can you fix this, dwarfs?'

Gotrek stepped forwards, shaking his head. 'The same hand that shattered the runes shattered this.' He pointed to a hole in the side of the crumpled piston. It was in the rough shape of a hand, and the steel all around it was cracked and brittle – more like glass than metal. Gotrek poked it with his finger. It shattered and fell away.

'It would take a team of dwarfs with a proper forge a month to replace all these parts,' said Rodi.

'Snorri would guess two months,' said Snorri.

Von Geldrecht groaned. 'The walls, the moat. The villain is peeling away our defences like an onion. He must be found and–'

Gotrek held up a hand, cutting him off, and cocked his head.

Von Geldrecht looked around, nervous. 'What is it?'

'Quiet,' said the Slayer, then crossed to the wall of the

round room and put his ear to it.

Rodi and Snorri did the same. Felix and Kat exchanged a puzzled glance with von Geldrecht and von Volgen.

After a moment, Gotrek lifted his ear from the wall and turned to von Geldrecht. 'There is digging being done,' he said. 'Somewhere beyond this wall.'

Von Geldrecht's eyes widened. 'Digging? But what for?'

Rodi snorted. 'Maybe the corpses are planting a garden.'

Snorri frowned. 'Snorri doesn't think that's likely, Rodi Balkisson,' he said. 'Snorri thinks they're going to sap the walls.'

TEN

'So close,' said von Geldrecht, clutching his robe tighter around him. 'And yet so far away.'

Felix and Kat stood with the steward and von Volgen and the slayers on Castle Reikguard's wind-whipped battlements, staring out at the stone-flanked, oak-doored canal-lock dike that gleamed dully in the light of the two moons about fifty yards upstream from the castle's easternmost corner. Until less than an hour ago, the lock could be opened to let the river spill into the moat, and closed to allow for cleaning and repairs. Now, with the destruction of the lock mechanism, the saboteur had closed it permanently, leaving the moat dry, and the sea of zombies which the moat had kept at bay now reached all the way to the castle, pawing futilely at the huge granite blocks of the sturdy walls.

Von Geldrecht sighed and shivered, then turned to the slayers. 'And where is this digging?'

They led him back along the wall and pointed out and down. Felix, Kat, von Volgen and the steward leaned as far as they could over the wall, peering into the night. Felix couldn't see anything but zombies.

Von Geldrecht shook his head. 'I still don't see.'

'Snorri thinks humans have terrible eyesight,' said Snorri.

'They are in the moat,' growled Gotrek. 'Digging into the inner bank, straight for your walls.'

Felix looked again and finally, behind the shifting jumble of zombies that pawed at the walls, he thought he saw movement in the channel.

Von Geldrecht groaned. 'If only we could open the dike again, we could drown them out.'

'You couldn't, my lord,' said von Volgen. 'If you recall, zombies don't breathe.'

'And you don't want to open the dike again until that hole is filled in,' said Rodi. 'Or you'll have your moat in your cellar.'

'Snorri thinks that would bring down your walls faster than the zombies could,' said Snorri.

Von Geldrecht cursed and struck the wall with his fist. 'So how are we to stop them? We can't send men out to the digging. They'll be overwhelmed before they get there.'

'We dig to them,' said Gotrek. 'Then mine their tunnel and collapse it before it reaches the walls.'

Von Geldrecht stared at him. 'But... but is there time?' he asked. 'How long would it take to dig such a tunnel? I don't know if I have men enough to spare from strengthening our defences, nor if they will have enough strength.'

Gotrek held up a hand. 'Tell your men to finish blocking the river gate. We'll do this. Humans would only get in the way.'

The steward let out a sigh of relief and bowed to the Slayer. 'Thank you, herr dwarf! You ease my mind. It will be as you say.'

Felix saw von Volgen wince at this unleaderlike display of emotion and look away, only to catch Felix looking at him. They exchanged a guarded look, then von Volgen turned and walked off as von Geldrecht began giving orders to his men.

THE ZOMBIES STARTED climbing the walls less than an hour later.

After they left von Geldrecht, Kat and Felix helped Gotrek, Rodi and Snorri search through the castle's stores for picks and shovels, then carted dirt away as the slayers began digging down into the basement of the captains' residence – which was the point in the castle closest to where the zombies were digging. But weariness soon overcame them again and they returned to their room to try and sleep until morning. It was not to be, however – at least not for Felix.

Tired as he was, Felix could not quiet his mind. Draeger's description of the saboteur kept repeating in his head, and he couldn't stop comparing it to those he knew in the castle. A small man in robes, Draeger had said. And quick. Not much to go on, but it did rule out quite a number of suspects. With his wounded leg, von Geldrecht was neither small nor quick. Bosendorfer was a giant of a man, and the old priest, Ulfram, might have been gaunt, but he was tall too. He could rule out Sister Willentrude as well, who had the figure of a well-fed barnyard hen. Who did that leave? Tauber was a small man, but Tauber was locked up – wasn't he? Hultz of the handgunners was not large either, though he was broad in the shoulder. It could have been Grafin Avelein, hiding her sex, or even the graf himself. Felix had never seen him, and had no idea what he looked like. But then, what if the villain was a master of illusion as well as a shatterer of runes? What if his small size and quickness were only a guise? After too much of that, it was almost a relief when the rally horns sounded and confused shouting echoed through the courtyard.

This time Felix and Kat hadn't bothered to strip out of their armour before lying down, and were therefore quick to the walls to see the zombies' new trick. Under cover of darkness the undead had brought tall, crudely made ladders to the castle and leaned them against all the land-side walls, and were now pulling themselves up towards the battlements in droves.

This wasn't much of a threat – at least not on its own. The zombies were terrible climbers and fell often, and the handgunners found it easy enough to use a pike to lever the ladders away from the wall and topple them to the ground. The problem was, they never stopped. It didn't matter how many times the defenders pushed the ladders back and sent all the zombies smashing into the moat, they just got up again, righted the ladders and resumed climbing, single-minded and untiring.

The handgunners were quickly joined by spearmen and river wardens sent by their captains to relieve them, but even with reinforcements, the men on the walls were run ragged, hurrying from ladder to ladder in a never-ending foot race. Unfortunately, it was even more pointless to try to kill the dead who mounted the ladders, for Kemmler would never run out. No matter how many the defenders might decapitate, or shoot through the head, there would always be more zombies to take their place.

Felix and Kat joined in the dizzy dance of run and push, run and push, run and push until the sky began to turn grey in the east, when they were finally both so tired they could no longer handle the pikes they had been given, and collapsed panting against the crenellations, legs as weak as twigs.

Captain Hultz, who looked no less weary than they, took the pikes and shooed them away. 'Go and sleep,' he said. 'You've done the work of ten tonight, the both of you, and the morning watch comes on any minute. Away. Away.'

Felix saluted and helped Kat up, and they staggered down the stairs, arm in arm, towards the knights' residence. But as they stumbled along the quayside, Kat stopped suddenly and blinked at two boatmen who were using boat hooks to manoeuvre a stone from the dismantled captains' residence under their winch so they could lower it into an oarboat.

'What is it?' Felix asked, frowning.

'Boat hook,' said Kat.

'What?'

The girl was gibbering from fatigue.

'Just a minute,' she said, then shrugged out from under his arm and crossed to the men.

'I need that,' she said, pointing.

The boatmen looked at her askance.

'The stone?' said one. 'What d'ye want a stone for?'

'The hook,' said Kat. 'I want the hook. And some rope. A lot.'

The boatmen looked at her again, and Felix did too. He had no idea what she was on about. Still, it was clear she'd had some sort of idea.

'If you can spare it,' he said politely, trying to make up for Kat's almost dwarfish brusqueness.

The boatman who had spoken shrugged, then went back onto the sloop and returned a moment later with a third boat hook and a coil of rope.

'I'll need all this back, mind,' he said, but Kat was already hurrying back to the stairs, tying the end of the rope around the T-shaped handle of the hook.

Felix stumbled up the stairs after her, still baffled, as she found Hultz and held out the hook and rope to him.

'Here,' she said, weaving slightly where she stood. 'This will stop them.'

Hultz blinked. 'And what is it supposed to be? A weapon? Am I to hook the corpses' guts out with it?'

'Not the corpses,' said Kat. 'The ladders. They can't climb without the ladders.'

Felix goggled at her. So did Hultz.

'Sigmar,' he said at last. 'Sigmar, it might work.'

He took the roped hook from her and called to his men. 'Lanzmann, Weitz, Sergeant Dore, take the end of this.'

Felix and Kat followed him and looked out as he let the hook drop down the wall. Just to their left, a mob of zombies was laboriously righting a fallen ladder and angling it towards the battlements.

'Perfect,' said Hultz, and sidestepped until he was above them.

The ladder bounced as it slapped against the wall, just a few feet below the crenellations, then steadied as the first of the zombies started to mount it.

'Quickly now, quickly now,' Hultz muttered to himself as he flicked the hook towards the rungs of the ladder. 'Before they all pile on.'

He got it on the second try and pulled it tight. 'Now, lads, now!' he shouted. 'Haul away!'

The three handgunners pulled on the end of the rope, gathering up the slack, then began to drag the ladder up the wall. There were two zombies at the bottom of it, but as it started to rise, one lost its grip and fell away.

The other came up with the ladder, and clung to it as the gunners grabbed it and pulled it up hand over hand.

Hultz was waiting for it, and stove its head in with a flanged mace as the bottom of the ladder reached the top of the wall. The corpse fell away and the handgunners tossed the ladder down into the courtyard with a cheer.

Hultz turned to Kat with a grin. 'Girl, I do believe you have saved us a whole lot of bother.'

'And given us a nice supply of firewood,' said one of the gunners. 'Nice of that necromancer to provide for our cook fires.'

'Now all we need is food,' said Hultz, then turned to his men again. 'Lanzmann, Weitz, go tell them river pirates we need all the hooks and rope they have, and be quick about it!'

As they started back towards the stairs, Felix looked out over the wall at the fields beyond. The sun hadn't crested the horizon yet, but there was enough light to see all the way to the black line of forest, and a flurry of seething movement there caught his eye.

'What is that?' he asked, slowing.

Kat followed his gaze and they stepped to the wall for a better look. A tall, crooked shape was rising from the mist in front of the trees. It looked like a mummified giant, or an enormous cocoon, white and lumpy and asymmetrical, with a huge gaping mouth yawning and black at the top – and it was crawling from top to bottom with a constantly moving skein of zombies.

With growing horror and fascination, Felix realised that they were building the thing as he watched, like wasps constructing a hive, though instead of wood pulp and mud, they were using dead trees and bones and stretched skin. Angular black branches stuck out at random from the structure's mottled sides, and its base was affixed to giant curved tusks that looked like they had come from the skeleton of some long-dead leviathan.

'Taal and Rhya protect us, it's a siege tower,' said Kat.

Felix shuddered. That was precisely what it was. The curved tusks were skids so the thing could be dragged over the fields, and the hideous yawning mouth at the top would disgorge swarms of undead troops onto the walls. And another was just beginning to rise beside it.

'And look there!'

Kat pointed to the left of the towers, where two lower, wheeled constructions crouched in the shadow of the forest like monstrous insects – a heavy-timbered tre-buchet and a catapult, as strangely constructed as the towers.

'Siege engines too,' said Felix, his stomach sinking. 'They've been busy.'

No one else seemed to have noticed the things. They were all too consumed with the task of hooking or pushing away ladders, but at Kat and Felix's words, the men on either side of them looked up to see what they were talking about.

'Sigmar's blood!' said one. 'Look at that!'

'Captain Hultz!' cried another. 'The wood! Look to the wood!'

Hultz looked up from trying to hook another ladder and cursed, but then raised his voice to shout down the babble of fear that was spreading like fire along the wall as the rest of the men began to notice the towers and the engines.

'Easy, lads! Easy!' he cried. 'They ain't moving yet. And plenty of time to prepare when they do. Keep on them ladders for now and we'll see to the rest when they get here.' He turned to his sergeant. 'Dore! My respects to Steward von Geldrecht, and if he could come have a look-see when he has a moment.'

Sergeant Dore saluted and trotted off to the stairs, and Felix steered Kat after him.

'And we'd better tell the slayers,' he said.

THE DISTANCE GOTREK, Rodi and Snorri had dug overnight was astonishing. They had bored down through the floor of the captains' residence cellar to a depth of about eight feet, then tunnelled east through the earth under the castle walls, and were already a few paces beyond them. A steady stream of squires and kitchen boys went in and out of the hole, carrying out buckets full of dirt and mounding it up all over the room. Off to one side, Volk, the artillery captain, was directing his gunners as they packed blackpowder into sections of clay drain pipe and affixed fuses to them. He gave a grin and a salute as Kat and Felix lowered themselves into the hole.

Felix had to bend almost double to enter the tunnel, for the slayers had shaped it to dwarf proportions, and it was very low. A lamp was pegged into the wall at the far end, and he could see Gotrek and Rodi's broad muscled backs gleaming in its glow as they swung their picks at the workface. Snorri was a little bit behind them, shovelling the dirt into buckets for the squires to take away.

Felix was pleased to see that Gotrek and Rodi were still working side by side without growling at each other. The truce that had existed since they had discovered the broken runes of warding seemed to be holding. Felix only hoped it would stay that way.

'Slayers,' he called, picking his way down the tunnel. 'Kemmler's undead are building siege towers and siege engines. It looks like they will try the walls tonight.'

Gotrek nodded without breaking his rhythm. 'We will reach the corpses' tunnel soon after sunset,' he said. 'We will return to the walls once... once it is collapsed.'

Felix frowned. It sounded as if Gotrek was out of breath. That was almost unheard of. Felix had seen him fight a whole day and spend hours digging through solid rock and hardly do more than breathe hard, but now he was gasping.

'Gotrek?'

The Slayer cleared his throat and spat. 'I'm fine. Just dust.'

Rodi shot a look at Gotrek at that, but said nothing. Felix swallowed, unnerved by Gotrek's ragged voice and Rodi's glance.

'Ah,' he said. 'Dust.' He hesitated, wanting to say more, but then just nodded. 'Send word when you're nearly through. We'll return.'

'Aye,' said Gotrek.

Felix and Kat exchanged a look as they made their way back out of the tunnel, but neither spoke what they were thinking. Was it truly dust, or was it the slivers from Krell's axe doing their evil work? Could the vile specks really kill Gotrek? And if so, how long did the Slayer have?

As FELIX AND Kat stepped back into the courtyard they saw a very bleary Steward von Geldrecht limping down from the walls and stroking his beard with nervous fingers.

'Hultz must have shown him Kemmler's towers,' said Kat.

Felix nodded. The man looked overwhelmed. His face was grey and slack, and he limped unseeing through the sawhorses and timber stacks of the hoarding crews as he headed for the stairs to the keep. Before he reached them, however, Sister Willentrude saw him, and stepped from where she had been praying before the ever-burning pyre of the dead. Her habit and apron were covered in blood, and she looked like she hadn't slept since Felix had seen her last – which was likely true.

'My lord steward!' she cried after him. 'I demand you release Tauber and his assistants!'

Von Geldrecht turned towards her, blinking like a sleepwalker, as all around him the construction crews raised their heads. 'Sister?'

'Twenty-two men died last night, my lord,' she said, her eyes flashing. 'Twenty-two men that would have lived with a surgeon's care. I and my initiates can keep disease and infection at bay with our prayers and purified water, but we are not adepts of the knife and the needle. We cannot stop men from haemorrhaging to death, or drowning in their own bile.' She raised an accusing finger to the steward. 'You have killed these men, my lord. By locking Surgeon Tauber away, you doomed them to unnecessary–'

Von Geldrecht caught the sister by the arm and started to drag her towards the keep, a ghastly smile plastered to his face. 'Let us discuss this in *private*, sister,' he hissed. '*In private!*'

Felix smiled grimly to himself. He hoped she gave him even more of an earful in private, for she was right. When von Geldrecht had caved in to Bosendorfer's threats against Tauber, he had endangered the lives of every man in the castle. If there was anyone other than Kemmler to blame for the fix they were in, it was the steward and the greatsword captain.

Quite a few of the men in the courtyard, however, didn't seem to see it that way. They stared after von Geldrecht and Sister Willentrude as Felix and Kat stumbled through them, murmuring amongst themselves.

'Does the old cow think Tauber would save us?' scoffed one. 'After he poisoned all the rest.'

'I don't know,' said another. 'I would have died after Grimminhagen if not for him. He saved my arm and no lie.'

'Men can change,' said a third. 'He wouldn't be the first who came back south a different man than marched north.'

'Bosendorfer says he was a bad'un *before* he went north,' said the first man. 'A poisoner from the start.'

Kat shook her head angrily as she and Felix entered the knights' residence. 'Sometimes,' she said, 'I think words are more poisonous than poison.'

WHEN FELIX AND Kat woke again that afternoon, they found that Kemmler's second siege tower and another trebuchet had been completed at the edge of the woods, assembled by the ceaseless, swarming industry of the undead. More unnerving, the zombies who surrounded the castle had learned their lesson, and were no longer throwing their ladders up against the walls to have them stolen by the defenders' hooks. Instead, they held fresh ladders at their sides and stared up at the battlements with dead blank eyes – waiting.

And while the dead waited, the defenders scrambled to finish all their tasks before the storm broke. Men were levering apart the last stones of the officers' residence tower and winching them onto the oarboats for their last trips to the water gate. The powder monkeys were laying out the powder and shot beside the cannons that faced the land side of the castle, and the carpenters were cobbling together rickety hoardings out of the last few scraps of usable wood and sending them up to the walls to be fitted into place.

Felix and Kat joined the men on the walls, muscling the sides and roofs of the hoardings into place, while more skilled men made final adjustments and nailed them together. It was heavy, nervous work, done with one eye always glancing over the battlements to make sure the horde hadn't started its advance, and Felix therefore jumped a while later when a polite young voice piped up behind him.

'Herr Jaeger?'

Kat looked up as Felix turned.

A dirt-smeared squire was hovering near the work gang. 'Slayer Gurnisson's compliments,' he said, bowing. 'He and the others are almost through to the zombies' tunnel.'

'Thank you,' said Felix. 'Tell him we're coming.'

He and Kat turned to the lead carpenter as the boy scurried off.

'All right?' asked Felix.

'On your way,' said the man. 'And give 'em hell.'

ARTILLERY CAPTAIN VOLK and four of his men stood around the hole in the floor of the cellar. Each of the men held a pipe charge in his arms, and had picks, trowels, even metal spoons tucked through their belts, as well as lines of matchcord that snaked away behind them like tails, while more pipe charges were piled at their feet. In the centre of them, hunched over a spindle upon which all the match cords were wound, was Volk himself. He grinned when he saw Felix and Kat, his fire-scarred face forbidding in the light of the tinder pot that glowed at his side.

'Your mates are nearly through,' he said, stepping aside so they could get to the hole. 'Can hear the zombies through the dirt now – leastwise, they can. I can't hear nothing. Too many years around the guns.'

Felix nodded as Kat started down the ladder into the hole. 'Is there a plan?'

'Oh aye,' said Volk. 'You and the dwarfs push them

dead bastards back to the mouth of their tunnel. We work in behind you and set the charges. When we're primed all the way to the far end, I call "fire in the hole" and y'run like blazes back to here, then…' He spread his fingers wide, eyes dancing with glee. 'Boom! The tunnel caves, the zombies are squashed, the castle is saved.'

Felix swung onto the ladder and started down. 'And we'll be able to get clear in time?' he asked.

'Aye,' said Volk. 'The slayers've rigged a door in their tunnel that'll close behind them and cut off the blast. Should go as smooth as silk.'

Kat glared as they turned to go into the low passage. 'That was a jinx if ever I heard one,' she muttered.

'Aye,' said Felix, and crossed his fingers. He wasn't normally a superstitious man, but there was no sense tempting fate.

As they ducked into the tunnel, footsteps clattered down the stairs from above and six spearmen entered the cellar.

'Sergeant Abelung reporting,' he said. 'Steward sent us to help. Where do we go?'

Volk pointed at Felix and Kat. 'With them.'

Felix looked the spearmen over as they climbed down the ladder. They looked as tired as he felt, and no wonder. They had been working all day on the defences as well.

'Hope this doesn't take too long,' said Abelung, hunching into the tunnel after Felix and Kat. 'The zombies will be coming over the top soon.'

'I think you'll get your fair share down here,' said Felix.

As they all crouched along towards the distant ringing of picks on hard earth, Felix felt a tension in his chest that had nothing to do with the prospect of fighting zombies in cramped quarters. After a whole day and night of digging, would Gotrek's problem be worse? Would he be able to fight? Would he retire if he couldn't? Felix knew the answer to that, and it worried him.

After passing three lanterns, they saw the slayers in the distance, still swinging away. Now it was Snorri and Rodi at the workface, and Gotrek behind, shovelling the dirt into a barrow. Felix eyed him uneasily, but to his relief, the slayer's earlier breathlessness seemed to have passed.

About five paces back from the workface Felix and Kat came to a strange arrangement of logs and rope that Felix surmised must be the slayers' blast door. A sturdy log that looked like it had once been a dock piling stretched across the top of the tunnel, with both ends well set into the walls. Hanging from it by means of heavy ship's cables was a thick wooden door propped open by a spear. The contraption reminded Felix of the sort of trap a hunter made by propping up a heavy rock with a stick and placing food under it, hoping that an animal would nudge the stick and bring the rock down on itself.

'Nothing could possibly go wrong here,' Felix muttered, edging around the precarious spear.

'Oh no,' agreed Kat. 'Perfectly safe.'

Abelung laughed like a cat being strangled as he and his men squeezed in behind them.

There was a clink and clatter of falling stone, and suddenly a freezing, foetid wind blew in Felix's face. He and Kat and the spearmen choked at the smell.

'That's done it,' said Rodi. 'We're through.'

Tattered grey hands were reaching through a ragged black hole in the workface and clawing at the dirt from the other side. Not all were human. Some were the huge, gnarled claws of beastmen.

Rodi and Snorri put down their picks and picked up their axe and hammer as Gotrek tossed aside his shovel and took up his rune axe. Felix and Kat drew as well, watching as the hole got rapidly larger.

Gotrek looked over his shoulder. 'Stay back and make sure the ones who fall down stay down.'

The zombies must have heard them talking, or smelled them, for their clawing became suddenly frantic, and there was a mournful groaning from the other side of the workface. One of the spearmen flinched back.

'Steady,' said Abelung, licking his lips.

A huge impact rocked the tunnel, and a beastman's horned head smashed through the workface in an explosion of dirt, making a big hole. Snorri caved in the beast-corpse's skull with his hammer as Rodi cut it off at the knees. It toppled forwards and a tide of zombies surged through the hole to crawl over its back into the narrow tunnel, groaning and swiping with claws and broken swords.

The three slayers slammed into them with axe, hammer and shoulder, and quickly drove them back into their tunnel, then followed them in. Rodi was first, cutting down a dead knight without breaking stride, then Snorri and Gotrek followed, smashing aside a beast and a bowman, and vanished into the darkness beyond.

'Right,' said Felix, taking a breath. 'In we go.'

He pulled a lantern from a hook and stepped to the hole with Kat while the spearmen crept hesitantly after. The zombies' tunnel was at least four times as wide as the slayers' narrow one, more than twice as high, and was filled wall to wall, for as far back as Felix could see, with dead men and beastmen.

In the lantern's flickering light they jumped into sharp relief as they swarmed forwards – a vision out of a nightmare, their teeth and claws flashing yellow, their shadows raking the walls and ceiling behind them as they attacked. Maggots crawled from holes in their faces and chests, and flies buzzed around their heads. Their eyes were wilted grapes, and their hair and fur was falling out in patches, while rips in their skin showed decaying, pus-leaking meat. The smell of them was like a hammer to the face, quite literally staggering.

Kat retched, then tied her scarf over her nose and mouth to block the smell. Behind her some of the spearmen were vomiting, though they spewed only water. There was nothing else in their stomachs.

The slayers spread out across the width of the tunnel as they butchered their way into the shambling throng, but without the wall at their backs, the zombies started to edge around their flanks, and the spearmen saw their duty.

'Come on, lads,' Abelung quavered. 'Fill in their line.'

'Not too close,' said Felix, holding up a hand. 'Slayers sometimes, ah, *forget themselves* in battle.'

Abelung's eyes widened. 'Much obliged, mein herr. Right then, lads, stay back and keep them spearpoints busy.'

The spearmen stepped behind the slayers and began stabbing between them, finding eyes, necks and knees. Felix and Kat capped their line at either end, closing off the space between the slayers and the sides of the tunnel, and killing the zombies that tried to edge around. Against living opponents, the flashing spears would have been devastating, crippling and blinding them and making them defenceless against the slayers' attacks; but even against the unfeeling dead they did enough, blocking the zombies' flailing claws and making them stumble, so the slayers never had to worry about defending themselves, only attacking – sending withered limbs and heads and rotting organs spinning away from them like they were red whirlwinds.

It was a glorious slaughter, thought Felix, but how long could it continue? The slayers would never tire, of course, but the spearmen were as exhausted as he and Kat. Would they have the stamina to fight all the way to the end of the tunnel? It looked like it went back more than fifty feet!

The slayers took another stride forwards, their boots sinking ankle-deep in rotting entrails as they tromped through the dismembered dead to smash another rank of groaning corpses, and Felix, Kat and the spearmen paced forwards with them. A moment later, two artillerymen ducked through the door behind them, laying matchcord along the walls as they went, then digging holes close to the ceiling of the tunnel. Felix looked back and saw them casting uneasy glances at the undead throng that moaned and flailed only yards away from them, but they kept to their work, and once they had dug their holes, they wedged the pipe charges into them, spliced the matchcord to them and ran back towards the cellar for another load.

They continued in this fashion for what seemed an eternity, Gotrek, Rodi and Snorri carving through more zombies, and Felix, Kat and the spearmen advancing behind them as artillerymen came and went behind them, planting their charges. After a while, Felix felt like he was part of a plough being dragged the length of a farmer's field by a trio of scarred old plough horses. The slayers were tilling the ground, while the artillerymen, like bloodthirsty farmers, were sowing bombs in the furrow, which would later sprout into beautiful red and yellow explosions on harvest day.

A gasp from Abelung snapped Felix from his delirious fancy. The young sergeant was fighting spear to spear with a corpse that had somehow stumbled between Gotrek and Rodi unscathed, and he suddenly staggered back, eyes wide.

'Captain?' he quavered. 'Captain Zeismann?'

ELEVEN

FELIX LOOKED AROUND as Abelung's comrades cried out. It was true. The zombie Abelung fought was the corpse of Captain Zeismann, still recognisable though his ready smile had become a lipless grimace, and his kindly eyes were birthing maggots. And he had brought his men with him. They were pushing through to the front, their spears stabbing erratically at the slayers. Some instinct, perhaps burned into their sinews through training, had kept them together and following their leader, even in death.

'Captain,' whimpered Abelung, edging back. 'Please, captain, don't–'

The zombie that had been Zeismann stabbed forwards, and Abelung, frozen by shock and grief, did not block in time. The spear point glanced off his breastplate, then skidded up and punched through his throat. He collapsed, wide-eyed, clutching at Zeismann's spear as blood bubbled from his neck.

'Damn you, sergeant!' shouted Felix, and leapt for Zeismann as the other spearmen shrank back.

The zombie captain thrust straight for Felix's heart, but though his aim had survived his death, his speed hadn't, and Felix swept the point aside, then hacked off Zeismann's head.

The living spearmen moaned as their old captain's body collapsed, and continued retreating as more of their dead comrades staggered past the hard-pressed slayers.

'Don't be fools!' shouted Felix, trying to hold back all the dead spearmen by himself. 'You must kill them to free them! Cut them down! Let them truly die!'

Still the spearmen hesitated, on the tipping point between fight and flight, as Felix decapitated another zombie spearman and dodged three more.

'On!' he shouted desperately. 'For Abelung! For Zeismann! On!'

The names did it. With tears in their eyes and sobs in their throats, the spearmen fell in beside him. 'For Abelung!' they shouted. 'For Zeismann! For Zeismann!'

Their spears flashed forwards, stabbing their dead comrades in the chests, and after a wild few moments, the hole was plugged and their line restored and Felix was able to stagger back to his position behind Gotrek, panting and out of breath.

But as he did, he realised that his wasn't the only breathing he could hear. Though Gotrek fought on beside his fellow slayers as tirelessly as ever, and had lost no strength or speed that Felix could see, his breath was once again raw and thick, as if fluid filled his lungs. And while he seemed in no way impaired by the constant rasping, his face was even redder than usual, and his single eye angrier, as if he was furious at his body's sudden betrayal.

Again the image of the black slivers burrowing through the Slayer's organs forced its way into Felix's mind and he couldn't push it out again. He suddenly feared that Gotrek's next strike or block might be the one to jar the flecks through his heart and kill him. He wanted to tell the Slayer to step back, to let him fight at the front for once. But Gotrek would never allow that. Nor would he care about the slivers. If they killed him in the middle of battle, so be it. He would have died a slayer's death, and all would be well.

Felix glanced ahead and grunted with relief as he saw that the tunnel mouth was only a few paces ahead. They were almost there. He shot a questioning glance at Kat, on the far side of the tunnel. She gave him a weary nod and took another step through the reeking swamp of decapitated corpses, but as Felix did the same, a deep rumbling shook the tunnel, jarring him sideways and nearly knocking Kat and the spearmen off their feet.

'What is it?' asked Kat, as the noise grew louder and the shaking more violent.

'The siege towers,' said Gotrek. 'The attack has begun.'

From behind came footsteps and shouting.

'Slayers! Spearmen! Fall back!' called an artilleryman. 'We are needed at the cannons! Sappers, plant your last charges! We are lighting the fuses now!'

Gotrek and Rodi nodded to Felix, Kat and the spearmen as the artillerymen holding the last two charges shoved them hastily into their holes and hurried back down the tunnel.

'Start running,' said Gotrek. 'We will follow.'

'But there are still zombies,' said Snorri.

'Plenty more on the walls, Father Rustskull,' said Rodi.

Felix and Kat backed away with the spearmen, leaving the three slayers alone against the roiling wall of zombies, then turned and ran – although 'running' was perhaps too fine a term for what they were doing. They were so weary from fighting, and the floor so littered with butchered zombies, that they stumbled and swerved like drunks passing through a slaughterhouse.

A young spearman crashed down behind his comrades, tripping on the crushed skull of a beastman and twisting his leg. Felix and Kat hauled him up and he limped on, hissing and lame.

From the direction of the cellar came a distant cry. 'Fire in the hole! Fire in the hole!'

Felix got the boy's left arm over his shoulder and Kat did the same with his right and they staggered after the rest towards the narrow hole to the slayers' tunnel. Two sparking flames raced out of the hole as the spearmen squeezed through it, and Kat cried out in alarm. Two of the matchcords that were laid along the walls of the tunnel were sizzling towards their charges.

'That bastard Volk!' cried the spearman. 'He's blowing us up too!'

Felix's heart lurched with fear, but the matchcords burned past the first charges and sparked towards the end of the tunnel.

'No,' he panted. 'He's lit the furthest ones first.'

'Still cutting it damned fine,' said the spearman.

Kat and Felix helped him through the hole as two more sparks sizzled past them. A shout and heavy thud boomed down the tunnel from the direction of the cellar. Felix couldn't see what had happened. The tiny space was filled with the sulphuric smoke of burning matchcord, but someone was screaming.

They stumbled on and the haze thinned, and Felix could see that the heavy log-built blast door had fallen closed, pinning a spearman to the ground. Shouts and pounding came from the other side of the door, and three more spearmen were trying to lift it from this side, but it wasn't moving.

Felix, Kat and the limping spearman hurried to help them, and all of them together lifted the door enough to get it off the pinned man's back. Someone pulled him clear, but they couldn't raise the door any further. Two more flames hissed under their feet and sped down the tunnel towards the bombs.

'You on the other side!' called Felix. 'Heave on my count. One, two, *three!*'

Muffled groans came from beyond the door, and Felix could feel pressure from the other side adding to their lift. They had it up to their knees.

'Go, Kat,' said Felix. 'Get under.'

'I won't,' she said. 'Not alone.'

'Damn you, girl! There's no reason–'

'Stand aside, manling.'

Felix looked around. The three slayers were striding up the narrow tunnel in single file, Gotrek at their head. Felix shifted aside and Gotrek lifted the door over his head as if it weighed no more than a window sash.

'Run,' he said.

Kat, Felix and the spearmen all ducked gratefully under the logs and staggered along the tunnel as fast as they could go. Felix looked back and saw Rodi and Snorri side-step past Gotrek through the door as calmly as if they were squeezing through a crowded market. Then the Slayer stepped forwards and dropped the door behind him.

The logs banged closed and the world turned upside down. It was as if the slamming door had struck a trigger, for just as it hit, the tunnel shook and a battering-ram of hot air punched Felix off his feet. He and Kat and the spearmen tumbled down the tunnel like leaves before a wind as an enormous boom battered his ears and made everything else go silent.

He came to rest on top of Kat with the spearmen on top of him, and someone's knee in his kidneys. The tunnel was swirling with grey smoke. He looked back along it. He couldn't see the slayers.

'That… was loud,' said Kat.

Felix coughed and rolled off her, then pushed to his feet. 'Gotrek? Rodi? Snorri?'

Nobody answered him. He limped down the tunnel, afraid of what he would find. A squat body lay on the floor.

'Gotrek?'

The body coughed and sat up, shaking its nail-studded head. It was covered head to toe in grey dust. 'What was that, young Felix?'

'Nothing, Snorri,' said Felix. 'I thought you were Gotrek.'

'Say again? Snorri can't hear you.'

Felix edged past him, peering into the smoke.

'Gotrek? Rodi?'

Two short, sturdy silhouettes staggered out of the cloud, slapping dust off themselves. One was waggling a finger in his ear.

'Why are you whispering, manling?' asked Gotrek.

'Do you hear bells?' asked Rodi.

A muffled tantara of rally horns and the thunder of cannon echoed from above. The two slayers cocked their ears and looked up. They could hear *that* well enough.

'Come, manling,' said Gotrek, sucking in a breath and striding past with Rodi. 'Time for some real fighting.'

FELIX, KAT AND the spearmen followed the slayers out of the officers' residence and into hell. In every direction was noise, flames and confusion. Lobbed missiles arced out of the night sky to crash down all over the courtyard – boulders, flaming corpses and dead cattle that exploded in showers of rotting entrails. Fires roared wherever Felix looked. The upper storey of the knights' residence was ablaze, as was the remaining river boat, and the hoardings were catching too. On the parapet, the knights, spearmen and handgunners fought off an endless tide of zombies that poured over the battlements as swooping bats slashed at any who tried to shove or steal their ladders away. And under all the shouting and shrieking, under the crack of the guns and the boom of the cannons, came the deep rumble of the approaching siege towers.

Gotrek was looking at none of it. Instead, his one eye swept the sky, glaring at it as if demanding an answer.

'Where is he?' he rasped. 'Where is the coward?'

'Don't be picky, Gurnisson,' snorted Rodi, brushing by him with Snorri and starting for the stairs. 'There are plenty of dooms here.'

Gotrek grunted and started after them, still looking at the sky. 'I already have my doom.'

Felix scanned the walls to see where they were most needed as he, Kat and the spearmen followed the slayers across the courtyard and up the stairs. On the far side of the main gatehouse, the westernmost section of the wall was thick with the mustard and burgundy surcoats of von Volgen's Talabeclanders, fighting in a tight line at the battlements, with spearmen detachments ranked behind them and stabbing over their shoulders. On the eastern walls, von Geldrecht called encouragement to Castle Reikguard's household knights, who were lined up like the Talabeclanders, with ranked spearmen backing them up, while closest to the gatehouse, Bosendorfer and his greatswords had staked out a section of wall for their very own, and were slashing wildly at the zombies with no spearmen to back them up. And on the towers, Volk's crews, shirtless and sweating, were loading, priming and firing the castle's great-cannons while Hultz's handgunners clustered around them, blasting away at the giant bats that harried them and tried to ruin their aim. Even Draeger's militiamen were on the walls, dragged out of their cells as von Geldrecht promised, but apparently not entrusted with weapons. They ran amongst the others, wielding hooked ropes and boarding pikes to steal and shove back the ladders of the zombies all along the wall.

Felix nodded with grim satisfaction. For all the fire and noise and crashing stones, all seemed to be going well. The hoardings were protecting the defenders from the bats and the blazing barrage that Kemmler's catapults and trebuchets were raining down upon them, and the defenders were holding their lines and making short work of the corpses that managed to make it to the walls.

Unfortunately, it looked as if all that was about to change.

As Felix, Kat and the slayers and spearmen squeezed onto the parapet behind the surging lines of knights, the deep rumble that had churned their guts since they had stepped into the courtyard grew so strong that it shook the castle walls, drowning out the shouts of the captains as they bellowed orders to their troops. Felix craned his neck to see over the battlements, and saw at last the source of the sound.

'Sigmar,' he breathed.

The towers had been frightening enough seen at a distance, when he had watched them being constructed at the edge of the woods. Now, lurching out of the night and crawling with nightmare crews, they were enough to make him want to turn and run. Up close, he saw they had been covered with the shaggy skins of beastmen, stretched across a twisted framework of dead trees, the hides crudely stitched together and the empty bags of head skin flapping and ballooning in the wind so that it looked like the eye and mouth holes were blinking and trying to say something.

More revolting still, the tower was being pulled by the dead beastmen that had been flayed to make it. Hundreds of skinless beast-corpses were harnessed to the towers, pulling them forwards by ropes that pierced them through their chests and strung them together like grisly fetishes on a shaman's braid. The bestial zombies trudged forwards as one, straining against the thick knots that pressed against their sternums as the towers skidded slowly over the uneven ground, swaying and shaking like they were in a high wind.

The boarding crews were just as hideous – naked, white-skinned ghouls with clawed hands and filed teeth. They hung from the fighting tops by the score, gibbering and howling for human flesh, and shaking shin-bone spears and thigh-bone clubs.

'Corpse-eaters,' moaned Kat, shuddering.

Felix fought down nausea as the reek of death and defecation washed over them. 'Gods,' he choked. 'The smell alone will kill us!'

The spearmen gave Felix and Kat a farewell salute, then hurried to rejoin the ranks of their comrades. Felix and Kat returned the salute, then followed the slayers as they went left, heading for where the nearest tower was trundling towards the wall.

But as it loomed closer, hope swelled in Felix's chest. It looked like the crew of the menacing tower were going to drag it straight into the empty moat, where it would tip forwards and crash flat before it reached the wall – and the further tower seemed about to do the same.

'That's it, you brainless puppets!' shouted Captain Hultz from where his handgunners blazed at the ghouls. 'Do our work for us!'

'They're going to crush their own crews!' laughed a spearman.

The cat-calls died away, however, as the long trains of zombies that had been following the towers all at once surged ahead and began throwing themselves into the moat in front of them.

'What are they doing?' asked a knight. 'They'll be flattened!'

'Oh, Sigmar,' moaned a handgunner. 'They're making a bridge.'

And as he and Kat stared, Felix saw the man was right. The zombies kept piling into the moat in their hundreds until, just before the harnessed teams of beast-corpses reached them, they were level with its banks.

At first the dead beastmen lost their footing on the uneven surface of their comrades' stacked bodies, but then they recovered, digging their hooves into the faces and ribcages and guts of the undead bridge and using them for traction. The skids of the towers had less trouble. They slid across the mound of crushed corpses as if they were greased, and the towers picked up speed.

Cannons belched smoke from the castle walls, and the top of the further tower smashed to splinters, sending the ghouls that clung to it spinning away to their deaths, while the cannonball from the right-hand gun crashed through the waist of the nearer, snapping timbers and braces within before punching out the far side.

The men on the walls cheered, but though smashed and sagging, the towers kept coming, screeching ghouls swarming up from their depths.

Rodi and Snorri stopped behind Bosendorfer and his greatswords, who readied themselves at the place where the nearer tower would strike the wall.

'Here,' said Rodi, hefting his axe.

Gotrek shot a last disappointed look at the sky, then fell in beside him. 'Aye,' he said.

'Snorri wishes these humans would get out of the way,' said Snorri.

'Here it comes,' said Kat.

'Not one step back, greatswords!' yelled Bosendorfer.

'Not a step, lads!' shouted his sergeant, a hulking veteran with a grizzled beard. 'Not a step!'

With an impact that shook the whole castle, the hellish tower struck and the ghouls launched forwards, straight onto the sword-points of the greatswords – but they didn't come alone. As the first wave died screaming and tumbling off the battlements to crash amongst the skinless beast-zombies below, a cold wind exhaled from the maw of the tower and a shrieking spectre burst forth, shadows flapping around it like a shroud. An eyeless female face stared from the centre of the darkness as claws like sabres reached for the greatswords.

The hairs stood on Felix's neck as the thing came forwards, and he took an involuntary step back. Every fear he had ever had – of the dark, of losing his mother, of illness, death and tortures beyond the grave – all welled up in him at once as he looked into her empty eyes, and every fibre of courage he possessed dried up and crumbled in the scathing wind of her shriek. He wanted to turn and flee – to hide in a corner and weep.

And perhaps he would have, but Kat stumbled back too, bumping into him, and somehow, that contact, and the opportunity it gave him to put his hand on her shoulder and reassure her, reassured him too, and the panic passed.

The greatswords, unfortunately, had no one to reassure, and were edging back and dying as the ghouls took advantage of their terrified paralysis, raking out their eyes and ripping out their throats. Bosendorfer swung his two-hander at the ghostly horror, but his blade passed right through it without touching and it came on, swiping with its claws.

They impaled him through the chest, and though they seemed to do no physical damage to him or his armour, their touch made him stagger and shriek.

'Fall back!' he cried, flailing with his sword. 'Fall back, we cannot prevail!'

The greatswords, already on the point of breaking, followed this order with a will, and fled down the wall, Bosendorfer in the lead and the sergeant taking up the rear, as a score of ghouls flooded onto the parapet unopposed after them.

'Cowards!' growled Gotrek, and charged forwards into the corpse-eaters with Rodi and Snorri milling at his sides, and Felix and Kat following behind.

'At least they got out of the way,' said Snorri.

The banshee howled at the slayers as they slaughtered the ghouls, but one swipe of Gotrek's axe and she dissipated into fading curls of mist, her miasma of fear fading with her. The slayers pressed on, but they were like a boulder in a wide stream. Though they cut down ghouls with every swing of their weapons, without the greatswords to hold their flanks, many more spilled around them and swarmed down the wall, attacking the lines of the knights and spearmen from the rear. The ranks were crumbling and falling back in confusion, allowing the zombies to top their ladders and gain a foothold on the wall. The greatswords needed to come back!

'Bosendorfer!' shouted Felix, hacking down a ghoul. 'Turn about! She's gone!'

A few of the greatswords looked back, but Bosendorfer didn't seem to have heard. Felix cursed, then filled his lungs. It had worked with the spearmen in the tunnel. Perhaps it would work here.

'Greatswords!' he shouted. 'To me! Hold the wall! Hold for Castle Reikguard!'

A few of the greatswords slowed and turned, and then called more of their comrades back. The grizzled sergeant hesitated, looking towards Bosendorfer, then back to Felix again.

'To me!' shouted Felix again. 'We can hold them here!'

The words seemed to galvanise the sergeant, and he started back along the wall. The others followed, and fell upon the ghouls that had got behind the knights and spearmen.

'That's it!' cried Felix, as they worked their way back along the wall. 'For Graf Reiklander! For the Empire!'

With the greatswords pushing back the ghoul incursion, the slayers pressed forwards to stem the tide at its source. They cut a bloody path to the battlements, then leapt from them to the siege tower and battled through the ghouls towards the maw from which they spewed.

Felix and Kat watched their progress uneasily as they and the greatswords fought to hem in the ghouls that still swarmed past the slayers to the wall. The tower was listing decidedly to the left and creaking noisily as the skinless beast-zombies, no longer needed to pull it forwards, climbed its sides, still strung together on their long ropes.

'Don't the brainless things know it's broken inside?'

cried Kat. 'They're going to pull it down!'

'Aye,' said Felix. 'And the slayers with it.'

A roar from above brought Felix's head up. He cursed. Hurtling out of the sky on the back of his undead wyvern was Krell, aiming straight for the three dwarfs.

'Slayers!' shouted Felix.

Gotrek, Rodi and Snorri dived aside as the patchwork monster slammed down on the precarious tower and nearly rocked it off its runners. Ghouls and skinned beasts spun away to the ground as the slayers clung like limpets, and more ominous crackings and grindings sounded from within.

'Mine!' roared Rodi as Krell dismounted and slashed at him with his black axe. The gauntleted hand and forearm Gotrek had previously severed seemed to have completely regrown.

'Find your own doom, Balkisson!' roared Gotrek, throwing himself forwards. 'This is mine!'

'Take it if you can, Gurnisson!' laughed Rodi and charged in as well.

Krell blocked both attacks with a scrape of steel, but Gotrek shouldered into his legs and sent him crashing back into his wyvern. The ugly beast flapped into the air, shrieking, and left the wight king lying at the edge of the tower as the slayers advanced.

'Snorri wants it to be his doom!' called Snorri, limping after them.

A skinned beastmen pulled itself up onto the fighting top and lurched in Snorri's way as Krell and the slayers clashed. Snorri crushed the beast-corpse's head with his hammer, only to find more of the hulking horrors pulling themselves up all around him, all still linked together like some grisly charm bracelet come to life.

'Get out of Snorri's way!' shouted Snorri.

Felix cursed. This was bad. He had to get Snorri off the

tower before he found his doom. Unfortunately, there were more than a score of ghouls in the way.

'Drive them back!' he shouted to the greatswords. 'Drive them off the walls!'

The greatswords cheered, and the grizzled sergeant echoed him. 'Aye, lads! Drive 'em back to the grave-yard!'

The greatswords fell upon the ghouls like a single man, their weapons rising and falling as one, and doing terrible damage to heads, shoulders and necks as Felix and Kat fought in their centre. Still, Felix wasn't sure they would be quick enough.

On the leaning tower, Snorri fought in the centre of a handful of skinned beasts, roaring joyously, while Gotrek and Rodi chopped at Krell from opposite sides. The wight king turned and slashed in their centre, his odsidian axe making a choking cloud of grit all around him. Rodi caught a mouthful and stumbled, coughing, and Krell struck him a blow so strong that, though he blocked it, it knocked the young slayer to the very edge of the fighting top.

'Ha!' snarled Gotrek, charging in. 'Now we'll see whose doom it is!'

Krell backed from Gotrek's blurring axe, and his ancient black armour was quickly scored with a dozen metal-bright scars, but the surge was taking its toll on Gotrek too. His ragged breathing had returned, and his face glowed like a hot coal.

Rodi struggled to his feet and started up the slant again, but the skinned beast-corpses were surrounding him as well. 'Wait, Gurnisson!'

Gotrek coughed as he drove Krell to the edge. 'A slayer doesn't wait!'

The undead champion's boot-heel slipped on the uneven lip of the fighting top, and Gotrek took advantage, hacking a huge divot out of his right greave. Krell threw himself to the side to avoid another strike and Gotrek turned after him, blowing like a steam tank.

At the same moment, Felix, Kat and the greatswords finally chopped down the last of the ghouls and leapt up onto the battlements to hack at the ring of skinless beasts that surrounded Snorri – only to find the old slayer in a terrible predicament.

His peg leg was wedged between two planks at the very edge of the slanted platform, and he couldn't get it out. He swung mightily with his warhammer as the dead beasts pressed him from all sides, but he could not move or dodge, and they were clawing him to pieces.

Felix, Kat and the greatswords charged in, chopping at the ring of beasts, but there were too many, and they were too big. They weren't going to make it before Snorri was driven over the side.

'Gotrek!' shouted Felix. 'Snorri!'

Gotrek looked to the old slayer as he smashed Krell's legs out from under him and sent him crashing down the slant. He hesitated, and Felix read his expression. If he went after the wight king, he could finish him, and cross out a thousand grudges in the dwarfs' ancient book. He could be known forever as the slayer of Krell the Holdbreaker. But if he did, Snorri would fall to his death.

With a savage snarl, Gotrek charged at Snorri, and slammed into the wall of beasts around him, hamstringing one with his axe and shoving it over the edge. It jerked to a stop and swung like a hanged man as the rope that connected it to its fellows pulled taut. The next in the string staggered sideways at the jerk and Gotrek shoved it too. That did it. As the second beastman pitched over the side, its weight, combined with the weight of the first beastman and the steep angle of the platform, pulled all the rest off one after the other in rapid succession. It was like watching a string of ugly sausages slip over the edge of a cliff.

But as the last beast-corpse toppled, it impaled itself upon a dead tree branch that jutted out through the stretched skins of the tower's side, and stopped dead. All at once, all the weight of all the beasts on the string jerked the crippled tower hard to the left, and something vital broke within it.

Gotrek cursed and stumbled to Snorri, ripping his trapped peg from the planks as the tower began to sink slowly but inexorably to the side.

'Fall back, Nosebiter,' he wheezed, and shoved him at Felix and Kat, who dragged him back towards the battlements.

'Where did the beastmen go?' asked Snorri.

'Forget the beastmen, Snorri,' snapped Kat.

Gotrek turned back to Krell. Rodi was already there, driving him back across the tipping fighting top with brutal cuts as the wight king roared at the sky. Gotrek plunged after them, panting and rasping, but before he could reach them, the wyvern flashed down, flaring its wings, and Krell vaulted into the saddle.

Gotrek and Rodi rushed at him, but they were too late. The wyvern launched forwards and plunged away out of sight, and the tower tilted drastically under their feet.

'Coward!' roared Gotrek.

'Come back and fight!' bellowed Rodi.

'Slayers!' called Felix. 'Get off it!'

'Hurry!' cried Kat.

The slayers stood for an agonising second, staring after Krell, then turned and walked back onto the battlements just as the collapsing tower finally sank away beneath them. Gotrek's face was hot and his chest heaved, but his single eye was as hard and cold as Felix had ever seen it.

Along the wall, the men pushing back the ladders and fighting the zombies cheered as the tower crashed to the moat, crushing scores of zombies and ghouls, and the cheer was echoed from the right as the second tower went down as well, burning like a kite in a furnace, but the slayers did not seem in a celebratory mood.

Snorri, bleeding from a dozen claw wounds, was frowning at Gotrek as he struggled to stand. 'Snorri doesn't think it was right of you, Gotrek Gurnisson, to stop him from–'

'And Gotrek Gurnisson doesn't give a damn what Snorri thinks!' Gotrek bellowed in the old slayer's face. 'Until he remembers his shame, Gotrek doesn't want to hear another word out of Snorri's mouth!'

Felix, Kat and Rodi stepped back as Snorri blinked, stunned by Gotrek's outburst. The greatswords didn't seem to know where to look.

'And what if Snorri thinks he'd like to punch Gotrek Gurnisson's ugly face in?' asked Snorri, his fists balling.

Gotrek's brows lowered, but before he could gather enough breath to reply, von Volgen and a pair of knights shoved past him, running towards von Geldrecht.

'Lord steward!' called von Volgen. 'The harbour! Look to the harbour!'

Felix, Kat and the slayers turned and looked down into the harbour, searching for what von Volgen was speaking of. Felix frowned. The sloop was still burning, and rocks and flaming corpses were still splashing down all over it, but he saw no new threat.

'What is it?' he asked. 'I don't see anything.'

'There!' said Kat, pointing towards the water near the quayside.

Felix followed her gaze. The water was filled with bobbing heads and thrashing hands as men tried to climb out onto the quayside.

No. Not men.

'Zombies,' rasped Gotrek. 'From under the river gate.'

TWELVE

'SIGMAR'S BLOOD!' CURSED Felix. 'How have they got in? We blocked it!'

The zombies were pulling themselves onto the docks in a mass now, like sludge-covered crabs crawling over each other to escape a roiling stew pot. The massive forms of dead beastmen heaved up amongst them, water pouring from their filthy fur, and they staggered towards the doors of the main gatehouse while the human corpses shuffled for the stairs to the walls and clawed up the sides of the burning riverboat as the river wardens hacked at them and shoved them back.

'So many,' moaned Kat. 'What do we do now?'

Felix turned to ask Gotrek the same question. The Slayer was walking after von Volgen with Snorri and Rodi following. Felix shot an uneasy look at Snorri, afraid he might still be angry at Gotrek, but the old slayer's face was as placid as it always was – as if his oldest friend hadn't just shouted in his face. Felix sighed. That was one advantage to Snorri's memory problems, he supposed. He forgot an insult as quickly as he forgot anything else.

Felix saluted the greatsword sergeant as he and Kat turned to follow the slayers. 'Thank you, sergeant.'

The big man gave him a sheepish smile. 'Thank you, mein herr,' he said. 'Thank you for bringing us back.'

'You are thanking him, Sergeant Leffler?' rang a voice behind them. 'For countermanding my order?'

They all looked around. It was Bosendorfer, his eyes blazing.

'If I tell you to fall back, you fall back,' he said, stepping forwards. 'If I tell you to hold the walls, you hold the walls, is that clear?'

'Yes, captain,' said the sergeant. 'Very clear.'

'Good,' said Bosendorfer, then pointed to the now-empty battlements. 'Hold the walls!'

The men hesitated, and Leffler glanced at Felix as if to ask his permission. Felix nodded automatically, then saw that Bosendorfer had witnessed the exchange, and was rigid with rage.

The sergeant saluted hastily, then led the others back to the battlements.

Felix stepped back, feeling like he should say something, then turned away with Kat, growling. He felt Bosendorfer's eyes on him the whole way as they followed the slayers down the wall.

'I don't think I've made a friend there,' he said.

'Who wants a coward for a friend?' sneered Kat.

They found the slayers on the top of the easternmost tower, waiting impatiently as von Geldrecht gave orders to his officers while von Volgen stood at his side, whispering advice.

'One in every five men on the wall shall descend and defend the gatehouse!' called von Geldrecht, then turned to von Volgen, frowning. 'One in five? Are you sure? Will the walls hold?'

'With the towers down,' said von Volgen calmly, 'the zombies on the ladders can be contained. The harbour breach is your greatest threat, lord steward. It must be stopped and the gatehouse held, for if it falls, you will have to retire to the keep – and that will involve a great loss of life and treasure.'

'But how are we to stop the hole?' said von Geldrecht, and Felix could see he was an eye blink from panic. 'I thought we had already blocked it.'

'Leave that to us,' said Gotrek, his breathing slowly returning to normal. 'You keep the corpses out of the gatehouse, and we'll plug your hole for you.'

Von Geldrecht breathed a sigh of relief. 'Thank you, slayers. You shall have all the assistance you require.'

'Rope, lamp oil, pipe charges and matchcord,' grunted Gotrek. 'Also an oarboat, and some men to keep off the zombies while we work.'

'It shall be done,' said von Geldrecht. 'And you will have Bosendorfer's greatswords to defend you.'

Felix coughed. 'Uh, no need to trouble them,' he said quickly. 'Perhaps some spearmen instead.'

'Certainly, certainly,' said von Geldrecht, then turned back to von Volgen as Felix, Kat and the slayers started for the stairs. 'And you will see to the defence of the gatehouse, my lord?'

Von Volgen bowed. 'Of course, lord steward. We will hold it to the last man.'

Felix thought he did a remarkable job of keeping the contempt out of his voice.

A FEW MINUTES later, Felix, Kat and Snorri were prowling back and forth along the embankment of the harbour, fending off the giant bats that wheeled down out of the sky and chopping at any zombies that dared rear their heads above the waves while Rodi tied a rope around Gotrek's waist, and Gotrek chained his rune axe to his wrist. They were all tucked into the furthest corner of the harbour, behind the stairs that rose to the keep, and beside the river gate. The spearmen Gotrek had requested were posted between the stairs and the embankment, blocking any zombies that shambled towards them from the courtyard. That didn't stop the ones who tried to climb out of the water, however, and Felix, Kat and Snorri had their hands full.

'Sure you have enough breath?' asked Rodi, pulling the rope tight.

'It won't take much,' said Gotrek.

Felix swallowed. He could think of no more unpleasant experience than jumping into a dark harbour full of undead men and beastmen, but it would be impossible to patch the hole until they knew how big it was, and the only way to learn that was to sink down and look. Gotrek also wanted to know how the zombies had made it. Had they pushed aside the stones? Had they dug through the mud? How could they have done it in such a short time?

Rodi tied off the rope, then ducked aside as a great boulder smashed down next to them, shattering the flagstones and bouncing away, proof that the battle had not stopped so that they could carry out their investigation. Indeed, it had become worse. On the towers, Volk's cannons continued to blaze away, trying to knock out Kemmler's catapults and trebuchets, which still bombarded the courtyard with filth and stones and flaming death. On the walls, von Geldrecht's knights and spearmen kept up their never-ending battle to push back the zombies' ladders. And in the courtyard, von Volgen and his company of chosen men guarded the gatehouse doors against the ever-growing swarm of zombies that continued to surge up out of the harbour in a never-ending tide and attack them with mindless focus.

Unless Gotrek found some way to block the hole in the river gate, the outcome of that battle was inevitable. Von Volgen's men were holding up well, but faced with a force that would not break or tire or diminish, they would eventually die of attrition, and the gatehouse would fall. Then the zombies would open the gates and the rest of the horde would pour in. The lower courtyard would be lost, and likely the keep too. Castle Reikguard would be in the hands of Kemmler, and the relief force, when it at last arrived, would take the roll of besieger, rather than rescuer.

Gotrek stepped to the edge of the embankment.

'Leave off, Nosebiter,' he said. 'It's time.'

Snorri put his hammer on his back and wrapped the end of Gotrek's rope around his massive fist. 'Snorri is ready.'

'Ready,' said Rodi, taking up a jug of lamp oil and a torch.

Gotrek nodded, then dived into the water, his axe in one hand. As soon as he vanished beneath the waves, Rodi cracked the jug of lamp oil on the stone embankment and let the contents spill onto the water, then touched the torch to the spreading sheen.

With a sudden *whump*, the oil went up in a ball of flame, then burned brightly on the waves, snaking like it was alive through the ripples and splashes.

A zombie came up in the middle of it and tried to climb onto the bank as the flames clung to its head and shoulders. It didn't seem to notice, and reached for Kat with a burning hand. She dodged back, then split its skull with one hatchet, and its throat with the other. The thing fell back, clawing weakly and fizzling as it sank beneath the waves.

A second later, the flames burned themselves out, and

a second after that, Gotrek's rope began wildly jerking and thrashing in the water.

'Pull, Snorri!' shouted Rodi. 'Pull!'

The old slayer heaved mightily on the rope, and began to reel it in fist over fist, but there was a lot of resistance. Rodi joined him and they pulled together as Felix and Kat stepped close to the edge, weapons raised.

The water churned at their feet, and then a shaven head and broad shoulders shot backwards up out of the waves, followed instantly by the horned goat head of a dead beastman, and the rotting, thrashing limbs of human zombies. Gotrek was infested with them. The beast-corpse had its ursine teeth clamped around his left shoulder, and the humans clung to his legs and torso, all clawing and biting as he swung his rune axe and roared sputtering defiance.

Felix struck the goat-headed monster a glancing blow. It was enough of a distraction for Gotrek to bury his axe under its jaw, and it fell away. Kat severed the spine of one of the men, and Gotrek peeled off the other two with his axe, then flopped on the embankment, coughing violently, as Felix and Kat drove the rest under the waves.

'Well?' said Rodi, throwing down the rope.

Gotrek sat up, still coughing, and slicked his crest back out of his eyes. 'Big enough for a beastman,' he said. 'But no bigger. And right through the gate.'

He opened his left hand to reveal a stub of metal bar. Felix and Kat looked at it over their shoulders. It was a broken piece of the iron lattice that made up the river gate doors, but it had a curious brittle look to it, and when Rodi poked his finger at it, it crumbled away like chalk.

'The saboteur,' he grunted. 'I thought Lord Lard-Guts was going to "take steps".'

Gotrek grunted and pulled himself to his feet. He had deep bite marks in his left shoulder, and claw marks everywhere. 'Forget the saboteur. We have to close the hole.' His eye focussed on the temple of Sigmar across the harbour. 'And that is the patch.'

'You CAN'T TAKE my door!' cried Father Ulfram, as his acolyte, Danniken, cowered in the background. 'This is a temple of Sigmar! You are committing sacrilege!'

The slayers ignored him, just continued banging at the hinges of the huge iron-bound door with their hammers and chisels.

'I'm sorry, father,' said Felix, 'but it's the only way. It is strong enough and big enough, and–'

'You've prayed to Sigmar to protect us, haven't you, priest?' interrupted Kat, an edge to her voice.

'Of course I have,' said Ulfram. 'Constantly.'

'And what if this is his answer?' Kat asked.

The priest opened his mouth to retort, then paused, his brows furrowed behind the rag that hid his eyes. 'Here it comes,' said Rodi, and stepped back as the massive door suddenly dropped from its hinges, then toppled forwards to crash down on the temple's front steps with a deafening boom.

Ulfram wailed at the sound and turned towards the altar at the back of the temple, making the sign of the hammer on his sunken chest. 'O Sigmar, if this be your will, then grant me–'

'We'll be back for the altar,' said Gotrek.

'What!' cried Ulfram. 'No! At this I draw the line! You cannot–'

But the three slayers had already picked up the heavy door and were walking it out to their commandeered longboat.

BY THE TIME the boatmen had pushed the heavy-laden longboat away from the quay and started rowing towards the river gate with Gotrek, Felix, Snorri, Rodi and Kat crouching on top of the precariously balanced door and altar, it was clear to Felix that Kemmler had figured out what they were doing and was trying to stop it.

The zombies that emerged from the waters of the harbour were no longer shambling towards von Volgen's beleaguered square of defenders before the gatehouse. Now they were bobbing up on all sides of the longboat and reaching for its sides with their water-bloated claws, while at the same time, every giant bat in the sky was now streaking down and trying to smash them all into the water.

It was a nightmare. Felix, Kat and Rodi crawled up and down the boat, slashing at the zombies in a frenzy, as Gotrek and Snorri stumped back and forth and fought off the bats that clattered and shrieked above them, while the terrified river wardens prayed to Manann and spent as much time bashing zombies with their oars as they did rowing.

Felix feared every second that the overloaded boat would capsize and they would sink into the roiling stew of zombies, but somehow – by Sigmar's grace? – they reached the river gate with only a foot of water in the bottom and only two of the oarsmen pulled to their deaths.

Gotrek lashed the boat length-wise to the iron bars of the gates, which allowed the boatmen to abandon their oars and take up their cutlasses and join Kat, Felix and Snorri in the defence, while Gotrek and Rodi bent to their work.

Felix had never been in so hectic a fight. It was a non-stop onslaught from water and air, a whirling madness of arms and wings and claws and snapping teeth, with the boat rocking and bumping under his feet. A bat clawed his forehead and he fought on blinded by blood. A zombie bit his ankle, and its jaws remained locked around it even after he had cut its head off. Kat weaved like she was drunk, her whole left side covered in black slime. The boatmen fought like cornered rats, snarling with rabid fear.

In the few brief over-the-shoulder glances he managed, Felix saw the two slayers working feverishly – fixing the door to the gate with long chains looped around its hinge posts, then tying ropes around the massive altar, and doing the same to it.

By then the boat was wallowing so low in the water that Felix feared that a single zombie laying its hands on its gunwales would send it sinking to the bottom.

'Any time, Gotrek,' he hissed through clenched teeth. 'Any time.'

'Nearly there, manling,' said Gotrek.

He and Rodi turned to the bow where two of Volk's tunnel charges sat half-submerged. They took lengths of slow-burning gunner's match from their belts then turned to the boatmen.

'The blast will stun the zombies in the water and knock back any coming through the hole,' said Gotrek. 'It will also sink the boat.'

'Sink the boat!' cried a boatman. 'You didn't say–'

'You should have time to swim to the bank before the zombies recover,' smirked Rodi. 'But if you don't, well, at least you died saving your mates.'

The boatmen wailed at this, but there was little they could do. Gotrek and Rodi touched the gunner's match to the matchcord of the charges then pitched them towards the centre of the harbour where they splashed into the water. Felix had been a little sceptical of this part of the plan, but he changed his mind as he saw the sparking flame of the matchcord still burning as it sank towards the bottom.

The zombies, being zombies, paid no attention and

just kept on attacking, as did the bats, but Felix's heart raced in his chest as he waited for the bang to come. How big would the explosion be? What if it smashed them all into the gate?

A dull thud, felt as much as heard, punched the soles of his feet and rocked the boat violently beneath him, then a geyser of water, smoke and zombie parts erupted in the middle of the harbour, spraying them all and sending a great mounded ring wave spreading in all directions.

'Here it comes!' shouted a boatman, dropping his cutlass.

The swell lifted them high, and as Felix had feared, banged the boat against the gates, but then the water passed through the bars and dropped again. The boat went with it, wallowing, then slipping out from under the chained temple door and roped altar to sink into the water.

The boatmen swam frantically for the embankment through a sargasso of floating, unmoving zombies, but Felix and Kat remained clinging to the bars of the gate and slashing at the wheeling bats as the last pieces of Gotrek's plan literally fell into place.

As the boat sank, the heavy temple door swung down on its chains until it vanished under the water and Felix felt it clang flat against the river gate.

'So,' said Felix, ducking as a bat smashed into the gate. 'That seals the hole?'

'Aye,' said Gotrek, then slapped the bulky stone slab of the altar, which still hung from its ropes, half-submerged, against the gate. 'And this is the lock. Not even a beastman could shift the door with this wedged behind it.' He raised his axe and turned to Rodi and Snorri. 'Ready, Balkisson? Nosebiter?'

'Snorri is ready,' said Snorri, pulling himself around

so that he held the outer edge of the altar.

'Aye, Gurnisson,' said Rodi, lifting his axe.

As one, he and Gotrek cut the ropes holding the stone table, and it sank swiftly into the water.

The slayers went with it, holding its sides to guide it, and disappeared beneath the dark water. Felix looked around – the floating zombies were beginning to twitch and groan.

'We'd better swim for it,' he said, sheathing his sword.

Kat nodded and they struck out for the embankment, only a few yards away. The boatmen helped them out of the water then looked back towards the gate.

'Have they done it?' asked one.

'It doesn't seem possible,' said another.

But as the slayers' heads broke the surface again and they began swimming for shore, Felix noticed that all the bats banked away from them and began to attack von Volgen's men again, harassing them from the air as they defended the gatehouse against the huge mob of zombies that surrounded it.

'Aye,' said Felix. 'They did it. Kemmler has given us up for another target.'

The three slayers heaved themselves out of the water and turned towards the battle at the gatehouse.

'Come on,' said Gotrek, wheezing as he started forwards with Rodi and Snorri. 'Only a few left now.'

Felix exchanged a weary look with Kat. It felt like they had been fighting forever, but the Slayer was right. Patching the hole would be pointless if the zombies that had already got in broke through the front gate. He drew his sword and Kat drew her hatchets, and they slogged after the slayers.

WHEN IT WAS all over, when the last trapped zombie had been decapitated and thrown on the pyre, when the fires in the residences had been put out and the handgunners on the walls had stolen so many of the zombies' ladders that they could no longer continue their assault, von Geldrecht and von Volgen approached the slayers with Captain Hultz and Father Ulfram and Danniken in tow. They all inclined their heads respectfully.

'Thank you, slayers,' said von Geldrecht. 'If not for your quick thinking, we would have been overwhelmed. Castle Reikguard owes you a debt of gratitude it cannot repay.'

'Even if it cost us a temple door,' said Father Ulfram.

'But how did they get in?' asked von Volgen. 'Did they burrow under the stones? Were they not piled high enough?'

Gotrek caught his breath, then spoke. 'The gate was shattered. Like the lock mechanism. Like the runes.'

Von Geldrecht closed his eyes and groaned. 'The saboteur.'

Von Volgen turned grim eyes on him. 'You have learned nothing more of him, lord steward?'

'My captains assured me they would report any suspicious goings-on,' said von Geldrecht, shaking his head. 'But they have given me no reports.'

Felix saw von Volgen's jaw clench with suppressed anger. 'My lord, rooting out such a powerful traitor is of utmost importance. You – you must do more.' He turned to Father Ulfram. 'Cannot the good father discover the identity of this warlock through his prayers?'

Von Geldrecht coughed as everyone looked at the priest. 'I have asked,' he said. 'But–'

'But I am not what I was,' said Ulfram, raising his bandaged eyes towards von Volgen. 'The fight with the pestilent champion I slew at Grimminhagen was not won without sacrifice. It took my sight and – and the strength of my prayers. Danniken here has done his best to help me recover, but I am much diminished, and Sigmar has not seen fit to answer me in this matter.'

Von Volgen bowed, chagrinned. 'Forgive me, Father. I did not know.'

Felix looked wonderingly at Ulfram as he nodded and looked down again. The frail old man had slain a champion of the dark powers? Did that mean he had been a warrior priest during the war? It hardly seemed possible, looking at him now.

'Nonetheless, it was a worthy suggestion, Lord von Volgen,' said Von Geldrecht. 'And you are right. I must do more. I – I had thought to keep the sabotage quiet until the fiend could be apprehended, but – but I see now that drastic measures are required.' He sighed and stared at the ground for a long moment, then looked up, his sagging face haggard. 'Hultz, inform the officers, and you von Volgen, tell your men. I will address the whole of the castle in the courtyard tomorrow after morning mess. Everyone who is not on duty will attend – knights, foot soldiers, servants and staff. Everyone. I will expose this villain before them once and for all.'

'My lord,' said von Volgen, uneasy. 'What do you intend?'

'It is better that no one know in advance.' Von Geldrecht turned to Ulfram. 'Father, if I could see you in the temple.'

'Of course, lord steward,' said the priest. 'Come with me.'

Danniken took Ulfram's arm and led him towards the now doorless temple as von Geldrecht limped beside him, talking in low tones. Felix was amazed at the contrast between his memories of the cheerful and robust von Geldrecht he had met only days before, and the frail old man who shuffled away from him now.

Hultz gave Felix, Kat and the slayers a salute as he

turned to start back to his men. 'Well done, tonight, friends. When we have beer again, the first round's on me.'

'Hultz,' said von Volgen, calling him back. 'One moment.'

'Aye, my lord.'

Von Volgen shot an uncomfortable glance at the retreating von Geldrecht, then lowered his voice. 'It is not my place to order you, but perhaps someone should put a guard on the river gate so this does not happen again.'

Hultz too looked after von Geldrecht, then nodded. 'Aye, my lord. A very good suggestion. I'll put someone on it right away.'

He started away again and von Volgen turned to Felix, Kat and the slayers. 'I know we did not start well, and I expect no friendship from you after having locked you up for something you didn't do. But I wish you to know that I value your presence here as much as I value that of my own knights. Thank you.' He clicked his heels together and bowed, then turned and strode off, ramrod-straight, and did not look back.

'He's still a blind fool that can't tell his own son from a corpse,' said Rodi, snorting.

Gotrek spat. 'He's not the fool that worries me,' he said, then looked after von Geldrecht, who was just entering the temple with Ulfram and Danniken. 'You don't catch saboteurs with speeches. You catch them in the act.'

'A trap?' asked Kat.

Gotrek looked around the courtyard. 'A watch on his next target.'

'You know where he'll strike next?' asked Felix.

'Well, it won't be the river gate,' said Kat. 'Not if Hultz guards it like he said.'

'The hoardings,' said Rodi. 'He's already taken away

the wards, the moat, the river gate – what else is left?'

Gotrek nodded, then turned for the stairs to the walls. 'Find places to hide. We'll watch until the rat comes out of his hole. Then we spring.'

Felix groaned. He was weary beyond description. 'Tonight?'

'Aye, manling,' said Gotrek. 'Tomorrow could be too late. And tell no one what you're about. I trust no one in this madhouse.'

As they spread out, looking for likely vantage points, Felix felt eyes on him and turned to see Bosendorfer leading his greatswords into the underkeep and looking over his shoulder at him. The hate in his eyes almost singed Felix's hair.

KAT FOUND A shadowed spot on the roof of the temple of Sigmar from which to watch the courtyard, while Snorri and Rodi chose places in the ruined stables, and half-burned residences respectively. Felix and Gotrek chose a dark section of wall on the river side of the castle, far from where the hoardings had been placed, but offering a view of all of them.

Now that he had stopped fighting and running and swimming and shouting, all of Felix's weariness and hunger and pain caught up to him, and he sagged against the battlements like an empty sleeve. He had cuts and bruises from head to toe, a loose tooth, a missing thumbnail – neither of which he could account for – and was covered in a grimy patina of smoke, sweat and harbour water.

How long had he been fighting? How long since he had more than a swallow of water and a single biscuit at a sitting? How long since he had more than a few hours of sleep at once? He was too tired to work out any of the answers. He was too tired to keep his head up, but at the same time, when he closed his eyes, his mind scuttled about like a nervous cockroach, and wouldn't let him sleep.

Who was the saboteur? What madness was von Geldrecht planning for tomorrow? What would happen with Bosendorfer? But the image his mind returned to more than any other was Gotrek bellowing in Snorri's face. The friendship between the two slayers had had its ups and downs in the time that Felix had known them, but never anything like this.

Snorri had now cost Gotrek at least two certain dooms, and had forced him to bully Rodi into turning from a doom as well. The price of Gotrek's vow to make sure that Snorri reached Karak Kadrin was getting unbearably high, and if things progressed as it looked like they were sure to, it could only get higher.

'You can't blame him, you know,' he said, lifting his head from the wall.

'Can't blame who?' rumbled the Slayer, his one eye continuing to scan the hoardings.

'Snorri,' said Felix. 'You can't blame him for not remembering things.'

'Can't I?' growled Gotrek. 'If Nosebiter had found his doom twenty years ago like a proper slayer, none of this would be necessary.'

Felix glared at the Slayer's hypocrisy. 'Isn't that the pot calling the kettle black?'

Gotrek spat over the wall. 'Leave it alone, manling.'

Felix shrugged then laid his head back down on the wall. 'I don't know why you bother, anyway. None of us is getting out of here alive. Not you. Not me. Not Snorri. Not Kat or Rodi. None of us will make it to Karak Kadrin.'

Gotrek shrugged. 'A vow is a vow,' he said. 'And a dwarf doesn't give up a vow just because it's impossible.'

THIRTEEN

'WAKE UP, MANLING,' whispered Gotrek.

Felix jerked his head up. He didn't remember going to sleep, but apparently he had. It was still night, though the first hints of a red dawn were smudging the sky above the trees to the east, and all seemed quiet. Handgunners were patrolling the walls, spearmen were standing guard on the embankment by the river gate, night watch crews were dragging debris out of the partially burnt residences and repairing other wounds the castle had suffered in the battle, and the pyre of dead zombies and defenders was still burning in the courtyard.

'What is it?' he croaked. 'Did he not show?'

'He's here,' said Gotrek, and nodded towards the hoardings that covered the easternmost corner of the castle. 'There.'

Felix squinted, trying to see into the blackness under

the hoarding, but then his eye was caught by movement on top of it. A grey shadow, almost the same shade as the shingles that covered the slanting roof, was crawling along on hands and knees, as delicate and careful as a spider, and as Felix watched, it paused and reached over the side for perhaps the space of five heartbeats, then crawled on again.

'He'll hear if we try for him,' said Gotrek. 'But he won't hear an arrow.' He looked towards the temple of Sigmar. 'Go to the little one. Point him out. She can't see him from where she is. Then go and block the underkeep door.'

Felix looked down at the courtyard then back up to the hoardings. 'He'll see me.'

Gotrek shrugged. 'Lots of people about. You'll only be one more. Just don't look at him.'

Felix nodded, and crept off. He took the internal stair down through the left-hand river gate tower, then sauntered as casually as he could along the front of the knights' residence around the harbour to the courtyard. It was almost impossible not to glance in the direction of the shadow on the hoardings.

Instead, he focussed on the roof of the temple of Sigmar, and as he neared it, he saw a movement in the shadows where it butted up against the charred wall of the officers' residence, and Kat's face appeared, looking at him questioningly.

Felix nodded his head in the direction of the figure on the hoarding, twice, then, as casually as he could, brought his hand up to his chest and made a small drawing and firing motion, as if he were pulling back on a tiny bow.

Kat seemed to get the idea, for she nodded and ducked back into the shadows to lift her bow off her shoulders and draw an arrow from her quiver.

Felix turned away from the temple and crossed to the entrance to the underkeep. The big doors were shut, but the little inset door was open. He stopped beside it, then leaned against the sturdy oak, as if just getting some air while watching the comings and goings of the courtyard.

Now he allowed himself a glance up at the hoarding, and saw that the crawling shadow was still there, and still obliviously at its work, whatever that might be. It stopped again at a point just parallel to the officers' residence, reached down over the outer edge of the roof, paused for a few seconds and continued slowly on.

Unbeknownst to the shadow, however, forces were moving against it. From the ruins of the stables to Felix's left came Snorri, walking towards the stairs to the wall in the west corner as if he hadn't a care in the world. The squat silhouette of Rodi crept out the front door of the half-gutted knights' residence and started for the stairs in the east. Gotrek trudged along the parapet, looking out over the battlements as if the zombie horde was the only thing on his mind. And on the peaked roof of the temple of Sigmar, Kat crept up the slant until she could see over the officers' residence, then ducked back down and drew her bow to full extension.

Felix held his breath as Kat stepped out, pivoted and fired all in one fluid motion. It was too dark to see the shaft fly, but the there was no question that it had flown true. With a squawk like a frightened goose, the shadow on the hoarding reared up, clutching its shoulder, then crashed down on the shingles and rolled towards the edge.

Freed from the need of caution, the slayers sped forwards, Snorri barging through the upper room of the gatehouse then bursting out the other side, Rodi pounding up the stairs, Gotrek rounding the east corner and passing him. Kat stood and drew back another arrow, but before she could fire, the shadow dropped off the edge of the hoarding.

Felix expected it to crash down dead on the roof of the officers' residence, but to his surprise, it hit on all fours like a cat, and though the fall had definitely hurt it, it kept moving, scrambling down through a blackened hole in the slates that had been made by the fires.

All three slayers jumped from the walls after it, then stomped down the roof to the hole and dived in.

By now, men all over the courtyard were looking up at the noise, and as Kat swung down from the temple roof and ran for the residence's door, several fell in with her, drawing swords and daggers as she drew her hatchets. Felix stayed at the underkeep door with difficulty, wanting to be in on the action, but he had to stay where he was. In a game of cat and mouse, one had to guard all the holes.

From inside the half-burnt residence came thuddings and crashings and the roaring of dwarfs.

'Snorri has him!' shouted Snorri, and a second later, 'No he doesn't!'

Then Gotrek's voice, enraged. 'Stay in your rooms! Close your doors!'

And Rodi's. 'Get out of the way!'

A second later, the residence's door burst open and a black shadow shot out. Kat leapt at it first, swinging both hatchets, but somehow it slipped past her and drove through the crowd, knocking them left and right. The men fell all over themselves trying to catch it, but it fought through and broke away, then ran for the underkeep.

Felix stepped in front of the small door and raised his sword, smiling grimly. He had done right staying at the hole – the wise cat who would get the mouse when all the others had failed.

The shadow came on, neither slowing or swerving, as Kat and the slayers and the men of the castle ran after it. Felix raised Karaghul even higher as it ran straight at him, then swiped down, aiming for the clavicle, and connected... with nothing. The blade cut through the shadow as if it wasn't there, and yet a second later it had shouldered him in the sternum hard enough to knock him flat, then ran over him into the underkeep.

Felix sprang up again, coughing and sucking air, and plunged in after it. It ran straight down the main hall, past the mess and the stores in the direction of the barracks at the end. If it reached them it would find plenty of places to hide within, and clothes to change into to disguise itself. Felix couldn't let that happen. He surged on, pumping his legs as fast as he could, and wonder of wonders, he gained on it.

Halfway down the hall he sprang forwards and made a diving tackle at its legs. It was only as he was flying through the air that he noticed that the figure had no arrow sticking from its shoulder.

He grabbed at the figure's berobed legs and they went down together, but something felt very wrong. Felix didn't feel legs under the robes. Indeed the robes didn't feel like robes.

They hit the floor as one, but as the figure slapped down, it exploded into a swarm of squeaking black shapes that fluttered around his face then up into the air. Felix clutched at them wildly and crushed one in his hand. It sank needle-sharp claws into his index finger as it stilled – a tiny little bat, but rotten with mould and decay.

The rest of the swarm looped up and around and shot for the door just as Kat and the slayers and the rest of the men pushed through. They shielded their faces as the little beasts battered past them and vanished into the night.

'Where is he?' growled Gotrek, walking towards Felix.

Felix stood and held out his hand to show the mangled bat corpse. 'Here,' he said. 'And the flock that flew out the door.'

Kat shook her head. 'No,' she said. 'I hit a man. I heard him yelp. This was a decoy.' She started running towards the door. 'Back to the officers' residence! Quickly!'

Rodi shook his head. 'He won't be there. He sent us chasing in here so he could slip away.'

Gotrek nodded, disgusted. 'We lost him.'

'But we haven't,' said Felix. 'We just have to look for a man with a wounded shoulder.'

Gotrek raised a shaggy eyebrow. 'How many men in Castle Reikguard *don't* have a wounded shoulder?'

Felix's heart sank. The Slayer was right. After all the fighting, everyone in the castle was hurt in some way. Even if they found a man with a puncture wound, how would they prove it had been Kat's arrow that made it?

'Do you have a better plan?' Felix asked.

'Aye,' said Gotrek, walking away. 'Kill everybody. Then we're sure to get him.'

THE STEWARD, WHEN he was roused from his bed and given the news, seemed close to tears. 'Again?' he said, pacing before the underkeep doors. 'Again?'

He stopped suddenly and turned to his officers. 'Wake everyone,' he said. 'Assemble them before the temple of Sigmar. I will not wait until after morning mess to speak. We will begin now. This will end today!'

'My lord,' said von Volgen, who had followed von Geldrecht down from the keep like a dour shadow, 'as the Slayer says, everyone is wounded. It will be difficult–'

The steward waved that away. 'There will be no need to check for wounds,' he said. 'I have a better way. We will find him out, you can be certain of that.'

But as he watched von Geldrecht limp away, Felix thought von Volgen didn't look very certain at all.

WHILE THE PEOPLE of the castle began to gather in the courtyard for von Geldrecht's speech, Felix, Kat and the slayers went up to the walls and looked at the sections of the hoardings that the traitor had visited during his shadowy prowling, and it was Felix who found the first sign of sabotage – and nearly died for it.

Remembering that the saboteur had stopped and reached over the outer edge of the hoarding roof at regular intervals, Felix climbed out onto the battlements and began to examine the shingles and walls from the outside, though he wasn't sure what he was looking for. He saw nothing on the shingles, nor anything on the shoulder-high panels that protected the defenders from airborne attacks and enemy fire, but as he looked at one of the support posts that held up the roof, he saw a strange black squiggle drawn on the wood.

At first glance, Felix took it for a carpenter's mark, made in charcoal, but something about the shape of it looked wrong. He grabbed the post to pull himself closer for a better look, but the wood around the mark splintered and gave way and the post slipped sideways under Felix's weight. Only a frantic scramble and a wild grab at the panels kept Felix from falling backwards off the walls to the sea of zombies below.

'Felix!' cried Kat, from the roof.

'All right, manling?' asked Gotrek, looking up.

Felix's heart was pounding so loud as he clung to the panel he almost didn't hear them. With infinite care, he pulled himself back onto the solid stone of the crenellations, then let out a breath.

'I believe,' he said, 'I may have found something.' He pointed a trembling hand at the next post. 'Look there, near the top. But don't put your weight on it. It won't hold.'

Kat and the slayers stepped to the next post, and when Felix could get his legs working again, he joined them, and saw that it too had a squiggle drawn upon it. It was most definitely a symbol of some kind, but not one a carpenter ever made. It had the look of the kind of arcane glyphs he had seen carved upon ancient tombs and other places of unfathomable evil that his travels with Gotrek had led him to, and it hadn't been made in charcoal, but in blood, now dried and brown.

The wood around the symbol was a different colour than the rest of the post, pale and grey, as if it had been exposed to the elements for centuries. Gotrek grunted when he saw the discolouration, then pinched the wood between his finger and thumb. It crumbled like dry cheese.

Kat shook her head, dismayed. 'Taal and Rhya, had he marked every post…'

'The hoardings would have collapsed entirely,' said Felix.

'But likely not until the start of the next battle,' said Rodi, grinning. 'A nasty little trap.'

'See how many he marked,' said Gotrek.

But before they were able to check more than a few, a horn blared, and Classen's voice rang from the courtyard.

'Fall in! Fall in! Lord Steward von Geldrecht will speak!'

Gotrek ground his teeth and glared down at the assembled crowd. 'There are things to be done.'

'Aye,' said Rodi. 'Replace these posts. Open the dike

and flood the moat again...'

'Kill more zombies,' said Snorri.

But the three slayers turned and started for the stairs nonetheless, and Felix and Kat followed them down into the crowd.

The mood of the men as they squeezed through to the front was sullen at best. Soldiers who had only a few hours ago killed off the last of the river gate zombies were grumbling about not being allowed to sleep nor getting to eat or drink before lining up. Men from the morning watches, whose job it was to repair the damages incurred in the battle, grumbled about not being able to get on with their work. The servants grumbled about being dragged away from preparing the biscuit and water. Felix felt for them all. He and Kat hadn't had a minute's rest since he didn't know how long – nor did it look like they would get another minute anytime soon.

But they were hardly the worst off in attendance. Even the wounded had been trundled out to the courtyard and lay or sat or slumped where they had been put, while Sister Willentrude and her initiates stood wearily among them, looking angrier than everyone else in the audience combined.

When everyone had quieted, von Geldrecht walked up the steps of the temple of Sigmar and turned to stand with Sergeant Classen, Lord von Volgen and Grafin Avelein Reiklander. Father Ulfram and his acolyte waited behind them, while Bosendorfer and his greatswords flanked the steps, their huge blades drawn and point down at parade rest. What was the reason for that, wondered Felix?

'Defenders of Castle Reikguard,' called von Geldrecht, his haggard face stark in the light of the still-burning corpse-pyre. 'I have gathered you here today in Graf

Reiklander's name…'

He inclined his head to Grafin Avelein at this, but she did not acknowledge it, only stared glassy-eyed into the middle distance, a strange half-smile on her lips.

Von Geldrecht coughed and began again. 'I have gathered you in Graf Reiklander's name, I say, in order to broach a serious matter – and to end it!' His voice cracked as he tried for emphasis, and his eyes, as he glared around at them all, glittered wildly. 'There is a traitor among us, a sorcerous saboteur who is weakening our defences!'

A murmur rose at that, but von Geldrecht waved it down with a weary arm.

'Yes!' he cried. 'A traitor! A collaborator with that foul necromancer who hides in the woods and sends his filthy corpses against us. It is this traitor who shattered the runes of warding that protected our walls, he who drained the moat, he who tore the hole through the river gate. But his reign of sabotage ends today! This morning – here and now – we will flush him out!'

The murmuring of the crowd grew louder as von Geldrecht turned to Father Ulfram.

'Father,' he said, 'let us begin.'

Father Ulfram hesitated, seemingly reluctant, then signalled to Danniken. The gaunt young man bowed, then stepped to a rough wooden table set to one side. On it was something wrapped in sable fur. He hesitated and seemed to pray, then gathered up the bundle in his arms as carefully as if it were a bomb, and returned with it to Ulfram. As the priest bowed before it, Danniken delicately unfolded the bundle to reveal a gold-filigreed, jewel-encrusted warhammer of incredible workmanship, gleaming red at the edges in the light of the pyre.

'Behold!' said von Geldrecht, holding out a hand to it. 'The Hammer of Judgement, first carried by Frederick the Bold, the great-grandfather of our beloved Emperor, Karl Franz. Long has it sat in the family vaults of Castle Reikguard, but whenever there is evil to be vanquished, it is brought forth, for its very touch destroys the unrighteous, and burns them with the holy fire of Sigmar's twin-tailed comet.'

Danniken's hands trembled as he held out the massive sacred hammer to Father Ulfram in its bed of furs. 'It is here, father.'

The blind priest reached out until he touched it, then lifted it with one hand and began a prayer as he held it over his head. He might be a shadow of his former self, thought Felix, but he must have retained some of his strength to lift a weapon like that. It looked as if it were made of solid gold.

As Father Ulfram prayed, von Geldrecht surveyed the crowd with too-bright eyes. 'Each of you,' he said, 'will come forwards, one at a time, and lay hands on the hammer. Our traitor will be the one whose impure flesh burns at the touch of so holy a relic! At which time...' He nodded to Bosendorfer and the greatswords. 'We will kill him immediately. He who refuses this test will *also* be killed immediately.'

Felix turned uneasily to Gotrek as the courtyard burst into anxious whispering. 'Do you think this will work?' he asked. 'Do you think the hammer has the powers he says it has?'

'That doesn't matter,' Gotrek grunted. 'The traitor won't touch it.'

'But von Geldrecht said everyone has to touch it,' said Kat.

Before Gotrek could answer, an angry voice called out from among the wounded. 'You have forgotten some suspects, my lord! Shouldn't Tauber and his assistants take the test as well?'

The whole courtyard turned to see Sister Willentrude glaring at von Geldrecht with haggard eyes.

Felix looked around, his anger rising. Was she right? Was Tauber not there? Had von Geldrecht forgotten him? Or had he left him out on purpose? Was this another sign of the strange connection between the two men that had caused von Geldrecht to hide him away from Bosendorfer – and keep him from his duties? His anger boiled over, when he saw that Draeger and his militiamen had been brought out from their cells, but not Tauber.

'Yes!' Felix cried. 'Where is Tauber? Let him prove his innocence so he can get back to work.'

'And if he burns?' muttered Gotrek.

Felix's heart lurched. He hadn't thought of that, but if Tauber was a traitor after all, then that was all the more reason for him to take the test.

'We already know what Tauber is,' called the steward, looking nervously from Felix to the sister. 'There is no need to test him.'

'Then you lied before, lord steward!' cried Willentrude. 'You said you were holding him until you could determine his guilt. If you know he is guilty, why haven't you killed him? Bring him out!'

The courtyard began to murmur in agreement, some because they wanted Tauber to burn, some – mostly the wounded – because they wanted him freed, but all seemed to agree he should be tested.

Von Geldrecht looked like he was going to explode. 'This is not about Tauber!' he said. 'This is about finding a further man!'

'But what if Tauber is the only one?' said Felix. 'What if he has the power to slip through his bars like mist? Or a swarm of bats?'

Von Geldrecht opened his mouth to make another

argument, but voices were crying out from all around the yard now, drowning him out.

'Test Tauber!'

'Let him burn!'

'Free him!'

Von Geldrecht's eyes darted around, frightened. Felix smirked. The steward would have to bring Tauber out now, or he'd have an insurrection on his hands. But then Felix glanced towards Bosendorfer, and saw that his eyes were gleaming with excitement, and his hands were clenched around the hilt of his two-handed sword.

'Very well!' shouted von Geldrecht over the cries of the crowd. 'Very well! Tauber will be tested!' He turned to two of his household knights and gave them a key. 'Bring the surgeon and his assistants.'

Felix groaned as the knights saluted and trotted to the stairs to the keep. 'Sigmar,' he said. 'We've signed his death warrant.'

'Whose?' asked Kat. 'Tauber's? You think he's guilty?'

Felix shook his head. 'Look at Bosendorfer. Do you think he'll wait for Tauber's guilt to be proved before he strikes?'

Kat's eyes widened. 'Shallya's mercy.'

'Now,' rasped von Geldrecht, leaning heavily on his cane. 'If there are no further interruptions, we will begin.' He turned to Grafin Avelein. 'Grafin, if you will go first, we will keep you no longer.'

Avelein woke from her daze and nodded. Bosendorfer's men tensed and the whole courtyard held its breath as she stepped up and without hesitation laid both hands on the sacred hammer, bowing her head in prayer. When she failed to burst into flames, the crowd let out their breath.

'Thank you, Grafin,' said von Geldrecht.

She curtseyed to him, then drifted off towards the

stairs to the keep, the half-smile still on her face. Felix watched her curiously, her behaviour breaking through his anxiety about Tauber and Bosendorfer. What had happened to her earlier sadness? Was the graf recovering?

'Spearmen,' called von Geldrecht. 'Step forwards.'

The spearmen marched forwards, led now by a sergeant Felix didn't know. There were less than twenty of them now. The crowd quieted again as the sergeant reached out and touched the hammer, and again let out a breath when nothing happened. As the rest of the spearmen advanced and laid their hands on the hammer one by one without incident, the tension before each touch lessened, but still, no one looked anywhere else.

After the spearmen had finished, Bosendorfer's men pointed them to the big open doors to the underkeep, and sent them inside to wait. This was to make sure that no one who hadn't yet taken the test could slip in amongst those who had.

Halfway through testing Hultz's handgunners, the two knights who had run off returned, leading a sad, shuffling coffle of filthy men. It took Felix a moment to recognise the skinny, unshaven figure at their head as Tauber. The surgeon's superior sneer and the sharp eyes were gone, replaced by a dull, slack-mouthed stare.

Felix watched Bosendorfer as Tauber was brought to the front of the crowd, afraid he was going to attack then and there, but the greatsword only stared at the surgeon, hard and cold, and stayed at his post.

Felix thought von Geldrecht would test Tauber immediately and get it over with, but he did not. Instead he called up Classen and the household knights, and had them touch the hammer while Bosendorfer and his greatswords stood ready to strike them down, then he had Bosendorfer and his greatswords touch the hammer while Classen and his knights stood ready to strike *them* down. No one burst into flames.

After that came Sister Willentrude and her initiates and then the wounded, while Tauber and his assistants continued to stand and wait. Why was von Geldrecht doing it this way, Felix wondered? Was he saving the best for last? Was he afraid Tauber wouldn't burst into flames, and wanted to delay the inevitable anticlimax? Then it came to him. He wasn't afraid nothing would happen. He was afraid Tauber would actually burn.

'He thinks Tauber's guilty!' he whispered. 'And he doesn't want him to be.'

'Aye,' said Kat. 'You're right. But why?'

Felix shrugged. He had no idea.

It took almost a half-hour for the wounded to be tested, for many had to be carried up and lifted so that they could touch the hammer. Some were so weak they had to have their hands placed upon it for them. Some had no hands.

'How is a man like that supposed to have crawled across the hoardings?' growled Kat. 'Von Geldrecht is a fool.'

The servants came next – cooks, menials, maids, grooms, the blacksmith, carpenter and all the rest, and then the refugee farmers and all the other 'guests' of the castle.

Von Volgen and his Talabeclanders went first, as dignified as they could, under the circumstances, then Draeger and his militiamen, as sullen as ever, and then it was Felix's turn. He scowled as he put his hand on the hammer, but made no complaint, only gave von Geldrecht a withering look as he stepped aside to wait for Kat and the slayers. Kat slapped the hammer contemptuously and made the horns of Taal right after. Gotrek turned the hammer by the head and squinted at it.

'Not bad for human work,' he said.

'Better than elvish at least,' said Rodi, running a thumb along the gold scrolling.

'Snorri thinks it sounds hollow,' said Snorri, tapping it with a thick forefinger.

As they reached the door to the underkeep, Felix turned to watch as von Geldrecht called the men off the walls one at a time and then sent them back. Then, finally, there was no one left but Tauber and his assistants.

Von Geldrecht glared and chewed his lip, then motioned for them to be brought forwards. He was almost cringing as they approached, and his brow was beaded with sweat.

Felix shot a glance at Bosendorfer. The greatsword's eyes were gleaming and his sword was rising. Felix's heart thudded. He was going to do it! And no one would see until it was too late. They were all too busy looking at Tauber.

'Bosendorfer!' he cried. 'Will you strike before you know?'

The shout snapped the greatsword around, and turned every head towards him and Felix. Bosendorfer froze in the glare of their scrutiny, his sword still held high, ready to strike, and rage and guilt quickly reddening him to the roots of his hair. He turned on Felix, snarling.

'You seek to embarrass me with a lie? I do not disobey orders, mein herr!'

Felix held his eye for a moment, then bowed. 'Forgive me, captain. I must have been mistaken.'

Bosendorfer didn't look like he wanted to forgive, but von Geldrecht stepped forwards and banged his cane. 'Captain! Your duty!'

Bosendorfer pulled his eyes away from Felix with difficulty, then turned back to Tauber and his assistants and went on guard. Felix let out a relieved sigh. Now that he knew everyone would be watching him, Bosendorfer wouldn't dare strike Tauber without cause.

Von Geldrecht had the surgeon's assistants touch the hammer first – still delaying whatever it was he feared – but at last it was Tauber's turn. The crowd in the underkeep doorway became absolutely silent, staring intently as the surgeon reached out his trembling hand towards the hammer. Felix's eyes flicked ceaselessly from Tauber to Bosendorfer to von Geldrecht.

Tauber touched the hammer.

He didn't burst into flames.

Felix let out his breath as Bosendorfer only stared, his greatsword trembling in white-knuckled hands, but he did not strike. He seemed genuinely surprised that the surgeon had passed the test.

The surgeon stepped dully back, then turned and shuffled for the underkeep door with his assistants as von Geldrecht let out a sigh of his own. He seemed more relieved than Tauber himself.

The steward motioned weakly for Father Ulfram to put the hammer away, but before Danniken could step forwards with the furs, someone behind Felix called out, 'And yerself, lord steward?'

Von Geldrecht glared towards the speaker, but then stepped to the hammer and laid both hands on it, bowing his head over it like Grafin Avelein had. He didn't burst into flames either.

There was a snickering from the crowd in the underkeep door as Father Ulfram laid the hammer back into the furs and Danniken folded them up.

'And what exactly did that prove, Goldie?' shouted another voice from the back.

Von Geldrecht turned and snarled at them, his face salmon-red. 'Out!' he roared. 'Out of that hole and fall in! I will address you all!'

Everyone groaned and cursed, but no one refused, and all shuffled out to stand before von Geldrecht again as he paced the top of the temple steps.

'It seems our traitor is wilier than I thought,' he said. 'Either he has used his dark powers to protect himself from the great hammer's purity, or he has hidden himself where we cannot find him. So it seems I must appeal, again in Graf Reiklander's name, to your love of your Empire and your fellows.'

He straightened and looked around, his eyes flashing from man to man. 'One of you must step forwards and save us all, for one of you knows who the traitor is!'

This raised a confused muttering, and Felix could hear some angry whispers as well.

'I do not mean that you are also a traitor,' said von Geldrecht against the ugly drone. 'I do not mean anyone is intentionally hiding this villain from the rest of us. I mean that one of you, perhaps more than one, has seen a comrade do something, something strange or out of character, something that made you frown for a moment, but which you then dismissed as nothing. You told yourself you must not have seen correctly. It must have been some harmless gesture or innocent eccentricity. Well, it was not!' Von Geldrecht brought his voice to a cracking roar. 'It was witchcraft! And though you knew it not, you saw it! What was it? Who was it? I want each one of you to think back and remember. Where were you? Who were you with? What did they do? Was it a strange twist of the hand? A whisper in a foreign tongue? Did they lurk in certain places for too long with no reason?'

The whispering grew louder. The men started glaring

around at each other while their sergeants barked for order. Von Volgen stared at the steward like he wanted to kick him down the stairs.

'Fat fool,' muttered Gotrek.

'Aye,' said Felix. 'They'll be burning each other at the stake before he's done.'

'And when you remember,' continued von Geldrecht, 'when those seemingly innocent actions are revealed in your mind for what they truly were, come to me. Not to anyone else! Not to your captain, not to your comrades. Only me. I will do what must be done.' Von Geldrecht spread his arms and bowed his head. 'Now, I thank you for your patience. You are dismissed. Return to your duties.'

But as the steward, the priest, von Volgen and Classen turned to talk amongst themselves, the crowd did not disperse. Instead they clumped together in little knots and began to argue amongst themselves, with many a wary glance over their shoulders at everyone else.

Felix groaned to see it.

Kat shook her head. 'How are they going to fight together when none of them trust each other?'

'Aye,' said Felix. 'He's–'

But he cut off as he saw the household knights falling in around Tauber and his assistants and motioning them back towards the keep along with Draeger and his men. What was this? He started forwards, but Sister Willentrude beat him to it.

'My lord,' she shouted, pushing towards von Geldrecht, 'are you going to lock Surgeon Tauber up again now that he has passed your test? Surely if he has touched the Hammer of Judgement of Frederick the Bold and not burst into flames, that is proof that he is innocent, and if he is innocent, you must free him so that he can care for the wounded.'

Von Geldrecht turned on her again, looking as sick as a mutant confronted by witch hunters, but then he composed himself as the whole crowd quieted to listen.

'The test was inconclusive,' he said, lifting his bearded chins. 'Since it proved no one's guilt, it did not prove Tauber's innocence. I cannot allow him to go free.'

There were murmurs at this. One of the wounded shouted, 'Free him!'

Another shouted, 'Put Bosendorfer in his place! Let him rot!'

'Then will you lock the rest of us up?' shouted Felix, stepping forwards to stand with the sister. 'As it didn't prove our innocence either?'

Von Geldrecht's eyes flared. 'Herr Jaeger, if you speak another word, I will certainly have *you* locked up! Now, disperse, all of you. Tauber remains our prisoner. That is an end to it!'

He turned away, limping angrily towards the keep as the men of the castle watched after him, muttering and whispering dangerously.

'I'm beginning to think we should do it Gotrek's way, and kill everybody,' said Kat, then turned to follow the slayers, who were crossing the yard to tell Carpenter Bierlitz about the weakened hoardings.

Felix nodded, distracted, but continued to stare after von Geldrecht. There was most definitely something between the steward and Tauber. That was the only way to explain his actions. He had been deathly afraid Tauber would burst into flames, and relieved when he didn't. Yet he would not release him. Why?

Perhaps later Felix could get von Geldrecht alone and get an answer out of him, but not just now. He didn't seem in the mood for talking at the moment. Felix sighed and made to follow Kat, but instead found himself chest to chest with Captain Bosendorfer, who was staring at him with pure hatred blazing from his ice-blue eyes.

FOURTEEN

Felix stepped back, his hand dropping to his hilt. 'You wish to speak to me, captain?'

'I wish to have your head, mein herr,' Bosendorfer snarled. 'You have been a disrupting presence since you entered these walls, countermanding my orders to my men, and now accusing me of dishonourable conduct, and I demand satisfaction.'

Felix sighed. Did this have to start now? He was so tired. Too tired to argue. Too tired to fight. He just wanted to walk past the captain and go to sleep.

Bosendorfer's eyes widened. 'Do you sneer at me, mein herr? Was that a laugh?'

Felix rolled his eyes. 'That was a sigh, captain. A weary sigh. I have been awake a full day now, and have done a little fighting along the way. So-'

'And you suggest that I haven't? That I have less reason to be weary than do you?'

'Of course not, captain,' said Felix. 'We have all fought hard. I just want to go to sleep, that's all.'

'Not before you apologise for your actions,' he said. 'Not before you admit your accusations of dishonourable conduct are false.'

Out of the corners of his eyes Felix saw Kat and the slayers turning back to see what the matter was on one side, and Bosendorfer's greatswords moving in on the other. All over the yard, people were turning their heads.

'I never accused you of dishonourable conduct, captain,' said Felix, rubbing his forehead. 'I may have warned you against it just now, but I am willing to believe you never intended it. And, on the wall?' he shrugged. 'I apologise for calling orders to your men, but there seemed no other way to get them back after they had fled–'

Bosendorfer slapped Felix across the cheek. It nearly knocked him to the ground. Kat cried out and ran forwards, drawing her skinning knife, with the slayers striding in after her. Felix caught her arm as she made to put the blade to Bosendorfer's throat.

'No, Kat!' he shouted. The sting of the slap was making him tear up. 'Slayers, stay back!'

'You lie, mein herr!' cried Bosendorfer. 'We did not flee! Not for an instant!'

Felix held Kat back as the three dwarfs ranged around to his left, ready to join in at his word. The greatswords were on guard on his right, but one, the grizzled sergeant who had fought beside Felix against the ghouls from the siege tower, was stepping to Bosendorfer and putting a hand on his shoulder.

'Captain, please,' he said. 'What's to fight about? We broke, and we came back. No one will say–'

'I did not break, Leffler!' shouted Bosendorfer, knocking the sergeant's hand aside and turning on him. 'I retreated in good order for your safety, and we would have taken up a new position had not Herr Jaeger, against all standards of military conduct, countermanded my orders and usurped my authority!'

The sergeant looked uncomfortable. 'That's as may be, captain. But we don't need to be fighting each other over things that happened in the heat of battle. Not when there's ten thousand dead bastards out there and we need every man in here. Herr Jaeger–'

'Are you defending him, Leffler?' cried Bosendorfer. 'Against your own captain?'

'No, captain, no,' said Leffler, holding up his hands. 'I'm only saying, if you want to challenge him, why not wait until we're clear of this? Until we can do it proper. Until you're all rested and ready.'

Bosendorfer looked at the sergeant for a moment, his eyes level and cold, then dropped his gaze to himself. He looked as battered at Felix felt – his armour dented, crusted rimes of blood on his arms, neck and chin, and a bandage around one hand that was stiff and black.

'Very well,' he sighed at last. 'Very well, when we are clear.' He turned on Felix again, eyes blazing as fiercely as before. 'But I *will* have satisfaction, and if you insult me again, or come between me and my men, I will not wait. We will resolve it between us then and there!'

Felix inclined his head. 'Very good, captain.'

Bosendorfer snorted and stalked away, head high.

Sergeant Leffler started after him, then looked back to Felix with an apologetic shrug. 'He's a good lad, mein herr,' he murmured. 'But younger than his brother was.'

Felix nodded wearily, then let Kat out from the prison of his arms.

'You should have let me kill him,' she said, curling her lip. 'And done us all a favour.'

'Aye,' said Rodi. 'That one will never be old enough to

be a captain.'

Gotrek shrugged. 'Don't worry,' he said. 'No one here will get much older.' He nodded to Felix. 'Get some sleep, manling. When you wake, we'll see about the moat.'

Felix nodded again, and it almost carried him over. He caught himself against Kat, and they staggered towards the residences.

'Let's hope,' said Kat, 'our room isn't one that burned.'

WHEN FELIX WOKE again, the day had already tipped past noon, and Kat was not beside him. He lifted his head up, afraid she had answered some call to action that he had slept through, but all that came through the room's shattered window was the normal hammering and thudding of repairs, and he sagged back, groaning. His muscles were so stiff it felt as if he had been dried on a rack like hard-tack, his head throbbed like he had a hangover and his mouth tasted like he had eaten a muddy shoe. He desperately needed a drink of water, but felt too tired to get out of bed. This was the time when one needed a servant. A servant would bring one water at the pull of a rope.

He looked up over the bed. There was no pull rope. There was hardly a ceiling. Though the room had not, as Kat feared, burned, one of Kemmler's trebuchets had dropped a boulder through it sometime during the battle last night. The boulder had missed the bed by inches, and now lay where the chair had been. Ah, well. He would just have to get the water on his own, then.

He levered himself up out of the bed, hissing and barking with pain, then pulled on his padded jack and chain shirt and strapped on Karaghul. The sky, when he stepped out into the courtyard, was low and grey, and the air wet and cold. He looked around for Kat and spotted her at last up on the parapet, leaning against the battlements and looking out over the walls near where Bierlitz and his men were replacing the hoarding posts that the saboteur had weakened with his sorcery. The slayers were down at the far eastern corner of the walls, looking down towards the closed dike and talking amongst themselves.

Felix stepped into the underkeep and waited in line for his swallow of water and his single biscuit, then came back out to the courtyard and crossed the stairs to the wall. Around him teams of men were continuing the seemingly endless task of piling decapitated bodies on the eternal pyres, while others fished bloated corpses out of the harbour with boat hooks. The river wardens were all by the river gate in their remaining oarboats, adding to the makeshift patch that Gotrek and the slayers had made last night and making it more permanent, while everywhere the men sharpened their weapons and repaired their kit in preparation for the battle that was sure to come with the sunset.

Despite all this activity, the mood of the castle could not have been more poisonous. The aftermath of von Geldrecht's speech was just what Felix had feared. The men of the various companies all whispered amongst themselves and shot suspicious looks at all the other companies, looking for signs of sorcerous behaviour. Some were muttering about freeing Tauber and bringing him back to the surgery. Some were muttering about breaking into his cell and murdering him.

Father Ulfram and Danniken shuffled from group to group, apparently trying to ease the tension, but it didn't seem to be working. Whoever they talked to just pointed fingers at one of the other groups or told them to go preach at von Geldrecht and Bosendorfer.

When he reached the top of the stairs, Felix crossed to

where Kat was staring out over the misty fields and the sea of zombies, her chin in her hands. Felix leaned beside her and followed her gaze. Off by the tree line, new bone-and-skin siege towers were being erected, three this time, as ugly as the others, and more ballistae and trebuchets were growing as well. He groaned as he saw them.

'We'll have it to do all over again, eh?' he said.

Kat didn't answer.

'At least this time we can be fairly sure they won't get into the harbour.'

She still didn't answer.

Felix looked at her. 'Something wrong?'

Her jaw bunched and her brow lowered. 'I hate them,' she said.

'The zombies?'

'Not the zombies.' She glared over her shoulder at the yard. 'Them. The men. The knights and spearmen and gunners. All of them.'

Felix frowned. He was feeling less than charitable towards them himself, just then, but he didn't know why she should be. 'If this is about Bosendorfer, forget him. I've already put him out of my mind. He hasn't been giving you trouble, has he?'

Kat blew out a breath. 'It doesn't have anything to do with him. It's all the whispering, and the backbiting and the… I don't belong here, Felix.' She pointed out to the dark band of the forest. 'I belong there, in the wood, doing what I'm good at. I just don't understand these… these… Why do we help them when they're so awful?'

She turned to face him, her eyes glistening. 'I have sworn to rid the Drakwald of beastmen and protect the Empire, but when I come into the towns, or to a castle, people are just – vile! They cheat each other, they fight each other, shout at each other. They might join together when things are at their worst, but as soon as the trouble is over, they're back to blaming each other for what went wrong and trying to take more than their share!'

Felix shrugged, feeling helpless. 'That's just human nature, Kat. We've always been a–'

'Then I don't want to be human!'

Felix looked around to see if anyone had heard her outburst. That was not the sort of thing one said in a land of witch hunters and mutants. He turned her around to face him, meaning to speak, but she clung to him suddenly, hanging her head.

'I'm sorry, Felix,' she said. 'I don't mean it. Not really. I just – sometimes I wish I could go into the forest and never come out again.'

Felix sighed and stroked her hair. 'I know how you feel,' he said. 'There are times when I wish Gotrek and I had never come back to the Empire. But there are other times,' he kissed the top of her head, 'when I wish I had come home sooner.'

'I wish you had too.' Kat smiled up at him. 'I will be better when we get free of this place – if we get free. I'm always better when I am moving.'

Felix wondered if that was the case with him too. It had been so long since he had stayed in one place for any length of time that he had no idea how he would fare settled down.

A curse from down the wall drew their attention to the slayers, and they broke from their embrace.

Gotrek was still leaning out over the battlements and chewing his thumb with a distracted air, while Snorri appeared to be trying to spit on as many zombies as he could, but Rodi was pounding the battlements with his fist.

'And why not?' he bellowed. 'It would be a glorious doom.'

Felix and Kat started down the wall towards them and heard Gotrek reply without looking around.

'You can go over the side anytime you want, Rodi Balkisson, but I'm not wasting so much blackpowder on a glorious failure.'

'It won't fail!' said Rodi. 'You think I can't cut my way through a pack of corpses with a few kegs of blackpowder on my back? Do you think I'm some weak human?'

'Look at it, Balkisson,' said Gotrek, pointing down at the dike with a stubby finger. 'Blowing yourself up in front of it would hardly splinter the wood.'

Felix and Kat leaned through the gap in the hoardings and looked where Gotrek was pointing. The dike was set into heavy stone ramparts built at an angle to the riverbank, so that when its doors were open, the water would rush easily into the moat like it was a branch of the river. When the doors were closed, however, as now, the water smashed into them in a constant foaming crest, angry at being denied its natural path. They therefore needed to be strong – and they were. Each of the foot-thick oak and iron titans looked to Felix to be about twenty feet high, and they were held closed against the pounding water by two great oak beams that slotted out across them from the stone banks, one near the top, and one near the bottom.

'At least four charges must be set,' said Gotrek. 'Two behind each beam, and fuses laid to blow them all as one.'

'What of it?' said Rodi. 'I can do all that.'

Gotrek snorted, then nodded towards the scores of zombies that milled around on the stone banks of the dike. 'And can you also keep the corpses from ripping out one fuse while you set the next? Or knocking the charges loose?'

Rodi opened his mouth, still defiant, but had no answer.

'There are some things even a slayer cannot do alone,' said Gotrek, then looked back down at the dike. 'We wait for tonight's attack, when the necromancer's attention is on the walls. Then we will go.'

Rodi turned away, disgusted, but Snorri wiped the spit from his beard and looked up.

'Snorri likes this plan,' said Snorri. 'Snorri has been growing a little tired of staying inside this castle.'

'You will stay on the walls, Nosebiter,' said Gotrek. 'Only I, Balkisson and the manling will go.'

Snorri's face fell. 'Snorri doesn't like this plan.'

'Neither does Kat,' said Kat, sullen.

Gotrek looked at her. 'You will keep us safe from spying eyes, little one,' he said. 'Flying eyes.'

Kat nodded as she realised what he meant, but Felix could see that she was still disappointed. Snorri wasn't the only one tired of staying inside the castle. Felix, on the other hand, would have been perfectly happy to remain on the walls.

With a sigh he pulled his head back through the hoarding, but as he did, something caught his eye. On the support post next to him was a familiar little squiggle, and the wood around it was withered and dry. Felix frowned and looked down the wall. Bierlitz and his men were replacing a post about fifty paces along.

'Have the carpenters not got to this post yet?' he asked.

Gotrek turned to him. 'They replaced it this morning. Why?'

Felix pointed to the symbol as his guts sank. 'Then when could this have been done?'

Kat and the slayers stepped closer and looked at the post. Gotrek touched the blood with his finger. It smeared. It hadn't fully dried yet.

'Today,' he said. 'Within the hour.'

Rodi scowled. 'We've been talking almost that long. Did the bastard do it while we were standing here?'

Gotrek stumped to the next post with the others following. It too had been marked, and its blood not yet dry.

'Snorri remembers they replaced that one too,' said Snorri.

All of them looked around, scanning the people in the courtyard and on the covered parapet. Felix cursed. It was impossible. There were too many, and it could be anyone – one of the men who was clearing rubble with the work gangs, one of the Shallyans carrying another body to the pyre, one of the handgunners who stood at their posts on the wall. It could be von Geldrecht or von Volgen or Classen or Volk or Bosendorfer, all of whom were peering out towards the zombies' new siege towers. Then there was Bierlitz and his crew putting up the new posts – was the old carpenter putting the mark on them as he erected them? Or was it Father Ulfram walking the walls with Danniken and giving encouragement to the men?

'We should tell the steward,' said Kat, looking towards von Geldrecht and von Volgen, 'though Bosendorfer will likely accuse us of it just for spite–'

'Wait,' said Felix. 'Wait!'

Kat and the slayers looked at him.

He nodded towards Ulfram and Danniken. 'Watch the acolyte,' he said. 'Watch Danniken.'

The others turned. Felix bit his lip. Was he right? Was he seeing what he thought he was seeing? It was hard to tell in the shadow of the hoarding roof.

The gaunt acolyte took Father Ulfram's elbow as the priest finished talking to a group of handgunners, then walked him along the wall to the next group. As Ulfram hailed the men and began asking them questions, Danniken stepped back demurely and leaned against a support post, as if waiting for Father Ulfram to finish, but as he waited, he idly took out a little knife and cleaned his fingernails, then, accidentally – or so it seemed – cut the tip of his index finger.

He hissed and squeezed it, then circled his hand around the outside of the post and traced his bloody finger back and forth across the wood, never once looking at what he was doing.

'Clever,' said Rodi.

'But how– how can he…?' stuttered Kat. 'He held the Hammer of Judgement and did not burn! When all the others were ordered to touch it, he brought it to Ulfram and–'

'He didn't!' said Felix, remembering suddenly. 'It was wrapped in furs! He never once touched it with his bare hands!'

'Enough talk,' said Gotrek. 'He dies now.'

'Wait,' said Felix. 'We must tell von Geldrecht. We don't want anyone crying murder.'

Gotrek grunted with impatience as Felix hurried down the wall to where von Geldrecht, von Volgen, Classen, Bosendorfer and Volk still watched the zombies and talked amongst themselves. He checked the post next to von Geldrecht. It too had been marked, and was already rotting.

'My lord steward,' he whispered.

Von Geldrecht and the others looked around.

'What is it now, Herr Jaeger?' asked the steward, witheringly. 'Do you wish to upbraid me again?'

Felix pointed to the flaking post. 'New marks.'

'What!' he cried, and stepped forwards with the others crowding in.

Von Volgen sighed when he saw the rotting wood. Von Geldrecht cursed and slapped the wall.

'Quietly, my lord,' said Felix, glancing back at Danniken and Ulfram. 'We have found the traitor.'

'What? Who?' said von Geldrecht.

'Watch Danniken,' said Felix. 'Watch his hands.'

'Danniken?' said the steward, again louder than he should. 'What has he–'

Felix gripped his arm to quiet him, and nodded in the direction of the acolyte and the warrior priest. Von Geldrecht turned and watched with the rest as Danniken led Ulfram to the next group of men, then retired to lean against another post. Again, he followed the same routine, taking out his knife, paring his nails, reopening the cut on his finger, then drawing with his blood on the outside of the post.

'But…' said Bosendorfer. 'But, but…'

'Sigmar's beard!' breathed von Geldrecht. 'The acolyte! A man of the cloth!'

'A vile saboteur,' snarled von Volgen.

Classen started forwards, reaching for his sword. 'Come, let us show him Sigmar's mercy.'

Von Geldrecht held him back. 'No! I wish to interrogate him.'

'Yes!' said Bosendorfer, his eyes glittering. 'We must learn who his associates are!'

'No good comes from waiting to kill warlocks,' said Gotrek, coming up with Kat, Snorri and Rodi.

The steward ignored him and motioned to Classen. 'You and Bosendorfer go down and come up behind him, through the gatehouse. We will trap him from this side. There will be nowhere for him to go.'

'Aye, lord steward,' said Classen and Bosendorfer in unison, then started for the stairs.

Von Geldrecht beckoned to the others. 'Come,' he

said. 'Let us take a stroll around the walls.'

'He has his back to us,' grumbled Kat as they started forwards. 'Why can't I just shoot him?'

Felix and the other humans made horrible attempts at miming casualness, but the dwarfs just walked along at their normal pace, glaring ahead with undisguised loathing. Felix almost said something, but then realised that they always looked like that, so were unlikely to raise Danniken's suspicions.

Something did, however. Perhaps it was Classen and Bosendorfer's wary posture as they came out of the gate-house on his left, or the fact that eight people were bearing down on him from the right, or perhaps his dark powers warned him, but as von Geldrecht got within twenty paces of him, the acolyte's head came up and his eyes darted left and right, widening.

'He's on to us,' said Rodi.

Gotrek, Rodi and Snorri pushed past von Geldrecht and von Volgen, taking their weapons off their backs, as Felix, Kat and Volk fell in behind them. On the far side of the acolyte, Classen and Bosendorfer hurried forwards as well.

With a wild look, Danniken leapt to Father Ulfram and pulled him in front of him, putting his little knife to the priest's neck as the handgunners cried out in surprise.

'What's this?' barked Ulfram. 'Who's that? What's happening?'

'Kill me and I kill him!' said the acolyte.

'Fair enough,' said Gotrek, still walking forwards with Snorri and Rodi as everyone else stopped.

'Dwarfs! Hold!' cried von Geldrecht. 'We cannot risk Father Ulfram's life.'

'What is going on?' said Ulfram, turning his bandaged head this way and that as the slayers reluctantly stopped. 'Danniken, is that you?'

'Your acolyte is the traitor, father,' said von Volgen. 'The foul warlock who closed the moat and weakened our defences.'

'And did you also poison the water, villain?' asked von Geldrecht. 'And ruin the food?'

'Who are your accomplices?' barked Bosendorfer. 'Is Tauber in league with you?'

Danniken's face split into a maniacal grin. 'Yes, I spoilt the food!' he cackled. 'And the water! And blinded Father Ulfram's witch sight as I treated his eyes after Grimminhagen.'

'You whelp!' cried Ulfram, struggling. 'I'll–'

Danniken pressed the knife deeper into the priest's throat, drawing blood. 'And yes, Tauber is in league with me,' he continued. 'And dozens of others. We are legion, my lords! Legion! You will never root us out!'

'Who?' asked von Geldrecht, his jowls quivering. 'Who are they? Tell me their names!'

'You are all traitors!' said Danniken. 'Your bones are traitors, lurking within your flesh, waiting only for death to betray you! And I will free them!'

And with that he tipped his head back and began keening in an ancient and arcane tongue.

The handgunners cowered back in superstitious fear, and Felix, Kat and the other humans hesitated, afraid to endanger Father Ulfram's life, but the slayers had no such compunctions. They started forwards, raising their weapons. Father Ulfram, however, acted first.

'Hammer of Sigmar give me strength!' roared the old priest, and drove the back of his head into Danniken's jaw, snapping his teeth shut and cutting off his chant. The acolyte staggered against the battlement, spitting blood and pulling the priest with him.

'Well done, father!' cried von Geldrecht.

As the others surged in, the priest turned and threw blind fists at Danniken, shouting, 'Heretic! In Sigmar's name I cast thee out!'

A wild blow knocked the acolyte flat between two crenellations, but Ulfram overbalanced and fell on top of him, his head and shoulders over the wall.

'Stop them!' called von Geldrecht. 'Catch them!'

Bosendorfer reached them first and grabbed for Ulfram's ankles, but Danniken, with surprising strength, bucked under Ulfram, dragging the priest another foot over the edge, and the greatsword's hands were kicked away in the flailing.

Gotrek shoved Bosendorfer aside and grabbed Ulfram's long white surcoat, but too late. The priest and the false acolyte flipped over the side, still fighting and bellowing, and the slayer was left holding a long strip of white cloth.

Felix and Kat pressed to the edge with everyone else and saw the two bodies smack into the thick mud of the empty moat amongst the milling zombies. For a long second, they and the others just stared as the bodies lay there, unmoving, but then, amazingly, the old priest coughed and gasped and flailed an arm.

'Father Ulfram!' called von Geldrecht. 'Father, are you all right? A rope, someone! A rope!'

It was Danniken, however, who rose first, pushing up from the priest's body, broken and bedraggled. He looked up at the parapet and laughed, his mouth full of mud and blood, then hauled Ulfram up by the collar and raised his little knife high as the priest pawed feebly at Danniken's legs with broken hands.

Danniken stabbed him in the chest. 'At last I am free to join my master!' he cried, striking again. 'As you will all join my master, to march with him on–'

An arrow appeared in his mouth, buried halfway to

the fletching like some sword-swallower's trick. The acolyte's words cut off in a gargle of blood and his eyes showed white all around. Felix looked to his right. Kat's bowstring was still quivering. Her eyes blazed.

Danniken fell slowly backwards to lie beside Ulfram, who sprawled face down in the mud, blood spreading out below him in a red pool.

Gotrek grunted and glared at von Geldrecht. 'Should have done that at the start.'

The steward didn't seem to have heard. He just continued to stare down at the priest. 'Volk,' he said quietly, 'ask Bierlitz to rig a rope and harness. We will recover Father Ulfram's body, and give him the proper rites. We will also sever Danniken's head and search his body for–'

He paused as Father Ulfram's body twitched and he tried to get his hands under him.

'Father – Father Ulfram!' he cried. 'Father, do you still live? Sigmar be praised! Volk, the ropes! Quickly!'

Volk ran off towards Bierlitz, but as Father Ulfram pushed himself unsteadily to his feet in the ankle-deep mud, Danniken sat up beside him, staring straight up because the arrow through his mouth wouldn't let him lower his head.

'Blood of Sigmar!' swore von Geldrecht as the acolyte stood. 'Danniken lives too. Shoot him again, archer, before he does Father Ulfram further harm!'

Kat dutifully put another arrow to the string, but Danniken did not attack Ulfram. Nor did Ulfram attack Danniken. Instead, the two of them turned as one, and began to shuffle together into the milling horde of zombies all around them. By the time Volk had come back with Bierlitz, Felix had lost them in the horde. It had swallowed them whole.

Von Geldrecht leaned against the battlements and let

his head sink down until it touched the stone. 'Forgive me, Bierlitz,' he said in a tired voice. 'There is nothing for you to do here. Continue replacing the damaged posts. Classen, Bosendorfer, Volk, spread the word. Our traitor has been found – and he is dead.'

Classen and Volk nodded, but Bosendorfer stayed where he was. 'And what shall we do about the other traitors, my lord? Tauber, and the scores of others Danniken mentioned.'

Von Volgen snorted.

Von Geldrecht closed his eyes and pushed himself upright. 'Don't be an ass, greatsword. There are no other traitors. He only said it to sow discord among us. Go and do as I have ordered.'

Bosendorfer glowered, but saluted and went off with Classen without another word. The slayers fell in with Volk, asking him about blackpowder and fuses, but Felix hesitated near von Geldrecht and von Volgen.

'Er, my lord steward,' he said, 'I apologise for bringing it up again, but if you believe Danniken was the only traitor, then do you believe Tauber is innocent?'

Von Geldrecht frowned, then sighed. 'Yes, Herr Jaeger,' he said. 'He is most likely innocent.'

'So, you'll release him?'

'Sadly, I cannot.'

Von Volgen grunted, anger flaring in his eyes. 'My lord, why not? The man is needed.'

The steward looked from Felix to the lord, then turned away, his face haggard and glum. 'I am sorry, but it is Graf Reiklander's decision, not mine. Please let it lie.'

He started to limp for the stairs, but von Volgen stepped in his way, his jaw set. 'My lord, I would like to hear this order from Graf Reiklander's own lips. It is not only the lives of the men of Castle Reikguard that are at stake. Many of my knights have died these past days for want of care. I would like to hear from him the reasons why.'

Von Geldrecht's face reddened. 'That is impossible,' he said. 'The graf is too sick to be disturbed.'

'Aye?' asked von Volgen. 'And perhaps too sick to give orders?'

The steward froze, glaring. 'What are you implying, my lord? Speak plainly.'

Von Volgen held his gaze for a moment, then coughed and looked down. 'I do not blame you, lord steward. I think it only natural that, with command thrust upon you as it has been, you would use the graf's name to add authority to your orders... regardless if the graf was giving them or not.'

Von Geldrecht looked like he was going to explode, then he too looked away. 'Your suspicion is understandable, my lord,' he said. 'But Graf Reiklander does still rule here, and he wishes Tauber to remain imprisoned. I am sorry. You will have to take my word on it.'

And with that he turned away, limping to the stairs and cracking his cane angrily with every step.

Von Volgen's fists clenched and it looked like he was going to call after him, but he restrained himself, and turned back to the wall to stare out over the zombie horde.

Felix looked at von Volgen for a long minute, then stepped away from Kat to lean beside him. 'My lord,' he whispered, 'why don't you take his place?'

FIFTEEN

Von Volgen turned from the wall, eyes hard. 'I don't know what you mean, mein herr.'

Felix grunted, impatient, and looked over his shoulder as Kat joined them. 'Yes you do, my lord. Von Geldrecht is no general. You know that. He isn't much more than a jumped-up quartermaster, and he is leading us to ruin! You could lead us to victory – or survival at least.'

Von Volgen fixed him with a cold stare. 'You speak of mutiny.'

'I speak of saving men's lives!' Felix blurted, then lowered his voice again. 'He has already killed half of us with his hesitations and his refusal to free Tauber. Will you sit and watch while he kills the rest? You could save us! You *want* to save us!'

'Yes, my lord,' said Kat. 'Please.'

The knuckles of von Volgen's hands were as white as

bone, and the veins in his neck stood out like ropes. Felix was afraid he was going to hit him, but when he spoke, his words were quiet and measured.

'Herr Jaeger, I thank you for the high opinion you have of my abilities,' he said. 'But it doesn't matter what I want. I have no authority here. I may advise. I may suggest, but it would be mutiny, indeed, treason, for me to try to wrest command from the man the rightful lord of this castle has given it to, and I will not commit treason.'

'But your men may die!' whispered Felix. '*His* men may die! Sigmar's beard, if Kemmler takes Castle Reikguard and leads us all to Altdorf, it might be the Empire that dies! Isn't that a greater treason?'

Von Volgen turned and looked back out over the endless army of corpses, his brow furrowed. 'You make a compelling argument,' he said at last. 'But I cannot agree. Law is the strength of our Empire, Herr Jaeger. More than strength of arms or faith in Sigmar, the laws that bind lord to lord and lord to peasant protect us. They allow us to trust one another, to unite and to know that the strong will not take advantage of the weak in times of crisis.'

'But you won't take advantage,' said Kat. 'You aren't that sort of ruler.'

Von Volgen cut her off with a raised hand. 'Today I am not,' he said. 'Today I usurp the rule of Castle Reikguard for the noble cause of saving the Empire. But what will tomorrow's excuse be? Will I take command of my neighbour's forces because he is losing a war against beastmen? Will I overthrow the elector count of Talabecland if he rules poorly?' He shook his head. 'A man may break the law with the best of intentions, but when he sees the ease of it, it becomes habit, and he is lost. I am sorry, friends. I will give Steward von Geldrecht what aid I can, but he rules here, and I will not change that. Nor,' he said, turning hard eyes on them, 'will I allow anyone else to try. Do you understand?'

Felix looked down to hide the anger in his eyes, and he heard Kat grunt beside him. He understood von Volgen's reasoning, but what did it matter what a man might be tempted to do far in the future when what he did now could save hundreds of lives? It was maddening! Unfortunately, there seemed no point in arguing it further. The lord had made up his mind.

'I understand, my lord,' said Felix at last. 'Forgive me for suggesting it. It seems all I can hope for now is that the lord steward listens to you.'

He started down to the courtyard towards the slayers, who were still deep in conversation with Volk, and left von Volgen at the wall, still gazing out over the endless zombie horde.

'NOT YET,' SAID Gotrek, as he looked down over the eastern battlements towards the dike. 'Not yet.'

'Don't leave it too late, herr Slayer,' said von Geldrecht anxiously. 'We no longer have enough men to mount a proper defence.'

'And whose fault is that?' muttered Kat.

Felix shot her a warning glance, then looked out towards the woods. After a long day of repairs and preparations, dusk was falling, and the horde was coming, in force this time. The men along the walls were already snagging ladders and lopping heads as the zombies began their ceaseless climbing. Beyond them, Felix saw the three new towers being dragged forwards by fresh gangs of skinned beast-zombies, while five trebuchets pitched stones, burning zombies and putrid corpses over the walls. A new weapon was trundling forwards as well, a long low contraption that was aimed straight for the front gate. It was roofed like the hoardings, and wheeled like a cart, and a huge battering-ram swung on chains beneath it, capped at the front with what looked like the skull of some knobby, mutated giant, crested with a ridge of iron spikes down the centre.

'That reminds Snorri of something,' said Snorri.

'It reminds me of Snorri Nosebiter heading for the privy,' said Rodi.

'No,' said Snorri. 'That wasn't it.'

Felix shifted his gaze to the dike. Just as Gotrek had predicted, the zombies guarding it were beginning to drift towards the walls, drawn like moths by the noise and violence to join their dead brethren in climbing the walls.

'Now,' said Gotrek. 'Lower the charges.'

Volk nodded and signalled to two men who held a rope, at the end of which were looped four knapsacks, each bulging with blackpowder charges. A third man shoved the knapsacks off the battlements, and the men with the rope started lowering them down as Gotrek and Rodi tied other ropes around their waists and stepped to the wall. Snorri took up the slack in Gotrek's rope while three more of Volk's gunners did the same with Rodi's.

'Ready,' said Gotrek and Rodi together, and stepped backwards off the battlements as Snorri and the gunners began to pay out the ropes.

Felix held his breath for the duration of the slayers' descent, and Kat put an arrow to her bow and scanned the sky for bats or other spying eyes, but they were not spotted. They reached the ground without incident, then untied themselves and drew their axes while the rope slithered back up the wall. Then it was Felix and Volk's turn.

'Don't worry, young Felix,' said Snorri, as Felix tied the rope around his waist and the old slayer drew in the slack. 'Snorri won't drop you.'

'That is the least of my fears, Snorri,' said Felix.

He gave Kat a nervous little salute, then stepped back off the wall and began to walk his way down beside Volk as Snorri and the gunners let out their ropes hand over hand.

As he descended, Felix's eyes darted nervously from the sky to the ground to the dike, expecting any second to see the zombies stumbling back around the corner, or the bats wheeling out of the sky towards them. To be caught dangling halfway down the wall by those flying slashers would be a nightmare. But despite his fears, he and Volk made it safely to the narrow strip of bulrushes beside the rushing Reik, and sank to their ankles in cold mud.

Volk hooked a flickering glass storm lantern to his belt, then grunted one of the packs onto his shoulders and held the other out to Felix.

'Here y'are, Herr Jaeger,' he said, grinning. 'Yer very own bundle o' joy.'

Felix smiled weakly as he stuck his arms through the straps and humped the thing up high between his shoulders. He was never at his most comfortable with explosives strapped to his back. It made him itch.

'Stay low. Stay quiet,' said Gotrek, and turned and strode into the river.

Felix, Rodi and Volk slipped in after him. The water was freezing and the current strong and very swift, even so close to the bank, but the bulk of the zombies were just on the other side of the sawgrass-covered mound that ran parallel to the river, and if the men and the slayers didn't want to be seen, they had to remain as low as possible for as long as possible.

They trudged east along the river for about forty paces, but as they neared the dike, the bank began to narrow further, while the shallows grew steeper and the current swifter, until they came at last to the heavy stone flanks of the dike, looming up out of the water like the entrance to some massive, algae-covered mausoleum. Here the shallows fell away completely and the muddy bank disappeared into a roaring roil of crosscurrents.

Unable to continue in the river, Gotrek, Felix, Rodi and Volk climbed out onto the sloping stone shoulder and raised their heads just high enough to look over it. Felix shivered.

Seen from the ground, the panorama of Kemmler's horde on the move was even more horrific than when looked down upon from the walls. Thousands upon thousands of undead staggered forwards in an endless shambling mass, while the twisted hive towers lurched and swayed above them like living things, and the ghouls howled from their tops. The towers were halfway to the castle now and closing fast, and the covered battering-ram was moving even faster, and would reach the main gate in mere minutes. And while the rest of the undead army surged ahead, the trebuchets had hunkered down like spiders crouching to spring and launched stones and flaming corpses towards the walls with clockwork regularity. How could Castle Reikguard's beleaguered garrison hope to stop such a vast and terrifying host? Felix found it hard to imagine that even the combined might of the Empire could do it.

'Work fast,' said Gotrek. 'We'll be in plain sight.' He pointed at Volk. 'You and the manling will set your charges behind the top beam. Balkisson and I will set the lower, then pass our fuses up to you. You will bring them back here, to the bank, out of view.'

'Aye, herr Slayer,' said Volk.

Gotrek held his eye. 'And you will not light them until I say.'

Volk swallowed, then nodded. 'Understood, Herr Slayer.'

'Then, go,' said Gotrek.

And with that, he and Rodi ran left to drop down into the moat. Felix and Volk scrambled up the stone bank to the top, keeping as low as they could, then looked down into the channel at the big oak doors. Up close, they were even more impressive than they had appeared from the castle. They were so thick Felix could have walked across the top of them to the far bank without narrowing his stride, and so tall a giant couldn't have looked over them, while the reinforcing bands of iron that criss-crossed them and bound the oak timbers together were inches thick.

Nor did any of the dike's strength or thickness seem less than necessary. The water beat against the doors with a constant deafening thunder that drowned even the rumble of the siege towers as they approached the castle. Felix could feel the power of it through the soles of his boots.

Volk pointed down to the upper of the two beams that held the doors closed. The bottom one stretched across the doors at a height of about five feet from the floor of the moat, while the upper one lay across them about five feet below the top. Both were as big around as tree trunks, and slotted firmly into holes in the stone banks.

'How do ye fancy dropping down to that while I pass ye the charges?' Volk asked.

Felix swallowed. The crossbeam might be thick, but balancing on it while trying to manoeuvre explosives into place didn't sound very appealing. 'Fancy would be too strong a term,' he said, taking off his pack. 'But it's what I came for.'

Felix gripped the top of the door and lowered himself to the beam. The wood thrummed under his hand with the rush of water behind it, and as his feet touched the beam, he could feel it flex as the doors pressed against it. He shivered. This would not be the place to be when those doors finally opened.

He glanced towards the horde again as he reached up to Volk, but none of the undead seemed to be looking their way. All the zombies were trudging towards the castle or crowding around the ladders, and the ghouls that swarmed the tops of the siege towers were too far away. A glance at the sky unfortunately told him nothing. It was too dark to see any circling bats.

Volk looped a coil of matchcord around his wrist, then leaned down with a pipe charge. 'Go to the middle and wedge it tight as you can between the door and the beam. Then come back for the second.'

Felix nearly overbalanced as he took the thing. It was heavier than he expected. He righted himself with a wild flail, then leaned back against the door and began sidestepping towards the centre, heart pounding, as the matchcord paid out behind him.

When he reached the middle of the doors he knelt and set the charge behind the beam in a gap between two of the iron bands. He pushed down on the charge to wedge it tight. Below him, the slayers were doing the same. Rodi had climbed up onto the lower beam, while Gotrek lifted the charges up to him.

When his charge was as well seated as he could make it, Felix crossed back to Volk, who handed him down the second charge.

'It seems a small amount of powder,' said Felix, cradling it more carefully this time, 'to break such big doors.'

Volk gave him a hideous half-melted smile. 'Ah, well, the water's doing most of the work, y'see. All the charges need to do is make a little crack, and the water will bust 'em wide.'

Felix carried the second charge back along the beam and set it beside the first, then looked down as he heard a hiss from below.

'Manling. Here.'

One at a time, Gotrek tossed up the two coils of matchcord that ran from the bottom charges. Felix caught them and slipped them onto his right arm, then walked to Volk.

'Well done, mein herr,' said Volk as he took the fuses. 'Them dead bastards won't know what hit 'em.'

He added the slayers' coils to the two from the top charges, then helped Felix onto the stone bank, and together they crept back down to the riverbank, Volk paying out the four lines of matchcord behind him.

The slayers joined them a moment later, then crawled up on hands and knees to watch over the embankment. Behind them, Volk braided the ends of the four fuses together into a single rope, then unhooked the storm lantern from his belt and set it beside them. Its flame flickered brightly inside its glass chimney.

'Ready when you are, Herr Slayer,' he said.

'Not yet,' said Gotrek.

Felix edged up beside the slayers and looked out over the field. The siege towers and the battering-rams were close enough now that the castle's cannons were taking shots at them. A ball punched through the nearest tower, and an explosion of earth and flying zombies erupted near the battering-ram, but not near enough. The thing crawled on, and a shot from a third cannon missed too.

'Damned bats!' growled Volk, glaring up at the swarms that clattered around the gun positions. 'Spoiling our aim.'

'They should save their shot,' said Gotrek.

'You're so sure, mein herr?' asked Volk.

Gotrek didn't answer, only watched the siege towers with unblinking intensity as they neared the dry moat. The zombies were doing the same thing they had done during the previous attack, swarming forwards to fill the dry ditch so the towers and their gangs of skinned beasts could use them as a bridge to cross the gap. More were doing the same for the battering-ram.

'Get ready,' said Gotrek as the first of the beast-zombie teams stepped out onto its bridge of corpses.

'Aye,' said Volk, and backed down the slope. 'Ready.'

Felix held his breath. The battering-ram was starting across its corpse bridge now, and the tower beyond it was nearly at the moat, while the middle tower was just beginning to cross. But as Gotrek raised his arm, the closest tower suddenly slowed as its team stumbled and became bogged down in its bridge of piled bodies.

Gotrek cursed. 'Hold,' he said.

There was a hollow boom from the gates. The ram had struck. Ghouls were locking off its wheels and driving long stakes down into the bank of the moat to hold it in place, while huge dead beasts swung the ram forwards and back on its chains in a ponderous rhythm – *boom… boom… boom…*

'Pull, you laggards,' Rodi growled as the near tower slowed even further. 'Pull!'

'Slayers,' said Volk, 'do we dare wait? They're knocking down our gates!'

'They'll hold a while,' said Gotrek, not looking around. 'I want them all.'

'Gotrek,' said Felix, grinding his teeth. 'You won't get any of them if you wait too long–'

A giant bat slammed down face first right in front of him, an arrow jutting from the back of its broken neck.

SIXTEEN

FELIX AND VOLK flinched back as the slayers looked up. Another bat jerked sideways in the sky above them and pinwheeled to the ground, an arrow in its eye, but there were more coming, screeching and swooping down at them, wings furled. They had been spotted.

'Now, gunner!' barked Gotrek, drawing his axe as Rodi and Felix drew as well. 'Now!'

'Aye,' said Volk.

He turned to lift the glass from the lantern, but as he bent, a bat crashed into him and knocked him flailing into the river.

'Volk!' cried Felix.

He sprang up, slashing, but two more bats slammed into him, driving him over the brink, and he too plunged into the waves.

The cold shock of it froze him for a second, but then he was smashed into the bank by the current and came up gasping as the water dragged him along, his knees scraping the rocky mud. Before he could find his feet, heavy wings flashed overhead and dropped towards the slayers as he finally got purchase.

'Krell!' he croaked, and tried to pull himself out, but then something grabbed him from behind and jerked him back into the water.

Felix turned and kicked and raised his sword before he realised it was Volk, thrashing and panicked. The captain clutched his arm and Felix pulled him close, kicking for the bank. After being dragged along the muddy bottom again, he got his feet under him, and hauled Volk up after him. Though they had been only a few seconds in the water, the powerful current had carried them almost back to where they had descended from the castle.

Felix looked back towards the moat as he stood. Gotrek and Rodi were surrounded by a cloud of bats and fighting toe to toe with Krell and the patchwork wyvern, who stood between them and the fuses – which remained unlit next to the storm lantern. Felix choked and started running back. This was bad. The charges had to blow *now*, while the siege towers were still crossing the moat!

The bats wheeled at him, shrieking and battering him with wings and claws as he ran for the fuses. He slashed through them desperately, but a glance towards the castle told him he was going to be too late. The furthest tower was already nearly all the way across the moat. The closest was halfway, and the battering-ram was continuing its relentless *boom… boom… boom…*

Gotrek smashed Krell's wyvern back and it flapped up in the air, its leg hanging by a string of sinew. The Slayer ducked under it with Rodi, hacking for Krell, but the wight king knocked them both back with a sweep of his black axe. The slayers weren't going to reach the fuses in time either.

A flash of flame shot down from above and struck behind Krell. For a second, Felix thought it was some new terror of Kemmler's, but then he saw it was an arrow, point down next to the lamp, a little flame just behind its head quickly fizzling out in the mud.

Felix blinked as he kicked a bat aside and gutted another. Who was shooting flaming arrows at them? And why? Then all at once he knew, and his heart surged.

A second arrow zipped down and quivered between the fuses and the lamp. So close!

'Come on, Kat!' Felix roared, chopping at the bats as Gotrek and Rodi exchanged ringing strikes with Krell.

Then the bats were gone from around him, flitting away and squealing. Sigmar! They were after the fuses!

A third arrow streaked down through the cloud of wings, and shattered the glass lantern, spraying its reservoir of oil in all directions and setting it alight. The bats flapped up, some of them on fire, and the little pool of flame spread. Then, all at once, there was a sparking and popping, and four lines of spitting flames began to crawl swiftly towards the dike. The fuses had lit!

'Slayers!' shouted Felix, backing away. 'Fire in the hole!'

The slayers, however, did not seem to hear. As the bats dived and snapped futilely at the sizzling fuses like crows trying to catch speeding centipedes, Gotrek and Rodi drove Krell back towards the dike with single-minded intensity, cutting deep gashes in his black armour and sending chunks of it spinning away. It seemed that, for this brief moment at least, they had both abandoned thoughts of individual glory, and were working in tandem to take the champion apart piece by piece.

Krell took another step back from the slayers' onslaught, and faltered on the edge. Rodi ducked in and smashed his axe into the wight king's knee in a burst of shattered iron and splintered bone. Krell fell sideways, and Gotrek leapt forwards and hacked at his neck with his glowing rune axe. The blade smashed through Krell's bevor, but before it could sever his neck, the champion toppled backwards into the moat and disappeared from Felix's sight.

The two slayers stepped to the edge, and Felix was certain they were about to leap in after him, but as they tensed, the four sparking fuses burned between their feet and vanished over the lip. Rodi laughed and stepped back, but Gotrek remained where he was, blowing like a bellows and still poised to jump.

'That isn't death in battle, Gurnisson,' said Rodi, turning back to him. 'That's just death.'

Gotrek growled. 'My doom does not require your approval, Balkisson.'

'No,' said Rodi. 'Only Grimnir's.'

And with that, the young slayer turned and ran back towards the bank. Felix held his breath, not daring to blink and miss the Slayer's last moment, though it might mean being caught in the blast himself, but after an interminable second, Gotrek cursed and raced after Rodi.

With a relieved breath, Felix sprinted for the corner of the castle, more than happy to use his long human legs to their fullest advantage, but even with his greater speed, he didn't quite make it.

As he neared the wall, he looked back to see how the slayers were coming, and the world behind him suddenly turned black and orange and yellow. One second, the bats were wheeling above the dike, and Krell's wyvern was flapping down into the moat the next second, all of them were eclipsed by a billowing fireball that rose above the dike like a phoenix. The air was suddenly as hot as the Desert of Araby, and lifted Felix off his feet as a sound like the sundering of the world battered his ears.

He slammed down again ten feet further on, blind and concussed, and felt heavy thuds strike on either side of him. Then, through the ringing in his ears and the clouds in his head, came a new noise – a roaring, crashing tumult. He opened his eyes and rolled over. He was lying between the two slayers, who were both looking back towards the moat and grinning like daemons. Felix followed their gaze and saw, frothing through the gap where the doors of the dyke had been, a rushing wall of water, twenty feet wide and twenty feet high, thundering down the moat like a stampede of white bulls.

Felix looked along the front of the castle, following the water's progress. The first tower was halfway across the moat now, its crew of skinned beasts obliviously straining at their ropes, but the ghouls clinging to the top had seen the wave coming and were shrieking and gibbering and trying to climb down. They were too late. The wall of water shot up over the bridge of zombies and hit the tower on its leading edge, lifting it and knocking it sideways and back. Screaming in terror, the ghouls rode the thing to the ground as it smashed to pieces in the ravaged fields.

The zombie mound was swept away like leaves in a gutter and the water rushed on towards the second tower. This one had almost reached the castle side of the moat. The flood slammed into its back edge, the froth climbing halfway up its height, and toppled it sideways, crashing it down right on top of the covered battering-ram and smashing it to pieces.

After that, the tide was spent, and it only rocked the third tower slightly as it streamed around its base before reconnecting with the Reik on the far side of the castle. Nevertheless, a huge cheer went up from the walls as the defenders saw the undead horde's attack reduced to a single tower, and the chances of the ram getting through the main gate reduced to zero.

Rodi laughed and pushed himself to his feet. 'We did it!' he said. 'We slew Krell and broke the back of Kemmler's army in one stroke.' He grinned at Gotrek. 'Not a bad night's work, was it, Gurnisson?'

Gotrek walked past him towards the ropes without a word, his chest working and his face as hard and cold as an anvil.

THE EAGER HANDS of Bosendorfer's greatswords helped Gotrek, Felix, Rodi and Volk over the battlements and back onto the parapet, then slapped them jovially on their backs.

'Well done!' said Sergeant Leffler. 'Saved our bacon, mein herr!'

Von Geldrecht limped towards them through the surging ring of well-wishers, his eyes wide. 'You did it, slayers,' he said, wonderingly, 'Krell dead, the towers fallen, the moat restored, a thousand zombies crushed and swept away, the battle over before it's begun–'

'The battle's not done,' rasped Gotrek, his face still hard.

He pushed roughly through the men and continued down the wall, towards where Snorri and von Volgen and his knights were holding off the ghouls who spilled from the last remaining tower. Rodi followed him, but Felix stopped and looked for Kat.

She was at the wall, watching him as she shouldered her bow.

'That was quite a shot,' he said, crossing to her and giving her a squeeze. Where did you find flaming arrows?'

Kat held up her thick wool scarf, which now had rough holes torn in the end of it. 'This and some naphtha from Volk's cannon crews.'

Felix laughed. 'Well done. The whole castle is in your debt. They owe you a new scarf, at least.'

Kat showed her teeth. 'I'll settle for a beast-hide coat.'

Felix looked after the slayers. 'If that's what you want, I think I can oblige you. As Gotrek says, "the battle's not done".'

Kat snorted at his pathetic imitation of the Slayer's sandstone rasp, and drew her hatchets. 'Lead on.'

As they started squeezing through the back-slapping greatswords, Felix felt someone's eyes on him, and glanced back to find Bosendorfer once again staring at him with undisguised loathing. Felix growled and hurried on. Was the greatsword angry that his men had offered Felix their congratulations? Ridiculous.

He hurried on with Kat, but by the time they had caught up with the slayers, the fight was over. The cannon crews had set fire to the last siege tower, and Snorri and von Volgen's knights had held off the ghouls until it had burned out from under them and crashed back into the moat in a hissing cloud of steam and smoke. As Felix, Kat, Rodi and Gotrek arrived, the knights were all cheering and wiping the sweat from their eyes, and Snorri was limping out from among them, his face covered in blood and his warhammer over his shoulder at a jaunty angle.

'Gotrek Gurnisson! Rodi Balkisson!' he boomed as he saw them. 'There you are! Snorri thinks you missed a good fight!'

Gotrek balled his fists at this, and Rodi shot him a

wary glance, but Gotrek only turned and stalked off again, pushing past Felix and Kat unseeing.

Rodi shook his head as he stared after him. 'Poor cursed bastard,' he said.

Felix frowned at him. 'What do you mean?'

Rodi looked up, seemingly surprised to have been heard. 'I shouldn't have spoke,' he said.

'Aye,' said Felix. 'But you did. What did you mean by it?'

The young slayer looked uncomfortable. He shrugged. 'Don't tell him I said it,' said Rodi, 'but I fear Gurnisson is cursed. He will never find his doom.' He slanted a glance at Snorri. 'He needs the intercession of Grimnir more than Nosebiter does.'

An hour later, Felix stared at the broken ceiling of his room as Kat slept soundly beside him, Rodi's words turning over and over in his head.

He had always thought of Gotrek as unlucky – at least as slayers thought of luck. He had survived encounters no one should have survived, and slain opponents he shouldn't have had a hope of defeating. Felix had also come to believe that the Slayer was partly culpable in his continued survival. Not that he ever shied from a fight or turned from danger, but as Rodi had said once before, he was sometimes choosy about his doom. He wanted it to be epic. He wanted it to have meaning. Dying in some pointless bloodbath was not the doom Gotrek envisioned for himself. He wanted to die saving the world.

But did his inability to find his doom stem from more than just bad luck and pride? Was the Slayer actually cursed? Had some god or daemon or mortal sorcerer somehow caused his quest to be endless? If so, why? What had the Slayer done to deserve such a fate? Was it tied in with the fate the daemon he had fought in the depths of the dark elves' black ark had spoken of? The vaporous being had said that Gotrek was to die fighting one greater than itself. Did this mean that the Slayer was being saved for some great destiny? Did it mean that nothing could kill him until that destiny manifested itself?

Felix grunted and shifted uncomfortably in the cot. There seemed to be precious little difference between 'destiny' and 'curse'.

THE MORALE OF the castle, so high after the restoring of the moat and the destruction of Kemmler's siege engines the night before, crashed down again with the coming of the dawn and the revelation that their great victory had been all for naught, and every gain the defenders had made had been cancelled out under cover of darkness.

Felix and Kat were pulled from sleep by cries of horror and dismay, and after struggling into their armour, made their way up to the walls under a lowering grey sky to find half the defenders huddled against a cold wind and staring silently down over the battlements.

The zombies were swarming near the ruins of the blasted dike, and like ants carrying bits of dirt to make an ant hill, they were carrying heavy rocks to it and throwing them into the water. Unlike ants, however, they were throwing themselves in as well – for the rocks were tied around their necks, and they were sinking to the bottom. Already the mound of weighted bodies had drastically constricted the flow of water through the channel, and the moat was half the depth it had been when it had swept away the siege towers.

'Is there nothing you can do, Captain Volk?' asked von Geldrecht from where he, von Volgen and his officers stood with the artillery captain further along the wall.

'Shooting at 'em might slow 'em a while,' said Volk, shrugging. 'But we're almost out of shot. And dropping pipe charges into the moat might shift a few, but they'll just pile more on.' He shivered. 'Look at 'em all. They're endless.'

Felix did just that, sweeping his eyes across the misty fields beyond the walls. Despite the thousands of undead that the bursting of the dike had swept away the night before, there seemed just as many zombies surrounding the castle now as there had been before, perhaps more. And at the tree line, three more towers were rising, and another battering-ram was taking shape.

'They don't need to eat,' said Kat. 'They don't need to sleep. They never run out of supplies. They don't care how many times we knock down their towers. They just keep making more.'

Von Geldrecht turned to Gotrek, who stood with Rodi and Snorri next to him at the wall, and held out his hands, pleading. 'Herr Slayer, you saved us last night. Is there nothing you can think of to fix this? Have you no clever trap to destroy them again?'

Gotrek grunted, his single eye never looking away from the zombies filling the moat. 'Sorry, lordling,' he said. 'There is nothing to do but fight.'

'That sounds good to Snorri,' said Snorri.

Von Geldrecht groaned, sagging as if something had broken within him, and turned back to the wall as his officers stared at him in dismay. Von Volgen grimaced and leaned in to speak to him again, then glanced up as he felt Felix looking at him.

Felix turned away. The mixture of fury and regret in the lord's eyes was too painful to see.

* * *

THOUGH THE HOPELESSNESS and the four days with little water and less food, had made the men of the castle listless, sick and weak, far worse for morale was the fact that there was no longer anything to do but wait for the end. The hoardings were all built and repaired, the river gate was patched, the saboteur had been caught and killed, the cannons supplied with all the remaining shot, and every weapon sharpened and polished until it shone.

Von Volgen kept his knights busy with exercise and wall patrols, but after his too-public display of despair, von Geldrecht disappeared into the keep without passing along any orders or words of encouragement, and his officers seemed to have decided to follow his example. They gave no orders, nor demanded any drill, just stood their watch when it was their time, and retired to their quarters when they were done. Consequently, their men did nothing as well, and sat huddled in little groups, griping and moaning and inventing rumours of more traitors. Even the weather added to the lassitude. Heavy clouds lowered over the castle, growing darker and more oppressive as the day went on and filling the air with a thick, undersea tension.

The mood was summed up perfectly by a spearman who Felix passed as he paced the walls. 'What's the point of doing anything,' he asked another spearman, 'when there's nothing to be done?'

There was a brief flurry of excitement in the middle of the afternoon, when von Geldrecht came out of the keep briefly to talk with Sister Willentrude, and von Volgen accosted him afterwards as he hurried back to the stairs.

'Lord steward,' he called, 'when may we expect to see you among us? Your presence is needed.'

Von Geldrecht waved him away and continued up the

stairs. 'Not now, not now,' he said. 'I have pressing business.'

Von Volgen stopped at the bottom of the stairs, glaring. 'What business could be more pressing at this time than the morale of your men? You must order them, my lord.'

Von Geldrecht turned, his eyes feverish and his beard unkempt. 'The graf summons me!' he snarled. 'And it is his orders I obey, *my lord*, not yours!'

He hurried up the stairs and vanished once again into the keep, and after a few minutes of murmured speculation about the incident, the men returned to their lethargy, and the day continued as before.

The slayers, being pragmatists, slept while they waited for the battle to come, but Felix and Kat were too restless, and wandered the castle ceaselessly, helping out where they could, but mostly just walking or staring out at Kemmler's siege towers as they grew like toadstools sprouting after rain. The swarm of activity around the looming constructs was as hypnotising as the gaze of a cobra before it strikes.

Another restless soul was Bosendorfer, who sat with his greatswords on the steps of the temple of Sigmar as they pounded out the dents in their armour and replaced damaged straps and buckles. Though he never moved from the spot, Felix felt Bosendorfer's eyes following him wherever he and Kat went, and all day long his talk was full of loud comments about honour and cowardice and disruptive outsiders – at which his men laughed uncomfortably.

Felix did his best to ignore it all, but then, towards the end of the afternoon, the tension, like the heavy clouds that were gathering over the castle, could no longer hold its burden, and burst into open conflict.

It started when one of Sister Willentrude's assistants

came out of the underkeep and said something to Bosendorfer. The captain and his men rose and followed her inside, and taking advantage of their absence, Felix and Kat came down off the walls and warmed their hands at the ever-burning pyre.

A short while later, Bosendorfer and the greatswords came back out of the underkeep in double file, carrying a corpse between them on a stretcher. Bosendorfer was at the back of the procession, carrying a two-handed sword outstretched in his hands and chanting a prayer, while Sergeant Leffler was at the front, the doublet, breeks and morion helm of a greatsword's uniform held neatly folded in his arms.

Felix and Kat stepped back as the procession shuffled to the pyre and the greatswords laid down the dead man and made the sign of the hammer over him.

'Best to make yourself scarce, mein herr,' said Leffler out of the corner of his mouth, then nodded at the corpse. 'That's Hinkner, who was wounded when we was fighting them ghouls with you. Captain blames you for his dying. Says he'd still be alive if we hadn't come back to the wall at yer call.'

Felix sighed. 'Very well, I'll retire. Thank you for the warning–'

'I told you not to speak to my men!'

Felix turned. Bosendorfer was striding towards them angrily, the sword he had held in reverence now gripped at the hilt and ready to strike.

Kat whipped out her skinning knife, but Felix held her back. 'He was just telling me to get out of the way, captain,' he said.

Bosendorfer laughed, harsh. 'Get out of the way? You could not go far enough unless you left the castle!' His hands shook as he pointed the sword at Felix's throat. 'That you are alive to witness the funeral of a man you killed is a travesty! It should be you on this pyre, not Hinkner.'

Felix knew he should back away. He knew he should say nothing and leave the captain and his men to their funeral, but that last jab had been too much, and his anger boiled over at last.

'I am indeed sad to witness the funeral of a brave man wounded in battle,' he said, as cold as he could manage. 'But if you want to throw someone on the fire for his death, captain, then it should be you who walks into the flames.'

'What!' cried Bosendorfer. 'What do you say?'

Felix stepped closer to him as men all over the courtyard turned to listen. 'The other night when we were raising toasts, you asked us all to pledge death to the man who had murdered the wounded who'd died in their cots. Do you remember?'

'Of course I remember!' said Bosendorfer. 'What has that to do with this?'

'Nothing, but the fact that you are the murderer,' said Felix. 'You are the one who killed those men. You are the one who killed Hinkner.'

Bosendorfer raised the two-handed sword over his head, snarling, but there was a cast of unease in his eyes, as if he feared he faced a madman. 'What are you saying? I've killed no one!'

'Haven't you?' asked Felix. 'Who forced von Geldrecht to hide Surgeon Tauber away for fear of his life? And how many men would still live had he been free to care for them? Hinkner didn't die in battle. He died from his wounds because Tauber couldn't see to them. You killed him, captain. You killed all of them. And if you wish to fight me over it, I am ready.'

He drew Karaghul and saluted, then stepped back into guard as the gathering crowd murmured and stared.

Bosendorfer glared at him, then answered his guard. 'Men may have died, but I saved the rest from worse. Tauber would have poisoned us all.' He raised his chin. 'When you are ready, mein herr.'

Kat remained crouched, her knife out, looking like she wanted to intervene, but finally she stepped back. This was an affair of honour now. It was between just Felix and Bosendorfer.

Or it would have been, had not a higher power intervened.

'Hold! Both of you!' cried von Volgen, striding across the courtyard at the head of his knights. 'There will be no fighting among us!'

Bosendorfer shifted around to face the Talabeclanders and his greatswords put their hands on their weapons.

'You are not my commander,' said Bosendorfer stiffly. 'You cannot order me.'

'It is not a matter of orders and command,' said von Volgen, stopping before them. 'It is a matter of survival. We must kill the enemy, not each other.'

'But he has accused me of killing my own men!' shouted Bosendorfer.

'You did!' called someone in the crowd.

'It matters not,' said von Volgen, his eyes blazing. 'You are *both* needed to defend Castle Reikguard.' He turned to alix. 'Apologise, Herr Jaeger, for the good of the Empire.'

Felix curled his lip, defiant. Why should he apologise for speaking the truth? But after a second in the heat of von Volgen's withering stare, he sighed. The Talabeclander was right. Fighting each other was insanity. He bowed to Bosendorfer. 'Forgive me, captain,' he said. 'I spoke out of turn.'

Bosendorfer sneered. 'That is all? You lied as well! You–'

Von Volgen turned on him, cutting him off with a gesture. 'Enough, greatsword! Accept the apology.'

'Damned if I will!' said Bosendorfer, stepping forwards. 'He has lied! He–'

Von Volgen barred his way with his sword. 'Accept it, captain,' he said, 'and continue with your funeral.'

'Who are you to order my troops!'

Felix, Kat and the others turned and saw von Geldrecht lurching down the stairs from the keep at the head of Classen and a handful of household knights, his sagging face crimson and quivering with anger.

Von Volgen bowed to him as the mob quieted. 'Forgive me, my lord, but would you have me let them murder each other?'

'I would have you leave the ordering to me,' von Geldrecht snarled, limping forwards. 'You have no authority here, no matter what your rank!'

'Nor do I seek it,' said von Volgen. 'But if you are absent when trouble starts, what choice have I?'

'You have the choice of leaving the castle if you dislike the way I am conducting its affairs,' said von Geldrecht.

Von Volgen paused at this, his square jaw clenching, and Felix waited for the explosion. Here, he thought, was the breaking of the Talabeclander's principles. Here was where the axe fell. In the face of such arrogant incompetence, could von Volgen really demur once again and let von Geldrecht continue to rule? Could he really let such stupidity pass without comment? Felix certainly hoped not.

Von Volgen bowed, as stiff as a board. 'Thank you, lord steward, but I will stay. We must remain united if Castle Reikguard is to stand. I only ask – I only ask that you return to us as soon as possible, and prepare us for the battle ahead.'

Felix grunted, disappointed. The man's moral code

was going to doom them to von Geldrecht's leadership, which would doom them to destruction.

The steward, however, did not seem pleased with von Volgen's answer. 'You are ordering me again, Lord von Volgen!' he cried. 'You are telling me what to do!'

'No, my lord,' said von Volgen through clenched teeth. 'I am asking to be ordered. I am asking you to take command!'

Von Geldrecht's face turned red with fury, and he looked like he was going to lay into von Volgen, but then a cunning look came into his eyes and he raised his chins. 'Very well, my lord. Then I command you to surrender your sword to me, and turn over the leadership of your men to Sergeant Classen. You will be the guest of the keep until we are relieved.'

Von Volgen stared, stunned, and didn't seem to know what to say, but his men were not so dismayed. One of his captains drew his sword, and the others followed suit.

'He will not take you without a fight, my lord,' said the captain.

Von Geldrecht stepped back at this show of aggression and waved at Classen and Bosendorfer. 'Knights, greatswords,' he said, 'arrest them.'

The two captains hesitated, then stepped forwards with their men lining up behind them. Von Volgen watched them come, and Felix could see him weighing his options. Did he defend himself? Did he surrender? Did he order his men to attack?

Felix looked at Kat. She nodded, and they fell in on either side of von Volgen as the courtyard looked on, and Bosendorfer and Classen continued forwards with their troops.

'We are yours to order, my lord,' murmured Felix. 'We will do as you ask.'

Von Volgen grunted, his fist white-knuckled on the grip of his sword, then at last he raised his bulldog head and made to speak.

A loud rumble from above interrupted him, and the flagstones shook beneath everyone's feet. The lords and their men froze and looked to the walls, but the hand-gunners had raised no alarm. The sound had come from the sky. The low clouds over the castle had grown dark and pregnant while the drama below had unfolded, and lightning now flashed in their depths. The men stared, rooted to the spot, swords hanging slack in their hands, and then someone said what they were all thinking.

'Rain! It's going to rain!'

'Fresh water!' called a spearman.

'Get a wash tub!' cried a handgunner.

All over the courtyard men turned and ran for their quarters, the confrontation between von Geldrecht and von Volgen forgotten. Even their own troops were staring at the sky.

But as men began setting out pans and tubs and buckets, von Volgen returned his eyes to von Geldrecht, who looked back to him as well, and their men went on guard again. Felix held his breath as von Volgen clenched his jaw and raised his sword – then reversed it and held it out.

'My lord steward,' he said, 'I will not shed the blood of Empire men. You may do with me as you will.'

Von Geldrecht slumped in relief, and motioned Bosendorfer and Classen forwards again, but they stopped as von Volgen put up a hand.

'But,' he said, with a flat smile, 'I would be forever in your debt, if you would wait to take me to my cell until I had a drink of water.'

Von Geldrecht, who had stiffened when von Volgen

spoke again, now relaxed and smiled. 'But of course, my lord. I would not be ungracious.' He bowed. 'You have the freedom of the courtyard until it rains.'

Von Volgen nodded his thanks and turned to his knights. 'Fetch your kit,' he said. 'Buckets, helmets, anything that will hold water. Go.'

The knights did not listen. They clustered around him, protesting his arrest, but he waved them down and told them to do as he ordered, and Felix let out a breath as they broke up and ran to collect their pots and pans.

He would have stood with the Talabeclanders, but the idea of fighting Empire men was just as abhorrent to him as it was to von Volgen, and he was glad it hadn't come to that – though it was a pity von Geldrecht was still in command.

'An ill wind,' said Kat, echoing his thoughts.

Felix nodded and looked up at the clouds, as Classen and Bosendorfer dismissed their men to find pots as well. It was going to be a brutal storm. He had rarely seen thunderheads so menacing. But was it his imagination, or did the lightning seemed tinged with red?

SEVENTEEN

ALL OVER THE courtyard, the men not on wall duty feverishly laid out every receptacle they could find. In addition to bowls, pots and buckets, they were setting down helmets, wine glasses, tankards, even chamber pots and empty powder kegs. Some genuflected towards the temple of Sigmar to thank him for the blessing. Sister Willentrude knelt and prayed to Shallya. Von Volgen's and von Geldrecht's men, who only moments ago had been ready to kill each other for their commanders, laughed and rubbed elbows as they set out their rain-catchers.

Felix, however, was finding it hard to get into the festive mood, and continued to shoot uneasy glances at the burgeoning clouds. Their bellies were now the bruised purple of an over-ripe plum, and the lightning that flickered through them still left a crimson after-image on the backs of his eyes when he looked away. A thick fog had risen too, oily and cold, washing up against the walls of the castle like a grey sea, then spilling down into the courtyard so it was hard to see across to the opposite walls.

The thunder had woken Gotrek, Rodi and Snorri, and they had joined Felix and Kat by the harbour to scowl at the sky with suspicious eyes.

'Something's not right,' said Gotrek.

'Can Kemmler have poisoned the clouds?' asked Kat.

Rodi shrugged. 'Necromancers are tricky.'

'Snorri doesn't think it smells like rain,' said Snorri.

Felix inhaled, but couldn't smell anything but unwashed bodies, smoke and over-ripe dwarf.

'Double water rations!' called one of the cooks from the door to the underkeep. He and the rest of the kitchen help were rolling out handcarts with open water barrels on them. 'Steward von Geldrecht has declared two ladles for everyone!'

A great cheer rose up, and the knights and foot soldiers started streaming towards the barrels, snatching up cups and glasses from the ground as they went.

Kat stared after them. 'But... but what if it doesn't rain?'

With unease slithering through his chest, Felix started across the yard with Kat at his side, searching for von Geldrecht, and found him in the door to the underkeep, watching the throng around the barrels like a benevolent lord on a feasting day.

'My lord,' he said, lowering his voice as he stepped up to him, 'this is a grand gesture, but are you sure it's wise?'

Von Geldrecht turned cold eyes on him. 'You think I am interested in anything you have to say, Herr Jaeger? You stood against me with von Volgen.'

Felix swallowed, then shrugged. There was no denying

it. 'I did,' said Felix, 'but that doesn't change–'

'What can be wrong with giving my men something they desperately need?' snapped the steward.

'Nothing, my lord,' said Kat through gritted teeth. 'Unless it doesn't rain.'

The steward gave them a comical scowl. 'Really, Herr Jaeger. You and your…'

His voice trailed off as an icy wind whipped through the courtyard, swirling the fog and flickering the torches that were set at either side of the underkeep door. There was a moaning on the wind that sounded like the cries of the wounded after a battle, and as it grew louder, the last purple tint of twilight faded from the heavy clouds and darkness fell in an instant.

All over the courtyard men looked up, shivering at this unnatural advent of night, but then, in the very next second, there was a blinding flash of lightning and a huge peal of thunder directly overhead, and the clouds let go at last.

Whoops of joy echoed from every corner of the castle as a deluge of fat drops rained down on them, battering their faces and drenching their clothes. Men ran around with their arms outstretched and heads tilted back, laughing hysterically. Felix couldn't help himself. Despite his worries, he joined them. He closed his eyes and spread his arms, letting himself get soaked to the skin, but as he opened his mouth to let the drops fall on his tongue, he smelled a strange but familiar metallic odour and wrinkled his nose.

The rain felt thicker than it should too, and slick, almost greasy. Felix opened his eyes and turned to Kat, who was looking down at her cupped hands. He choked. In the yellow light of the torches, it almost looked like she was covered in–

'Blood!' screamed someone. 'Sigmar have mercy on

us all, it's raining blood!'

All over the courtyard the defenders were coming to the same realisation, and it stopped them in their tracks. Some only stared uncomprehendingly up at the clouds, letting the red rain splash on their faces. Others shook and vomited, utterly repulsed, or threw themselves in the harbour to try to cleanse themselves, but the vast majority just raged and wept, the crash of disappointment after their hopes for salvation had been raised so high too much for them to bear.

A servant holding a soup pot in shaking hands stared at the blood pooling in it. 'It's not right. It's not right.'

'What are we to drink?' asked a greatsword, wiping at his face. 'It's got into everything.'

Then, from beyond the walls came the now-familiar rumble of Kemmler's siege towers, and the gibbering of the ghouls.

'They're coming!' bellowed a handgunner from the walls. 'To the walls! To the walls!'

Kat and the slayers started immediately for the stairs, while captains and sergeants shouted at their men and tried to pull them together, knocking pots out of their hands and hauling them to their feet, but as Felix started after his comrades, von Volgen stepped past him to von Geldrecht and saluted.

'It seems I won't be getting my water, my lord,' he said, holding out his sword. 'So I am your prisoner.'

Von Geldrecht pulled his eyes away from the haemorrhaging clouds and stared at him, blood-rain streaming down his face. 'Are – are you mad?' he choked. 'Get to the walls! Lead your men!'

Von Volgen inclined his head, his face impassive. 'Very good, my lord. Thank you. And may I suggest you do the same?'

Von Geldrecht glared after von Volgen, enraged all

over again, as the Talabeclander turned and hurried to his men, but the goad seemed to have worked, for as Felix ran after Kat and the slayers, he heard the steward shouting behind him.

'To the walls, Reiklanders!' he roared. 'For Castle Reikguard! For the graf!'

THE ZOMBIES WERE already coming over the battlements as Felix, Kat and the slayers mounted the walls. Rotting claws and maggot-spewing jaws swiped and snapped at the defenders as they raced to drive back the dead and throw down their ladders. But the corpses were only the first wave. Beyond them, emerging out of the fog like the ghosts of lurching, shrouded giants, came Kemmler's siege towers, their gangs of skinless beast-corpses marching over bridges of the dead, and their fighting tops crawling with shrieking, red-eyed ghouls. As before, two of the towers were aiming for either side of the gatehouse, while the third groaned towards the corner nearest the blasted and replugged dike, and all three were going to hit before the men of Castle Reikguard could mount a solid defence. There was no way they would keep the dead from gaining a foothold on the walls.

'We will defend the gatehouse until the humans clear the parapet,' said Gotrek, bulling for the door into the gatehouse's upper floor. 'Snorri Nosebiter, you and Rodi Balkisson hold this door,' he said. 'The manling, the little one and I will hold the opposite door.'

'Are you ordering me, Gurnisson?' snarled Rodi, pulling up.

Gotrek didn't look back. 'Do as you will, Balkisson.'

'Snorri doesn't need any help, Rodi Balkisson,' said Snorri. 'He can hold the door himself.'

Rodi shot an angry glance at the old slayer, then

strode on with the others. A handgunner was just pushing the door closed. Gotrek stopped it with a hand.

'Let us through.'

The gunner cursed and stepped aside. 'Hurry, then,' he snapped. 'They're here.'

Felix looked back as the wall shook under their feet. The middle siege tower had slammed into the battlements and ghouls were diving under the hoarding roof and tearing at the defenders with teeth and claws and sharpened bones.

'In,' said Gotrek.

Felix and Kat stepped through the door after him as Snorri and Rodi turned to defend it.

'Snorri will see you in Grimnir's halls, Gotrek Gurnisson,' said Snorri over his shoulder.

Gotrek whipped back, glaring. 'You are not going to Grimnir's halls, Snorri Nose–'

The handgunner slammed the door shut, cutting him off, then dropped a stout iron bar across it and led them across the small room as Gotrek cursed. In the centre of the room was the mechanism that raised and lowered the drawbridge and portcullis, and opened the gates. This was the reason the gatehouse must be defended at all costs. If the ghouls broke in there would be nothing to stop them from throwing open the main gate and letting the whole ten thousand zombies pour through and swarm the castle.

Another impact shook the room as they reached the opposite door, and the handgunners who crouched at the arrow slots looked up, uneasy.

'Let us out,' said Gotrek.

The handgunner paled as he looked through the slot next to the door. 'But they're coming! They're on the wall!'

Gotrek fixed him with his single-eyed glare. 'Let us

out,' he repeated.

The handgunner swallowed and unlocked the door, then pulled it open. 'Go! Go!'

The ghouls were indeed coming. As Gotrek, Felix and Kat strode out into the red rain and the handgunner slammed the door behind them, a gibbering white tide of them launched themselves off the siege tower into the thin-stretched knights and spearmen who defended the battlements.

The first wave drove them back from the battlements and the second wave swarmed left and right around them – half towards the defenceless cannon crew at the far end, and half bounding straight at Gotrek, Felix and Kat, shrieking like deranged apes.

It was a mad, miserable fight. The blood-rain was slashing in under the roof of the hoarding in nearly horizontal torrents, blinding them and making the stones of the parapet slick and uncertain. Felix hacked at the ghouls as if on ice, his feet slipping and skating out from under him and hampering his attacks and blocks. His weakness didn't help either.

It had been four days since he had eaten anything other than a biscuit, and he felt hollow inside. His head spun. The wall and the hoarding and the sky reeled around him, refusing to stay in their proper places. Beside him, Kat weaved and staggered like she had drunk a whole keg of brandy. The only reason either of them was still alive was because the space was narrow and Gotrek was taking the brunt of the attacks – but Felix was beginning to wonder how much longer the Slayer would last.

As he fought, the Slayer's wheezing and coughing came back worse than before, and his face grew as red as a poker. Even so, his mighty arms never stopped moving and his axe remained a flashing steel streak that chopped tirelessly at the encroaching horde. The ghouls fell before him in pieces – heads, arms and legs flying every which way – and their bodies toppled left and right. Their blood added to the blood that fell from the sky and ran in the gutter along the battlements to pour out through the rain spouts.

The cannon crew at the far end of the wall unfortunately had no Gotrek to protect them, and Felix saw them go down under a swarming mass of pale flesh, defending their gun to the last, then the ghouls were hurtling down the far stairs and into the courtyard. Felix's blood chilled as he glanced after them. They were not the only undead who had made it over the walls.

Zombies were everywhere, left to crawl unopposed over the battlements as the men tried to deal with the more desperate threat of the siege towers and the ghouls. But the ghouls had fought their way in too. The knights on the eastern wall were overrun, and the horrors were scrambling over their corpses to leap to the roofs of the residences and drop to the harbour-side. More were loping towards the knights who had gathered to defend the gatehouse's lower doors, and billowing black shapes floated amongst them – shades and banshees that drove the defenders back with their unearthly shrieks.

'Gotrek, they're in,' said Felix. 'And they'll be through the gatehouse's lower doors before they get through us.'

The Slayer nodded and started forwards, his axe blurring. 'To the stairs, then,' he wheezed.

Felix and Kat crept along behind him, stabbing and swiping over his shoulders as he cut down the fiends in a whirlwind of blood and steel. The ghouls' claws and bone daggers could not stab past his flashing blade, nor could they defend themselves against it, and after a handful were reduced to meat and splattered brains, the rest fled in terror, but the way was not yet clear. There were zombies behind the ghouls now, spewing up out of the bowels of the siege tower and clogging the wall in a mindless mass.

Gotrek ploughed into them like a bull crashing through a cornfield, and they died dismembered, headless and trampled underfoot. Before he and Felix and Kat fought halfway down the wall, however, a cry and splintering crash from below told Felix it was all for naught.

The banshees had sent the knights fleeing in terror from the gatehouse's lower doors and a hulking beast-corpse was ramming its way through the left-hand one, using horns like a balled fist to splinter the wood. Bosendorfer and von Volgen and the other remaining defenders ran across the courtyard to stop them, but they were too late. The ghouls swarmed around the beast-zombie as the door caved in, and poured through the door like terriers down a rat hole.

Gotrek cut down the last of the zombies and reached the stairs only a second later, and he, Kat and Felix plunged again into the bloody downpour and down to the courtyard to join the others. A huge hollow boom rocked them as they got close, and the portcullis shot up in a clattering whine of gears and chains. Felix cursed. The ghouls had done it. They had killed the handgunners and reached the mechanism. The drawbridge was down, and the main gate was swinging open.

'Fall back!' shouted von Geldrecht from somewhere across the courtyard. 'Up the stairs! To the keep!'

From much closer, von Volgen countermanded the order. 'Hold! Hold! Block the gate!'

Both were drowned out by the rumble of hooves

pounding across the drawbridge. Felix looked around. Thundering through the gate four abreast were the armoured skeletal riders that had chased down von Volgen's column as they had raced for Castle Reikguard five days earlier. They had a new leader, a skeletal, unarmoured wight with long blonde hair fixed to its skull by a golden crown and the decaying kirtle of some barbarian queen around its pelvis. The dead war queen rode a flame-mouthed black horse and held aloft a flanged mace that burned with viridian fire.

She and her riders smashed through von Volgen's hastily assembled line like it wasn't there, trampling knights under their flashing hooves and fanning out across the courtyard to ride down fleeing men as a black tide of dire wolves flowed in after them to tear out the throats of the fallen.

Gotrek set his eye on the queen and started through the red rain with a growl as she dashed out a spearman's brains with her mace. Felix and Kat followed as the Slayer cut down everything between him and her – zombies, ghouls, wolves and the mounted wights that slashed at him as they galloped by.

Before the gatehouse, von Volgen was bowing to the inevitable as he picked himself up and looked around. His line had been smashed and the gates could no longer be held. The zombies were spilling through after the wolves a thousand strong to spread like grey, slow-moving lava across the courtyard.

'Fall back!' he called. 'Bring the wounded! Protect the inner gate!'

His knights rallied around him and moved in a well-formed square for the stairs that rose to the keep. The household spearmen and knights and handgunners, abandoned by von Geldrecht – who was nowhere to be seen – rallied to von Volgen too, and began to retreat in good order.

Bosendorfer and his greatswords were not retreating. In a mad display of courage, they were plunging into the heart of the dead riders' ranks, their greatswords carving synchronised figure-eights in the air before them like the blades of some oversized threshing machine.

Gotrek ploughed into the ancient warriors' centre from another angle, shattering bone horse legs and ripping through bronze armour with each swing of his axe. Kat and Felix staggered and fought at his flanks and were soon joined by Snorri and Rodi, who were head to toe in blood, brains and bile.

'Snorri thinks we guarded the wrong doors,' said Snorri, chopping through the neck of a skeletal horse.

Gotrek decapitated a wing-helmed rider and took another step towards the wight queen, who was sowing crimson death amongst a knot of spearmen only a few paces away. 'They would have got in wherever we weren't.'

'Aye,' said Rodi. 'If we'd had a slayer at each door, the gates would still stand.'

Beneath the blood that covered him, the young slayer looked as pale as an elf, and he weaved as if drunk as he fought. He had a knight's surcoat tied around his middle that bulged, wet and red, just above his belt.

'Rodi,' said Kat, 'you're hurt.'

Rodi shrugged. 'A ghoul got lucky. Hooked my guts out. Had to stuff them back in.'

Felix and Kat blanched at this revelation, but Rodi fought on undisturbed.

Gotrek brought down another rider and the ancient queen was at last before him, slashing around with her mace as her flame-mouthed mount kicked in heads with its hooves and crimson rain flung from her golden hair.

'Turn, bone hag!' roared Gotrek. 'Turn and die!'

But as the queen wheeled to face him, Bosendorfer and his greatswords chopped through the riders on her right and crashed into her from the side, their two-handed swords rising and falling. The war queen shrilled with fury and swung her flaming mace, shattering a handful of long blades and clubbing Bosendorfer to the ground. Her riders and her wolves surged around her, slashing and snapping at Bosendorfer and his men.

Gotrek roared and bulled ahead, as if angry at being upstaged, and Kat, Felix and the slayers slogged after him, smashing through the riders to the queen. She swung down at Gotrek with her mace, and he slashed up with his rune axe to meet it. The evil weapon shattered as if it had been made of ice, flaming green chunks spinning everywhere, and she fell back with an unearthly wail.

Gotrek's next blow took the queen's arm off at the elbow, and she turned her horse, trying to flee, but Snorri and Rodi cut the legs out from under it and the three slayers chopped her into dust as she fell to the ground.

Her riders howled, and fell upon the slayers and the greatswords in a frenzy.

'Protect the captain!' shouted Sergeant Leffler, standing over Bosendorfer, who lay unconscious on the red wet ground, his breastplate crushed and his leg a bloody ruin.

Felix looked around as he and Kat fought their way to them and the slayers traded blows with the ring of riders. They were almost the last men in the courtyard. Von Volgen and his knights were protecting the bottom of the stairs that rose to the keep, while Classen and the household knights were escorting Sister Willentrude and a line of limping wounded from the underkeep. Almost everyone else had retired.

'Get him up,' said Felix to Leffler. 'Make for the keep.'

'Aye, mein herr,' said the sergeant. 'I don't know what got into him, but it was brave work. Damn brave.'

Felix turned to Gotrek, Rodi and Snorri. 'Slayers, lead us to the stairs.'

Gotrek nodded and Rodi smiled.

'Aye,' he said. 'Then we hold them – to the death.'

'To the death!' repeated Snorri.

Gotrek shot the old slayer a glowering look at this, but said nothing, only stepped in front of the greatswords with Felix and Kat at his sides, and began cutting a path through the riders and the wolves and the rain towards the stairs. Snorri and Rodi took up rearguard positions and the greatswords started forwards in double file, guarding the flanks as Leffler carried their fallen captain between them.

Ahead, Sister Willentrude was guiding the last of the line of wounded up the stairs as Classen's knights joined von Volgen's in protecting their retreat. A surging mass of undead crushed in on them from all sides – zombies reaching and groaning, wolves lunging, ghouls slashing, shades shrieking, dead beastmen looming above and swinging ponderous claws, while bats flashed down from above and the skeletal riders charged in with spears lowered, trampling the living and the dead alike in their homicidal desire to reach the knights.

Into the back of this murderous mob slammed Felix, Kat, the greatswords and the slayers, axes and swords and two-handers flashing and spraying blood as they severed spines and necks and crushed heads and chests. On the walls, under the hoardings, the greatswords had not been at their best, but here, in the open, where they had room to swing, their effectiveness was astonishing. Nothing could reach inside the great sweeping arcs of their cuts, and they mowed down zombie and ghoul and beast-corpse alike without breaking step.

The knights around von Volgen and Classen cheered to see them coming and fought with renewed vigour, cutting a hole in the undead's front line for them to pass through.

Von Volgen clapped Felix on the shoulder as he stumbled out of the melee after Gotrek. 'Up you go, mein herr,' he said, grinning through bloody teeth. 'I believe you are the last.'

'*We* will be the last,' said Gotrek, turning back to the wall of undead as the greatswords carried Bosendorfer through the lines with Snorri and Rodi following. 'Tell your men to retire, lordling. We will hold the rear.'

Von Volgen nodded. 'Very good, Slayer,' he said. 'A good doom to you.' Then he raised his voice and began shouting orders to his troops.

Gotrek turned to Felix. 'Go with them, manling, and take Snorri Nosebiter with you. Rodi Balkisson and I will hold until the gate is closed – and after.'

Snorri turned, looking confused. 'Snorri wants to hold the gate too.'

'Snorri has to go to Karak Kadrin before he finds his doom, remember, Father Rustskull?' said Rodi.

'Yes,' said Snorri sullenly. 'Snorri remembers.'

'Come, Snorri,' said Felix, and started for the stairs with Kat. 'Guard the greatswords' retreat.'

Snorri scowled, but took up the rear as Felix and Kat led the greatswords up the narrow, curving stairs to the gatehouse of the keep. Though the zombies could not reach them on the steps, they were open to the sky, and the huge bats swooped down at them in roiling clouds as they climbed. Felix must have cut half a dozen out of the air by the time they reached the top step, and Kat had done the same, while two greatswords had been torn from the steps by their claws, and the rest were bleeding.

More bats were attacking the gatehouse as they turned towards it, and Felix saw Sister Willentrude and a handful of tattered spearmen fending them off as the tail end of the column of wounded men limped in behind them.

'Foul beasts!' cried the sister, waving a broken spear. 'Get away!'

Cursing, Felix and Kat ran to help, but just as they reached her, a bat slammed into the sister's back, smashing her face-first into a pillar that flanked the gate, and biting her neck.

'No!'

Felix slashed at the thing, half-severing a wing. It flailed, shrieking, and ripped away from Sister Willentrude to flap at him, clawing his forearm. Felix shoved it back as it tore mail and flesh. It was too close to hit with his sword. Then it was gone, its head caved in by Snorri's blurring hammer, and flopping to the ground.

Felix let out a breath and wrung his bloodied arm. 'Thank you, Snorri.'

Kat helped Sister Willentrude to her knees as the greatswords filled in all around them. Blood was pumping through the Shallyan's fingers as she pressed them to her neck.

'Get her in!' said Felix to the spearmen who fought off the bats. 'And take Captain Bosendorfer. We will hold the gate! Snorri, greatswords, form a line!'

The spearmen looked relieved, and gladly took Bosendorfer and the sister as the greatswords and the old slayer turned to defend the gate. It wasn't until he and Kat had ranked up with them and begun hacking at the bats that Felix realised he had likely overstepped his bounds.

He glanced at Leffler, fighting at his side. 'My apologies. I didn't mean to order you, sergeant.'

Leffler grinned. 'Why stop now, mein herr? Yer just gettin' good at it.'

Felix laughed uncomfortably and fought on, swinging at the clattering bats as von Volgen's men topped the stairs and ran for the shelter of the gate. The wounds in his forearm, which Felix had hardly felt when the bat had clawed him, were throbbing now, and his arm was stiffening like it had been beaten. Blood was running down his wrist and slicking Karaghul's hilt.

He glanced down to the steps. A double file of armoured wights was halfway up, hacking at Gotrek and Rodi, who were backing up, one step at a time, and protecting Classen's knights as they retired.

Felix allowed himself a tiny sigh of relief as he killed another bat. Thanks to von Volgen and the slayers, the retreat into the keep was going as smoothly as could be hoped. There had been terrible casualties, of course, but after the initial panic, von Volgen's orders and the slayers' impenetrable defence had stopped it from being a complete slaughter. It could have been much worse.

Kat's shriek brought his head around and snapped him from his optimistic daydream. A huge shadow swept overhead, cutting off the rain for an eyeblink, then banked and shot down straight at the gate – straight at him.

Felix and Kat and the greatswords dived aside as Krell's wyvern landed hard in front of the gate, its claws scraping trenches in the flagstones, and Krell flung himself out of the saddle to stand before them, slashing with his axe.

Felix stared, stunned. Krell shouldn't be standing there. Felix had seen him fall into the moat just before the doors exploded. His mount too. The fireball had engulfed them, and yet here they were. Krell looked none the worse for wear. Indeed all the great gashes that Gotrek and Rodi had chopped into his armour when they had knocked him into the moat were gone as if they had never been. His wyvern, however, looked more patchwork than ever, with fresh stitches holding together the disparate hides that made up its torso, and its head and neck were burned black and showed skull and vertebrae through the charred meat.

Two of the greatswords died by Krell's axe before they could stand again, but the rest attacked the towering wight king as one, their long blades whirling in their customary synchronisation. Snorri led the charge, bashing at Krell's knees with his hammer and driving him back towards the wyvern.

'Stand back, manlings!' he roared. 'Snorri needs some room to swing!'

'No, Nosebiter! You will not fight!'

Felix looked up as he and Kat joined the greatswords' line. Gotrek and Rodi were elbowing through Classen's knights to the top of the stairs, axes high.

'Leave him to us, Father Rustskull!' shouted Rodi.

The surcoat he had wrapped around himself had come loose, and his entrails were hanging out of his belly. He didn't seem to notice.

Krell turned from Snorri and the greatswords as Gotrek leapt on the wyvern from behind and severed its long neck with a single blow, then ran on with Rodi. Krell roared and swiped as they launched themselves at him, gashing Rodi's shoulder with his axe and cutting two inches off Gotrek's crest.

The two slayers rolled past him to come to their feet before the gate while Classen's knights swarmed after them and surrounded him.

Gotrek waved them on. 'Go in,' he growled. 'Close the gate. This is our doom.'

'Aye,' said Snorri, stepping out from the greatswords' line to join him and Rodi. 'This is slayers' work.'

Krell slashed at them and nearly took Snorri's head off, but the old slayer got his hammer up in time, and the cut only knocked him off his feet.

'Curse you, Nosebiter!'

Gotrek charged forwards with Rodi to drive Krell back from Snorri, and Classen and his knights took advantage and ran for the gate. Felix and Kat hesitated as they ran past. The greatswords waited with them.

'Will you stay?' asked Kat, as Snorri picked himself up and the oak and iron doors of the gatehouse began to swing slowly closed.

Felix chewed his lip. The armoured wights were topping the stairs now, and surging in to support Krell, while Snorri hefted his hammer and started forwards again. Which vow did Felix honour? Gotrek had told him to keep Snorri safe, but after so many years fighting beside Gotrek, it seemed wrong to turn away.

'Go in, manling,' shouted the Slayer as Krell and the wights knocked him back and drove Rodi towards the gate. 'And take Snorri Nosebiter with you.'

Snorri kept walking ahead. 'Snorri doesn't want–'

'I don't care what Snorri doesn't want!' roared Gotrek as he blocked and backed away. 'Go in!'

Snorri snorted, but then stopped, fists bunched, and watched as Gotrek and Rodi fought in the centre of Krell and the wights.

Felix looked back towards the doors. The gap between

them was getting awfully narrow. 'Uh, Snorri…?'

With an enraged snort, the old slayer turned and walked through the gate, as angry as Felix had ever seen him. Felix and Kat breathed a sigh of relief and followed him in as the greatswords filed in behind them. Once inside, Snorri turned and glared back through the closing doors. Felix and Kat joined him, staring as Krell and the ancient wights battered Gotrek and Rodi inexorably back towards the gate.

A tremor of realisation went through Felix as he watched. This was it. This was Gotrek's doom at last. He faced too many opponents. He would never survive. At least it was a good doom – certainly better than dying from slivers in the heart – and if he killed Krell, then the Slayer's fame was assured. He would be remembered as one of the greatest heroes of dwarf history. Felix's eyes brimmed. And what a poem it would make! A last stand. A closing door. Two rivals united against deathless evil, fighting shoulder to shoulder.

But then, with the doors almost too narrow for a dwarf to pass through, Rodi suddenly dropped his shoulder and slammed into Gotrek from the side, surprising him and knocking him off balance, then shoved him back through the gap.

'Sorry, Gotrek Gurnisson,' called the young slayer as Gotrek crashed down inside the doors. 'You will not rob me of another doom!'

Felix and Kat and Snorri stared in shock as Gotrek bounded up and tried to squeeze back through the gap, but it was too small now and he couldn't get between the doors.

'Treacherous beardling!' Gotrek roared, pulling desperately. 'We'd both have had our dooms!'

'No, Gurnisson, we would not!' cried Rodi as he slashed at Krell and the armoured wights. 'Even here, even with a belly wound, even with the doors closed, we would have survived! You are cursed, Gurnisson! You will never find your doom! Nor will anyone around you! Grimnir mocks you, and I will not be part of the joke!'

Gotrek pulled with all his might, but at last he had to snatch his hands from the gap to keep them from being crushed. He turned on Classen as the doors boomed shut.

'Open them!' he shouted. 'Let me out!'

The knight sergeant edged back in the face of the Slayer's fury, but shook his head. 'No, herr dwarf. I will not risk the keep for your personal wishes.'

Gotrek glared at him for a long moment, breathing heavily, then grunted and turned back as the muffled clash of steel against steel rose to a feverish tempo beyond the doors, and a whoop of fierce joy sang above the tumult – then was cut short.

After that, all that could be heard was the hiss of the crimson rain and the chop of axes and swords against the oak and iron of the doors. Gotrek's shoulders slumped and he stood facing them, head bowed, while Classen called for men to man the murder holes and drive Krell and the wights away with gunfire and boulders.

Kat and Snorri bowed their heads too, and so did Felix, though he wasn't sure how he felt. Rodi had been a sharp-tongued companion, and hot-headed as well. Nonetheless, Felix had liked him. He had been quick and funny and brave, but now that he had stolen a doom from Gotrek, those memories were beginning to sour.

'Cursed,' said Gotrek, then turned and started into the keep's courtyard.

Felix and Kat fell in behind him, with Snorri hobbling

along after them, mumbling under his breath.

EIGHTEEN

'How many still live?' asked von Geldrecht, then amended his question as he looked around. 'How many can still fight?'

Felix looked around too. He, Gotrek and Kat stood with the steward, von Volgen and the remaining officers at the side of Bosendorfer, who lay wincing upon a cot in the back corner of a large cellar room within the keep. In normal times the room was a chapel belonging to Karl Franz's personal retinue of Reiksguard knights. Now it was carpeted with the wounded and the dying, and the prayers were to Shallya, not Sigmar.

Felix had made a fair number of prayers to the Lady of Mercy himself since the retreat to the keep. Kat had cleaned and bound the claw wounds on his forearm as best she could, but the bat's talons must have been diseased, for the arm was now stiff and hot, and the edges of the gashes red and painful to the touch. Still, he could hold a sword, and he could walk, and in this company, that ranked him among the able. Most of von Geldrecht's remaining officers were no better off, and some were worse – with splinted arms, seeping head wounds, missing fingers and missing eyes.

At least the mad anger that had driven Bosendorfer to challenge Felix to a duel, and which had caused von Geldrecht to order von Volgen's arrest, seemed to have bled out with the blood they had all lost. The steward seemed in no danger of sending von Volgen to the dungeon, and Bosendorfer hadn't even looked at Felix since he had woken from unconsciousness. They were all too weary for such nonsense now.

'Six,' said the greatsword captain, glancing to where Sergeant Leffler and his greatswords sat, binding each other's wounds. 'But there would be seven if someone would see to this leg. Where's that damned sister?'

'She is in need of a sister herself,' said von Geldrecht. 'Lord von Volgen?'

'Fourteen,' said von Volgen. 'Though even the fittest can barely stand in his armour.'

'There's only me,' said an artilleryman Felix didn't know. 'But all the powder's down in the underkeep where we can't get to it, and there's no cannon shot for the top guns anyway.'

Looking at him, Felix realised almost all the officers were unfamiliar to him now. Volk was dead, Hultz of the handgunners was dead, and Felix was too numb to mourn their loss, or remember if he had seen them die. Even the young spearman who had taken the place of Abelung, who had taken the place of Zeismann, had been replaced by an even younger spearman. The boy had peach fuzz on his chin and a thousand-yard stare. Only Bosendorfer and von Volgen were left of those who had commanded before the fighting began, and the wound in Bosendorfer's leg that he had taken from the wight queen's mace would be the death of him.

The boy from the spearmen wiped at his cheek. It was caked in blood. All the men were, from head to foot. Drying, it looked like they were iron statues, gone to rust. 'Eleven, my lord,' said the boy. 'Eleven. Eleven.'

'I don't know,' said a young river warden. 'The rest took shelter in the underkeep. I couldn't get to them, so I came up here. There – there was fifteen before the battle.'

'They will be dead by now,' said von Geldrecht blankly. 'Handgunner?'

'Nine,' said the handgunner. 'And we've no powder or shot either.'

Classen had to be nudged awake.

'Eh?' he said, looking around.

'How many of your company can still fight, knight sergeant?' asked von Geldrecht.

'Nineteen,' said Classen. 'Though it'll be less by morning.'

Von Geldrecht swung his head around to Gotrek, Felix and Kat. 'And we are less one slayer, yes?' His eyes glittered angrily. 'Died outside the gate when he could have backed through the doors and fought again.'

'A slayer's doom is no one's business but his own,' rasped Gotrek.

'Even when he may have doomed the rest of us with it?' asked Bosendorfer. 'We may die tonight for want of his axe.'

'We will all die tonight,' said Gotrek. 'Rodi Balkisson's axe would make no difference.'

Von Geldrecht looked at him sourly. 'Less of that talk, dwarf. Would you have us give up hope? Would you have us give up fighting?'

Kat snorted. 'You certainly did,' she muttered, but

fortunately only Felix heard her.

'I will fight,' said Gotrek. 'The dwarfs would have died out long ago if we only fought when there was hope.'

'Aye,' said von Volgen. 'We must fight. There may be no hope for us, but we are still the hope of the Empire. We fight now to slow Kemmler as long as possible, and give Karl Franz time to prepare for his coming.'

'Well said,' said von Geldrecht, looking as if he wished he'd been the one who had said it. 'Though I'd hoped we might survive at least one more night.' He looked around at them all. 'Is that impossible?'

Classen raised his chin. 'We will try, my lord. We will die fighting to make it...'

A figure moving towards them caused him to trail off in mid-sentence. The others looked around. Sister Willentrude was shuffling through the ranks of the wounded, the makeshift bandage that had been wrapped around her terrible neck wound as blood-soaked as her once-white Shallyan robes. She was staring at von Geldrecht with a look of dull despair on her ravaged face.

'Sister,' said von Geldrecht, 'you should not be up from your bed. What is the matter? Is there some new calamity?'

'She's come to look at my leg,' said Bosendorfer. 'Let her through.'

But Sister Willentrude didn't look at him, only raised her arms as if she wished to be comforted and stumbled on towards the steward, moaning.

Von Geldrecht stepped back, eyes widening, as the others began to stand. 'Sister? Are you well?'

'Draw your sword, fool!' shouted Gotrek, pushing forwards. 'She is–'

Before he could finish, the sister fell upon von Geldrecht, her hands clawing at his chest and her jaws snapping at his neck. The steward barked in terror and shoved her back, and Gotrek's axe bit deep into her side, then severed her head as she sprawled to the floor.

Von Geldrecht and the other leaders looked down at the headless corpse in stunned silence, as from all over the room, the wounded shouted and tried to stand.

'The dwarf killed the sister!' cried one.

'Kill him!'

'Lord steward, arrest him!'

Von Geldrecht held up his hands as some of the men started lurching towards them, balling their fists.

'Go back to your beds,' he said. 'She was already dead. She – she had turned.'

The angry looks turned to masks of grief and disbelief. The fists lowered.

'Not the sister,' said one. 'Not her.'

Beside Felix, Kat sobbed quietly. 'But we saved her,' she murmured. 'We *saved* her.'

He put his arm around her shoulder. She didn't seem to notice.

Von Geldrecht stared at the sister's headless body, then sighed again. 'Thank you, gentlemen,' he said. 'I will go inform Graf Reiklander of our numbers and our prospects. Please begin your preparations for tonight's attack. I will rejoin you soon.'

He turned and limped away, leaning heavily on his cane, as the others began to disperse and Bosendorfer stared at the corpse of Sister Willentrude.

'But who's going to look at my leg?' he asked.

Felix glared at him, and had to restrain himself from leaping up and throttling him. The man most responsible for the deaths of the wounded since the siege began, and now he was moaning about his leg not being seen to? It would be the most poetic of justice to see him die for want of a surgeon, but… but he wasn't the only one wounded, was he? There was a whole chapel full of hurt men. And Felix's arm needed attention as well.

Felix grunted to his feet and started after von Geldrecht.

'My lord steward,' he said as he caught up to him. 'I know you must be weary of my asking, but with Sister Willentrude dead, I must try again. Will you release Tauber and let him do his job?'

Von Geldrecht turned, and Felix was afraid he was going to get another earful, but instead the steward just stared at him for a long moment, and then nodded. 'Very well, Herr Jaeger,' he said. 'Very well.' He pulled his ring of keys off his belt and unhooked the clasp, then selected an age-blackened skeleton key and drew it off. 'I'm afraid I've left it too late,' he said, holding it out. 'And for that, I apologise. But as your dwarf friend says, just because there is no hope, doesn't mean one should stop fighting.'

He dropped the key in Felix's outstretched hand, then turned and started off again. 'Good luck, Herr Jaeger.'

FELIX AND KAT followed an old servant down narrow steps as he held up a lantern. 'Steward said I wasn't to let no one down here,' he said. 'Not on no account. But as you have the key...'

He stepped from the stairs into a cramped corridor then led them through a barred door into a rectangular room lined with sturdy iron-banded doors, each with a tiny window and a slot at the bottom for food.

'Herr Doktor is in this one,' he said, pointing. 'His assistants in that.'

Felix and Kat started to the door he indicated, but then a scuffling noise brought their heads around. There were noises coming from another cell.

'Who's that?' came a sharp voice. 'Are y'zombies?'

A hang-dog face appeared at the window of a door on the opposite wall. More crowded in behind it.

'Draeger!' said Kat.

'The dwarf-lover and his cat, is it?' asked Draeger. 'What's happened? We heard fightin', but nobody came for us – not that I'm complainin', mind.'

'The lower courtyard's been lost,' said Felix. 'We're all in the keep now.' He turned to the servant. 'Will this key open this cell?'

'Aye,' the servant said. 'Opens all of 'em.'

'Hang on!' said Draeger. 'Who says we want t'come out?'

Felix shrugged. 'Stay if you want, but next time it'll be the dead who come knocking.'

Draeger bit his lip and turned, and there was a whispered conversation behind the door, then he turned back. 'Let us out, then. We'll go down with our swords in our hands, thanks.'

Felix nodded and opened the cell. Draeger and his militiamen staggered out wearily, and blinked around.

'Much obliged, mein herr,' said Draeger, touching his brow, then started for the guard room. 'Our kit's this way, lads. Come on.'

As they filed out, the servant crossed to Tauber's cell and held up his lantern so that Felix could put the key in the lock.

'You have visitors, Doktor Tauber!' he called.

There was no response from within.

The key shrieked and stuck as Felix twisted it, but turned at last and the bolt shot back. He pulled on the handle, then peered in with Kat as the door creaked open. At the back of the cell was a low cot, and lying upon it, face to the wall and arms hugging his knees, was a filthy, emaciated figure.

Felix lit a candle from the lamp and gave the key to

the footman. 'Let out his assistants, please.'

'Yes, mein herr.'

As the man shuffled away, Felix stepped in. 'Doktor Tauber?' he said. 'Doktor Tauber, are you awake? I have water for you.'

There was still no response. Kat drew her skinning knife and crept forwards at Felix's side. Felix understood her caution. If Tauber had died, he might well rise and attack them.

Felix reached out and shook his shoulder as Kat held the blade ready.

'Doktor Tauber?'

The man jerked and grunted, and Kat and Felix stepped back, wary, but when he turned his head to look at them, there was intelligence in his blinking, squinting eyes.

'So,' he said, in a voice like dry paper. 'Von Geldrecht is gone then?'

Felix smiled. 'No, herr doktor, he still lives. But he has relented at last. He wants you to see to the wounded.'

Tauber frowned at this, then rolled back over and closed his eyes again. 'Let them rot.'

Felix sighed. He had been afraid of this. 'Doktor, they need you.'

'What could they possibly need a warlock for?' croaked Tauber. 'Are they begging for poison now?'

'You are no warlock,' said Felix. 'You didn't poison anyone.' He pulled the stopper from a jug he had found with half an inch of water in it. 'Here. I have water.'

Tauber didn't look around. 'Bosendorfer certainly thought I did,' he said, sneering. 'Or *wished* I had. And the rest believed him. Why should I help the fools who wanted me killed?'

'For the good of the Empire,' said Felix. 'We have to hold back Kemmler's force as long as we can.'

Tauber rolled over and looked up at him, smiling thinly. 'Mein herr, I may have been locked down here, but even I know that the castle will fall no matter what I do – and soon.' He chuckled. 'Would you like to try again?'

Felix opened his mouth, but he didn't know what other argument to make. Maybe he should try threatening the man. Maybe he could force him to work.

Kat laid a hand on Tauber's shoulder. 'Because you are a doctor,' she said. 'If you are to die, it should be doing what you do.'

Tauber stared at her for a long moment, his brows lowering as if he was going to snarl at her, but then he closed his eyes. 'You… you said there was water?'

Felix held out the jug as Kat helped him to sit up. He seemed to have lost nearly half his weight, and looked more than ever like a starved crow with a bad disposition.

He took the jug in clawed hands and drank, but only in sips, moaning and shivering with relief. Felix shot Kat a grateful look over his head. Why hadn't he thought of that argument? She shrugged, embarrassed, then steadied Tauber as he lowered the canteen with a gasp and opened his eyes.

'Help me up,' he said. 'I am ready.'

TAUBER STOPPED JUST before the door of the Reiksguard chapel, making Felix and Kat and his assistants jolt to a stop behind him. He peered through at the men who lay in groaning rows on its polished stone floor, and his hands clenched at his sides.

The hate in the doctor's eyes made Felix swallow, and he wondered if he had made a terrible mistake. Tauber may not have been a poisoner when Bosendorfer and the others had accused him of it, but what if his unjust imprisonment and their loathing of him had made him one? What if Tauber went into the chapel and proceeded to kill everyone he touched?

'Don't let them turn you into what they think you are, doktor,' he said.

Tauber gave him a ghastly smile. 'Fear not, Herr Jaeger. I have too much pride for that.'

The doctor straightened his shoulders and took a deep breath, then strode into the room with something approaching his old hauteur. As Felix and Kat followed him in, Felix saw the men look up at him, and winced at the fear and mistrust that flashed in their eyes. Tauber paid their reactions no mind.

'Who is most grievously hurt?' he asked, raising his voice. 'Who is closest to death?'

There was a chorus of pleading at this, but as Tauber raised up his hands for order, Sergeant Leffler stepped next to Felix and whispered in his ear.

'Please, mein herr, I know he won't like to do it, but if you could ask him to look at the captain?'

Felix grunted. Tauber likely wouldn't like it at all, considering, but Leffler was right. Bosendorfer would be dead within the hour if his leg wasn't seen to.

'This way, doktor,' he said, and led him to the cot where Bosendorfer lay as Leffler murmured his thanks behind him.

The greatsword turned pale as he saw the doctor approach, and gripped the sides of the cot as if he wanted to flee.

Tauber smiled down at him like a wolf. 'Don't worry, captain,' he said. 'It will be my greatest vengeance to make you whole again.'

FELIX SAT AGAINST the chapel wall, trying to stay awake long enough for Tauber to get around to him, but it was a struggle. Despite the throbbing pain in his arm, sleep pulled at him like an anchor, dragging his head down to his chest. He was so tired from the five days of endless fighting and rebuilding and fighting and rebuilding that he felt encased in lead. Beside him, Kat looked as weary as he felt, staring at nothing while Gotrek and Snorri snored thunderously next to her.

A few minutes later, Tauber finally hissed down before Felix, and gave him a weary smile. He was moving like a man twice his age, but despite that, he seemed almost cheerful. Kat had apparently been right. There was no greater tonic than letting a man do what he did well.

'Now, Herr Jaeger,' he said, 'what can we do for you?'

Felix folded back his sleeve to show the makeshift bandage Kat had tied around the claw wounds. Tauber snipped through the cloth with a pair of scissors and pulled it away. His smile faded.

A cold lump formed in Felix's chest. 'Is it that bad?' he asked.

Tauber sighed. 'Were Sister Willentrude still alive, you would be in little difficulty, for her prayers would have driven out the infection and the wounds would have eventually healed on their own. As it is, they are too far gone. I can only wash and bandage them and tell you to pray.'

'There's nothing else to be done?' asked Kat.

Tauber pursed his lips. 'If you were strong enough, your body might fight off the infection, but none of us is at our strongest at the moment, eh?' He looked over his shoulder at the rows of wounded. 'They are all in the same fix. A proper field hospital, with water and Shallyan prayers and food, and most of them would live. Here, despite my best efforts, most will die within a day – perhaps sooner.'

Felix swallowed, his stomach sinking, and Tauber saw it.

'I'm sorry, Herr Jaeger,' he said. 'My bedside manner leaves something to be desired, I know. Forgive me. You will have perhaps a little longer. You may even pull through, for you have a good constitution, but unless you receive proper attention soon, your chances are slim.' He shrugged, then snapped his fingers at the assistant who stood behind him with a satchel full of bandages and makeshift implements. 'But here, let us do what we can do. Even a little attention may help, no?'

WHEN TAUBER HAD moved on, Kat and Felix sat silent for a long while, leaning against each other and holding hands. The crippling weariness that had dragged at Felix still weighed him down, but now sleep would not take him. Tauber's words had struck too hard.

'I hadn't really given up hope until now,' said Felix at last. 'Gotrek and I have been in helpless situations so often, and we've always cut our way out somehow, but… but you can't fight sickness with axe and sword.'

Kat nodded. 'What day is it? How long before the relief is supposed to come?'

Felix tried to think back. It was difficult. It all seemed like one long, miserable night. 'Four days since von Geldrecht sent the pigeon?' he said. 'Five?'

'And seven days to get here from Altdorf,' said Kat.

Felix nodded. 'They will get here too late.'

'Then this may be our last day alive,' said Kat. 'Our last day… together.'

Felix looked at her and swallowed, then forced a smile. 'Don't be ridiculous, Kat. We'll be together forever, marching side by side behind Kemmler's banner.'

Kat's eyes widened, but then she laughed and circled

his arm with hers. 'As long as it's side by side, Felix, I am content.'

FELIX BLINKED UP out of a dream in which he had got into a contest with Gotrek over who could keep their arm in a roaring fire the longest. Gotrek had been laughing and sneering at Felix as he held his hand uncaring deep within the flames, while Felix had sweated and gritted his teeth even though he had only held his arm at the very edge of the fire.

The dream faded as he took in the murmuring hubbub that was going on around him, but the throbbing heat in his arm did not. He looked down at his wound and saw that the sick red of infection had spread beyond his bandages now. His head seemed to pulse with it too, and his vision was blurry and doubled.

'What's happening?' murmured Kat. 'Another attack?'

'I don't know,' said Felix.

'It's not an attack,' said Gotrek, sitting up beside Snorri, who snored on, undisturbed.

Felix squeezed his eyes shut then opened them again and the double vision went away, though the blurriness remained. At the far end of the room, beyond where Draeger and his militiamen had made their berth, the officers were again gathered around Bosendorfer's cot, and appeared to be arguing.

'But he can't!' Bosendorfer was saying. 'He's a Talabeclander.'

'He is also a lord,' said Sergeant Classen.

'Come on, manling,' said Gotrek, standing.

'Stay here, Kat,' said Felix. 'We'll see what it is.'

She nodded, and Felix pushed himself up from the wall, then had to hold himself there as the world did somersaults around him. When at last everything stopped moving, he stepped over Snorri and stumbled after the Slayer.

'You haven't asked if I want it,' von Volgen was saying as they joined the circle around Bosendorfer.

'Well, do you?' asked the handgunner.

The lord looked around at them all, ending on Bosendorfer. 'If I am asked, I will do it. But I will not ask it for myself.'

'What's going on?' asked Gotrek.

Classen looked up at him. 'Lord Steward von Geldrecht has disappeared,' he said. 'He is nowhere in the keep.'

NINETEEN

'SMALL LOSS THERE,' grunted Gotrek.

'You insult our commander?' snapped Bosendorfer. 'Have a care, herr dwarf!' The greatsword seemed much recovered, his leg wound neatly bound and his eyes alert. Tauber had been as good as his word.

'What happened to him?' asked Felix.

'No one knows,' said Classen. 'And until we find him, we need a new leader.'

'Has anyone gone to speak with Graf Reiklander?' asked von Volgen.

'I asked to see him when we found von Geldrecht gone,' said Classen. 'But Grafin Avelein turned me away. She said the graf was too sick to speak.'

'He was never too sick to speak to von Geldrecht,' muttered the spearman.

'Does this mean no one has been in the graf's apartments?' asked von Volgen. 'Could the steward be within?'

'The grafin said he was not,' said Classen.

Felix suddenly remembered his last encounter with the steward, and a sinking suspicion iced his guts. 'When was von Geldrecht discovered missing?' he asked.

'No one has seen him since he went to tell the graf our situation,' said Classen. 'I assumed he retired to his rooms afterwards, but he is not there now, and no one has seen him since he entered the keep.'

'I think he has escaped,' said Felix.

Every head turned to him.

'Escaped?' said Bosendorfer.

'How?' asked Classen. 'We are trapped.'

'Why do you think this, Herr Jaeger?' asked von Volgen. 'Did he speak to you?'

'It – it wasn't so much what he said, but…' Felix frowned. 'It was when he gave me the key to Tauber's cell. He said he was afraid he'd left it too late, and he apologised, then – then he said "good luck".' He looked around at the others. 'It didn't occur to me at the time, but now that I think back on it, it sounded like he was saying goodbye.'

A dark laugh came from behind them and they turned. Tauber was limping towards them, an evil smile wrinkling his pinched face.

'That is exactly what he was saying, meinen herren,' he said. 'Lord Steward von Geldrecht has fled, and left you all behind.'

'What?' barked Bosendorfer. 'And how would you know this, locked in your cell?'

'Because he asked my help to do it,' said Tauber.

'What do you mean?' said everyone in unison.

'Why would the steward want to leave?' asked von Volgen.

Tauber laughed. 'Don't you want to leave, my lord? I certainly do.'

'Answer the question, curse you!' barked Bosendorfer.

'I would imagine he left,' said Tauber, shrugging, 'because he finally convinced the grafin to give him the last of her husband's gold.'

'Are you saying,' asked von Volgen as the others murmured in surprise, 'that von Geldrecht was stealing from the graf?'

'For years,' said Tauber. 'And he might have gone on indefinitely except that the graf had the temerity to die – which complicated everything.'

The men stared, stunned, at this casual pronouncement, but Bosendorfer jolted up, struggling to rise from his cot.

'What lie is this?' he cried. 'The graf isn't dead, you villain! The steward has given us his orders every day since we came back!'

'Indeed,' said Tauber. 'And who but the steward has seen him since then?'

The men looked around at each other, waiting for someone to speak, but then Classen cried out.

'His wife!' he said. 'The grafin never leaves his side!'

'Yes!' said Bosendorfer, turning on Tauber. 'The grafin! If the graf was dead, don't you think she would have said something?'

'Aye, the grafin,' said Tauber, nodding sadly. 'It was for her sake that I became part of this.'

'Part of what?' asked von Volgen. 'Tell it from the beginning.'

Tauber nodded, then pulled up a stool and hissed down into it, grimacing. 'I'm sorry, gentlemen,' he said. 'It is too long a story to tell standing.'

'Just get on with it,' said Classen.

Tauber inclined his head politely, then began. 'As I said, von Geldrecht had been embezzling from the graf for years, and when Archaon invaded, von Geldrecht was well pleased to stay behind when the graf marched north, for with everyone away, his thieving could be even bolder. Unfortunately for him, the graf took a terrible wound at Sokh, and though I did my best, and kept him alive all through our long march back from the north, he died of it within a week of returning to Castle Reikguard.'

The men groaned at this, and Bosendorfer cursed.

'I don't believe it,' he said.

Von Volgen waved him silent and motioned for the surgeon to continue.

Tauber sighed. 'When von Geldrecht found the graf dead in his bed, he came to me before he went to the grafin. He said the lady was nearly mad with grief over the graf's suffering, and he didn't want to push her over the edge by telling her he had died. He begged me to tell her instead that he was comatose, and that with rest and care, he would recover.' Tauber scowled. 'I thought this was foolish, but eventually allowed myself to be convinced. Unfortunately, while I was lying to the grafin, von Geldrecht was lying to me. The real reason he wanted her to think her husband was still alive was greed. With the death of the graf, Castle Reikguard would pass to his son, Dominic, a much more suspicious fellow than his father, and von Geldrecht feared his embezzlement would be discovered.'

He coughed, then continued. 'Von Geldrecht therefore decided to leave before Dominic returned, but, greedy fool that he was, he didn't want to go without taking all he could, and the most valuable, portable, untraceable treasure in the castle was a chest of dwarf gold locked away in a secret chamber in the graf's rooms. The difficulty was, Von Geldrecht couldn't open it. Both the key and lock were cunningly hidden, and only two people knew their secret – the graf and the grafin – and the graf was dead.'

'So he went to work on the grafin,' said Felix.

'Very good, Herr Jaeger,' said Tauber. 'He did indeed. He told her her husband could be brought out of his "comatose state" by a great physician in Altdorf, but that the man charged a fortune to perform his miracles. He told her she would need all the gold in the secret chamber to pay him.' He smiled. 'I learned all this when von Geldrecht came to me a second time. The grafin had grown suspicious of his story, so the steward asked me to back him up, and was willing to give me a share of the gold for my cooperation.'

'Which you gladly took,' said Bosendorfer, glaring.

Tauber curled his lip. 'I did not. The graf was a good master and a true nobleman, and I had no intention of helping that fat villain rob him, but he reminded me that I had already lied to the grafin about the graf, and he threatened to tell her I had killed him.' The surgeon looked down. 'I – I should have still said no. But I feared the noose. So, in the end, I agreed to do as he said, but–'

He laughed suddenly. 'But even with my "learned" opinion backing up his lies, the grafin still hesitated. She said she'd had visions of a kindly old wise man who told her that if she waited and prayed to Sigmar, her husband would rise from his bed again.'

'And she believed this?' asked von Volgen.

Tauber nodded. 'I believe her fears for her husband twisted her mind.' He chuckled. 'And wasn't von Geldrecht vexed to find that he suddenly had a rival in a mad woman's visions? He did his best, telling her the dreams were false visions sent by some evil sorcerer, but she would not be dissuaded, and would not give him the gold.'

He shrugged and looked around at them all. 'Then, as

you know, Kemmler's horde surrounded the castle, and von Geldrecht's departure grew even more complicated. Fortunately, he knew of an escape tunnel built by Karl Franz's great-grandfather, but despite his dire warnings to the grafin that the graf would be killed when Kemmler conquered the castle, she still refused to give up hope that the kindly old wise man would come and save him.'

Tauber nodded to Felix. 'This is the real reason von Geldrecht had me locked up, mein herr, and why you could not convince him to let me go. He had me visit the grafin every day, telling the poor lunatic that the graf's condition was worsening, and that he must get away swiftly to Altdorf with all the gold.' He shook his head. 'The ruse still failed when last we tried it, but it seems he finally got her to do it – or perhaps he decided he couldn't wait any longer, and fled without the gold. Either way, he is gone. And now,' he said, standing with a groan, 'I must be getting back to my patients. Good day to you, gentlemen.'

He inclined his head to them all, then turned and limped to the next cot in the row.

The men looked around at each other, stunned.

'It must be lies,' said Bosendorfer. 'It must be.'

'And if it isn't?' asked the handgunner. 'If the steward's fled and Graf Reiklander is dead, is there any reason to stay here? Let's find this secret passage and go meet the relief column.'

'Aye!' said the young spearman. 'Now *that* is a plan.'

Von Volgen glared at them both. 'The reason for staying is the same as it ever was. We stay to slow Kemmler's hordes and allow a force to be assembled against him. No one will be taking that passage.'

Gotrek grunted his approval, as did Classen.

'I nominate Lord von Volgen as commander,' he said.

'Talabeclander or no, he is the wisest and most experienced of us.'

'Seconded,' said the artilleryman.

Classen looked around at the rest of them. The spearman and handgunner nodded, but Bosendorfer looked truculent.

'We must see if Graf Reiklander is truly dead first,' he said. 'I'll not give over command of the castle if our lord still lives.'

Von Volgen nodded. 'On this I agree,' he said. 'Let us go to the graf's apartments and discover the truth of the surgeon's story.'

Felix, Gotrek and the officers rose stiffly while Sergeant Leffler came forwards to help Bosendorfer to his feet, then tucked his shoulder under his arm. As they all followed von Volgen towards the door, Kat left Snorri snoring and joined them.

'What happened?' Kat whispered.

'Von Geldrecht has fled,' said Felix, 'and we go to see if the graf still lives.'

'He fled?' she asked, surprised.

'Aye,' said Felix. 'He had been waiting all this time while he tried to get some gold out of the grafin. We don't know if he got it, or gave up, but he is gone.'

They stepped from the Reiksguard's residence and blinked in the dreary light of an overcast afternoon. On the walls, the few remaining spearmen and handgunners shuffled through their patrols, while a mixed force of Reikland and Talabecland knights piled stones and barrels and whatever else they could find against the main gates to block them. Felix shivered. It would be night again soon, and the end would come at last.

A FEW MOMENTS later, after they had climbed to the middle floor of the keep, von Volgen knocked on the oak doors of the graf's quarters.

'My lord!' he called. 'Grafin Avelein, are you there?'

There was no answer. Felix and Kat and the others looked around at each other as they waited. Gotrek only stared at the door, arms folded across his massive chest.

Von Volgen knocked again. 'Grafin Avelein, if you do not open the door, we will be forced to break it in for fear of your safety.'

There was still no answer. Von Volgen sighed and drew his sword, but Gotrek pulled his axe from his back.

'Let me,' he said.

Von Volgen stepped aside, and Gotrek smashed the lock plate, then kicked in the double doors.

A gust of hot cloying air boiled out of the dark room, and everyone choked and covered their noses. Felix's eyes teared up. It smelled strongly of cinnamon and cloves and Estalian incense, but underneath all the spice was another, more worrying smell.

Felix and Kat followed Gotrek, von Volgen and the others into the dim interior. There were no lamps lit. The only light came from cracks between the drawn curtains, and was barely enough to see by.

'My lady Avelein?' called von Volgen, as he crossed the entry hall. 'Are you here?'

A sobbing came from somewhere further inside the apartments. Von Volgen started towards it and the rest followed, edging uneasily through an arched doorway into a larger room. The incense was stronger here, as was the second, underlying stench, which Felix could no longer deny was the reek of rotting flesh. Von Volgen crossed to a window and threw back the drapes, letting the light of the overcast afternoon illuminate a strange sad scene.

The room was a grand and richly furnished

bedchamber, with panelled walls and a massive canopied bed in the centre, and slumped beside the bed, head down, was Grafin Avelein Reiklander, her vermillion dresses spreading across the Araby rugs like a pool of velvet blood. Her right hand was stretched out to hold the shrivelled claw of a corpse that lay propped up amidst tasselled pillows upon the bed – and there was no doubt it was a corpse. The face was sunken and gaunt, its lips pulled back from its teeth and its eyes withered in hollowed sockets. A wound on its neck had been sewn shut, but the edges had pulled away from the stitches, revealing dry, black meat within. There were flies everywhere.

Bosendorfer stared, pole-axed. 'He was telling the truth,' he mumbled. 'Tauber was telling the truth.'

He let go of Leffler's shoulder and sank, still staring, into a chair. Felix didn't wonder at his reaction. The greatsword had erected his tower of rage against Tauber upon the belief that he was a villain and liar in all things, but here was proof that the story the surgeon had told of Graf Reiklander was true, and if that much was true…

Von Volgen stepped to the grafin and hovered above her, uncomfortable. 'Lady–'

She flinched at his voice, but did not otherwise move. 'Go away,' she sobbed. 'Leave us alone!'

'Lady,' he said again. 'I apologise for intruding upon your grief, but with your steward apparently fled, we had to learn if Graf Reiklander was dead so that–'

'He is not dead!' she shrieked, raising her head to glare at him with red-rimmed eyes. 'He is only sick! Very sick!' She had a purpling bruise under one eye.

Von Volgen looked back at the others, his square, bulldog face a mask of discomfort, but no one else seemed inclined to speak up. He clenched his jaw, then turned back to her.

'Grafin,' he said, 'I understand von Geldrecht and the surgeon, Tauber, told you that your husband lived, but... but they lied. He is dead, lady. I am sorry.'

Avelein stood, eyes blazing, and slapped him hard across the face. 'He is not dead!' she cried. 'I have been promised! He will rise from his bed! He will return to me!'

'Who promised you this?' asked von Volgen. 'Von Geldrecht? Has he–'

Avelein turned away from him. 'Von Geldrecht betrayed me!' she snapped. 'I knew I shouldn't have trusted him! I knew the old man was telling the truth.'

'Von Geldrecht betrayed you?' asked Classen. 'How?'

Avelein put her hand to her bruised cheek and closed her eyes. 'He said the necromancer's hordes would over-run the castle before the old man could revive my lord, and he promised to take us away and use my lord's gold to heal him in Altdorf, but...' She gestured to the wall. 'But when I opened the secret chamber, he – he struck me and stole it all.'

Sobs overcame her again and von Volgen stepped forwards to comfort her, putting awkward hands on her shoulders.

'I am sorry, lady,' he said. 'His deceptions have hurt us all.'

Felix glanced towards where Avelein had gestured. A panel on the far wall was not quite flush. He crossed to it with Gotrek and Kat as the grafin continued to weep.

'I should never have listened,' she said. 'I knew he was lying. But he told me the outer walls had fallen.'

Felix pulled on the panel. It was heavier than he expected, and as it swung out he saw it was affixed to a door of stone a foot thick. Inside was a small closet with jewellery and jewelled weapons on shelves, and in the middle, an iron-bound chest, its lid thrown back and entirely empty.

'I only I hope I haven't offended the old man by losing faith in him,' continued the grafin as Felix blinked at the empty chest. 'I only hope he still comes, now that I have opened the door for him.'

Von Volgen and the others froze at these words, and Felix, Kat and Gotrek looked around. Opened the door? What door? Suddenly the grafin's fancy of the old man sounded more concrete, and more threatening. The image of Kemmler in his guise as Hans the Hermit flashed through Felix's mind. If the necromancer could wear one guise, he could undoubtedly wear another. Had he been appearing to the impressionable grafin in her dreams?

'My lord,' said Felix, starting back towards the bed with Gotrek and Kat. 'My lord, I fear I may know–'

Von Volgen waved him down and leaned towards the grafin, forcing a smile. 'Forgive me, Grafin, but I was not listening closely before. Please tell me more of this old man, and the door you have–'

He broke off as footsteps clattered in the corridor. Everyone turned, hands falling to their weapons, but it was no undead host striding in, but Captain Draeger and his militiamen, with a few of the castle's spearmen and handgunners skulking at the back – more than twenty men in all. Only Bosendorfer did not look up at their entrance, just continued to slump in his chair, staring at nothing.

Von Volgen glared at Draeger. 'What is this, captain?'

'Aye,' said Classen. 'You scum aren't allowed in here!'

Draeger snorted. 'Way I see it, everything's allowed now. It's every man for himself.' He jerked his thumb at his chest. 'And this man wants to leave, so where's this escape tunnel, then?'

Felix groaned. Apparently their discussion about von Geldrecht had been overheard.

Von Volgen's face grew hard and cold. 'There is no escape tunnel. No one will leave this castle. We will fight to the end or until we are relieved.'

'Very brave of you, m'lord,' said Draeger. 'But I think I like the steward's way better. Now–'

One of his lieutenants grabbed his arm and pointed towards the hidden closet, the door of which was still ajar. 'Captain!' he cried. 'The passage!'

Draeger's eyes lit up and he started towards it. 'Good eye, Mucker. This way, lads!'

'That is not the passage!' barked von Volgen. 'Get away from there!'

He and Classen tried to block the way, but the militiamen swarmed past them, laughing and jeering, and Draeger hauled open the door to the closet. The laughing stopped as they looked in. Draeger cursed, and his men grumbled.

'You see, fool,' said von Volgen, pushing to him. 'Only a closet. Now get back to your posts.'

Draeger ignored him and turned, laughing, to his men. 'No tears, lads,' he said. 'It ain't a way out, but I do see our back-pay, eh?' He reached into the closet, grinning. 'Look at all them sparklers.'

Von Volgen grabbed Draeger and threw him back into his men, then stepped in front of the panel. 'Back to your posts.'

Gotrek, Felix, Kat and the young officers joined him and blocked the closet. Only Bosendorfer and Sergeant Leffler remained where they were, the captain still and unseeing in his chair and Leffler kneeling beside him.

Draeger snarled and drew his sword as his men went on guard. The officers reached for their weapons and Gotrek raised his fists, but von Volgen held up a hand.

'No blades, gentlemen,' he said. 'These men must be fighting fit when we are done here.'

'Oh, we will be,' said Draeger. 'Killing unarmed men is easy.'

A horrendous crash boomed overhead, jarring both sides from their fighting stances, and everyone looked up at the ceiling. Heavy mailed footsteps clanked across it – dozens of them.

'What is that?' asked Classen.

Grafin Avelein rose from her husband's death bed and lifted her hands to the ceiling as if in welcome. 'He has come,' she said. 'The old man has come through the door.'

TWENTY

BEFORE ANYONE COULD stop her, the grafin ran out of the bedchamber, calling joyously. 'Old man! Thank Sigmar you've come! My husband awaits you!'

'Grafin! Stop!' barked von Volgen, and hurried after her.

Gotrek was right behind him, pulling his axe from his back, and Felix, Kat and Classen swiftly followed. The other young officers fell in behind them, the handgunner and artilleryman drawing their backswords, and the spearman brandishing his spear with trembling hands. Draeger, however, stayed where he was, staring at the ceiling with wide eyes while his men huddled around him. In his chair, Bosendorfer continued to stare at nothing as Sergeant Leffler whispered urgently in his ear.

'The escape tunnel,' murmured Classen as they trooped into the entry hall. 'The madwoman has let them through Karl Franz's escape tunnel.'

As Gotrek and von Volgen strode for the broken

doors, a rank wind blew in at them, carrying with it a graveyard stench that overpowered the room's incense and made Kat and Felix choke and retch.

'Old man!' came Avelein's voice from the corridor. 'Old man, this way–'

Then suddenly her glad cries became a wail of abject terror, which was immediately eclipsed by a high, crazed laugh. Felix groaned as he heard it, all his fears confirmed. But as he and the others followed Gotrek and von Volgen into the corridor, it wasn't Hans the Hermit that was waiting for them, but a figure infinitely more terrifying.

Grafin Avelein lay shrieking at the base of the flight of stairs that led up to Karl Franz's private apartments as more than two dozen enormous, barbarically armoured wights clanked down towards her in a verdigrised tide, and a sinister figure on the landing above laughed like a jackal.

The figure looked nothing like the old hermit who had led them from Brasthof to the Barren Hills. His grin was not toothless, his shoulders were not hunched, nor were his robes and beard black with filth. Instead a tall, cadaverous sorcerer in a peaked hat and long grey robes grinned down at them, a gnarled, skull-topped staff clutched in one taloned hand. Gone was Hans the Hermit's sagging scabrous flesh. Gone were his weak, watery eyes. In their place was skin like scarred leather stretched over bones as sharp as blades, and eyes like black pits of hate, five hundred years deep. Only his voice was the same.

'Greetings, my masters!' he said. 'Are you not pleased to see old Hans again? Do you not like the bits of bone and bronze I found in those old tombs?'

Half the armoured wights trampled over Grafin Avelein and continued down the stairs to the ground floor, but the other half charged straight for Gotrek and the others, green-fired eye sockets blazing. Gotrek roared a wordless challenge and sprang to meet them, and his first axe swing sheared through the armour and bones of the leader like they were so much cheese and chalk. His second cut the legs out from under two more.

The Slayer couldn't fight them all, however, and too many surged past him for von Volgen, Felix, Kat and the officers. Felix and Kat fell back instantly, the axe blows of the wights as heavy as a house falling, and the others were in trouble too. The young spearman was backing away, the head of his spear sheared off, and the hand-gunner and artilleryman were retreating with him, their backswords no match for the corroded axes. Von Volgen and Classen fought shoulder to shoulder, but staggered with every impact. Even Gotrek was having difficulty holding his ground, and his breath was again coming ragged and raw.

Felix glared back towards Reiklander's apartments as he ducked a vicious swipe. 'Draeger! Get out here! Fight for once in your miserable life!'

But it wasn't Draeger and his militiamen who charged out of the door, but Bosendorfer, arm in arm with Sergeant Leffler, and lurching like they were in a three-legged race. Both had their side weapons out – a long sword for Bosendorfer and a mace for Leffler – and they threw themselves into the fray like men possessed. The sergeant shattered the skull of the wight that threatened the handgunner, and Bosendorfer knocked back another with a wild strike, then fell and dragged Leffler down as his bad leg buckled under him.

Cursing, Felix and Kat kicked back a wight and hauled the greatsword to his feet.

'Fall back, captain,' said Felix. 'You can't fight on one leg!'

'I tried to tell him, mein herr,' said Leffler, getting

under Bosendorfer's arm again.

'No, I must!' cried the greatsword, lunging forwards again. 'I must do the work of the men I killed.'

Felix and Kat fought forwards with them, protecting their flanks as wights came in from all sides. Felix had a lump in his throat. Confronted at last with Tauber's innocence, Bosendorfer had finally realised what he had done by keeping the surgeon from his work, and had decided he must die for it.

Nor was Bosendorfer the only one with regrets. At the same time as he flailed at the wights in suicidal fury, Grafin Avelein stood and shouted at Kemmler, tears streaming down her bruised cheeks.

'You promised me!' she cried. 'You promised me my husband would rise from his bed. You promised me he would take me in his arms again!'

'And so he shall, dearest heart,' said Kemmler. 'Indeed he comes to you even now. Look!'

Avelein turned towards the apartments and wailed, bringing everyone's heads around. Staggering stiffly through the desperate melee came Graf Reiklander, a stained night shirt hanging loose about his shrunken limbs.

Felix and Kat stared at the graf as Classen and the younger officers fell back in superstitious horror, but Gotrek and von Volgen knew no fear and swung for his neck as he passed.

The wights blocked their strikes and crowded them back, allowing the graf to shamble on, and Avelein flew to him, weeping.

'Grafin!' called Felix. 'Beware!'

'Oh, Falken,' she sobbed, throwing herself into his arms. 'I knew you weren't dead. I knew it!'

Graf Reiklander tore her throat out with his teeth.

As she slumped in his bony arms, artery spurting,

Gotrek at last broke through the wights, but he didn't attack the zombie graf. Instead, with a roar of fury, he charged straight up the stairs for Kemmler, the rune on his axe flaring bright.

Kemmler cried out in fear and raised his staff, and the landing was all at once choked with mist and shadows that blossomed like flames from his cloak. The Slayer plunged into the swirling darkness, axe high, but a second later the cloud dissipated again and revealed him slashing around at nothing, alone on the landing.

At the same time, as Felix and Kat fell back another step before the wights' attacks, tendrils of darkness began to curl around Graf Reiklander and Avelein, who now stood on her own, dead-eyed, as blood streamed down her neck. Kemmler appeared out of the mist behind them, then opened his cloak and enveloped them in its black folds.

'Come, children, we have work to do,' he said, then raised his voice to the wights. 'Finish them, then join your brothers at the gate.'

Gotrek bellowed and thundered back down the stairs, but the graf and the grafin and the necromancer vanished into the cloud of smoke, and by the time he reached it, it had dissipated into nothing and a trio of howling wights was turning to surround him with slashing bronze axes.

Felix and Kat tried to fight to him, but they could make no headway. Nor could any of the others. Indeed they were being driven back on all sides. Von Volgen was fighting one-handed now, his left mangled and missing fingers, and the young handgunner and spearman fought back to back above the butchered body of the artilleryman. Beside them, a wight dashed Sergeant Classen's brains out, and his body crashed into Bosendorfer and Sergeant Leffler. Bosendorfer stumbled at the impact and dropped his guard, and the wight's verdigrised axe bit deep into his guts.

With a cry of rage and grief, Leffler crushed the wight's skull, then dragged Bosendorfer back out of the way.

Felix and Kat surged forwards to guard their retreat and ended up beside von Volgen, who was falling back before two other wights.

'Do you hear it?' he asked, blood spraying from his lips. 'There is fighting at the inner gate. We must go. We must defend it.'

Over the clash and clang around him, Felix did hear it – a faint roaring and clashing from outside. He laughed bleakly, and was going to make a remark about not being able to defend themselves, but the words died as, in a single stroke, a wight cut down the young spearman and handgunner, chopping them both nearly in two, and Kat had to twist aside to avoid being butchered too. Felix cursed and shoved forwards to protect her, driving it back in a flurry of strokes, but as it stepped back, Gotrek suddenly flew back and crushed it flat as he crashed to the floor, a bloody gash across his chest.

The three wights strode after him, raising their axes, and he scrambled up again and leapt at them as fiercely as ever, but his breath was whistling like a bellows with a hole in it, and his crimson face was running with sweat.

This was the Slayer's doom, thought Felix, as wights slashed at them from every direction and anger began to boil in his guts. What a misery! It might be better than dying from poisoned slivers, but not by much. Instead of the doom he should have had, instead of dying a grand death at the hands of Krell the Holdbreaker, the Lord of the Undead – a truly fitting end to an epic life – the Slayer was going to be overwhelmed by nameless wights in a pointless skirmish, as the final battle for the gates of Castle Reikguard happened offstage. It didn't seem right. The only consolation Felix could find was that when the Slayer died, he would die too, and wouldn't have to write such an anticlimactic finale.

A deafening bang punched Felix's ears, and the skull of the wight he and Kat fought exploded in a spray of bone shards. Another bang, and a hole appeared in the breastplate of one that was driving back von Volgen.

'At 'em, lads!' cried a voice from behind. 'They're between us and the tunnel!'

As Felix stumbled back from the collapsing wight, Draeger's men flooded past him, hacking at the ancient warriors in a frenzy and cutting their way to Gotrek.

Kat blinked around in wonder. 'They're fighting.'

'Even a rat will fight when cornered,' grunted von Volgen.

Draeger strode past them, sword in one hand, smoking pistol in the other. His pockets were overflowing with necklaces, and he had a jewelled sword strapped around his waist. 'That's the way, lads! Through them and we're free!'

Felix, Kat, von Volgen and Sergeant Leffler lurched after the militiamen and joined their line. With escape so close at hand, the men fought with a will Felix had not seen in them before. Even so, they were letting Gotrek do most of the work, but the Slayer didn't seem to mind. With his flanks protected, he chopped through the wights like a vandal smashing statues, shearing through ancient breastplates and shattering bones in clouds of dust and bronze shrapnel as he drove them onto the landing. He kicked one back through the stair-rail to smash on the floor below. A half-dozen more followed as the militiamen crowded in around them, and finally there were none left, and Gotrek stood at the broken rail, panting and hawking noisily.

'Down!' said von Volgen, limping for the stair and beckoning the others to follow. 'We cannot rest yet. There are more at the inner gate!'

But the militiamen stopped where they were, and Draeger, who hadn't done much during the fight other than wave his sword about, did so again now.

'Well done, lads!' he cried. 'Now up and away! Karl Franz's bolt hole awaits!'

The militiamen cheered and turned to scramble up the stairs as von Volgen turned towards Draeger, furious.

'You may not leave!' he barked. 'You are needed at the gate! We may yet hold out!'

Draeger backed away, smirking. 'Sorry, m'lord. As I said all along, this ain't our posting. Best of luck to yer.'

And with that, he turned and ran after his men. Von Volgen cursed and staggered after him, but he was too winded and hurt to catch him.

'Forget them,' Gotrek grunted as he gulped in reedy swallows of air. 'You don't need cowards. Let's go.'

Felix mopped his brow and turned to the stairs with the others, but a weak voice stopped them.

'Sergeant. Jaeger.'

Bosendorfer was raising himself up on one elbow. Felix winced as he turned to see the man's guts spilling through a hole in his breastplate.

He crossed to him with Leffler and knelt beside him.

'I wasn't leaving you, captain,' said the sergeant. 'I–'

Bosendorfer waved him silent. 'You must. I go to Sigmar's halls, to beg forgiveness of the men I sent there.' He turned fevered eyes on Felix and gripped his arm. 'Jaeger. You led my men better than I. If–' He stopped as bloody coughing racked him, then continued. 'If they will have you, lead them now.'

Felix swallowed, not knowing what to say. It wasn't a duty he wanted, but he couldn't deny a dying man. 'If they will have me, captain,' he said.

Bosendorfer nodded, seemingly content, then lay back, clutching his chest with a gauntleted hand. 'Sigmar, that hurts.'

It was the last thing he ever said. With a mechanical rattle, his last breath escaped him and his arms slumped to his sides.

Felix and Kat bowed their heads as Sergeant Leffler covered his face.

'May Sigmar welcome you, greatsword,' whispered Kat, closing his eyes. 'May Morr keep you from Kemmler's clutches.'

Von Volgen coughed from the stairs. 'Come. There will be time later to grieve,' he said, 'if we live.'

ALL WAS DARKNESS and clamour as Gotrek, Felix, Kat, von Volgen and Sergeant Leffler ran out into the keep's courtyard. The screams and clashings of battle filled the night, and the sickly green light of Morrslieb, glowing through the clouds like warpstone at the bottom of a pail of soured milk, glinted on the thrashing of armoured limbs and the wet red of bloody weapons.

The four humans and the Slayer hurried towards the action along a trail of butchered bodies – spearmen, knights, ghouls and wights – that led across the courtyard to the inner gatehouse, where the last of von Volgen's men and the few remaining household knights guarded the doors of the gatehouse from a surging ring of ghouls, zombies and towering bronze-armoured wights that hacked and clawed at them with tireless savagery.

To the left of the gatehouse, a handful of greatswords were holding the parapet stairs against a stream of corpses that poured down them, while on the walls above, a weary crew of spearmen and handgunners ran back and forth along the battlements, trying to drive back and topple the ladders of the zombies and ghouls that were climbing over at a dozen points.

But though these were all desperate battles, it was the fight that raged on the top of the gatehouse, silhouetted against the moon-bright clouds, that made Felix's guts sink and Gotrek grunt with anger. Snorri Nosebiter, his booming laugh echoing loud across the courtyard, was going toe to toe with Krell, the Lord of the Undead.

'Curse you, Nosebiter,' growled Gotrek, and veered for the stairs at a run.

Felix was about to follow, but then remembered the greatswords. He turned to Leffler.

'Sergeant,' he said. 'Forgive me. I cannot lead you. I am oathbound to the Slayer, and must follow him. You are their leader now.'

Before the sergeant could answer, however, von Volgen turned to both of them.

'Take the greatswords with you, Herr Jaeger,' he said. 'I and the knights can hold the doors, I think, but not if the dead keep pouring in from above. Hold them at the battlements until we can finish the wights, and we just may have a chance.'

'Yes, my lord,' said Felix.

But as he ran after Gotrek with Kat and the sergeant, and von Volgen ran towards the gate, Felix wondered if they did have a chance. The men were weary and starving and desperately outnumbered, and even if they could stop the wights and hold the doors closed, Kemmler was already somewhere inside. What hope had they against him? The necromancer had taken the graf and the grafin and said they had work to do. What would be the fruit of that labour? Felix shivered with anticipatory dread.

'Make a hole, lads!' cried Leffler as Gotrek raced up behind the greatswords who held the base of the stairs.

'Let the Slayer through!'

The greatswords glanced back, then parted as Gotrek shoved to their front line and slammed into the clot of undead at the bottom of the stairs.

From Felix's vantage, it looked like an orange-crested bomb had hit them. A shockwave of force ripped through them, knocking down zombies and ghouls further up the steps, and limbs and heads and trailing viscera flew in all directions.

'Follow the Slayer!' shouted Felix. 'To the walls!'

The greatswords glanced around from their fights, wary, as he and Kat pushed through after Gotrek.

'Where's the captain?' asked one.

'I'll not go against him again,' said another.

'The captain fell to the wights,' called Leffler. 'He told Herr Jaeger to lead us.'

'I'll not order you,' said Felix, looking back at them. 'I haven't earned that. But I'd have you with me if you'll come.'

And with that he turned with Kat and hurried after Gotrek, not looking back to see if they followed.

'To the walls!' roared Sergeant Leffler, and to Felix's surprise, the cry was echoed tenfold.

'To the walls!'

Gotrek was halfway up the stairs, corpses and fiends toppling before him in a rain of butchered flesh and body parts. Felix and Kat fell in behind him, severing the heads of those that Gotrek had only wounded, and Felix stole a glance to the wall.

Krell was driving Snorri back towards the river side of the castle, knocking him around like a bear slapping at a pit dog. The old slayer got up and charged back in every time, but Krell just knocked him down again and took another step forwards. Felix tried to see if Snorri had taken a cut from Krell's axe, but he was covered in cuts from head to toe, and there was no way to tell what had made which.

'Manling,' coughed Gotrek, as they fought on. 'You will take Snorri Nosebiter to the escape tunnel.'

'Aye, Gotrek,' said Felix, then looked unhappily around at the battle. 'But–'

'The castle will fall,' said Gotrek. 'No matter how hard we fight. Fulfil your vow. Bring Nosebiter to Karak Kadrin.'

'Aye, Gotrek.'

The Slayer smashed a beast-corpse from the top step and he, Felix and Kat surged onto the parapet as the thing toppled to the courtyard below. The greatswords followed behind as they started towards Snorri's fight, and they all moved along the wall like some centipedal killing machine – Gotrek, Felix and Kat at the front, carving a path through the dead that were climbing over the battlements, and the greatswords at the sides, their two-handed blades scything down anything they missed.

A great cheer went up from the beleaguered spearmen and handgunners, and they took advantage of the greatswords' clean sweep to stave off and knock down a dozen ladders while the walls were clear. But as Felix looked back, he saw that without reinforcements, the reprieve would only be temporary. Already new ladders were slapping up against the wall and new zombies climbing them.

Felix turned to the greatswords. 'Leave me,' he said. 'Spread out on the walls. Hold back the zombies.'

The greatswords looked unhappy at this, and stayed in formation.

'Damn you!' Felix shouted. 'Now I *am* ordering you! The Slayer needs no help! Defend the walls!'

'You heard him!' roared Leffler. 'Face left! Spread out! Drive the bastards back!' And as the men slowed and turned, he gave Felix a smile and a sharp salute. 'On yer way, captain. They'll do you proud, I promise.'

Felix nodded, embarrassed. 'Thank you, sergeant,' he said, and almost added 'goodbye,' but decided that was too pessimistic. 'Sigmar watch over you.'

He turned and ran after Gotrek and Kat, who were charging towards the tower above the river where Krell had driven Snorri.

'Back off, Nosebiter! He's mine!' roared Gotrek as Snorri picked himself up and flung himself at Krell again. 'Turn, butcher! It's me you want to fight!'

Krell turned as Gotrek leapt, and the Slayer's axe – its rune blazing – sliced through his breastplate, opening a ragged hole that showed bone beneath. Krell bellowed and fell back, swiping his axe in wild desperation. Gotrek ducked the swing and came in again, chopping at the undead champion's legs and forcing him back.

Snorri whooped and charged in too, swinging his warhammer in a blurring arc, but Gotrek stiff-armed the old slayer and sent him stumbling back.

'Enough, Nosebiter,' growled Gotrek. 'Your pilgrimage starts now.' He shoved Snorri towards Felix and Kat. 'Get him out. Go.'

'Aye, Gotrek,' said Felix, shocked at the suddenness of it. 'Then I guess this is good–'

But the Slayer was already charging Krell again, his rune axe raised over his head. The wight king roared in to meet him, and sparks and grit flew as their axes struck and counter-struck in a hurricane of rune-glow and obsidian.

Felix put a hand on Snorri's shoulder. 'Come, Snorri,' he said. 'We'd better go.'

The old slayer politely removed Felix's hand without looking away from the fight. 'No thank you, young Felix. If Gotrek Gurnisson meets his doom, Snorri must avenge it.'

Felix clenched his jaw. 'But Gotrek doesn't want that, Snorri. He wants you to go to Karak Kadrin.'

'Snorri knows,' said Snorri. 'He will go after this.'

Felix groaned and glanced down to the courtyard, then back along the wall – the way they would have to go to get to the escape tunnel. His guts filled with ice. Von Volgen's strategy was failing. There weren't enough defenders left to make it work. At the gate, von Volgen and the last few knights fought with their backs to the doors, the wights and ghouls and zombies eight deep around them. On the battlements, the greatswords and the spearmen and the handgunners were being over-whelmed as more and more ladders rose and more and more zombies and ghouls crawled over the crenella-tions to surround them. If Felix didn't get Snorri away soon, there would be no leaving.

'Snorri,' said Kat, touching his arm. 'Please. Are you willing to give up going to Grimnir's halls to avenge Gotrek? Do you want to wander forever in the afterlife?'

Snorri continued to watch as Gotrek and Krell bat-tered each other, but his jaw set, and his face grew harder than Felix had ever seen it. 'Gotrek Gurnisson is my friend.'

Kat bit her lip, and a lump formed in Felix's throat. Both the slayers were willing to die for each other – *more* than die! To save Snorri's afterlife, Gotrek was prepared to dismiss Felix and allow his doom to go unremem-bered, and to avenge Gotrek's death, Snorri was prepared to give up his afterlife. Who would dare inter-fere with a bond as strong as that? And yet, a vow was a vow, so Felix must.

He wondered if he should try to knock Snorri uncon-scious and drag him away, the way Rodi had done at the battle of Tarnhalt's Crown, but he feared it wouldn't work. If a slayer couldn't hit Snorri hard enough to keep him under, Felix doubted he could do it.

A blood-chilling shriek of victory brought Felix's attention back to the courtyard, and he groaned. The last of the knights were falling under the crush of the undead, and the ghouls and wights were pouring through the smashed-in doors of the gatehouse. Felix saw von Volgen hack off the skull of an armoured ancient before being gored and trampled by a beast-corpse with the horns of a bull.

A second later, there was a ratcheting clatter and the heavy doors of the inner gate began to swing ponderously open, letting in a spreading mass of shambling undead. The inner court was breached. Castle Reikguard had truly fallen.

He looked back to the walls. The defenders were dying there too, the spearmen and handgunners and greatswords disappearing beneath a tide of zombies and ghouls that poured over the walls. Sergeant Leffler was the last still on his feet, reeling and whirling his two-handed blade around his grizzled head, but as Felix watched, a ghoul leapt on his back and bore him down, and the rest fell upon him like swarming rats. He had held to the end.

The lump in Felix's throat became a brick.

'Well,' said Kat, edging back as the zombies began staggering their way and the ghouls started loping out ahead of them. 'There's no leaving now.'

Felix went on guard. 'So it seems.'

As the ghouls bounded forwards, Gotrek bellowed with rage behind them, and Felix and Kat glanced around. While they had been watching Castle Reikguard fall, Krell had got the upper hand on the Slayer, and was bashing him back towards the battlements in a storm of strikes.

Snorri growled in his throat as he watched Gotrek stumble and weave, and his hands clenched his hammer convulsively.

'Behind you, Snorri,' said Felix. 'Turn around!'

Snorri whipped around, still growling, but his eyes went wide as he saw the swiftly oncoming ghouls.

'Snorri's!' he roared.

Felix and Kat charged in behind the old slayer as he slammed into the leaping fiends, and for a brief moment, they made a good account of themselves. Kat's hatchets severed fingers and shattered kneecaps, while Felix's sword lopped heads and severed arms, and the heavy head of Snorri's hammer was everywhere at once, cracking skulls, breaking legs and crushing chests in a whistling blur, but there were just too many facing them, and the weight of the zombies lumbering ever forwards at the back of the ghouls drove them back, foot by grudging foot, until they found themselves fighting shoulder to shoulder with Gotrek as Krell pressed him from the other side.

Felix laughed bitterly as their enemies closed in around them. When Gotrek had freed him from his oath to witness his doom, and told him that all he had to do was get Snorri to Karak Kadrin and his vow would be fulfilled, Felix had thought he was getting off easy. He'd had wild dreams of freedom, of future, of a life of peace at Kat's side. Well, those dreams were dead now. Indeed, all of them would lose what they most wanted here. Snorri would die without memory or peace, Kat would die far from the forests that she loved, Felix would die without having had a chance at a normal life and, with his death, Gotrek's saga would never be written. The Slayer would die unheralded and forgotten.

Felix saw Gotrek glance back at Snorri as they crowded together. The Slayer didn't look good, and he sounded worse. He was cut in a score of places, his one eye was nearly swollen shut and his breathing sounded like two bricks being rubbed together. Krell aimed a cut at his head, and he blocked it like he was being held up by a drunken puppet master.

A roar turned Felix back around. A huge beast-corpse was crashing through the crowd of ghouls for Snorri, swinging a club the size of a man. The old slayer easily ducked the swipe and swung up sharp with his warhammer, burying the head deep within its prodigious gut, but though he killed it, the beast felled him too, for with a gush of gelatinous black entrails, it toppled forwards, smashing Snorri to the parapet as the ghouls shrilled and surged around him.

Kat and Felix hacked desperately to keep them back, but without Snorri's steadfast hammer, the fiends swiftly drove them back. Felix took a cut on the arm, and Kat kicked to shake grasping claws from her leg as more ghouls clambered towards them over the dead beast. But then it shook, staggering the ghouls, and flopped to the side.

Snorri roared up from beneath it, covered in guts and slime and swinging his hammer – and went down again immediately, his peg leg snapped off at the stump. The ghouls pounced as he fell, piling on and weighing down his arms so that he couldn't swing his hammer as more clawed for his neck and eyes.

Felix and Kat cried out and fought forwards to protect the fallen slayer, but Felix knew they wouldn't last long. Already one had Kat by the hair, and another was throwing itself on Felix's sword so the others could drag him down.

Then something red and bloody and blowing like a blast furnace shoved past them and smashed back the clutching horde. It was Gotrek, breath ragged and blazing rune axe slicing through ghouls in every direction.

The ghouls fell back, shrieking, and Gotrek hauled Snorri up to his one leg. The old slayer grinned through a crimson river that was pouring from his scalp as Felix and Kat fell in beside them and Krell roared in from the left.

'Well met, Gotrek Gurnisson,' said Snorri, spitting blood. 'Snorri thinks we have found our dooms at last, eh?'

'No,' gasped Gotrek, levering himself up onto the battlements and pulling Snorri after him. 'We… have not.'

And with that, he shoved Snorri off the wall.

Felix and Kat stared as the old slayer dropped out of sight towards the river, flailing and howling in surprise.

'Gotrek!' cried Felix. 'You–'

Gotrek ducked Krell's axe, and pulled Felix up too.

'After… him… manling,' he wheezed, pushing Felix towards the drop. 'Little one… too.'

Krell's axe swept again towards Gotrek's head, trailing its black cloud of grit. Gotrek blocked with the rune axe, but the blow was so powerful it drove the haft of it back into the Slayer's cheek and smashed him into Felix.

For one brief, sickening moment, the two of them tottered on the very edge of the battlements, scrabbling at the stones, then gravity won out, and they too plunged from the wall.

Felix gaped as the scene on the parapet receded and the wall shot up beside him. Kat appeared on the battlement, screaming his name and bracing to jump, but Krell swung his axe at her and she fell back out of sight.

'Kat!' Felix screamed.

The river hit him in the back like a giant's club and he plunged into its depths, the cold waves closing over him and blocking out everything that meant anything to him in the whole world.

TWENTY-ONE

AFTER AN ETERNITY of sinking blackness, Felix's feet touched bottom and he kicked up as hard as he could, fighting the weight of his chainmail and the rushing water and the ringing numbness of his body. He broke the waves for just a second and caught a ragged breath, then went down again, but this time he touched bottom almost instantly, though he was dragged along it by the current, and couldn't stand.

He kicked up again, flailing and straining to find the top of the castle walls against the night sky. Was Kat alive? Had Krell killed her? Had she jumped? He couldn't see anything! Already he was far down the river, and the castle was receding fast.

'Kat!' he shouted. 'Kat! Jump!'

Nothing.

'Kat!'

His chainmail pulled him down again, and the

current dragged him on. He sheathed Karaghul and floundered for the bank, but just as he got his feet under him, he saw moving figures on it, lurching and turning towards his splashes. The fields were still crawling with zombies.

He sank back and looked around, searching the moon-rimmed waves.

'Gotrek? Are you there?' he whispered. 'We have to go back! Kat is still in the castle!'

There was no response. Where was the Slayer? Had he already gone back?

'Gotrek?'

A pale shape bobbed near him. He blinked water from his eyes and saw it was the Slayer's broad, muscled back, blood welling from a score of wounds. He was face down in the river, unmoving.

'Gotrek!'

Felix splashed to him and tried to lift his head out of the water, but they were still being dragged sideways by the current and he couldn't get leverage. He cursed and tried again, catching Gotrek's heavy wrist and pushing for the shore. Something sharp bumped his knee as he kicked, and he felt under the water. It was Gotrek's axe. The Slayer still clutched it in an iron grip.

'Is that you, young Felix?' came a voice from nearby.

'Snorri!' Felix cried, staring around. 'Snorri, come here!'

A dark shape with nails sticking from its head sloshed up out of the waves beside him.

'Snorri thinks Gotrek Gurnisson shouldn't have pushed him like that,' said Snorri. 'That was a good fight.'

'Snorri, help me. Gotrek is drowning.'

Snorri snorted. 'Gotrek Gurnisson can't drown. Snorri has seen him swim many times.'

Nonetheless, the old slayer caught Gotrek's shoulders and rolled him over in the water so that he was face up. Gotrek's head hung to the side, and a trickle of water flowed from his mouth. Felix couldn't hear him breathing.

Felix's heart lurched at the sight, then he looked back towards the dark silhouette of the castle, dwindling further into the distance with every passing second. What did he do? He had to go back for Kat, but he couldn't leave Gotrek. Or could he? He could leave him with Snorri and head back alone, but how was he to storm the walls and fight Kemmler and Krell and the wights by himself? It was impossible. He'd be torn apart by the zombies before he even reached the castle. As shameful as it was to admit it, Felix needed the Slayer's help.

'Wake up, Gurnisson,' said Snorri. 'Snorri wants to go back and finish that fight.'

'Gotrek's hurt, Snorri,' said Felix. 'And you've lost your peg leg.'

'Oh,' said Snorri. 'Snorri forgot.'

'We'll go back as soon as Gotrek wakes up,' said Felix, staring towards the disappearing castle. 'We *have* to.'

A MILE OR so down the river, they came upon a small village, so dark Felix would not have noticed it but for the little dock sticking out into the river that he banged his head on. No light burned among the low cottages, nor did Felix hear any sounds of movement. He feared that they had not travelled beyond Kemmler's sphere of influence, and that the place might be populated with zombies, but the cold of the river had penetrated all the way to his heart now, and his teeth were chattering uncontrollably. He could wait no longer.

'H-h-here, Snorri,' he whispered. 'Help me pull him onto the beach.'

'Aye, young Felix,' said Snorri.

Together they dragged Gotrek out of the water onto a narrow strip of mud. This was not easy, as Snorri had to do the whole thing on his knees, but finally they managed it and rolled Gotrek on his side. More water spilled from his mouth, but Felix still could not tell if he was breathing. He put an ear to the Slayer's chest and heard it at last, a faint, thready whisper. There was a heartbeat too, but it was soft and uneven, like waves sluicing over a broken wall. Felix swallowed, hardly relieved.

He slapped the Slayer's cheek and whispered in his ear.

'Gotrek, wake up!'

There was no response. Snorri frowned, concerned.

'Let Snorri try,' he said, then slapped the Slayer so hard it sounded like a pistol shot.

Felix cringed and glanced around, afraid the noise might attract attention, then turned back to Snorri.

'I-I don't think that's going work, Snorri. Gotrek is... sick or-or, I don't know.' He shivered as the night wind nosed through his wet clothes, then looked towards the town. 'We have to get him someplace warm and dry. Can you...' He paused and looked at Snorri's stump. 'No, of course you can't. I'll go look for a cart.'

'Snorri doesn't need a cart,' said Snorri, and pushed unsteadily up onto his one leg, then tucked the head of his warhammer under his arm.

The old slayer grabbed Gotrek's wrist, then pulled. Felix stood and helped and, with a lot of grunting and cursing, they got Gotrek onto his feet, then Snorri bent and put his shoulder against Gotrek's belt buckle and heaved him onto his shoulder.

Felix cursed as Snorri swayed alarmingly under Gotrek's weight, but then the old slayer steadied, bracing with the hammer-crutch as Gotrek's head and arms hung limp down his back, dripping water. Felix noticed that, even though he appeared completely unconscious, Gotrek still had a death-grip on his rune axe, which dragged on the ground.

'Lead on, young Felix,' said Snorri, turning towards the village. 'Snorri hopes they have beer.'

Felix doubted it. There were lines and grooves on the muddy beach that showed where small boats had been, but they were gone now, and he had the feeling the people of the village would be gone too.

He drew Karaghul and they started forwards into the middle of the dark huddle of cottages, Felix as quiet as a thief, and Snorri as quiet as an ogre fist-fight, stumping and thudding and hitching and grunting with every step. If there was anything hiding there, it would certainly hear them coming, but perhaps it would be frightened away.

Felix couldn't see any damage to the village, nor any bodies on the ground, but at the same time, the place didn't look or sound occupied. In a normal village, he would have heard the clucking of hens in their roosts and the shifting of livestock in their pens. There would have been carts and barrows at the backs of the cottages, and the dull red of banked hearths showing through the shuttered windows. There was none of that here. The carts were gone, the windows were dark, and it was as quiet as a graveyard.

To the left a cottage door was hanging open, the interior as dark as a cave. The tiny tavern across the way, however, was boarded up tight, heavy planks nailed across the front door and all the windows.

Felix stopped just outside the open cottage, peering uneasily into the darkness until his eyes adjusted, then went in. It was empty. He beckoned to Snorri.

'Lay him by the hearth,' he said. 'I'll make a fire.'

Snorri hobbled in as Felix dried off his flint and steel and found some tinder.

'Snorri thinks Gurnisson has gained some weight,' said Snorri as he settled Gotrek to the dirt floor in front of the fireplace, then peeled his stiff fingers off his rune axe and leaned it beside the hearth.

After a few damp strikes, Felix finally knocked a spark from the flint and it kindled the tinder, then found a stack of chopped wood to one side of the hearth, and built it up around the tiny flame.

A few minutes later, once the fire was going nicely, he went and shut the door to hide the light, then looked around. The shack was a lot like the village as a whole – undamaged, unoccupied and stripped. The few cupboards along the walls were empty of plates and cups. The crude table was bare, and the bed stripped of linen and blankets. The people must have fled when Kemmler's hordes arrived. The question was, had the necromancer's unnatural blight spread this far? Was the food rotten and the water poisonous?

Felix crossed to a row of jars, his stomach suddenly howling. He tore off their lids, hoping for anything – flour, lard, honey. There were dried traces of something in the last one. He scraped at them with a finger, then stuck it in his mouth. Mustard, as crumbly as chalk.

Still, it tasted like mustard, with no mildew smell or sour reek of rot. In fact, to his starved tongue, it tasted better than grilled beef. Sigmar, he was hungry!

He turned to Snorri, who was wringing out his beard by the fire. 'Snorri, see if you can get into the tavern. Look for food and drink.'

Snorri grinned. 'That is the best idea you've had in a long time, young Felix.'

He gave his beard a final twist, then started out the front door as Felix went out the back. The garden was little more than a bare-earth dog run, but there was a tiny vegetable plot at the back and the wooden hatch of a cold cellar next to a chicken coop. Felix stumbled to the coop and threw open the door. Empty. He fumbled through the stinking straw at the bottom. Not even an egg. He pulled up the hatch of the cold cellar and looked in, then gave a glad cry – two small carrots and a head of cabbage that had seen better days.

He pulled them out and stuffed one of the carrots in his mouth immediately. It was dry and rubbery and covered in dirt, but still good – not rotted through like all the food in Castle Reikguard had been. He chewed it noisily as he crossed to the vegetable patch, and moaned as the juices ran down the back of his throat. In other times he would likely have thrown the thing aside as not fit for pig fodder, but these were not other times. This was the best carrot nature had ever grown!

The vegetable patch was a disappointment. It was barely spring, and nothing had sprouted yet. Still, the carrot and the cabbage were better than nothing, and the rest of the cottages would have cold cellars too.

He heard a splintering crash from the street and crouched, on guard, then realised it was only Snorri breaking into the tavern. He went back inside and sat down by the fire next to Gotrek, then began to stuff the cabbage leaves in his mouth, groaning with happiness. He eyed the other carrot lustfully, but put it aside. He couldn't be greedy. Snorri would be hungry too. And Gotrek as well.

'Gotrek,' he said, shaking the Slayer's shoulder. 'There's food.'

The Slayer didn't move. He lay sprawled where Snorri had laid him, eye closed. Felix stared at him uneasily, certain now that Gotrek's unconsciousness had no external cause. It hadn't been the fight, or the fall or the water. What was causing this had been in him for days – the poisoned black slivers from the axe of Krell.

The door of the cottage slammed open and Snorri limped in on his hammer-crutch, a keg on one shoulder and a mouldy sausage on a string dangling from his mouth. He spit it out, letting it fall to the dirt, and beamed.

'Beer, young Felix! Beer!'

Felix was more interested in the sausage, mouldy as it was, but he stood and helped Snorri lower the keg gently to the ground, then went and collected two of the empty jars from the side board.

Snorri knocked in the top of the keg with his hammer, then took one of the jars from Felix and plunged it in.

'Careful, Snorri,' said Felix as the old slayer made to down the jar in one go. 'It might be spoiled like the stuff in the castle.'

Snorri paused, then took a cautious sip as Felix watched. A broad smile spread across his ugly face. 'No, young Felix,' he said. 'It's fine – for human beer at least.'

And with that, he tipped the jar back and drank it off, almost, it seemed, without swallowing. Felix dipped his own jar into the keg and filled it up. He inhaled as he brought it to his face, and the yeasty smell of the hops almost, brought tears to his eyes. He put it to his lips. Felix didn't know what Snorri was talking about. It was the best beer ever brewed, better by far than the best carrot ever grown.

He drank a few delicious swallows, then lowered the jar and let out a satisfied sigh. After starving for so long, he would be drunk in seconds from the beer, but he didn't care. It tasted too good.

A thought came to him and he looked at Gotrek. The Slayer had not been tempted from unconsciousness by a cabbage. Then again, who would be? But beer had been known to perform miracles of resuscitation upon dwarfs. Hadn't Felix seen Snorri sit up out of the depths of a concussion at the mere mention of the word?

Felix knelt beside Gotrek and raised the jar. Snorri saw what he was doing and joined him, holding up Gotrek's head as Felix tipped the jar and let a dribble of beer spill between his slack lips.

They waited.

Nothing.

Felix poured more beer into Gotrek's mouth. It spilled out again and sank into his beard.

Snorri's face, which until that moment had still worn the remnants of the smile the beer had placed upon it, fell with worry. 'Snorri has never seen Gotrek Gurnisson spit out beer before,' he said quietly. 'Snorri thinks something may be wrong.'

Felix nodded and sat down with a thump. 'Snorri isn't the only one.'

THERE HAD BEEN times in Felix's life when he had thought that there was nothing that could make a man more miserable than fighting for his life. At other times he had felt that the moments before battle, when dread and anticipation filled a man's guts with cold fear, were the worst, and at still other times he had believed that nothing could make a man more miserable than regret, but now he knew that none of those miseries could even come close to the feeling of powerlessness that came when a man knew his friends were dying and in danger and there was nothing he could do about it.

With a stomach full of not very much sausage, but quite a lot of beer, he had managed at last to fall asleep near dawn, but it was not an easy sleep. It was full of dreams of running for Castle Reikguard to save Kat, but never getting there no matter how fast he ran, and other dreams of Gotrek getting up out of his sick bed, but not being Gotrek – not being alive at all – and turning on him with dead eye and axe glowing green. In some dreams, he reached Castle Reikguard at last, then ran through its halls, chambers and cellars, calling Kat's name, but never finding her. In other versions, he did find her, but she was shuffling with the other undead, pointing stiff, grey fingers at him and whispering, 'You did this. You left me behind.'

Sometimes he fled from her, ashamed. Other times, he ran to her, begging her forgiveness.

'I will forgive you,' she said in a hollow, faraway voice. 'But you must let me feed.'

In the depths of his guilt, Felix agreed, and offered her his arm, which she accepted, and began to gnaw on with needle-sharp teeth, and hot, foetid breath. The pain was excruciating, but it was only what he deserved.

'Wake up, young Felix,' said Snorri. 'Snorri thinks you're having a bad dream.'

Felix blinked slowly awake, and Kat's sad grey corpse-face was eclipsed by Snorri Nosebiter's ugly pink one. Grey daylight was streaming through the cracks in the shutters, and there was birdsong in the distance. He hadn't heard birds in… Sigmar, it felt like years.

'Thank you, Snorri,' he said.

He levered up onto his elbow, then hissed and nearly vomited as agony stabbed through his arm. The pain of Kat chewing on him had continued after the rest of the dream had faded, and he looked down. The bandage Tauber had wrapped around his wounds was now brown with dried blood and crusted with river mud, and the skin around it purple and bulging. He drew his dagger and cut off the gauze, then felt nauseous all over again. The deep gouges left by the bat's claws were like volcanic fissures that spewed a lava of stinking pus, and there was a network of black lines spreading under the inflamed skin around them. The volcano analogy was apt in another way too, for it felt as if his forearm had a molten core – as if his bones were white-hot – and were radiating heat like a stove.

Snorri clucked like a hen. 'Snorri thinks that might be infected.'

'Possibly,' said Felix. 'Yes.'

Felix turned to Gotrek, who lay unmoving beside him. The Slayer looked paler than Felix had ever seen him, and his lips had a faint bluish tinge.

'Is… is he…'

Snorri shook his head. 'No, young Felix. But he still won't drink any beer.'

Felix sat up, wincing and fighting dizziness as he moved his arm, then put his ear to the Slayer's chest again. The faint slushy sound of his heartbeat was still there, but even weaker than before, and he couldn't hear the Slayer's breathing at all.

Felix groaned and lay back. After his years of fighting and hard travel he could dress a wound well enough, even set a bone if he had to, but he had no idea how one fixed glassy slivers that crept through the heart and lungs. He was helpless to save Gotrek, just as he was helpless to save Kat. He doubted he could even save himself.

Still, he had to try. With a grunt he pushed himself unsteadily to his feet. 'Come, Snorri,' he said. 'We have to find food.'

But as he took a step towards the door, nausea and dizziness overcame him again and he found himself face-first on the floor, the world going black around him.

'Stay here, young Felix,' said Snorri out of the darkness. 'Snorri will find the food.'

* * *

AFTER THAT, FELIX was unable to follow the passage of time. He drifted restless and uneasy between consciousness and unconsciousness, between waking nightmares and nightmares that seemed reality.

He woke to find Snorri standing over him, waving something in his face. 'Look, young Felix. A turnip!'

He woke to sunlight stabbing him in the eyes and the worst thirst of his life. The jar of beer was a mile away. He spilled it when he reached it.

He woke to find his fever gone and Gotrek healed. Under cover of darkness, they and Snorri went back to the castle to rescue Kat, dodging zombies and killing ghouls before slipping across the dry moat and stealing a siege ladder. Felix led the slayers over the walls and they found Kat bound for sacrifice in the defiled temple of Sigmar. Felix killed Kemmler while Gotrek and Snorri killed Krell, and they were all reunited until he woke again and found it was still day, and Snorri had brought him another carrot.

He woke to throbbing agony. The bruised lines in his forearm had spread to his neck and chest, and his pulse boomed in his ear like an orc war drum, shaking him with every beat. He was as hot as the jungles of Lustria, sweat beading on his brow and pouring down his neck, and yet, at the same time, as cold as he'd been that night he'd fallen through the ice in the Drakwald and nearly frozen to death. His teeth chattered like dice in a gambler's cup and he couldn't hold the jar of beer Snorri gave him, and had to let the old slayer pour it into him with a patient hand.

He woke to his brother limping into the cottage with his gold-handled walking stick and *tsk*ing over him.

'Well, you've certainly made a mess of things this time,' he said, his chins wobbling with disapproval.

'Aye,' said his father, who lay beside him, his face torn

with terrible scratch and bite marks. 'Just the sort of end I expected you to come to, you ne'er-do-well.'

Ulrika knelt down beside him and took his arm in her cool white hands. 'Let me kiss you, beloved,' she said, 'and we can live together forever, with no pain, and no partings.'

Felix looked up at her and thought she was the most beautiful woman he had ever seen. He wanted to open his mouth to say yes, but then Kat was at his other side, also dead, but not nearly as well preserved.

'Will you live on after I've died, Felix?' she asked. 'Weren't we to die together?'

Then, across the room, Gotrek got up and slung his axe over his shoulder. 'Come on, manling,' he said, glaring back at him. 'I've got a doom to find.'

Felix stared after the Slayer as he stumped out the door. He tried to rise. He tried to speak – tried to tell Ulrika and Kat that he couldn't go with them. He still had his vow to Gotrek to see to its finish – but he couldn't speak, couldn't move, couldn't even turn his head.

TWENTY-TWO

'ANOTHER NIGHTMARE, YOUNG Felix,' said Snorri, shaking his shoulder.

Felix peered up at him, having difficulty separating Snorri from the dream. He looked more unreal than the phantoms that had been surrounding him. He was at once too close and far away – his ugly face was glaring inches from his own, but the hand that touched his shoulder was at the end of a long arm that stretched from across the room. Felix looked away, unsettled, but got no relief elsewhere. The walls of the cottage were breathing in and out, and with each inhalation closing in a little closer – and it was blistering hot.

'Snorri,' he gasped. 'What are you playing at? Put out the fire. You're roasting us alive!'

'There is no fire, young Felix,' said Snorri. 'Snorri hasn't built it up yet.'

Felix looked past him to the fireplace and saw it was

true. The fire was down to ashy embers, and pink light was seeping through the shutters. It was morning – though which morning, Felix had no idea.

He rubbed his greasy brow with the back of his hand. 'I… How is Gotrek? Has he…?'

'Still asleep, young Felix,' said Snorri. 'Snorri doesn't know if he'll wake up again.'

Felix shivered, then tried to sit up. His head swam and his arms wouldn't support him. The wounded one, which had hurt him so much the day before, now felt numb and distant, but at the same time as fat and full as an overstuffed sausage. His fingers were black, and so thick he couldn't close them.

Snorri gently helped him to his feet and held him there. 'Do you need to go to the privy, young Felix?'

Felix shook his head. 'Take me to Gotrek.'

The old slayer dutifully put Felix's arm over his broad shoulders and crutched him over to where Gotrek lay by the hearth. Felix lowered himself unsteadily to the ground beside him, then once again put his ear to the Slayer's chest.

At first he could hear nothing but his own pulse pounding in his ear, but once he had listened past that, his overheated heart grew cold, for it seemed he could hear nothing at all. He pressed harder with his ear, hoping for anything, no matter how faint.

His heart flared with hope as he heard something at last, very soft, and hardly a beat at all, but something. He listened again to be sure. Yes, it was there, a low continuous vibration, like the roll of a snare drum, or surf, or distant thunder, or–

'Snorri thinks he hears horses coming,' said Snorri.

Felix looked up at him, marvelling. He could barely hear Gotrek's heart with his ear pressed to his chest, and Snorri could hear it standing a pace away. Truly, the senses of the dwarfs were… Then he heard it too – the same sound he had heard while listening for Gotrek's heart – the rumble of many horses on the move, but coming muffled through the walls of the cottage.

He looked at Gotrek again. What did this mean? Had he heard nothing? Was Gotrek dead? Or had the sound masked Gotrek's pulse? And how could he listen again if the horses were going to keep getting louder?

Wait.

Wait a moment.

Horses?

Getting louder?

'Snorri!' he said. 'Help me up!'

'All right, young Felix.'

The old slayer reached down and set him on his feet with one hand, then draped his arm again around his shoulders.

'Out,' said Felix. 'Out to the road.'

Snorri hitched forwards on his hammer crutch and hobbled Felix forwards. Slow and unsteady, they stumbled out the door to the muddy road which ran through the town. Felix looked west, in the direction the sound was coming from. The road turned through a stand of trees beyond the west end of the village, and he could see nothing, but the rumble was getting louder, and birds flew up from the wood.

'Take cover,' said Felix, pointing to the side of the village's last house, 'until we see who it is.'

Snorri obligingly crutched him to the house and they watched from behind it as the source of the rumble finally appeared from behind the trees. First came ten pistoliers on swift horses, cantering out and surveying the village and surrounding land while woodsmen with longbows crept out of the trees to either side of the road, scouting for dangers in the brush. Then a great company of knights and magisters and warrior priests followed on colourfully barded horses, pacing majestically towards the village, banners flying and lances high.

The relief force had come at last!

'Come on, Snorri,' said Felix, urging the old slayer forwards. 'We must go meet them. No time to spare.'

'All right, young Felix,' said Snorri. 'But it's only some humans.'

They lurched out from behind the house and started weaving towards the army like a pair of drunks heading home from the tavern. Felix waved and the pistoliers spotted him and galloped forwards, drawing their weapons.

'Who in Sigmar's name are you?' asked a young fellow with a dashing moustache as they thundered up and surrounded them, guns at the ready. 'Do you live?' The boy couldn't have been more than eighteen.

Felix threw up a hand in a limp approximation of a salute. 'Felix Jaeger and Snorri Nosebiter,' he slurred. 'The last defenders of Castle Reikguard.'

The pistoliers looked at each other, and the first one spoke again. 'Defenders?' he said. 'What do you mean, peasant? Y'don't seem to be defending a damned thing.'

'I mean,' said Felix, with elaborate precision, 'you have come too late, pistolier. Castle Reikguard has fallen.'

The pistoliers cried disbelief at this, and the dashing boy glared at him.

'What nonsense is this?' he snarled. 'Castle Reikguard has never fallen!'

Felix opened his mouth to argue with him, but realised it was pointless. 'If you would take me to your leader, I will tell him everything that has befallen.'

The pistolier scoffed. 'Take you, you sick old beggar? To see Horst von Uhland? How do we know you're not some pawn of Chaos, sent to give him the pox?'

Snorri gripped his warhammer at this, and raised it into a fighting position while balancing on one leg. 'Snorri Nosebiter is no pawn of Chaos!' he growled as Felix struggled to stay upright. 'And he'll fight any foolish human who says so!'

The pistoliers edged their horses back and thumbed back the hammers of their pistols, but before things could get out of hand, more hoof beats sounded, and Felix saw another contingent of riders trotting out from the main force.

'Easy, gentlemen,' called a white-bearded knight in the surcoat of the Reiksguard. 'Questions first. Shooting later.'

'My lord general,' said the young pistolier. ''Ware, please! They may be the undead. Or cultists. Or–'

The general barked a laugh. 'A trollslayer and a cultist? You need to see more of the world, lad.'

He pulled up in front of Felix and Snorri as his retinue of knights and companions reined in behind him.

'Now then,' he said, looking down at Felix and Snorri with a bright-eyed glare. 'Who are you? And where have you come from? Be quick.'

The eager pistolier saluted. 'They say they are the last defenders of Castle Reikguard, my lord. They say the castle has fallen.'

The general scowled at him. 'Why don't you let them tell–'

'Felix Jaeger!' cried a voice from behind him. 'And Snorri Nosebiter! As I live and breathe!'

Felix frowned and looked past the general. One of his companions, a tall man in a hooded beige travelling cloak, was getting down from his horse and hurrying forwards.

The general and the others looked around at him, surprised.

'You know them, magister?'

The man pulled back his hood, revealing a silver mane of hair and a lined, worried face. 'I do, general,' he said. 'Though I barely recognised them. Felix, Snorri, you look nine-tenths dead.'

It was Max Schreiber.

Felix's heart surged. He almost wept. He let go of Snorri's shoulder and stumbled forwards, reaching out to him.

'Max!' he said. 'Gotrek. Kat. I...' The world started to spin and dim. His legs wobbled. 'I think the Slayer has met his doom at–'

'Felix!'

The ground raced up and smacked Felix in the face. Far away, people were shouting, but he didn't care. The darkness was closing in around him again. It was warm and soft and lovely.

'HE'S COMING AROUND,' said someone.

'Thank you, sister,' said someone else. 'Now return to the others.'

Felix didn't want to open his eyes. The darkness had been too comforting, and he knew that leaving it would hurt, but already it was fading of its own accord, and he couldn't follow it. It was leaving him behind.

He lifted his eyelids and looked around, and for a moment was confused. He knew the roof beams above him from earlier wakings. He was back in the cottage. Had the coming of the relief force only been another dream? Had Max been a dream?

A balding, white-bearded man hove into his field of vision and looked down at him, his eyes hard, then Max stepped in to his right, followed by an anxious, dark-haired young man in armour, and... and... Felix blinked, thinking he was still hallucinating. Two men stood at Max's side, one in the black robes of a priest of Morr, the other in the midnight-violet robes of a wizard of the Amethyst College, but they both had the same long, sad face and shaved skulls. They were identical.

'Herr Jaeger,' said the white-bearded man, who Felix now recognised as the Reiksguard general without his helmet – von Uhland, the pistolier had called him. 'Are you well enough to talk? We have little time.'

Felix pulled his eyes from the unsettling twins and did a mental check of how he felt. Disorientated, certainly. In pain, oh yes, quite a bit, but not so much as before. And the freezing, fevered sweating had stopped, so, relatively speaking, not so bad.

'Yes,' he said.

'Good,' said the general, and sat, then motioned for the others to do the same.

Felix looked around as they did. He was lying in a military cot, his arm neatly bandaged and his fingers nearly returned to their normal size and colour. In the background, a Sister of Shallya was moving about, and through the door he could see that the village was teeming with soldiers. Gotrek's axe was propped near the hearth where Snorri had set it, but the Slayer wasn't there. Felix's heart thudded with sudden panic.

'We'll try to be as brief as possible,' said the general, as a scribe at his shoulder began to make notes in a big book. 'But we must ask you some–'

'Where is the Slayer?' asked Felix. 'Gotrek. Is he–'

Max leaned in, cutting him off. 'He's with the surgeons, Felix. They're doing everything they can.'

'No,' said Felix, heart thudding. 'You don't know. *They* don't know. The axe. Krell's axe. It struck him. It left poisoned slivers in the wound. They're killing him!'

The sombre twins raised their heads, and Max's eyes widened.

'Poisoned slivers?' he asked.

Felix nodded. 'The Slayer said they burrow to the heart. I fear they have already reached it.'

Max paled and turned to the general. 'My lord, if you would excuse me.'

'Go,' he said. 'We will make record of our conversation here.'

Max stood and hurried from the cottage. Felix wanted to get up and go with him. He should be with Gotrek, not here, talking.

General von Uhland turned back to him. 'He will be well taken care of, Herr Jaeger. I promise you. Now, we had the story from your friend with the – the nails in his head, but it was a bit confused. We'd like you to–'

'My father and mother,' broke in the dark-haired young man, leaning forwards with anxious eyes. 'Do they still live?'

Felix looked at him, bewildered. 'I– who are your father and mother?'

'This is Master Dominic Reiklander,' said the general. 'Son of the graf and grafin.'

Felix's face fell as he remembered the last time he saw them, when the undead graf had torn his wife's throat out. The boy read his expression and looked away before he could speak.

'I'm sorry. They…' Felix didn't want to go into details. 'They didn't survive.'

Dominic nodded, then stood abruptly and crossed to the hearth to stare into the fire.

Von Uhland looked at him, then turned back. 'This Krell you mentioned. He is the leader of the undead?'

Felix shook his head. 'Krell is a lieutenant. The necromancer who raised the horde is named Kemmler. I know little about him, but he is capable of raising thousands of undead, and blighting food and drink, and–'

'I know of him,' said the general, grim. 'Though I had heard he was dead, killed by Duke Tancred of Quenelles in Bretonnia.' He cursed, then looked back at Felix. 'And his plans? The message General Nordling sent said the fiend meant to march on Altdorf. Do you know his numbers?'

'I would guess more than eight thousand,' said Felix. 'Perhaps as many as ten. Men and beastmen alike, as well as picked troops of ancient warriors, giant bats, ghouls, spirits. And...' He looked apprehensively at Dominic's back. 'And, I fear he has some further plans for the graf and grafin.'

The young lord turned, dark eyes flashing. 'What? What do you say?'

Felix swallowed, wishing he didn't have to go on. 'He raised them, my lord, but I fear that was only the beginning...'

The young lord looked stricken, and had to sit down, but then looked up and fixed Felix with a hard eye. 'Tell me.'

Felix shrugged. 'I wish I knew more to tell. He raised them and took them away, saying they had "work to do". What that could have been, I don't know. But it kept him from the final battle.'

Dominic buried his head in his hands. 'He will pay,' he said. 'No matter what he's done. Their deaths and desecration cannot go unavenged.'

The sad-eyed priest of Morr cleared his throat. 'This does not bode well,' he said.

Von Uhland looked at him. 'You know what he intends to do, Father Marwalt?'

The priest shook his head, but it was his brother who answered.

'Not precisely,' said the Amethyst magister. 'But if he is using the graf and grafin in his ritual, it may mean that he is preparing something that will affect all of the Reikland.'

Von Uhland frowned. 'I don't understand, Magister Marhalt,' he said. 'How could their corpses help him?'

'In magic, there is power in name and place,' intoned Father Marwalt. 'Castle Reikguard is the ancient seat of the Reikland princes, the place from which the province was once ruled, and still the sometime home of the ruler of us all, Karl Franz.'

'And the graf and grafin are the rulers of Castle Reikguard,' continued Magister Marhalt. 'Therefore, symbolically at least, the rulers of the Reikland.'

'A ritual performed in Castle Reikguard, upon the rulers of Castle Reikguard, could be used to affect all the lands that make up its domain,' finished Father Marwalt.

Von Uhland stared at them. 'What could he do?' he asked. 'What would this ritual be? Could he raise all the dead from here to Altdorf?'

The father and the magister shrugged their narrow shoulders simultaneously. 'Who can know?' they said in unison. 'It might be anything.'

'And how long?' asked von Uhland, licking his lips. 'How long would such a spell take?'

The twins shrugged again.

'A ritual that powerful might take days or weeks,' said Magister Marhalt.

'And it has already been days,' said Father Marwalt.

Von Uhland paled and stood. 'No more time can be lost,' he said, turning to the door. 'I will survey the position, and then we will move.'

'I will come with you,' said Dominic, stepping to him. 'I know the castle as I know my hands, and the secret ways in and out as well.'

Felix thought of Kat, and struggled to push up from

the bed. 'I'll come too,' he said. 'I must return to–'

Von Uhland put a hand on his shoulder and pressed him back. 'Rest, Herr Jaeger. The Reiksguard has the situation in hand. But thank you for your insight and information.'

'But...' said Felix.

The general was already walking out the door with Dominic Reiklander on his heels. Felix glared after them. Who was Uhland to tell him to rest? He wasn't going to idle in bed when Kat was in danger. He threw off the covers and pushed himself to a sitting position, then clutched the edges of the cot while the room spun around him.

Felix took deep breaths until the sensation passed. He wanted desperately to lie down again, but he wouldn't. He had to go with von Uhland and Dominic. He shifted his legs over the side of the cot and wobbled to his feet, then paused for the spinning to fade again, and started for the door.

Max appeared in it before he reached it. 'Felix,' he said, his face grave. 'Gotrek is dying. Come with me.'

TWENTY-THREE

MAX LED FELIX through the red-bordered door of the sick tent, then stood aside. The Slayer lay on a cot against the back wall, his one eye closed, and his arms, legs and torso covered in bruises, bandages and stitches. Snorri stood beside him, a new peg on his stump, and stared down at him silently. Off to one side the Sister of Shallya was helping a surgeon pack up his scalpels, needles and thread.

'We did all we could, Felix,' said Max. 'The surgeon cleaned and patched every wound he could find, while the abbess prayed to Shallya to heal the damage done to Gotrek's internal organs. I performed every spell of cleansing and healing I know, but... but there has been no change. It seems we were too late.'

Felix nodded dully, then crossed to the cot and stood beside Snorri. Gotrek lay as if asleep, his brows furrowed, but his chest did not seem to rise and fall. He made no movement at all.

'He still lives,' said Max, 'but not for long. It is only a matter of time.'

Felix knelt beside the cot and leaned in. 'Gotrek,' he said. 'Please. Don't let your doom be a few specks of glass. Krell lives. Go back and finish him. Get your revenge and help me rescue Kat.'

There was no change in the Slayer's face. Felix hadn't really expected one, but it still hurt when it didn't come. He hung his head, then stood again, his fists balling at his sides.

'He should have his axe,' he blurted. 'He shouldn't die without his axe.'

'Snorri will get it,' said Snorri heavily, then turned and walked out of the tent.

Max coughed from the door. 'If there is anything you need, Felix,' he said.

Felix shook his head. 'Just– just some time.'

Max nodded and motioned to the surgeon and abbess, then stepped to the door as they filed out. 'I'll see you're not disturbed.'

Rage boiled in Felix's chest as he looked down at the Slayer. This was not how it was supposed to end. The Slayer was not supposed to die in bed. He was not supposed to go quietly. He was supposed to go down fighting, bleeding from a hundred cuts and torn to pieces by the death throes of the monstrous enemy he had just slain. This was pathetic, the worst end for Gotrek's saga that he could imagine. He would never have written it like this. Never!

Twenty years and more of travelling with the Slayer, fighting beside him, weathering his moods and sharing his triumphs – it had all seemed like it was building to something. He had felt that the epic would have a finish worthy of its chapters. Curse Krell! Curse him for a cheat and poisoning coward! And curse Rodi too, for robbing Gotrek of a true slayer's death while he was still well enough to take it.

Felix turned away, snarling. Everything was wrong now. Everything! The Slayer had died poorly, and though, because of that, Felix was now free of his vow to him, what did that freedom hold? Nothing. It was meant to have been a new beginning for him – a new life with Kat, where they would go where they liked and do what they wanted, alone together at last, but it had been at least two days since he and Snorri and Gotrek had fallen from the walls of Castle Reikguard. There was no way Kat could still be alive after all that time. He would of course go with General von Uhland and find out for himself, but he already knew the answer. She was dead, and with her death, his dream of a better future died as well.

Snorri limped back into the tent and held out Gotrek's rune axe. 'Here it is, young Felix,' he said.

Felix stepped to him and took the weapon, and almost dropped it. It was unsettlingly heavy. With a grunt, he heaved it up and crossed to Gotrek's cot, then laid it on the Slayer's bearded chest and crossed his heavy hands over it.

'There, Gotrek,' he said, standing. 'You'll need that in Grimnir's halls.'

Snorri stood on the opposite side of the cot and bowed his head. 'May Grimnir welcome you, Gotrek son of Gurni,' he said.

This at least was right, thought Felix – that he and Snorri were there, and that the right things had been said. He decided he would stay and stand vigil over Gotrek until the sisters told him he was dead. He had vowed to the Slayer that he would witness his end, and if this sad, silent passing was it, then he would not fail that vow. If only he didn't feel like he was going to fall over at any second.

Felix looked around and saw a camp chair off to one side. He dragged it to the cot and sat. He would sit vigil then. It would be the same.

FELIX SNAPPED AWAKE, panic seizing him. How long had he been asleep? He looked to the door. Red twilight filtered into the tent. No! It hadn't been noon when he'd sat down in the chair. How had this happened? How had he let himself fall asleep?

He turned to Gotrek's cot.

It was empty.

The panic in Felix's chest turned to cold dread, then crushing guilt. Gotrek had died. Snorri had taken him away to be buried, and Felix had missed it. He had not witnessed the Slayer's end. He had not been by his side in his final moments. He had failed in the duty that he had sworn to keep for twenty years. Now anger surged up to join the guilt. Damn Snorri! Why hadn't he woken him? Why hadn't he warned him when the end was drawing near?

Felix struggled up out of the chair and nearly fell on his face. He was much recovered from his wounds, and his arm no longer throbbed, but the dizziness still lingered, and he was so hungry he could barely stand.

He recovered and pushed unsteadily into a maze of tents. In the short time they had been here, the relief force had transformed the little village into a bustling camp, and one that was preparing for war. Knights and squires and grooms hurried by, carrying armour and saddles, and the harsh cries of sergeants echoed from every direction.

Felix took a right, heading – he hoped – for the main road through the village. He had to find Max or Snorri or the abbess of Shallya and ask them what had happened – and they would get a piece of his mind for letting him sleep through the death of his dearest friend.

After another turning, he found the road, and looked both ways. A large tent with the banner of the Reiksguard knights flapping above it sat beyond the shack he and Snorri had sheltered in. That would be the command tent. He started towards it, but before he had taken more than five steps, an intoxicating smell nearly stopped him in his tracks. Someone was roasting pork, and there was gravy too.

He turned towards the delicious scent just in time to hear a familiar voice say, 'Snorri would like more beer, please.'

Felix's heart lurched and he stumbled forwards. The old slayer sounded very calm. Did he not know what had happened to Gotrek? Or had he forgotten already? Sigmar, that would be a terrible thing! The mess tent was just ahead on the left. Felix ducked through the canvas flaps, scanning for the old slayer.

'Snorri,' he said. 'There you are. I–'

He cut off as the scene in the tent came into focus. Snorri sat at a long mess table in the middle of the room, with a feast of food before him and a huge mug of beer in his fist, and across from him, head down and fork shovelling food into his mouth like some sort of machine, was Gotrek.

'Hello, young Felix,' said Snorri, waving a well-stripped bone.

Gotrek raised his single eye to Felix, scowling. 'Finally awake, manling?' he asked. 'Now's not the time to sleep. There's work to be done.'

'Gotrek!' said Felix, but then a lump rose up in his throat and he found he couldn't say anything else, which was just as well, really. It would have only been something sentimental, and Gotrek would have thought him weak.

'Aye?' said the Slayer. 'What?'

He was not quite his old self. He looked as strong as ever, and he ate with his usual relish, but his movements were somewhat stiff, and he was uncharacteristically pale, while his face had lines and scars upon it that hadn't been there before they'd come to Castle Reikguard. But how was he alive at all? Max had said all their prayers and spells and surgery hadn't worked. Had they only taken some time to take effect? Had the Slayer recovered by sheer force of will? He thought of asking, but Gotrek would likely have snorted at that too.

'Nothing,' Felix said at last, forcing down the lump. 'It… it's good to see you, that's all.'

'Herr Jaeger,' called someone. 'Come here. Eat while we talk. We must be moving soon.'

Felix turned and saw General von Uhland. Indeed, now that he had got over finding Gotrek alive he saw that there was quite a gathering in the tent. General von Uhland and Lord Dominic Reiklander, still dressed for scouting, sat with a small circle of officers, while Max Schreiber, Father Marwalt and his twin, Magister Marhalt, sat beside them.

Felix sat and stabbed a few slices of ham from the platter, then slathered a slice of bread with butter. So this was how generals ate, he thought. No wonder they all got fat, no matter how much campaigning they did. Well, he was all for it now, and stuffed his mouth full with both hands. Sigmar, it was good! The juice of the ham ran down his throat like the elixir of life. He never wanted to stop eating.

'We have a challenge ahead of us, Herr Jaeger,' said

General von Uhland as he ate. 'Kemmler's undead are dismantling Castle Reikguard. Already all of the buildings of the lower courtyard have been put to the torch, and the exterior walls have lost most of their crenellations.' He gave a grim smile. 'Were we to wait long enough, he would tear down the walls entirely, and we could ride in and attack, but we cannot wait. We cannot allow Castle Reikguard to become indefensible. We must win it back as whole as we can.'

'But how are we to get in without smashing down the gates or the walls?' asked one of the general's officers. 'Can we climb in?'

'It would be a slaughter,' said another man. 'The dead would tear us apart as we topped the walls.'

'With luck, it won't come to that,' said von Uhland. He nodded to Dominic. 'Lord Reiklander knows of a secret way into the castle that comes out in Karl Franz's apartments. A picked squad of men—'

'Kemmler knows that route,' said Felix. 'He used it. It will be guarded.'

Dominic's head came up. 'How? How did he learn of it? Who betrayed the secret?'

Felix hesitated. He was fairly certain it had been Dominic's mother who had told Kemmler the way in – thinking she was inviting in the kindly old man who would cure her husband. 'I – I don't know,' he said.

'It doesn't much matter how he knows,' said von Uhland. 'The question is, how well will it be guarded?'

Gotrek raised his head from his shovelling and swallowed noisily. 'That doesn't matter either,' he said. 'Nothing will stop me from facing Krell again.'

'Same goes for Snorri,' said Snorri.

Gotrek shot the old slayer an angry look at that, but Snorri didn't seem to notice.

'I was hoping you would say that, Slayer Gurnisson,'

said von Uhland. 'Someone must get in and open the gates for us, someone who knows the castle and who has the ability to reach the lower gatehouse. Someone who is quite prepared to die.'

'A Slayer is always prepared to die,' said Gotrek.

'I will go too!' said Dominic.

The general pursed his lips. 'My lord Reiklander, I cannot of course forbid you, but with your father dead you are the last heir of Castle Reikguard. It would be wiser if you stayed with the main force, and fought in the storming.'

'No!' said Dominic, his jaw clenching. 'Reikguard is my castle. I will not have it handed to me by my uncle's honour guard. *I* will take it. *I* will lead the infiltration!'

The general looked like he wished to say more, but at last only nodded. 'As you wish, my lord.'

'I will come as well,' said Max. 'You will need someone to shield you from Kemmler's sorceries and his witch sight.'

'As will we,' said the magister and the priest of Morr in unison. 'We are well used to dealing with the undead.'

'And I,' said Felix. 'I'm in.'

Gotrek looked from him to Snorri and back, his eye hard. 'You have made a pledge to me, manling. Do you forsake it?'

Felix looked down, unable to meet his gaze. 'Kat is there, Gotrek. If she lives, I must save her. If she is dead, I must avenge her. I am willing to die for it. I'm sorry, but–'

'Forget it, manling,' Gotrek grunted. 'I won't stop you.' He turned his eye back to Snorri. 'But there is one who will not go.'

As GENERAL VON Uhland and his captains rose and left the mess tent to make ready to march, Max crossed to

Gotrek's table and sat down beside Felix.

'I am glad to see you recovered, Gotrek,' he said. 'It seems a miracle.'

Gotrek shrugged and kept eating. 'Dwarfs have strong constitutions.'

'Even so,' said Max, 'not three hours ago, I counted you among the dead, and now you seem fully recovered.'

'Not yet,' said Gotrek. 'It'll take a few more beers.'

Max laughed then paused and turned to Snorri, smiling quizzically. 'Yes, Snorri?'

Felix looked around to see that Snorri was staring at the magister across the table, his brow furrowed.

'You look familiar to Snorri,' said the old slayer. 'Does Snorri know you?'

Max raised an eyebrow. 'Max Schreiber, Snorri. You don't remember?'

'Snorri remembers Max Schreiber,' said Snorri. 'Do you know him?'

Max looked at Gotrek and Felix, confused. Gotrek just grunted and looked away.

Felix swallowed, and leaned in to speak in Max's ear. 'Snorri has some... difficulties with his memory.'

Max looked across the table to Snorri, then nodded, grim. 'I wondered if this might happen,' he murmured. 'There were already signs of it when last I saw him in Praag, twenty years ago. I had hoped he might find his doom before–'

Gotrek got up abruptly and strode off, batting out of the mess tent and into the night.

Max looked after him, confused. 'Did I say something wrong?'

Felix coughed, then drew Max further down the table. 'Snorri has forgotten his shame,' Felix said softly. 'According to Gotrek, he will not be welcomed into

Grimnir's halls until he remembers it, which means that–'

'That he cannot die until he regains his memory,' broke in Max, nodding sadly. 'He cannot act as a slayer should.'

Snorri looked up at them, puzzled. Apparently they hadn't moved far enough to escape his keen dwarfen hearing.

'Snorri doesn't know what you're talking about,' said Snorri as Felix reddened. 'Snorri remembers his shame.'

Felix blinked, his heart thumping with sudden hope. 'You – you remember?' he asked. 'Truly?'

'Of course,' said Snorri. 'How could Snorri forget? It was…'

Felix and Max waited as the old slayer's gaze turned inwards and he paused, his fork halfway to his mouth.

'It was…'

A look of panic began to spread over Snorri's cheerful, ugly face, and his eyes darted left and right, as if his memory might be hiding in some corner of the tent.

'It was…'

Snorri's hand slowly lowered, and he laid his forkful of meat back on his plate. Now his eyes stared off into some unimaginable distance. 'Snorri has forgotten his shame,' he said softly. 'This is bad.'

Felix winced. 'Snorri, you already knew this,' he said. 'You told us on the way to the Barren Hills. You're going to Karak Kadrin to pray for the return of your memory at the Shrine of Grimnir.'

Snorri stuffed the meat into his mouth and chewed angrily. 'Snorri remembers,' he said. 'He just forgot that he forgot for a moment.' But the pain on the old slayer's face told Felix that he was lying. The loss was as fresh as the first time he had realised it.

Felix and Max exchanged another look, then Felix had

to turn away. How horrible to have to experience over and over again the pain of learning that you had forgotten the most important thing in your life – the key to your only chance at redemption.

'Wizard, come here.'

Felix and Max turned. Gotrek was standing in the door of the tent, looking at Snorri, his face hard and closed. Max crossed to him, and Felix stood and went with him.

'What is it, Gotrek?' asked Max.

'Snorri Nosebiter will need a sleeping draught,' he said.

Max looked over his shoulder at Snorri. 'Now? But there is less than an hour before we start for the castle.'

'Now,' said Gotrek through gritted teeth. 'Snorri isn't going.'

Max frowned, then nodded. 'Ah. I see. Very well, Slayer. It will be done.'

Gotrek grunted and turned away again, walking off into the darkness. The pain behind his rage was almost harder to witness than Snorri's confusion. Gotrek was the most honest person Felix had ever met – not the kindest by any means, but he never lied or engaged in trickery – so to be forced to go behind Snorri's back and drug him so that he would stay behind and not seek his doom was obviously killing him – even though it meant saving his old friend's eternity.

TWENTY-FOUR

MAX BROUGHT SNORRI a huge stein of beer as he was having his third helping of sausages, and by the time von Uhland's army moved out for Castle Reikguard an hour later, he was snoring noisily, his head down on the table and his hand still clasped around the stein.

Felix didn't dare meet Gotrek's eye as they left the old Slayer behind and followed Max, Father Marwalt, Magister Marhalt, Dominic Reiklander and six picked Reiksguard knights out of the camp. Gotrek was as tensed as a bear trap, and Felix didn't care to get his leg bitten off. He hoped the others were smart enough to sense his mood as well, or there would likely be violence before they reached the castle.

While von Uhland's main force marched off due east along the main road, Lord Dominic led the infiltrators by the light of a slotted lantern through the trees to the woods north of the fields that surrounded Castle

Reikguard, where he said the entrance to the secret tunnel was hidden. Felix grew wary as they got close, for these had been the woods from which Kemmler's horde had poured. The bats had risen from this wood, and the siege towers had been built at its edge. But now, it seemed, they were deserted. He neither heard nor saw any evidence of the undead, nor of any other being. No birds sang in the branches. No rabbit or fox or badger rattled through the undergrowth, and with the winter branches as yet unbudded, it was as if they moved through a dead world – as if they might be the last men alive in the Empire.

As he trudged along at the back of the line with Gotrek, Felix kept finding himself staring at the twin brothers, Father Marwalt and Magister Marhalt, who walked side by side in the centre of the line, their heads together as if having a private conversation, but without speaking a word. Finally, his curiosity got the better of him, and he edged up to Max, who was just ahead of him in the line.

'Max,' he said softly, nodding ahead. 'The father and the magister, do... do they have some sort of connection?'

Max smiled slyly. 'Besides the obvious?' he asked. 'Yes, they can speak with only their minds. Indeed, that is partly how they came to choose their professions.'

He dropped back with Felix and continued, filling his pipe with tobacco. 'There was a third brother, Marnalt – another twin – and the three could speak to each other in this manner from birth, but then Marnalt was murdered by a necromancer, and used for foul experiments. After his death, however, the dead brother came to the living pair in their dreams, and they discovered that they could communicate together as they had when they were alive.' Max made a flame appear at the end of his finger and lit the pipe, then went on. 'Marnalt begged his brothers to find a way to free him from his ghostly unlife and let him pass on to Morr's realm, and so the brothers found their calling. Marwalt sought the answer to his brother's predicament in the teachings of Morr, while Marhalt entered the Amethyst College to seek a sorcerous solution, and in the process, each discovered that they had great natural abilities, which they have since used to fight necromancy in all its forms.'

'And did they free their brother?' asked Felix.

'Oh yes,' said Max. 'And exposed, ruined and destroyed the villain who had imprisoned his soul, and the souls of a thousand other children.' He smiled and started ahead again. 'They have been much in demand since then.'

A while later, with the moons both low in the sky, Lord Dominic slowed to a stop and pointed ahead.

'The passage is in front of us,' he said. 'About fifty paces.'

Max nodded. 'Go quietly then,' he said. 'There may be guards.'

Felix and Gotrek and the Reiksguard knights drew their weapons as Dominic closed his slotted lantern, and Max and the robed twins mumbled spells and invocations. When all were prepared, they crept forwards again, and after a minute came to a small clearing. There was a charcoal maker's hut to one side, long since burned to the ground and slowly returning to the forest. Creepers overgrew the exterior walls and dead weeds pushed up through the planks of the little porch.

'I sense no one,' said Max.

'Nor any necromantic construct,' said Father Marwalt.

'Nor spell of death,' said Magister Marhalt.

'On, then,' said Dominic.

They entered the clearing, and quickly saw that it had

been recently visited. The brush was crushed flat, and there were footprints in the leaf mould, some made by bare feet, some by heavy boots, and some by feet made of only bones.

'The entrance is in the hut,' said Dominic. 'It was hidden, but…'

The Reiksguard captain took the lead and stuck his head in cautiously. After a quick look, he motioned the others on.

Felix followed Gotrek in and looked around. The interior was as dilapidated as the outside, roofless and weed-choked, but in one corner, the charred planks had been pulled up, revealing a square hole of masoned stone below, with steps descending into darkness. A stone hatch lay cracked into two heavy pieces beside it. Dominic grunted as he saw it.

'Softly, friends,' said Max. 'There may be guards in the tunnel.'

'I'll go first,' said Gotrek.

No one argued, and the Slayer walked towards the steps with Felix following after. Dominic Reiklander stepped in at his side and opened his lantern again, but the Reiksguard captain coughed.

'My lord,' he said, 'perhaps we should go ahead.'

Dominic shook his head, though his face was pale. 'No, Captain Hoetker,' he said. 'I will not be given my castle. I will take it.'

The captain looked unhappy, but could only incline his head respectfully and form up behind him. Max and the twins took up the rear, and the procession followed Gotrek into the dark.

The tunnel was two men wide, and went straight south for as far as Felix could see – which was admittedly not very far. Beyond the glow of the lantern it was pitch-dark, but it was clear that Gotrek could see well enough, for he stumped forwards unconcerned, his axe swinging at his side.

A few moments later, something glittered in the darkness ahead of them, and Felix could make out a big lump blocking the passage. Gotrek didn't slow, but everyone else did, going on guard and whispering to each other as they went on. In a few more steps, the glittering became a spill of gold coins, and the lump became a body, slumped against one wall, its eyes bulging and its hands to its chest.

'Von Geldrecht!' gasped Dominic.

It was indeed the steward, his every pocket bulging with gold, and with packs, pouches and sacks heavy-laden with the stuff strapped and slung all over his body.

'And your father's treasure,' said Felix. 'He tricked your mother into unlocking its hiding place.'

'The thief!' snarled the young lord. 'He always *was* too fond of gold.'

'Well,' said Max, squatting by the body and looking into its eyes, 'then you will be pleased to hear he died of it. The strain of carrying it was too much.'

Gotrek snorted. 'Pathetic.'

Dominic looked uncertainly at the spilled treasure, then motioned for them to continue. 'We will have to leave it for the moment. None of you will speak of this until it is recovered. Understood?'

There was a general murmur of assent, though some of the knights looked over their shoulders as they went on, and Felix frowned back at it, puzzled.

'Why wasn't he picked clean by Draeger and his men?' asked Felix. 'This was their escape route.'

'Then they didn't get this far,' said Gotrek.

And about a hundred paces further in, the Slayer's prediction proved true. The passage was clotted with dismembered bodies and broken weapons, and blood festooned the walls.

'Who were these?' asked Dominic as he picked his way fastidiously through the carnage.

'A militia captain and his men,' said Felix. 'They tried to escape after Kemmler and his wights came in.' He grimaced as he found Draeger amongst the bodies. He was in three parts, and partially eaten. 'It seems they met some stragglers.'

Dominic shivered, then continued on.

The passage ended at last against a wall of massive, dwarf-cut stone that Felix realised must be the foundations of Castle Reikguard's outer walls. There was a thick, iron-bound stone door set in the blocks, wide open.

'Hold,' said Father Marwalt and Magister Marhalt, as Gotrek approached it. 'There are wards here.'

The Slayer stopped and waited impatiently as Max and the twins muttered and probed the air before them with cautious hands, conferring all the while. Finally, Father Marwalt turned and spread his long-fingered hands. All the colour seemed to drain out of the air between his palms, and a cloud of grey mist billowed forth, rolling towards the dwarf and the men. It was as cold as the grave.

Gotrek growled and lifted his axe. 'Curse your sorcery, death priest,' he snarled. 'What is this?'

'What are you doing?' barked Dominic. 'Desist!'

Magister Marhalt held up a hand as his brother continued the spell. 'Fear not,' he said. 'It is an invocation called Morr's Mask. It is harmless, if unpleasant. It will hide our warmth and heartbeats and make us appear dead to the undead. It is oft used by paladins of Morr to get close to their prey.'

A clammy chill permeated Felix's clothes, leaving a

sticky film of damp on his skin. His breath clouded, then grew too cold to make steam. The tips of his fingers were blue.

'You are making corpses of us,' said Dominic, revulsed.

'My lord, I promise you,' said Magister Marhalt, 'it is only a mask. With it, we should be able to walk past any undead, for they will believe us more of their own kind.'

Dominic and the knights whispered prayers and made signs of the gods as the cloud settled around them. Gotrek cursed in Khazalid and glared at the priest and the magister with one cold eye, but he stayed his axe.

A moment later Father Marwalt lowered his arms, then ducked his head apologetically. 'I'm sorry,' he said. 'I should have explained first. I am unused to fighting alongside those who are not of Morr's temple.' He motioned to the door. 'You may go in. The wards will not notice us now.'

Gotrek strode to the door and went in without pausing. The rest followed more hesitantly. Felix could feel nothing as they passed through except the cold mist of the priest's spell, which moved with them as they went. Inside, the passage turned right, following the castle wall until it ended at a narrow spiral stair. The stair was almost too thin for Gotrek to enter, and he had to turn sideways and hold his axe behind him in order to climb it. Felix couldn't imagine how the huge wights had done it – unless they had deformed themselves in some way.

The stairs went on and on, around and around and around until Felix thought he was in some horrible looping nightmare where he was forced to climb forever without getting anywhere. Finally, however, long after his knees were ready to give out and his mind ready to scream, the steps ended at a short corridor with one wall of stone, and one wall of wood. Rather, the corridor had once had a wooden wall, but it had been smashed through, as if by an explosion, and the panelling and struts and the remains of the secret door that had been set into it were now strewn across the carpeted floor of the ruins of a stately bedroom.

A canopied bed larger than the charcoal burner's shack through which they had entered rose against one wall, the initials KF picked out in gold on the headboard, and beautiful pieces of furniture and giant paintings of the Emperor's august ancestors lined the panelled walls, now all sadly smashed and slashed.

Gotrek brought his axe into guard and stepped through the splintered wall into the room, looking around, then motioned the others forwards. They ducked through behind him, swords and spells at the ready.

'Come,' said Dominic, shaking his head at the wreckage as he crossed towards the far door. 'The stairs are this way.'

They passed through an entryway lined with suits of armour, then through a shattered door to a landing that Felix recognised. It was there that Kemmler had appeared to them before taking the graf and grafin away in his cloud of shadows. Felix edged to the railing and looked down. Below was the door to Graf Reiklander's apartments, and the pile of bodies of the men who had died there – the young spearman, the handgunner, the artilleryman, Classen and Bosendorfer. At least, he thought with a glance at Dominic, the corpses of the graf and grafin were not among them.

Movement from further below drew his eye and he looked down the well of the stairway. The ground floor was crawling with shuffling zombies, wandering aimlessly and bumping into each other, as well as a few ghouls, their heads twitching nervously this way and that as they hunched over dead bodies and sucked the marrow from their bones. Felix tried not to wonder if any of those bodies, or any of the zombies, was Kat. He must focus on the task at hand.

He turned away and prepared to follow Gotrek with the others, but the Slayer stopped and raised his axe. The rune upon its head was blazing as bright as Felix had ever seen it, and reflected red in Gotrek's single eye.

'The necromancer is here,' he growled.

'Yes,' said Magister Marhalt, his eyes half-closed. 'Below us, on the ground floor. We must be careful.'

Father Marwalt put a finger to his lips. 'Quiet from here on and move slowly,' he said. 'The undead will not notice us.'

'And remember,' added Max, shooting a hard glance at Gotrek and Felix, 'our aim is to open the gates for von Uhland, *not* to have any unnecessary fights. You may fight as you like *after* we have let the army in.'

Gotrek grunted, but made no complaint, and they all turned and started down the steps at a ponderous crawl.

It was like something out of a nightmare, thought Felix – walking through a house full of the living dead as if invisible, and all the while fearing that one would come upon a loved one. With thudding heart, he scanned each pile of bodies they passed, looking for, but praying he wouldn't find, the tatters of a heavy wool coat, or a broken bow or hatchet, among the bones. He saw nothing, but that was no guarantee Kat still lived. She might have been eaten. She might be a zombie. She might have been chopped to pieces by Krell and left on the wall.

The ground floor as they reached it was thick with zombies and ghouls, and Felix found it difficult not to go on guard as they neared them. Some of the knights couldn't help themselves, and Max and the twins had to surreptitiously grasp their arms to remind them to lower their swords.

Felix clenched his teeth until they ached, expecting at any moment that one of the horrors would look up and see them as interlopers and groan warning to the others, but they didn't. Even the ghouls, who were living things, with almost human intelligence, gave them no more than a passing glance. Still, he couldn't help holding his breath, or gripping the hilt of his sword.

The keep's grand foyer was ten paces down a broad corridor – a high, marble-floored entry hall with the door to the courtyard around the corner to the right, and the open double doors of the great hall to the left, and as they shuffled towards it through the crowds of undead, Felix began to hear low murmurings and whisperings coming from within the dining hall.

'Eyes front,' whispered Max. 'He is there.'

But as they entered the foyer and turned towards the front door, Felix couldn't help but look back, and neither could any of the others – not Gotrek, not Dominic, not even Max or Father Marwalt or Magister Marhalt, who all slanted their eyes over their shoulders as they walked on.

Felix had had a brief glance at the dining hall once before, when he'd entered the keep with von Volgen and Classen and the others to confront Grafin Avelein, and he remembered it as a regal room with heraldic shields and tapestries on the walls, chandeliers hanging from the ceiling, long, richly set tables below a raised dais and tall windows looking out onto a formal garden.

It was regal no more.

The shields and tapestries had been torn down, and

in their place, strange symbols were scrawled in blood on the bare stone walls. The chandeliers had been replaced by inverted corpses, headless and dripping black fluids from the stumps of their necks. The tables had been smashed and thrown to the corners to make room for an eldritch circle, burned and gouged into the polished wood floor. Ringing the circle at nine points were bronze braziers in which burned mounds of severed heads, hands and arms, the fat and the flesh of them popping and hissing in the flames.

And in the centre of it all was a scene so strange it made Felix stumble in shock. It seemed to have been arranged as a sick parody of some old harvest ritual, where the lord and lady of the land would give their blessing to their peasants' crops and toast the bounty of nature. There were two thrones in the circle, each carved with the eagle and crown of the Reikland, and squirming in those thrones were the undead corpses of Graf Reiklander and Grafin Avelein – dressed in the full regalia of the ancient princes of the Reikland. Sable robes with ermine cuffs were draped around their bony shoulders, jewelled crowns slipped sideways on their shrunken skulls, chains of office hung across their sunken chests, swords and sceptres were clutched awkwardly in withered claws, and around them, mounded up on all sides of the thrones, was a bounteous feast of famine that was decaying as Felix watched.

Sheaves of wheat gone rotten were crossed at the corpses' feet. Cadaverous hogs lay trussed on platters, so gaunt their ribs had broken through their crumbling skin. Baskets of apples and cabbages and leeks, black and shrivelled, collapsed between spilled sacks of wormy flour and mouldy grain. The skulls of cattle and the bones of sheep, goats and geese lay in heaps. And standing before it all, his robes whipping in an unnatural wind and his arms flung wide like a priest giving a benediction, was Kemmler, his skull-topped staff gripped in one hand as he keened a cacophonous incantation.

A black nimbus flickered around him, curdling the air, and he seemed to be drawing it from the dead graf and grafin, and from the foul offerings that he had gathered around them. With each syllable of his chant the corpses and the bounty seemed to wither more, while the crowns and swords and chains the graf and grafin wore rusted and blackened and crumbled to dust as the rippling energy around the necromancer grew darker and more tangible.

It was the spell of blight again, Felix was sure of it – the same evil pall that Kemmler had cast upon the castle, poisoning the water and ruining the food, the spell that had starved and weakened the defenders and made them easy prey for his minions. Now he was casting it again inside Castle Reikguard, upon the rulers of Castle Reikguard, and if what Father Marwalt and Magister Marhalt had said was true, it would affect all the lands that made up its domain – the blight would spread across all the Reikland. Every well would be poisoned. All the food would wither, rot and die. The people would starve. The army would die on its feet. With one spell, Kemmler would defeat the forces of the Empire before his undead horde marched a single step.

'Mother,' choked Dominic. 'Father!'

Felix clamped a hand over the boy's mouth and looked around, afraid he had been heard, but a second later Gotrek pushed past them both, stalking towards the great hall as he ran his thumb along the blade of his axe and drew blood.

Felix gaped, and made to call after him. Max beat him to it.

'Gotrek!' hissed the magister, grabbing for him. 'What are you doing? I said you weren't to fight!'

Gotrek shrugged him off without breaking step. 'No one does that to a slayer,' he growled. 'No one!'

Felix had no idea what he was talking about. Slayer? Which slayer? Was Snorri here? Had he somehow woken from his drugged stupor and beaten them here?

Then he saw what Gotrek had seen, and he paled. Rodi Balkisson stood at one of the flaming braziers, feeding a severed head into the fire from a bucket full of body parts that he held in his left hand. There was a terrible axe wound in his chest, and his lower jaw and beard were missing, leaving a crusted red hole in his face where they should have been. There was no mistaking the braided slayer's crest or massive physique, however. It was Rodi, and he was dead, and yet he walked. Nor was he the only one. Kemmler had also raised others to be his servants – Tauber, Sergeant Leffler and von Volgen also held buckets and fed the grisly fires as well.

Max and Father Marwalt and Magister Marhalt tiptoed frantically after Gotrek, whispering after him to come back. The Slayer didn't heed them. He strode into the great hall and chopped off Rodi's head with a single slash of his glowing rune axe.

'Go to Grimnir, Rodi Balkisson,' said Gotrek.

TWENTY-FIVE

KEMMLER TURNED, HIS incantation faltering, as Rodi's body and jawless head thudded to the floor behind him.

'You have dishonoured the dead of the dwarfs, necromancer,' said Gotrek, launching himself at him. 'You will die for it.'

Kemmler leapt back, crying out in fear, and vanished into a cloud of darkness that erupted from his cloak.

The Slayer skidded to a stop, glaring around, then roared and charged out of sight to the right, bellowing, 'Stand aside, wight! The defiler dies first!'

'The dwarf is insane,' whispered Father Marwalt and Magister Marhalt, as Felix and Max hurried for the door.

'He is a slayer,' said Max over his shoulder. 'Sanity doesn't enter the equation.'

'Then I am a slayer too,' cried Dominic, and charged after them, drawing his sword. 'My mother and father must be avenged!'

'But, my lord, the gates!' called Captain Hoetker. 'We must open the gates!'

The young lord didn't listen. He shoved past Felix and Max as they reached the door, and plunged on in the direction Gotrek had gone.

Felix blanched as he saw what the boy was running towards. 'Lord Dominic! Come back!'

The right end of the great hall was a raised dais – the place where the graf and grafin's thrones should have been. A curtained musicians' gallery rose above it, and a mural of Young Sigmar killing Blacktusk the Boar was painted behind it. Now it was bare of furniture, and full of wights. Kemmler stood in the centre of a square of motionless skeletal warriors, crooning out another incantation while below him on the dais's broad stairs, Gotrek fought Krell, the Lord of the Undead.

Felix raced forwards, reaching after Dominic, but he was too far back. The young lord shouldered in beside the Slayer and started hewing at the wight king like a woodsman. Unfortunately, his sword strokes were wild and glancing and did nothing. He looked like a terrier trying to help a bulldog fight a bear, and quickly met a terrier's fate. As Krell slashed at Gotrek, Dominic got in the way, and was smashed backwards into the rotting bounty at the foot of his father's throne, his sword sheared in half and his armour crumpled at the shoulder.

Felix ran to him as the Reiksguarders thundered in. He was stunned, and groaning in pain, but thankfully seemed uncut by Krell's axe.

'He lives?' asked Captain Hoetker, hurrying past.

'Aye,' said Felix.

'Well, keep him back.'

The knights charged forwards to attack Krell, and were

followed into the room by a tide of zombies and ghouls.

'Father!' shouted Max. 'Magister!'

The twins turned, and Magister Marhalt backed from the door, mumbling cantrips and pulling something from his sleeves, while Father Marwalt pulled a stick of charcoal from his robes and began to recite a prayer to Morr.

Below the dais, Krell whirled his axe in a wide arc as the Reiksguarders fell in with Gotrek to attack him. Two of the knights tried to turn the blow on their shields and crashed down, shields sundered and arms maimed and flecked with black slivers.

'Get back, fools!' growled Gotrek, and Max echoed him.

'Knights!' he shouted. 'Leave Krell to the Slayer! Kill the wights! Attack Kemmler!'

At the door, Magister Marhalt held out a gold-chased human skull towards the undead who were shuffling into the room and cried an arcane phrase. The skull's jewelled eyes emitted a violet light that went through them like a shockwave. They flew backwards into the entry hall, knocking back those behind and disintegrating as they fell – arms, legs and torsos breaking into rotting chunks.

With the doorway momentarily clear, Father Marwalt rushed to it and drew a thick black line across the threshold with his charcoal, then dodged back. The zombies and ghouls came forwards again, but when they tried to step over the line, their flesh blackened and cracked as if they were being consumed by invisible flames. They could not cross it.

Felix looked back to the dais. The Reiksguarders had done Max's bidding and were attacking Kemmler's protective square of wights, leaving Gotrek to fight Krell all on his own.

The Slayer was revelling in it, raining blows on the wight king with a maniacal smile twisting his face. This, at last, thought Felix, was the fight Gotrek had been looking for since he had first crossed axes with Krell on the walls of the castle seven days ago. There were no distractions now – no undead wyvern to get in the way or allow Krell to escape, no interfering rivals, no worries about keeping Snorri alive. There was only a fight to the finish with a worthy enemy.

The dwarf and undead warrior were so evenly matched that it seemed neither would ever gain an advantage. No matter how fast Gotrek's axe blurred, Krell's was there to meet it. No matter how powerful Krell's strikes, Gotrek returned them with equal force, and the air shivered with the ringing of obsidian on steel.

Felix hauled the semi-conscious Dominic out of the way as Gotrek sent Krell crashing into Kemmler's ritual circle, then leapt after him.

'My lord,' said Felix, as Krell surged up again and the battle roiled their way. 'Can you stand?'

The boy only groaned and Felix dragged him further back.

Behind his protective wall of wights, Kemmler's arcane incantation was rising to a crescendo, but Max and Magister Marhalt and Father Marwalt were casting spells of their own to counter it. Magister Marhalt trained the jewelled sockets of his golden skull on the necromancer and bathed him in its burning violet stare. Max scribed glowing words in the air with one hand while brandishing a round metal mirror with the other. A white-gold light poured from the disc as if it were reflecting the light of the sun, and the beam seared Kemmler's eyes. Father Marwalt held a flickering black candle and recited traditional Morrian burial prayers, meant to lay the dead to rest and keep them there – and it appeared to be working, for the verdigised axes of Kemmler's wights seemed to be slowing, and the swords of the Reiksguarders were bashing through their defences and striking bronze and bone.

But, though Max's light blinded him and Magister Marhalt's fire burned him, Kemmler managed to shriek the last words of his incantation and thrust his skull-topped staff out before him.

A ripple of shadow burst from the staff and Max and the twins gasped and staggered. Felix did too, a wave of dizzying weakness buckling his knees. The Reiks-guarders were affected as well, and suddenly it was their swords that were faltering, and the wights that were smashing them back. Felix groaned. His arms were shaking and his heart beating fast but faint. It felt as if all the days of thirst and starvation he had experienced during the siege were happening to him now in the span of a minute.

Then, just as he felt he would collapse next to Lord Dominic, a shimmer of gold passed through him and the sick weakness lessened, though not entirely. He looked around. Max stood before the dais, braced as if against a high wind, his arms outstretched and shaking, pushing the walls of a sphere of golden light out to encompass them all.

Protected by Max's ward, the twins renewed their prayers and incantations, though their hands pushed though their ritual motions like they were neck deep in quicksand. Kemmler had also thrown up a shield – a whirlwind of spectral forms and half-seen faces that swirled around him, screaming and dying as they blocked the purple light.

The only ones apparently unaffected by all the prayers and spells and counterspells were Gotrek and Krell, who fought on, oblivious, to everything but their close-fought combat. Krell slammed Gotrek backwards into a jumble of tables, smashing them to splinters, then charged in as the Slayer rolled from the wreckage and slashed behind him with his axe. The strike tore away Krell's greave and boot, leaving him limping on a bare bone foot, but he came on regardless, and his next strike sent Gotrek crashing into the braziers that ringed the circle and sending burning hands, feet and heads flying everywhere.

Felix pulled Dominic out of the way again, and the boy finally stumbled to his feet.

'This way, my lord,' said Felix. 'Keep back.'

But as he drew Dominic away, he bumped into something behind him, and turned to find Sergeant Leffler swinging his two-handed sword at him.

Felix gasped and ducked, and the blade whooshed an inch over his head – and gashed Dominic's shoulder. From their left, the corpse of Surgeon Tauber lurched in, hands outstretched, and from their right, Lord von Volgen was stabbing at them with his long sword.

Dominic twisted aside and gashed von Volgen with his broken sword, but the wound didn't slow the corpse in the slightest, and it slashed at him again.

Felix parried the blow and kicked von Volgen back, then bulled into Dominic to get him out of the path of Leffler's two-hander.

'Stay behind me,' he shouted.

Felix chopped Tauber's head off as the zombies crowded in, then smashed the heavy two-handed sword from the sergeant's hands and ran him through the neck. That left only von Volgen. The corpse of the lord lurched towards him, but as Felix raised Karaghul to hack at it, its sword arm dropped, a sad expression on its face.

Felix faltered, but instinct carried the blow and he cut von Volgen's head from his body. His heart hammered as the corpse fell. It had seemed as if the zombie had allowed itself to be killed, almost as if it had been begging for it. But that wasn't possible, was it? Had some portion of von Volgen's soul remained trapped in its undead cage?

A movement brought his head around and banished the thought. Dominic was staggering once again towards the battle between Gotrek and Krell, and trying to raise his broken sword with his battered arm. Felix stepped after him.

'My lord,' he said, 'leave it to the Slayer.'

The young lord waved him back. 'I must do something! I must have some part in–'

He stopped as he found himself face to face with his mother and father. The corpses were writhing in their thrones and Felix saw that they had been tied there. They strained against the ropes, snapping at Felix and their son with mindless hunger.

Dominic stared at them, then choked back a sob. 'This is what I must do. I must do as the Slayer did, and free them as he freed his friend.'

The boy threw aside his broken blade and instead drew from its scabbard the sword strapped to his father's side. The corpse tried to claw at him, but the rope held it and it couldn't reach.

Aged by Kemmler's death magic, the blade was spotted with rust, but still whole enough to do the job. Dominic raised it over his head, then faced the grafin with tears in his eyes.

'Go to Sigmar, mother,' he said, then swept her shrivelled head from her neck. She made no noise as she died, but behind his wall of wights, Kemmler screamed as if the sword had struck him.

'Foolish boy! You're ruining it!'

His cry of rage turned into a shriek of pain as Max and Magister Marhalt's spells lanced through his lost concentration, but almost instantly, his shadows billowed forth again, growing stronger than before.

'Spoiler!' he shrieked. 'Vandal!'

'Finish it, my lord!' shouted Felix, stepping between the boy and the expanding darkness. 'Strike while you can!'

Dominic raised his sword over his father. 'Go to Sigmar, father.'

Again he struck true, and the graf's head tumbled off his shoulders.

Kemmler howled, and with a silent thunderclap the boiling ball of darkness around him exploded outwards in all directions, and his enervating power blasted Felix and Dominic and the other living men to their knees.

All the weakness that Max's sphere of protection had momentarily mitigated returned again tenfold. Felix's limbs would not support his weight. His heart beat so fast he felt it might explode, but it seemed to be pumping bile, not blood. His head swam and his vision blackened at the corners. Dominic dropped his father's sword. Max and Father Marwalt and Magister Marhalt were the same, arms shaking and struggling to rise. The knights who had been fighting the wights had collapsed too, and the ancient warriors were chopping them to pieces. And at the door, the black line of charcoal was greying and the zombies were beginning to push through it.

Even Gotrek seemed to have been stricken by the spell. He staggered back from Krell as if on his last legs, his torso a mass of bruises and his rune axe hanging heavy in his hands. The undead champion howled in triumph and strode after him, raising his black axe for a savage blow. But as it swung down, trailing its choking cloud, Gotrek jolted forwards and chopped hard at the haft of it, then twisted savagely and up.

Krell bellowed in surprise as the black axe flew from his gauntleted grip and spun up to the ceiling to bite into one of the great hall's gilded beams. It stuck there, quivering, twenty feet over his head.

Gotrek laughed and sprang, slashing for his legs, as the towering wight stumbled back.

'Two thousand years of grudges,' growled the Slayer, 'crossed out in a single stroke!'

Gotrek hacked at the undead champion's exposed leg bone and chopped through it like dry wood. Krell toppled to the floor in a deafening crash, and the Slayer straddled him, swinging down with his rune axe blazing red.

'No!' cried Kemmler, from the dais, and began incanting a new spell.

There was no stopping the axe's deadly trajectory. It cleaved through the champion's breastplate and buried itself in his rib cage. Krell struggled to rise, but Gotrek kicked him in the teeth and wrenched his axe free, grinning wildly.

'A single stroke, butcher!'

He raised the rune axe over his head for the final blow to the neck, but on the dais behind him, Kemmler thrust forwards with his staff and the skull that topped it opened its mouth, puking out a stream of roiling black energy.

Gotrek grunted and went rigid as the darkness struck him in the back, his grin turning into a rictus grimace as every muscle in his body tensed. Felix stared. It was a rare thing to see the Slayer affected by magic at all, let alone paralysed by it, but as shocking as that was, that wasn't all it was doing to him. As Felix watched, the lines in the Slayer's face deepened, and his cheeks grew gaunt. His body was growing leaner as well, every detail of his muscles and veins standing out from his skin as if he had been flayed.

Nor was he the only one affected by the spell. The flesh of Felix's fingers was shrinking and his knuckle bones poked through his tightening skin like tent poles. Max and the twins were the same. Max's silver hair was turning white at the roots, and the magister and the father were ageing before Felix's eyes, their spells and invocations weakening and flickering out. Kemmler's withering blast was pressing them all into the grave – a hand like that of time itself, crushing them with the weight of years – while more and more zombies broke through Marwalt's ward and shuffled into the room.

The Slayer turned, inch by straining inch, as if frozen in ice, and raised his rune axe in a shaking hand, but he couldn't turn fast enough. He was weakening with every half-step. He would never be able to reach the necromancer before the spell turned him into a walking skeleton.

Felix struggled to his feet, as weak as a broken reed, and drew his dagger, but as he raised it to throw at Kemmler, something flashed down from above and stuck in Kemmler's shoulder.

Kemmler barked in surprise and fell back, his stream of black energy boiling away to nothing as he turned, looking for the source of the attack. There was an arrow in his shoulder, and as Felix stared, another flashed down and sprouted from the necromancer's leg. He screamed again and fell.

An arrow?

Felix's heart thudded like it was trying to escape his chest. An arrow!

At the opposite end of the room, Gotrek broke free of

his paralysis and ran for the necromancer with a blood-curdling howl of rage. Kemmler saw him coming and raised his staff in a trembling hand, spitting out the beginning of another incantation, but before he could utter more than a few syllables, the Slayer bounded onto the dais, smashed his way through the necromancer's remaining wights, and slashed down at him with all his might.

Kemmler blocked with his staff and Gotrek's rune axe chopped it in two, sending its grinning skull spinning to the side as a chorus of screams, like the dying of a thousand souls, shook the room and weird half-seen entities burst forth and vanished into the shadows. Then the axe found flesh, and Kemmler screamed as well, a great stain of blood spreading across his abdomen to darken his grey robes.

'Now, necromancer!' roared the Slayer as he raised his axe again. 'You die for your desecrations!'

But as Gotrek lashed down, misty shadows boiled up from Kemmler's cloak and enveloped them both in swirling darkness, and when it cleared, Gotrek was alone, his axe buried in the splintered planks of the dais, and his one eye blazing with frustrated fury.

'Coward!' he shouted at the air. 'Defiler!'

He turned with a growl to where he had brought down Krell, and charged back across the room towards the wight's still-prostrate form, but even as he ploughed through the rotting rubbish around the Reikland thrones, shadows formed around the fallen champion and by the time the Slayer reached him he was gone as well – even his axe had vanished from the ceiling – and Kemmler's voice echoed through the hall, coming from everywhere and nowhere at once.

'You have not defeated me, fools,' he hissed, 'only delayed me. I have all the time in the world.'

Gotrek cursed as the necromancer's mad laughter faded away, and he lashed around with his axe at nothing.

'Cursed!' he roared. 'Cursed!'

Felix turned from him as he heard moaning and shuffling behind him, and found the horde of zombies that was spilling through the door nearly at his back. He caught Lord Dominic's arm and pulled him up, and they staggered back from the dead, raising their swords together. Gotrek fell in beside them, still grunting angrily, and Max and Father Marwalt and Magister Marhalt rose behind them, corpse-thin and shaking from Kemmler's withering, but preparing spells nonetheless.

But as the zombies shuffled towards them, rusty weapons raised and claws outstretched, their steps began to falter, and their arms to droop. A big one in the apron of a butcher tripped and fell on its face. A woman in the remains of a rich dress lost an arm, then her lower jaw, then collapsed entirely, her skin putrefying before their eyes. The corpse of a beastman crashed down, taking several smaller zombies with him. Some of the others struggled gamely on, but they didn't last long. They were dropping like flies – the ones outside in the entry hall too. Finally the last of them crashed to its knees in front of Felix, its clawed fingers scratching feebly across the toe of his boot before stilling forever.

'Kemmler is gone,' whispered Father Marwalt, dropping into a broken chair.

'And his influence goes with him,' said Magister Marhalt, sagging to the floor. 'It is over.'

'For now,' said Max, letting his hands fall to his sides. 'How long before he comes again?'

Nobody had an answer for him. The twins just shivered where they slumped, while Dominic

Reiklander staggered to kneel before the headless corpses of his mother and father, and Gotrek cleaned his axe.

Felix could not yet rest. His hope wouldn't let him. He looked to the dais where Kemmler had been struck by the arrows, then turned, trying to figure out where the shafts had come from. Somewhere high up. They had shot *down* at Kemmler. There. The musicians' gallery above the dais. He stumbled towards it, his heart beginning to pound.

'Kat!' he called. 'Kat, was it you?'

There was no answer.

'Kat?'

Still nothing.

There was a door in the wall below the gallery. He threw it open. It was a water closet. He cursed and started for the door to the corridor, stumbling over the mounds of rotting corpses that choked it. The door to the gallery must be on the floor above. He limped down the hall to the stairs, feeling as frail and light as a bird skeleton from Kemmler's withering.

The stairs were almost too much for him, but he crawled up them at last, then made his way down the corridor. There was a small door on the left-hand wall. He stumbled to it and pulled on the knob. It was locked. He pounded on the panel, desperate now.

'Kat! Kat, are you in there?'

Nothing. He yanked at the door, then kicked it, but it was useless. He was too weak. He couldn't budge it. He couldn't break it. A sob escaped him.

'Stand aside, manling,' said Gotrek.

Felix looked up. He hadn't heard the Slayer approach, hadn't known he had followed him.

Gotrek chopped at the door with his axe, knocking a great hole in the panel, then reached through and turned the latch from the inside. He pulled it open and stood aside.

'Go on, manling,' he said.

TWENTY-SIX

FELIX HESITATED ON the threshold, almost afraid to go on now that the way was clear. What if she wasn't there? Or it wasn't her? Or…

He swallowed and stepped through into the narrow, curtained balcony. At first he could see nothing but the silhouettes of chairs and stools set in rough rows, and the pale litter of sheet music scattered on the floor. But then in the lee of the balustrade, he saw a small form, slumped and still.

'Kat!' he cried, stumbling through the chairs.

She lay on her back, eyes closed, her bow in her hands and an arrow nocked on the string, but so thin Felix didn't know how she'd had the strength to draw it. Her face, already gaunt when last he'd seen her, was a sunken skull, her skin stretched across the bones drumhead-tight.

He put a hand on her shoulder. 'Kat,' he whispered.

'Do you live?'

She didn't respond, didn't even seem to breathe. The arrow slipped from the string and clattered to the floor. Panic thudded again in Felix's chest.

'Kat, hang on.'

He reached down and got his arms under her and lifted. She was so light that, even weak as he was, he could stand with her in his arms. He staggered back to the door and out into the hall.

'Gotrek, bring the Shallyans!' he cried. 'Bring food!'

'Bring her to Max, manling,' said Gotrek. 'The Shallyans will come when we open the gate.'

Felix nodded and started downstairs, rushing so fast that twice he tripped, and would have fallen if Gotrek hadn't steadied him.

'Max,' called Felix, as he carried Kat into the great hall. 'Help her. Look at her.'

Max and the twins looked up, then made room as Felix laid Kat down beside them on the floor.

'This is the archer, then?' asked Max, kneeling. 'Who turned the tide and saved us all?' He looked up at Felix. 'You know her?'

Felix nodded, his throat tightening. 'She – she is–'

Max nodded. 'Ah. I see.' He smiled sadly as he looked Kat up and down. 'You've always liked the brave ones, haven't you, Felix?'

Father Marwalt put his right hand over Kat's heart and his left on her forehead, then closed his eyes. Felix held his breath. Max seemed to as well. Gotrek stepped to Felix's shoulder and crossed his arms, glaring at Kat as if trying to shame her into surviving.

After a long moment, Father Marwalt sat back on his knees. 'She is not Morr's concern,' he said. 'She stands on the threshold, but she has not yet passed through his portal.'

Felix choked out a sob of relief, and the tears he had held back until now streamed down his cheeks. What a fool! To cry at good news. What was the matter with him?

Max put a hand on his shoulder, and Felix nodded his thanks, then looked around for Gotrek.

The Slayer was walking towards the door to the corridor.

'Come on, manling,' he rasped over his shoulder. 'It takes four hands to open the gates.'

THOUGH OF COURSE relieved that he hadn't had to lose any men fighting against Kemmler's undead army, General von Uhland seemed almost let down that the infiltrators had done it all themselves and hadn't given him a battle. All the zombies and wights in the castle had dropped dead with the necromancer's retreat, and the ghouls had fled. There was no horde left to fight, and the general's troops were faced with the much less glamorous, but just as necessary, challenge of disposing of ten thousand mouldering corpses before they diseased the whole region.

Snorri, too, was less than pleased to have missed the climactic battle, and he was still muttering about it late that afternoon, as he and Gotrek sat on either side of Felix's bed in the room in the keep in which the general's surgeon had put him.

'Snorri blames himself,' said Snorri, scowling. 'He hasn't been that drunk in a long time.'

Gotrek said nothing, and seemed to be having trouble meeting his old friend's eye.

'Snorri has never had manling beer that had such a kick either,' Snorri continued, licking his lips. 'He wonders who makes it.'

There was another silence, and then Gotrek grunted angrily.

'I am to blame, Snorri Nosebiter,' he said, forcing the words out as if they were heavy stones. 'I had you drugged, so you would sleep.'

Snorri raised an eyebrow. It made him look like a confused dog. 'Snorri doesn't understand.'

Felix saw Gotrek clenching his jaw and balling his fist, and cut in to save him.

'You can't find your doom until you get your memory back, Snorri,' he said patiently. 'And we knew you would forget and want to come with us.'

Snorri blinked at him, still seemingly lost, then lowered his head. 'Yes,' he said. 'Snorri forgot. Snorri always forgets.'

There was an uncomfortable silence after that, and none of them seemed to know how to break it. Fortunately, it was broken for them when Max entered the room, walking with the aid of a staff.

'Are you able to stand?' he asked Felix.

Felix nodded. 'I think so.'

'Then come with me.'

With Gotrek's help, Felix levered himself out of the bed and tottered unsteadily after Max as the slayers followed behind. He still felt like he was made of matchsticks and spit, and he was still as gaunt as one of Kemmler's ghouls, but food and drink and the healing spells and prayers of Max and the Shallyan Sister had for the most part banished the dizziness and nausea. Gotrek only had to catch him once on the way down the hall.

Inside another room, the Sister hovered over another bed, but as Felix and Max and the slayers approached, she stepped back.

Lying on the bed, looking scrubbed and unfamiliar in a clean white nightshirt and her hair combed back from her skeletal face, was Kat. Her eyes were closed and her withered hands were folded over her chest, and for a terrible moment Felix thought Max had brought him to her to pay his last respects, but then, as he stumbled to the side of the bed, she opened her eyes and looked up at him – and smiled.

'Hello, Felix,' she said in voice like the memory of a whisper.

Felix eased himself down beside her. 'Kat,' he said. 'It – it's good to see you.'

She reached out and he took her hand. Her fingers were trembling, and terribly thin.

'I knew you would come back,' she said. 'I knew it.'

He frowned. 'How did you survive?' he asked. 'How did you stay alive for so long with Kemmler's dead all around?'

Her face crinkled into a grin. 'Reiklander's secret closet,' she said. 'I hid myself inside and waited. Then I heard fighting, and knew it was you.'

Felix closed his eyes, imagining Kat lying in the dark for two long days and nights, not knowing if she would ever be saved, and praying the zombies wouldn't find her first.

He leaned down and kissed her. 'I'm just glad we were here in time.'

There was a polite cough. Felix looked up. Everyone was very busy looking somewhere else, but the Sister was smiling down at them.

'She should rest, mein herr,' she said. 'I only called for you because she insisted.'

Felix nodded and turned back to Kat. 'I will visit you whenever you wish,' he said.

'I'll be up and about soon,' she said. 'I'm feeling better already.'

Felix swallowed at that. Feeling better than when he had found her wasn't much to crow about, and she still looked more dead than alive.

'Good,' he said. 'Then I'll see you soon.'

She nodded and closed her eyes again and he stood, then limped to the Sister of Shallya and drew her into the hall.

'Sister,' he murmured. 'Will she live?'

The sister looked at him, then pursed her lips. 'I don't know,' she said. 'She has come as close to starving as is possible without succumbing. And you have both been subject to the enervation of the necromancer's spells. Neither of you may recover your full strength.' She shrugged. 'At least you were both in vigorous health at the start. Perhaps that will count in your favour. Rest and Shallya's blessing are what is needed now, lots of rest.'

Felix nodded, distracted, as the sister bowed and started down the hall. He looked back through the door at Kat, chewing his lip. What if the two of them were enfeebled like this for the rest of their lives? It might not be so bad for him. After all his years on the road, after all the fighting and running and chasing, it wouldn't be so bad to live quietly, to read and write and think for a time. But for Kat? She was a child of the forest, a hunter. What would she do if she couldn't survive in the wild on her own? What if she were housebound or bed-bound for the rest of her life? It would kill her. She would sicken and die, like a wolf in captivity.

He closed his eyes. If that was her fate, it might almost have been better that she had died.

'I am no doctor,' murmured Max, stepping though the door to join him, 'but my advice is, that while rest is indeed what is needed now, in the long run, you would both do better to go where Gotrek goes, despite the dangers.'

Felix looked up at him. 'I am bound to anyway,' he

said. 'But Kat too? Why do you say that?'

Max nodded at Gotrek, who was following him into the hall with Snorri. 'I mentioned before that some of your unusual vitality seemed attributable to your remaining near Gotrek all these years. Whatever the cause of it, it seems that your association with him has kept you healthy and mended wounds that should have been the end of your adventuring.' He looked towards Kat, sleeping in her bed. 'I cannot say if this strange influence would work on Kat as well, but it certainly couldn't hurt,' he said, smiling. 'Also, I don't think you could keep her from following even if you chained her to her bed.'

A glimmer of hope stirred in Felix's heart. He hadn't been sure he believed Max's theories about his health when the magister had first shared them with him, and he still wasn't now, but if it *was* true! It could be the saving of Kat. It might make her well again!

'Sounds like rubbish to me,' Gotrek grunted. 'But no one ever got strong lying in bed. She can come if she wants.'

Max smiled at Gotrek. 'Excellent. And where do you go now, Slayer? What unspeakable abomination do you intend to throw yourself at next?'

Felix looked at the Slayer, as curious as Max was. Their most recent journey had begun when they had gone north to fight the beastmen at the behest of Sir Teobalt of the Order of the Fiery Heart, and they had become caught in the web of Kemmler's schemes after that, but now, as far as he knew, Gotrek had no goal other than his perennial quest to find his doom, and that might lead him anywhere.

But as Felix waited for the Slayer to speak, he saw him slide his one eye towards Snorri, and suddenly he knew the answer.

'We go,' Felix said, turning back to Max, 'to Karak Kadrin, to accompany Snorri Nosebiter on his pilgrimage to the Shrine of Grimnir.'

ABOUT THE AUTHOR

Nathan Long was a struggling screenwriter for fifteen years, during which time he had three movies made and a handful of live-action and animated TV episodes produced. Now he is a novelist, and is enjoying it much more. For Black Library he has written three Warhammer novels featuring the Blackhearts, and has taken over the Gotrek and Felix series, starting with the eighth installment, *Orcslayer*. He lives in Hollywood.

Follow the further adventures of other characters from the tales of Gotrek & Felix

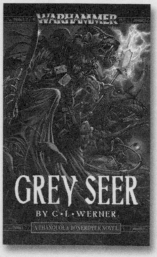

WARHAMMER

GREY SEER

BY C · L · WERNER

A THANQUOL & BONERIPPER NOVEL

WARHAMMER

Features characters from the Gotrek & Felix series!

TEMPLE OF THE SERPENT

BY C · L · WERNER

A THANQUOL & BONERIPPER NOVEL

ULRIKA THE VAMPIRE

WARHAMMER

BLOODBORN

NATHAN LONG

ULRIKA THE

SUMMER 2011

WARHAMMER

BLOODFORGED

NATHAN LONG

UK ISBN 978-1-84416-738-8 US ISBN 978-1-84416-739-5

UK ISBN 978-1-84416-824-8 US ISBN 978-1-84416-825-5